LOCKED . . . LOADED . . . READY TO ROCKET AND ROLL

Yates fired, loosing a silent gout of burning gas and strips of plastic packaging from the rear of the man-portable launcher. The Wyvern missile, kicked clear of the weapon's muzzle by an explosive charge, shot twenty meters toward the edge of the crater rim before its engine switched on, a tiny, white-hot point of light dwindling rapidly toward the UN base.

Long before the Wyvern could cross the distance to its target, however, the UN troops hiding in the trenches fired their own missile. The slam's back-flash was bright enough to be seen with the naked eye from eight kilometers away; the missile streaked skyward, scratching out a needle of white fire against the night as it arrowed into First Platoon's LSCP.

The detonation was a strobe of light banishing the stars, dazzling against the night . . .

LUNA MARINE

BOOK TWO OF

THE HERITAGE TRILOGY

IAN DOUGLAS

An Imprint of HarperCollinsPublishers

EOS
An Imprint of HarperCollins*Publishers*
10 East 53rd Street
New York, New York 10022-5299

Copyright © 1990 by William H. Keith, Jr.
ISBN: 0-380-78829-2
www.eosbooks.com

First Eos paperback printing: June 1999

HarperCollins® and Eos® are trademarks of HarperCollins Publishers Inc.

Printed in the U.S.A.

10 9 8 7 6 5

LUNA MARINE

BOOK ONE OF

THE HERITAGE TRILOGY

PROLOGUE

Cave of Wonders, Cydonia, Mars
1445 hours MMT

Sound did not carry well in near vacuum, but Dr. David Alexander felt the slight, ringing vibration of each step through the insulation of his Marsuit boots. There'd been no sound within this chamber in . . . how long? The team's best guess was half a million years.

"Halfway across the catwalk," he said, speaking into the needle mike positioned close by his lips. "Twenty meters." Over the headset clamped down over his ears, he could hear the unsteady rasp of his own breathing, the *hiss-thump* of his backpack PLSS. His breath, hot and moist, fogged his helmet visor with each exhalation, a white smear immediately dissolved by the stream of cool air blowing past his face.

"Ah, we copy that, Aladdin," a voice crackled in his ears. *"You're looking good."*

Aladdin. The radio handle was a last-minute joke concocted by Ed Pohl that morning, back at C-Prime. Naming this place the Cave of Wonders had been his idea, after he'd seen the first transmissions from the penetrator robot three days ago.

It could as easily have been Ali Baba. The cavern, apparently, required a human presence to operate it, a living *open, sesame* to switch on power and lights and to open doors. Robots massing one hundred kilos and programmed

1

to radiate at thirty-seven degrees—human body temperature—had failed to learn anything about the long-sealed chamber. Alexander, claiming the right as the one who'd found the cavern entrance in the first place, had volunteered to go in. He was, he estimated, a hundred meters into the vast and labyrinthine complex hollowed out beneath the Cydonian Face, and perhaps ten meters beneath the surface of the ground outside.

"Aladdin, we're seeing an increase in heart rate and respiration. Please check your O_2 mix."

"Copy." His eyes flicked to the med and PLSS readouts mirrored above and to the right of his visor, checking that all were well in the green. Of *course* his heart and breathing were faster, the idiots! "O-two at six-point-three. Systems nominal. Fifteen meters."

"Ah, roger that, Aladdin. Watch the hyperventilation."

That sounded like Doc Penkov. He could imagine all of the Team members back at Cydonia Prime, crowded into the radio shack as they followed his progress. Only Devora Druzhinova and Louis Vandemeer were on the surface today, now waiting just outside the tunnel entrance in case he needed help.

The catwalk of black metal trembled harder with his next few steps, and he stopped, gripping the pencil-thin guardrails to either side until the motion dampened itself out. His heart was pounding hard now, beneath the breastplate of his suit. At last, he was inside the Face. . . .

The Face . . . first observed on photographs transmitted to Earth late in the previous century by the Viking orbiters and subsequently confirmed by other robot spacecraft. The Face . . . enigma and lure, drawing scientists like David Alexander to probe its secrets, held in silence now for half a million years. Even now, with all the evidence of the ancient ruins uncovered on the Cydonian plain, with the uncanny discovery of flash-frozen and desiccated corpses of long-dead archaic *Homo sapiens* on Mars, there were some who yet thought the two-kilometer-long mesa's vague and sandblasted resemblance to a human face to be the product of chance and human psychology.

The discovery of the Cave of Wonders had all but put

to rest that notion. Sometime between four and five hundred thousand years ago, someone had reshaped a natural landform, giving it the vaguely apelike, vaguely human features that had attracted so much comment when they were first noticed sixty years before. At the same time, they'd hollowed out the Cave in the bedrock beneath the towering mesa, connecting it by a long, descending, and carefully sealed tunnel to the well-hidden entrance on the Face's eastern corner, just below the left end of the harsh-carved canyon slash that formed the Face's mouth.

Once, the Cave had been airtight, accessed through a series of airlocks that still worked at the touch of a gloved, human hand. But even solid rock is porous over geological time. The air within this enormous chamber—radar probings had established that it was a spherical cavern half a kilometer across—had leaked out long ago. The air pressure inside now stood at a little below ten millibars, the temperature constant at minus fifteen degrees Celsius.

Alexander tried not to look down. The catwalk seemed impossibly frail, a spider's web of black, interlacing threads woven into a deck that felt solid and metallic enough but was hard to see against the deeper black of the two-hundred-meter depths below. Ahead, a pale light—a white-yellow glow a meter across without visible source—illuminated the end of the catwalk; the only other light in the place came from the worklights mounted on the shoulders of his suit and from the telltales inside his helmet.

"Ten meters," he said.

"Hold it, Aladdin. Can you pan for us?"

"Roger. Panning to the right." Carefully, he turned himself in place, allowing the camera mounted on the outside of his helmet to relay the view across a full three-sixty. He could see nothing but black; the cavern swallowed his worklights in impenetrable darkness, but the camera would be picking up frequencies invisible to his eye. Perhaps they were enjoying a better view of things than he, back at the Team HQ.

Alexander thought of Howard Carter. On November 26, 1922, after a long dig and repeated disappointments, the British archeologist had chiseled a narrow hole through a stone door separating him from another world, in a long-sealed tomb in Egypt's Valley of the Kings. Air thirty centuries old, hot and stale, had gusted from the opening; a candle thrust through the hole flickered but remained lit, proving the air breathable.

Carter's heart must have been pounding as hard as Alexander's was now, his breathing as fast and as uneven, as he carefully enlarged the hole and peered through. The candle's flame had been captured and flung back at him by myriad polished surfaces of pure gold.

"Can you see anything?" Lord Carnarvon, his partner and the expedition's backer, has asked, close at his shoulder.

"Yes," Carter had replied, his voice cracking with emotion. "Yes, wonderful things!"

Alexander knew now exactly what Carter must have felt as he first addressed that sealed, stone door leading to the tomb of Tutankhamen.

"Still not a lot to see," the voice said over his headset, *"even at IR freaks. Maybe this thing is a bust after all."*

Alexander refused to even consider the possibility. "I'm moving again. Eight meters."

It could not be a bust. It couldn't. So far, except for the automated controls on the airlock doors on the way in, there'd been no positive indication that there was anything inside this sealed, empty sphere worth exploring. Even so, Alexander had suggested the name Cave of Wonders in what was for him an atypically romantic whim; no one knew what they would find in the chamber, though speculation had ranged from living quarters for the transplanted humans who'd worked here, to some kind of operational center for the yet-unknown intelligences who'd brought early hominids to this place, to a starship, intact and filled with secrets buried these past five hundred millennia.

The last few steps toward the end of the catwalk, suspended high above an invisible floor and surrounded by darkness absolute, were the hardest steps David Alexander had ever taken. He was drawn on, however, by wonder and by Howard Carter's ghost. Like Carter, he was standing at a doorway opening to another world.

But he still needed to find the key. . . .

"Five meters," he said. "I'm . . . I'm entering the lighted area now." The sourceless glow seemed to hover above a widening in the walkway, a structure that reminded him, disconcertingly, of the harpoon gunner's bowsprit platform on an old-time whaling vessel.

Light surrounded him. He raised his gloved hands, staring at the white material. St. Elmo's fire danced from the fingertips, cold and otherworldly. His fingertips traced blue arcs in the air . . .

. . . and the cavern was no longer shrouded in blackness. From his vantage point, suspended near the center of that kilometer-wide chamber, it seemed as though he was in the middle of a perfectly spherical swarm of stars, each star rigidly locked with the geometric perfection of the other stationary stars around it. There were thousands of them, in orderly, regimented splendor. Fainter glows floated among the ranked stars, forming oddly regular sweeps and streaks and dots that *might* have been words, an alien script felt more than seen.

"Ah, Control," he called, his breathing coming faster still. "Are you picking this up?"

"Roger that, Aladdin. We see . . . something, but we're not sure what we're seeing. What do you make of it?"

"I'm . . . not . . . sure. . . ."

As he focused on one section of that far-off wall of stars, one marked by one of the alien-script words, it seemed as though one section of the spherical surface—twenty degrees, perhaps—broke off and rushed toward him, each star becoming a tiny, polished facet, like a jewel.

Or . . . like a display screen or monitor.

How was the illusion accomplished? Was he seeing something real? Or was it in his mind?

Alexander blinked, hard. Sweat was trickling down his face, tickling his nose and stinging his eyes, and he yearned to be able to reach up and wipe it away. His mouth felt as dry as the thin, dry vacuum of the Martian atmosphere. He was looking now at an array of tiny, rectangular TV screens, an array at least fifty rectangles wide and fifty high . . . or were they, in fact, tiny? He had no way of judging scale. They might have been the size of a thumbnail, suspended a few centimeters in front of his eyes, or the size of a theater's holoscreen, each three stories tall. Without a frame of reference, there was no way to tell.

"Aladdin! We're not seeing anything here. Can you describe what you're seeing?"

The clear majority of those screens, he saw—perhaps two thousand of them or more—were blank. But on the others . . .

He picked out one that was alive with a reddish hue, straining to make out the scene he could just distinguish glowing in its depths. Abruptly, and silently, the screen expanded until it filled his field of vision.

"Aladdin!" the voice called, tinny in his ears. *"Aladdin! Can you see anything?"*

It took Alexander a long time to answer. "Yes," he replied at last. "Wonderful things! . . ."

ONE

Ramsey Residence
Greensburg, Pennsylvania
1635 hours EST

"Okay, gorgeous. Let's get you out of those clothes, first."

"But, Jack . . . *all* of them? How far do you want me to go? I mean, I'm outside, and the neighbors might—"

"I want you naked, babe." Not that the bikini top and tight, red slacks she was wearing now left all that much to the imagination. "Make yourself starkers. For me."

John Charles Ramsey—he preferred the name Jack—leaned a bit closer as he watched the young woman on the flatscreen that dominated one wall of his room. She gave him a sultry pout, one filled with lust-churning promise, then started slowly unzipping her pants. She was lounging on a folding chaise next to an outdoor pool, where the sunlight turned her long hair to spun gold, and she had to wiggle a bit to get the slacks down off her hips. Jack licked his lips once, then reached down to unzip his own pants.

Before long, the woman was naked, seated in that tailor's seat, show-all pose that Jack loved best. She leaned back with catlike grace, closing her eyes and smiling dreamily as she started gently fingering her blond-tufted cleft. "Oooh, Jack," she breathed.

"Yeah, Sam. Oh, yeah. Do it. *Do* it. . . ." His hand was inside his shorts, now, squeezing with slow, deep movements. *God*, she was beautiful. . . .

7

"I want you, Sam," he told her, leaning even closer to the screen. The way those big, hard-nippled breasts bobbed and circled with her quickening motions was pure heaven, especially when she reached up with her free hand and rubbed them. "Oh, God, I want you, Sam."

"Oooh, and I want *you*, Jack. I want you right here, inside me. . . ."

"Jack?"

"Mom!" He started violently, bumping hard against his desk top and nearly falling out of the chair. At the code word "Mom," the image of Sam and her breast-heaving passion dissolved in a cloud of rippling pixels, replaced in a startled heartbeat by an elderly man with a bushy mustache, bright eyes, and a white linen suit, standing in a library or book-filled study.

The door to Jack's room, just to the left of the screen, opened, and his mother walked in. She glanced at the screen, then at Jack, who was pulling himself and his chair awkwardly up close against his desk. "Are you okay, dear? I thought I heard you . . . talking to someone."

"Um, sure, Mom. I was just talking to Sam, here. You know, Sam Clemens? My agent?"

"Howdy, Ms. Ramsey," Sam said in a pleasant, home-spun Missouri drawl.

"Oh, of course, dear," she said, ignoring the AI agent. "I just wanted to tell you that your Aunt Liana just arrived. I think it would be nice if you came down and said hello."

"Aw, *now*?"

"That's the general idea."

"Uh, I'll be down in just a few, Mom. Sam here is helping me download some stuff."

"That's fine."

She paused to glance at the recruiting posters decorating much of the wall space not taken up by the monitor. Above Jack's bed, a grinning, life-size Marine in crisp Class As snapped a salute, held it, dropped it, then saluted again in an endlessly animated cycle. "The Marines Want *YOU*" was emblazoned across the bottom of the sheet, the letters cycling through the entire spectrum, as Valkyries streaked through the sky in the background. Nearby by was a large, full-color poster of the flag-raising at Cydonia, five US Marines in vacuum armor, hoisting a small American flag on a length of pipe against the pink sky and rusty stone backdrop of Mars. The photo was signed by David Alexander, the civilian archeologist who'd taken the photograph.

The man who also happened to be Jack's uncle.

"Come on down when you're ready. Just don't take too long."

She pulled the door shut behind her, and Jack loosed a long, heartfelt sigh of relief. That had been entirely too close; usually, he could hear her coming up the stairs, but that time he'd nearly been caught. He thought again about a pressure-sensitive switch with a PC-radio link he'd seen in World Electronics for fifty bucks. It might be worth it, to be able to flash an alarm whenever Mom started up the steps. If she ever caught on to "Sam's" alter ego . . .

"It's okay, Samantha," he whispered. "She's gone. But, uh, keep your voice down, okay?"

At the name Samantha, Samuel Longhorn Clemens pixel-flickered back into the guise of a blond, naked, twenty-year-old woman, standing this time in the Clemens library. Jack himself was seventeen, an age particularly susceptible to the charms of commercial AI net agents who looked and spoke and undressed like her. Software packages like Samantha—the thought of the word "software" made him vent a quiet, frustratedly longing groan—were supposedly restricted to people twenty-one and older, but it was easy enough to get around *those* rules, especially if you had a buddy with a valid Net ID. The net vendors, mostly, just wanted your recorded assurance that you were twenty-one so that *they* didn't get into trouble if you got caught. Damn it, the United States still had such uptight and puritanical laws about sex. It wasn't like you couldn't go to any public beach or download any movie these days without seeing plenty of nudity, all ages, all sexes, all orientations.

"Maybe I should go ahead and get those downloads," he told her.

Reaching up, she cupped her full breasts, rubbing her nipples between her fingers. "Whatever you say . . . Jack. But, oooh, I would just *love* it if you could download *me*." Watching her, it was impossible to think of her as anything other than a flesh-and-blood woman. Net agents, however, artificially intelligent programs designed to search the Net for information and to serve as secretaries, librarians, search specialists, data valets, and even personal stand-ins, were the most visible aspects of the ongoing computer revolution, and they could look like anyone, or any*thing*, their owners desired.

"Whatcha got for me?"

She leaned forward in the screen, drawing a deep, slow breath. "*Lots. . . .*"

A window opened to the left of the screen, the image adjusting itself so that none of Sam's lush anatomy was obscured. A succession of images—military aircraft, tanks, troops, and ships flashed across the screen window. "I have two hundred twenty-seven news downloads," Sam told him, "dealing with the war. Eighty-five of those are cross-linked with stories about the US Marine Corps."

"Just gimme a summary."

"Of course, Jack. In summation of the most important stories, extensive fighting is continuing near Chapayevsk and Saratov, where Moslem troops continue their advance into southern Russia, and at Vladivostok, where PRC troops are threatening to break through the Russian-American lines. US forces entered the towns of Navajoa and Ciudad Camargo yesterday, completing operations in Sonora and Chihuahua. According to Secretary of Defense Archibald Severin, 'The threat of Mexico forcing the creation of their so-called Aztlan Republic, carved out of the American Southwest, has been effectively and permanently neutralized.' "

As she spoke, she let one hand slide down between her legs, gently caressing. Jack's attention was torn between her and the rapid-fire succession of download imagery. On the screen, greasy black smoke boiled into the sky behind a war-damaged Capitol dome. Other scenes showed firefighters and disaster crews picking their way through tumbledown rubble and smoking craters.

"Four American cities," Sam continued, "Washington, Atlanta, Boston, and Miami, were hit by EU ship- or sub-launched cruise missiles last night. Damage and casualties are reportedly light. The president said today that—"

"Never mind that. Let's hear the stories about the Corps."

"Of course, Jack. In Cuba, the launch sites at Matanzas and Sagua la Grande are now firmly under US control. Elements of the 1st Marines are advancing on Habana, and reports of mass surrenders of starving Cuban soldiers have been reported by most major news networks.

"In the Russian Far East today, the 1st and 3rd Battalions of the 5th Marines, fighting alongside battle-hardened elements of the 43rd and 115th Russian Armies, repulsed what was described as a major human-wave assault south of Laka Khanka near the city of Ussuriysk—"

"Skip it, Sam. Space news."

"Whatever you say, Jack. There are fifteen new stories dealing with space, including one cross-indexed to the US Marines and to the war."

"*Shibui!* Now you're talking! Let me hear that one, Sam."

The window showed a stock photo of the moon, shot from space. "Reports of a military expedition to the moon by a special assault force of US Marines trained in space-combat techniques have been circulating in Washington today, but all attempts to confirm or deny these reports have so far failed. It has been confirmed that a Zeus II heavy-lift booster took off from Vandenberg early this morning with an estimated ninety to one hundred Marines aboard. Official agencies have responded only with 'no comment' to speculations that the Marines are bound for the UN-held base in the lunar crater Fra Mauro. There are no images associated with this story."

"Okay. Save it, and I'll look at that one a bit later. Anything on aliens?"

"There are twelve stories dealing with extraterrestrials

or aliens, including three new additions to the Cave of Wonders database.''

''*Sugoi shibui!* Lemme see those now.''

''Of course, Jack. One of those stories mentions your Uncle David.''

''Hey, *yatta*! Play that one first.''

''Whatever you say, Jack.''

Jack didn't mind admitting that he was space-crazy. A lot of his friends were, especially since the intriguing discovery of ancient humans on Mars had been publicized two years ago. The fact that his archeologist uncle, Dr. David Alexander, had been the sonic-imager technician on that expedition—and the man who'd smuggled out news of the discovery at the very beginning of the war—just made it that much better. And some of what they'd been coming up with, lately, from the incredible mass of data gathered within the Cave of Wonders . . .

His uncle's face came up in the window, as secondary windows opened to show the red Martian landscape, the now-famous Cydonian Face, and a montage of images taken from the immense chamber beneath the Face. Jack leaned a bit closer, his heart pounding, as he looked at those images.

Images from other worlds.

His uncle was talking. ''Full screen, Sam.''

''Of course, Jack.''

The view of David Alexander filled the screen, replacing Samantha's tanned and naked body. There *were* a few things that Jack found more fascinating than pretty women.

''. . . and so we've been able to identify another alien race from the data we've brought back,'' the man was saying. He was wearing a safari jacket with the Mars-Face emblem of the Cydonian Research Foundation over the left breast pocket. ''Of course we don't know what they called themselves, but we call them Race Eighty-four, because they're the eighty-fourth distinct species we've been able to isolate for study.''

Another window expanded in the picture, showing a . . . face. It was recognizable as such, at least, which was more than could be said with many of the eighty-three other beings glimpsed on the display screens found within the Cave of Wonders. The eyes were startling, large and golden and horizontally slit by a jagged black line that must have been a pupil; the head was more like that of a fish or reptile, a mottled apple green and green-yellow, with a low skull crest and glistening scales like fine chain mail. There were no external ears that Jack could see, but there was a recognizable nose and a lipless, black-rimmed mouth in a more or less human arrangement on the head.

Lizard-man, Jack thought, heart pounding. *Fish-man*. It looked so human it almost looked hokey, like one of those man-in-latex monsters that still occasionally waddled through the cheaper varieties of sci-fi late movies, the ones made decades ago, before the advent of digital characters and programmable AI agents. He wondered what its hands looked like, and whether or not it had a tail.

"The other end of this particular communications link," Alexander said, "is still working, apparently *has* been working for thousands of years. We think, from what we've learned so far, that the Eighty-fours must have been an advanced, technic species perhaps ten to twelve thousand years ago. Now, they seem to be barely above the stone age, if that. We have no idea what happened.

"We also don't know how the communications complex at Cydonia managed to connect with the Eighty-fours' home world, especially since Cydonia is something like half a *million* years old. Each of the active screens within the Cave of Wonders, however, has large amounts of encoded information, information which, we believe, includes data on that species's language, culture, history, and biology. In time, we might be able to learn more about the Eighty-fours, as well as the other races we've glimpsed so far, and discover what connection they may have with the Builders of so long ago.

"What makes this one especially interesting," Alexander continued, "is that we've been able to identify the home star of these people . . . and they're close. *Real* close!"

The alien face was replaced by a landscape and a dark-

ening, alien sky. It looked as though the scene had been
shot from the open-air top of some kind of high, flat-
topped building; in the distance, fading into the shadows,
something like an ancient Mayan step pyramid rose from
a black jungle, with stairways sloping up each face and
ornate carvings worked into the stone. Two moons, crescents bowed away from the red-orange twilight glow at
the horizon, hung in a purple sky. The stars were just
coming out. . . .

"It appears that their end of the communication link
with Cydonia is now an object of veneration, of sorts.
They have it set up atop one of their distinctive pyramids—we think it's a temple of some kind—and so we've
been able to watch a number of the local sunsets . . . and
we've been able to match the constellations we can
glimpse in their sky with constellations in our sky,
changed a little, of course . . . but recognizably the same
as constellations in our own sky."

Lines drew themselves from star to star in the landscape,
picking out a familiar hourglass shape with three bright
stars across the middle. The hourglass lay on its side instead of standing upright and was slightly distorted by par-
allax, but it was obviously Orion; it could be none other.

"What is truly spectacular about this find," Alexander
went on, "is the fact that these, these people, the Eighty-
fours, are living right now on a world circling the star we
call Lalande 21185. A star that is only about eight and a
quarter light-years away. . . ."

"Wow!" Jack said, the word long, drawn-out, and
breathless. Why, eight light-years was right next door as
far as interstellar distances went, just less than twice the
distance to Alpha Centauri. It meant that intelligent life
must be dirt-common throughout the Galaxy . . . though
the number of races represented on those display screens
in the Cave of Wonders had pretty well established that.

The face of the Eighty-four reappeared as Alexander
kept discussing the find. Jack found himself wondering
what they called themselves . . . and whether they'd had
anything to do with the structures on Mars.

Or with the ancient humans found there. It didn't sound

like their civilization was that old. But . . . what were they doing at the other end of that magical, faster-than-light communications device buried beneath the Face on Mars?

"Jack!" Another window opened on the screen, and his mother looked out at him. "Jack, *are* you coming?"

Jack started. Damn! He'd let the time get away from him. "Sorry, Mom! I'll be right down! Uh, halt program," he said. Windows closed, leaving only the bright-eyed electronic ghost of Mark Twain on the screen. The word "Mom" had reactivated his incarnation. "Uh, save all this stuff, Sam," he said. "I'll have to go over it later!"

"Whatever you say, Jack," Sam drawled. " 'Minds me that I still have t'run down that data on spacecraft converted to military operations you asked fer this morning. I got some, but I'm still followin' up some leads, like the good newsman that I am." He winked. "Catch you later."

He sighed. He was really proud of the Samantha–Sam Clemens crossover, which he'd hacked out himself from two separate sets of vendored software. Sometimes, he felt guilty about deceiving his mom . . . but, then, Mom wouldn't understand about Samantha. She didn't understand a *lot* of things. . . .

The display flicked to the screen saver his mother had bought him last year as an "educational" gift—a tedious succession of abstract animated light paintings by various modern artists. He had others that he preferred, but he let them run only when he was sure his mother wasn't going to come barging into his room. He checked his fly, steeled himself, then strolled out of his room and onto the open landing above the house's main den.

His mother was still seated at the downstairs computer where she'd called with her reminder. Aunt Liana, who looked a lot like her older sister, except for the short blond, green, and pink hair, sat in the conversation pit. Her eyes were puffy and red.

Uh-oh, Jack thought. *Looks like houseguest time again. . . .*

"Oh, good, Jack," his mother called as he trotted down the stairs. "Would you go bring your aunt's things in and put them in the spare bedroom? She's going to be staying with us a few days.''

''Sure, Mom.'' Liana's car, a bright red, yellow, and black '39 hydrogen-fueled Apollo, was parked in the drive just outside. Wondering just what ''a few days'' meant in real-world time, he hauled the two suitcases out of the backseat and carried them inside and down the hall.

When he returned to the E-room, his mom was seated next to Liana, her arm around the other woman's shoulders. Used tissues littered the rug around the sofa.

''This is *it*, Stacy,'' Liana sobbed. ''He just . . . he just won't *understand*! . . .''

''I know, Li. It was like that with Doug, before the divorce.''

''But I *can't* divorce David, I just *can't*. P-pastor Blaine would . . .''

Liana saw Jack standing uncertainly at the edge of the room. ''Oh, hi, Jack,'' she said with a sniff and a dab from the wadded-up tissue in her fist. ''Don't . . . don't mind me. How are you? How's school?''

''I'm all done with school, Aunt Li,'' he told her. ''I was doing Net homeschooling, remember? Got my diploma a couple of months ago. Soon as I turn eighteen, I figure on joining the Marines!''

''Good heavens! Why?''

He was used to the question. ''Well, because—''

''Jack doesn't really know *what* he wants, Sis,'' his mother said. ''He's been on this Marine kick for a couple of years, now.''

''Mom. . . .''

''Why, with his test scores, he won't have any trouble getting into just about any college he wants.''

''Mom! . . .''

''He's always been fascinated by space travel, of course. I've been telling him he should try to go to CMU, in Pittsburgh, and get into their AI and Cognitive Sciences program.''

''*Mom!* . . .''

''Why, as good as he is with computers and Net agents and all of that? I'll bet he could get a position with the

Space Agency, or maybe the Moravec Institute. They need good computer people in orbit, they say. . . .''

Jack rolled his eyes but gave up trying to bull his way through the barrier. Once his mother got going, there was no stopping her, and she *would* not listen. It was his fascination with space that had led to his determination to join the Marines, and she just didn't seem to understand that. Marines had gone to *Mars*, for Pete's sake! They'd recaptured the International Space Station from UN troops, and now they were on their way to the Moon. As a computer scientist, his chances of getting to go to space were about on a par with winning the lottery, he figured. But as a Marine, he *knew* he had a chance. . . .

Someday. . . .

''Your mother says you're really interested in all the news about the aliens, lately,'' his aunt said. ''I think it's so exciting, don't you?''

Uh-oh, he thought. *Here it comes.* He *hated* talking to her about this and had a pretty good idea why she wasn't getting along with his uncle.

''Uh, yeah!'' he said, brightly. ''Real yatta! Just now, upstairs, I DLed the goods on three new species from the Face. Really shibby stuff. I—''

''Jack! I wish you wouldn't use those ugly, made-up words!''

''What ugly? Everybody uses 'em!''

''Nonsense. What's that, that 'shibby,' you said? . . .''

''Oh, you know. Shibby. Like *sugoi shibui*! It means, I don't know. Max-slick. Iced. Um, really good.''

''And yatta?''

''That's a real word, Mom. It's just Japanese. Means great.''

''Seems like everything Japanese is popular, now,'' Liana said with another sniff. ''Ever since they left the UN and joined our side in the war. My hairdresser told me that pink-and-green geisha bobs were going to be all the thing this year.'' She turned to Jack. ''I heard that they've discovered the Divine Masters in that Martian cave, but that some people high up are trying to hide it from the rest of us!''

"I, uh, really don't think that's what's—"

"I mean, it's obvious that they've found something up there they don't want to talk about! It's obvious! David was the one who found the cave, found out how to open it. He came home with all that data, and all they can do is release a little bit of harmless stuff once in a while, nothing about who built the Face, or why."

"I think that's because they don't know yet, Aunt Li."

"Nonsense! They know more than they're telling! David's been a changed man ever since he came back from Mars! And the Space Agency! All they do is trot him around to one public-relations or fund-raising gig after another. Won't let him work. And of course they don't let him talk with his colleagues in Europe and China, with the war and everything. And so he takes it out on *me*! . . ."

Jack thought it might be a good idea to deflect the conversation from that particular topic. "They're *not* hiding anything, Aunt Li," he insisted. "I mean, the UN were the ones trying to cover things up. That's why they grabbed Mars, back at the beginning of the war, 'cause they were afraid the news would cause riots and stuff. That's why Uncle David arranged to broadcast everything he'd learned on the Net, so that the world would know the truth!"

Liana leaned forward, tapping Jack's kneecap with her forefinger to emphasize her point. "*I* think they learned a lot that they're not telling us, Jack! Maybe they released a little of what they learned, to mess up those other countries and stuff, but I think the *real* knowledge about the Cosmic Brothers and the Creator Space Gods is being kept secret! I mean, look at how the scientists . . . and David is among them! Look at how they attack Dr. Caulder's work! And Sitchen! And von Daniken! All the really great men in the field are just positively *vilified*, just because they tried to speak the truth! I told David, I said . . ."

Jack sighed and leaned back in his chair. Once his Aunt Liana got wound up about the ancient astronauts and the cosmic space brothers, there was no way to stop her. As she babbled happily about flying saucers using antigravity to build the pyramids and the stone heads on Easter Island, he thought about that glimpse of a genuine alien world he'd just had upstairs . . . dark-stone step pyramids against a violet sky, enigmatic beings with green scales and golden eyes, a world, a civilization only eight light-years away.

It made Liana's twaddle about ancient astronauts and godlike ETs seem like comic-book stuff. No wonder Uncle David didn't get along with her! He had the scientist's approach to life and the universe, a rational approach that demanded evidence, data, and proof. Liana was happy to snag any passing bit of fiction wrapped in the guise of wisdom from the ancients or the star gods or whatever and incorporate it whole into her eclectic and uncritical world-view. According to her, the star gods and cosmic brothers would be here any day to stop the war and lead humankind to a new and higher level of evolution.

God, was she actually thinking about staying here long? Jack wasn't sure he could stand it, not for more than a day or two.

As she kept talking, a growing resolve hardened within him. In two weeks, he would be eighteen and able to enlist in the Marines without a signature from his mother.

If he could just hold out until then. . . .

TWO

UN Base, Fra Mauro, The Moon
0435 hours GMT

Marine Lieutenant Kaitlin Garroway leaned forward and bounced, easing herself into the gently loping "kangaroo hop" that Aldrin and Armstrong had discovered, seventy-three years before, to be the most efficient way of maneuvering a space suit about the Lunar surface. Dust exploded in slow motion about her feet and legs as she bounded forward, exhilarated by speed, by strangeness, by the utter silence of her surroundings.

Shadowless hills burned in the arc-brilliant sunshine, mounds and swellings like silver-gray sand dunes, smooth-sculpted against the featureless black of the sky at a horizon too crisp, too clear, too near to be Earth's. The sun, close-guarded by a crescent Earth, stood almost directly overhead—high noon at Fra Mauro, with another seven days to go until sunset. Small and alone in the near-featureless emptiness of the Lunar landscape, the former UN base was little more than a half circle of hab cylinders partly buried in the mounds of regolith bulldozed over them as protection against flares and solar radiation. To her right, a bulky, Chinese-built Kongyunjian transport rested on splayed landing legs in the flame-scorched plain designated as the Fra Mauro Spaceport, flanked by the squat, black insect shapes of four Marine LSCP-K landers.

An American flag, stretched taut by a wire from hoist

to fly, hung breezelessly motionless from a jury-rigged mast raised above the landing-field control shack. Two Marines from Kaitlin's platoon, Anders and Juarez, stood guard outside, like bulky black-and-white statues in their combat rigs and active camo armor. The Marines had landed, as the old saying went, and the situation was well in hand.

The stark silence was broken by the click and hiss of a radio channel opening in her headset. "Hey, Lieutenant? Kaminski, on your six. Is the scuttlebutt true?"

She stopped, taking another couple of bounces to keep from falling headlong, then turned in place until she saw another space-suited figure coming toward her from behind. She couldn't see his face through the highly reflective visor, but the name KAMINSKI was picked out in block letters across the upper chest of his suit, while a sergeant's stripes had been painted on his left arm. The rest of his armor, with its active camo coating, reflected the grays, silvers, and night blacks of his surroundings, an illusion not good enough to render him invisible, certainly, but effective enough to make it difficult to precisely trace his outline. "And what scuttlebutt would that be, Sergeant?"

Kaminski stopped and gave the buttstock of the ATAR rifle he carried a slap, the gesture silent in hard vacuum. "That they already have another objective for us. Something about alien shit here on the Moon."

Kaitlin snorted. "I swear, Sergeant. The only thing faster than light is rumor in the Corps!"

"Is it true then, ma'am?"

"I don't know yet, Ski. I'm on my way to a briefing now. You'll know when I do." *More likely, you'll know before I do,* she thought. The resourcefulness of Marine noncoms in general in acquiring field intel on upcoming deployments and the resourcefulness of this Marine in particular in working the system were legendary.

"Yes, ma'am."

"Everybody done topping off their plissers?"

"That's affirmative, Lieutenant. Gunny Yates's cycled 'em through the pliss rechargers in the UNdies' barracks. Soon as they was checked for traps."

"Good. Pass the word for me, and tell them to swap out their PSMs now, while they have the chance. Otherwise the UNdies'll claim we're engaged in chemical-biological warfare."

Kaminski chuckled. "Y'know, Lieutenant, some of the guys are sayin' this had t'be the first time in the history of the Corps that two companies of Marines went into battle wearing full diapers."

"Execute, Ski."

"Aye, aye, ma'am!" Kaminski slapped the rifle butt again in lieu of a salute—such niceties as rifle salutes were impossibly cumbersome inside armor—then bounded off in a puff of gray, slow-falling dust, making for the space field. Kaitlin continued her trek toward the two-story hab that had originally housed the UN Lunar HQ, now commandeered as the Marines' Ops Center. Left, several Marines guarded the main personnel module, where the base's UN crew was being held until transport could be arranged for their removal back to Earth.

The battle for Fra Mauro had been Kaitlin's first time in combat, and she hadn't even come under fire. The battle proper had been over in all of five minutes.

Four days before, the First Marine Space Assault Group had shuttled to Earth orbit and rendezvoused with the former International Space Station. There, they'd transferred to the four ugly little LSCP-Ks, which had been ferried to LEO from Vandenberg in a pair of heavy-lift cargo transports the week before. The boost to Luna had been three days of claustrophobic hell, twenty-four Marines packed like ceramic-swaddled sardines into no-frills accommodations that barely left them room to move . . . and civilized notions like swapping out their Personal Sanitation Modules had been impossible.

One-SAG was organized as a special assault battalion, under the command of Major Theodore Avery—two companies, each composed of two twenty-four-man platoons. Kaitlin was CO of Second Platoon, Bravo Company, under the command of Captain Carmen Fuentes. For the actual assault, however, honors had been awarded to Alfa Company, under the command of Captain Robert Lee. Alfa had stormed the main habs, hacked through the airlock electronics, and secured the entire base before Bravo's two LSCPs had even touched down.

There'd not been more than a handful of UN troopers at Fra Mauro in any case; intelligence had reported at least sixty elite French Foreign Legion troops on Luna, but there'd been nothing more there than a small token guard, four Legionnaires and a couple of PLA security troops off the Kongyunjian heavy transport.

Fra Mauro was not the only Lunar base, however, though it was the oldest and best-established, dating back to the 2020s. There were numerous small outposts and research stations, too . . . and there was also the former US-Russian radio telescope facility at Tsiolkovsky on the Lunar farside, a base as large as Fra Mauro that had been taken over by the UN before the war. There was plenty of evidence to suggest that the UN had been busy indeed on the moon during the past thirty months; dozens of Lunar transport flights had been tracked during the past two years from Kourou in French Guiana, from Shar in India, from Jiuquan and Xichang in China, and—at least until Japan had defected from the UN camp—from Tanegashima Spaceport as well. One reason the Marines had been deployed here was to find out just what it was the enemy was up to.

Two Marines from Alfa Company stood guard in front of Ops. Stepping through the low, round outer hatch of the airlock, Kaitlin cycled through, wondering as the closet-sized chamber pressurized if anyone in 1-SAG knew what was really going on.

Given a choice, she knew she would trust Kaminski's scuttlebutt over almost any other authority available.

The inner hatch sighed open, and she stepped into the hab's lower deck. Ops, and Fra Mauro's control center, were up one level. Four more Marines greeted her, took her ATAR, helped her unlatch and remove her helmet, then detach the heavy PLSS—the Portable Life Support System, popularly called a plisser—and slide it from her aching shoulders.

"They're waitin' for you topside, ma'am," said one of

the men, a gunnery sergeant with JACLOVIC stenciled across his breastplate.

"Thanks, Gunny." She clanged up the ladder and emerged in a pie-wedge of a room, cramped by consoles, commo gear, and computers. The first thing that hit her as she emerged from the hatch was the smell of brewing coffee. Tradition. The Marines had been in control of the UN Lunar base for less than three hours now, and they already had the coffee going.

They were waiting for her there: Major Avery, Captain Fuentes, and Captain Lee; and the other platoon commanders, Lieutenants Delgado, Palmer, and Machuga; along with the four LSCP pilots and Captain White, Avery's number two. Twelve men and women, all still wearing their Class-One/Specials, more than filled the small compartment as they clustered about the light table in the center.

"So good of you to join us, Lieutenant," Avery said, an edge to his voice. Somehow, he'd managed to make himself clean-shaven, a bit of personal grooming that set him well apart from the stubble-faced men around him.

"I was checking my people at the spaceport and the vehicle bays, sir."

"*That* is why you have section leaders," Avery said. "That is why we have staff and gunnery sergeants, to look after those little details for us . . . so that we can show up on goddamn *time* for briefings!"

"Sir! I—" She clamped her mouth shut, angry, but unwilling to show it. "Yes, sir."

"See that you remember that in future, Lieutenant. I expect my officers to be punctual and BTFM. Do you understand?"

"By the manual, sir. Yes, sir."

The others shuffled aside enough to make room for her at the table. A dozen Marines in full armor left precious little room for movement. The photomemory plastic sheathing most of the armor captured ambient light and modified its own pigments to reflect the colors and tones of the surroundings. In these close quarters, the Marines' active camouflage armor reflected back the glare of the table and the overhead lighting and the close, dark gray mesh of the metal floors and walls, giving them a strange and alien patterning that the eye found difficult to cling to. With helmets off, their heads seemed to float above confusing masses of black, gray, and cool white reflections.

Kaitlin drew a deep breath, steadying herself as she slumped against the edge of the table. The Ops Center, broad and metallic, with low ceilings and harsh fluorescent lighting, stank of unwashed bodies and sweat. None of the people in that room had been out of their suits for the better part of a week, and the hab's air must have been pretty gamy to begin with. She could hear the low-voiced rumble of the hab's air circulators and wondered if they always labored that hard.

"So what's the deal, Major?" Carmen Fuentes asked. "Scuttlebutt says we have a new objective. What's the matter. This one wasn't good enough?"

Avery favored her with a scowl from across the table. "You got a problem with that, Marine?"

"Negative, *sir*!" Fuentes rasped out. She glanced at Kaitlin, and her eyes gave the slightest of upward flickers. Avery, Kaitlin had heard, was not universally loved by the Marines under his command, especially those with combat experience. He'd come to 1-SAG straight from four years in the Pentagon, where he had the reputation of being a number one i-dotter, t-crosser, and form-shuffler. How he'd rated a combat command like the First Space Assault Group was anyone's guess.

"Garroway," Avery snapped. "Your people in good shape?"

"Ready to rock and roll, sir," Kaitlin said, straightening up again from the table, pushing against the weary pain in her back and legs. Marine Class One/Special armor wasn't all that heavy in Luna's one-sixth-G gravity, but it had a full eighty kilos' worth of inertia, just like it did Earthside, and dragging the stuff around, hour after hour, was a real workout.

"Casualties?"

"Negative, Major. We didn't even get into the fight."

"What's th' matter, Garry?" Lieutenant Delgado said, teeth white in his dark face. "Movin' a bit slow today?"

"Screw you, Del."

"Hey, anytime."

"That's enough of that," Avery said. "Okay, Garroway, you and Machuga have point on this new op, then," He brought up a USCGS map on the surface of the light table's projection display, topo lines overlaid on a black-and-white photo. Several of the officers moved styro coffee cups out of the way. "Alfa took the brunt of the assault, turns out. Three dead. Damned Chinese fanatics. I'm holding Alfa in reserve here. Captain Fuentes, you will deploy your people to Objective Picard. First Platoon in assault, Second Platoon in overwatch and flank security."

Fuentes looked startled. "Flank security, sir? That hardly seems necessary when—"

"We are playing this one by the book, Captain. By the Corps manual. Now, listen up." He'd removed his suit's gloves, and one precisely manicured finger poked at the topo map projected onto the illuminated tabletop.

"This is the Mare Crisium, the Sea of Crisis," he said, indicating an almost featurelessly smooth expanse of darkness pocked here and there by isolated craters and ringed by bright, bumpy-looking hills, crater rims, and mountains. "It's located about two thousand kilometers east-northeast of our position here. Roughly circular, four hundred fifty by five hundred sixty kilometers, near enough." He touched a keyboard on his side of the table, and a white square picked out one of the two largest, isolated craters in the mare, then expanded sharply, expanding the crater until it covered the table's top. "The crater Picard," Avery said, pointing again. "Twenty-two hundred klicks from Fra Mauro, at fourteen point six north, fifty-four point seven east. Diameter of twenty-three kilometers, with a rim rising two thousand meters above the crater floor. As you can see, there's some interesting activity of some sort in here."

As Avery expanded the scale still further, a patchwork of shallow excavations, piles of tailings, and the broadly looping tracks of wheeled vehicles, startlingly white against the dark regolith, became clearly visible. Several habs and a pair of Lunar hoppers stood near one side of the heaviest activity.

"How recent are these?" Captain Lee wanted to know.

"The photos? Five days."

"So we don't know what they have out there right now," Lieutenant Machuga said.

"There's still the little matter of those sixty missing troops," Lee put in. "I can't believe intelligence could be off *that* much."

"Military intelligence," Fuentes said with a grim chuckle. "A contradiction in terms."

"All right, all right," Avery said. "Let's stick to the point of the thing." He tapped the surface of the table. "Earthside thinks the UNdies have uncovered something at Picard. Something important. They want us to go in and secure it, whatever it is. They'll have an arky team here in a couple of days to check it out."

Palmer gave a low whistle. "Alien shit, huh?" He glanced at Kaitlin. "We pullin' another Sands of Mars here?"

Kaitlin refused to meet Palmer's eyes but continued a pointed study of the map display of the floor of Picard Crater and the excavations there. Two years before, her father, then Major Mark Garroway, had made Corps history by leading a band of Marines 650 kilometers through the twists and turns of one arm of the Valles Marineris to capture the main colony back from United Nations forces at the very start of the war. "Sands of Mars" Garroway was a genuine hero within the Corps, and ever since she'd joined the Marines, Kaitlin had found it difficult to live up to that rather daunting image. Some seemed to assume that if her father was a hero, she must be cut of the same tough, Marine-green stuff. Others . . .

"This operation," Avery said with a dangerous edge to his voice, "will be strictly by the manual. No improvisations. And no *heroics*." He stared at Kaitlin with cold, blue eyes as he said it.

"Yeah, but what kind of alien shit?" Machuga wanted to know. The CO of Bravo Company's First Platoon was a short, stocky, shaven-headed fireplug of a Marine who'd come up as a ranker before going OCS, and his language tended to reinforce the image. "Anything they can freakin' use against us?"

Avery looked at his aide. "Captain White?"

"Sir. We know very little about any supposed ET presence on the Moon," White said. He was a lean, private man with an aristocrat's pencil-line mustache, a ring-knocker, like Avery. "The records we've captured here . . . well, we haven't had time to go through all of them, of course, but the UN people conducting the investigation apparently think that these are different ruins, artifacts, whatever, from what we found on Mars."

"What the hell?" Delgado said. "Different aliens?"

"More recent aliens," White said. "The Mars, um, artifacts are supposed to be half a million years old. I just finished going through some of Billaud's notes—"

"Who's Billaud?" Lee wanted to know.

"Marc Billaud," Avery said. "The head UNdie archeologist here. A *very* important man. Earthside wants us to find him, bad."

White ignored the interruption, forging ahead. "Dr. Billaud's report suggests that the ruins they've uncovered here are considerably younger. Perhaps even dating to *historical* times."

"Shit," Machuga said. "Startin' t'look like Grand Central Station around here."

"What difference does it make how old they are?" Palmer wanted to know.

"The astronuts," Kaitlin said. She'd talked about the subject a lot with her father.

"Would you care to explain, Lieutenant?" Avery said.

"Well, it's just that people all over Earth are going ballistic over what we've been finding on Mars. New religions. Predictions of the end of the world. New takes on the old ancient-astronaut theories. Claims that aliens were God, and that when He comes back in his flying saucer, we won't need governments anymore, that kind of thing."

Palmer chuckled. "Sounds reasonable."

"It's nonsense," Kaitlin replied. "Half a million years

is a *long* time. What could any alien visitors that far back have done that humans might still remember, as religious myth or legend or whatever? But if the aliens were *here* in just the last few thousand years, it . . . well, it could be a different story.''

''Gotcha,'' Lieutenant Dow, one of the LSCP pilots, said with a smirk. ''God help us! Jesus was an astronaut, and the Ark of the Covenant was a two-way radio tuned in to God.'' Those old chestnuts had received a lot of reawakened interest on Earth during the past couple of years.

''Maintaining civic order is becoming a serious concern,'' Avery said, ''not only in Washington, but all over the world. What the UNdies have found here could be of strategic importance in the war. And that, gentlemen, and ladies, is why we are here.''

Which made Kaitlin wonder if this expedition *was* becoming a reprise of her dad's experience on Mars. Though the UN war had a number of formal causes, ranging from US foreign trade practices to Latino demands for an independent nation of Aztlan carved from the American Southwest, the trigger had been the perception in Europe and Japan that the US and Russia were going to keep the secrets of newly discovered extraterrestrial technology for themselves. Close on the heels of that problem was the UN desire to keep the remarkable finds on Mars—*especially* those that suggested that aliens had somehow tampered with human evolution—a closely guarded secret. During the famous March, Major Garroway had arranged for Dr. David Alexander to publish news of some of the initial archeological finds on the Internet, a move that had started riots and caused unrest worldwide and shaken several of the governments arrayed against the United States.

That move had been instrumental in forcing Japan to switch her allegiance from the UN to the US, a shift of power that might well have marked a turning point in the war.

Of course, those reports about aliens and ancient humans on Mars had stirred up problems in the United States as well. Every man and woman in 1-SAG had signed Disclosure Oaths at Vandenberg just before the launch, swearing not to talk to *anyone* other than their debriefing officers about anything they might see or find on the Moon.

Kaitlin wondered what her father would have thought about that. It had been his idea to post the news of the Martian finds on the Net, to undermine the UN's efforts to clamp down on the activities on Mars.

"The evidence we've uncovered here," Avery went on, "suggests that an UNdie survey team found something important at Picard. We don't know what. Earth wants us to go in, secure the site, and hold it until they can send in their own arky team. And that, Marines, is exactly what we're going to do."

He began typing on his keyboard, accessing the table's display software to bring up two green arrows on the map. "Captain Fuentes, you'll deploy in your two LSCPs, coming in low and from the west, along here. Crisium's western mountain wall should shield you from radar . . . and in the final part of your approach, you can skim the surface and stay below the crater rim."

"They might have an OP on the crest of the rim," Fuentes pointed out. "Or a portable radar. That's what I'd do, if I was in their place."

"There is no evidence of an OP anywhere on the rim, Captain," White pointed out.

"Not as of five days ago," Fuentes replied, an edge to her voice. "But you can't imagine these bozos don't know that we're here. Or that we might be getting ready to come gunning for 'em."

"Your Second Platoon will come in first to secure the crater rim," Avery went on, as one of the arrows touched the southwestern edge of the circle of smooth-rounded hills defining the rim. "From here, you should be able to apply covering fire for First Platoon's approach, if necessary. First Platoon will cross the rim in their bug and descend to the crater floor . . . about here." The map expanded again, centering on a flashing landing point between the pressurized habs and the grounded hoppers. "The tactics we employed here at Fra Mauro should work well. Twenty-four men will be sufficient to overwhelm any personnel who happen to be outside the habs, hotwire the airlocks, and gain entry. You are to use care not to breach the habs' pressure integrity. HQ wants prisoners, not vacuum-dried corpses. We particularly need to take Dr. Billaud alive. Questions?''

Fuentes gave a low whistle. "It'll work, sir, if the bad guys do exactly what you think they're gonna do. In my experience, the enemy isn't usually that accommodating."

"Sir," Kaitlin added, pointing. "This facility is a good five or six kilometers from the crater rim. We're not going to be able to provide much overwatch fire support from way the hell out there."

"You'll have your Wyverns and two SLWs. That should be more than enough to provide adequate support." He gave Fuentes a hard look. "Remember, people, we're dealing with a tiny outpost here. From the number and size of those habs, we're looking at life support for fifteen people, tops! If anyone was shuttling in large number of troops and the hab modules to support them, we'd have picked up the deployment from Earth, both optically and by radar."

"AFSCOM has a recon spacecraft up," White said. He glanced at the LED time readout displayed on the back of his left glove. "They'll relay to Colorado Springs, and Colorado Springs will relay to us. We should have an up-to-the-minute report on what's going on in Picard within the next thirty minutes."

Captain Lee scratched the side of his face, making a bristly sound on the unshaven skin. "Sir, if I may suggest . . . Alfa, Second Platoon, ought to provide additional overwatch, at least as reinforcements. The UNdies know we're here, now, and we don't know where those sixty troops are supposed to be."

"Well, they're not at Picard, Captain," White said with a thin smile. "We'd have seen them if they were."

"Intelligence believes that the UNdies' main Lunar force is on the farside," Avery said. "At our old radio-astronomy facility at Tsiolkovsky. If the Air Force guys don't report anything unexpected at Picard, we're go."

"I still think it might be a good idea to have some of

my people in reserve, sir," Lee insisted. "Just in case. Captain Fuentes is right. You can't count on the bad guys to do what you expect."

Avery exchanged a glance with White, then shrugged. "I want at least one platoon here to hold Fra Mauro," he said. "You can have the other platoon as reserve. Not that you're going to need it."

"This," Captain White said, "is going to be a stroll in the park."

Kaitlin said nothing, but she had to suppress an icy shudder. The assault on Fra Mauro, sudden, sharp, and decisive, had been as close to a "stroll in the park" as anyone had a right to expect . . . and three of Alfa Company's people had died when a couple of Chinese special forces troops had opened up on them from the grounded Kongyunjian transport with a rapid-fire squad laser.

Even a minor hit, if it burned through armor, was deadly on the Moon; here, the usual battlefield ratio of three or four wounded for every man dead was reversed. And in this unfamiliar environment, things could so very easily go death-cold wrong, especially in a cobbled-together, *ad hoc* deployment like this one.

She found herself hoping that the Air Force mission *did* see something at Picard. Better to call this assault off and wait for a stronger and better-equipped follow-up force from Earth. Scuttlebutt had it that Army troops would be arriving in a few days, with transports for prisoners and a ticket home for the Marines. Let *them* deal with Picard and its "alien shit."

She checked her own glove-back timepiece. Zero-four-fifty-five GMT. Twenty-eight minutes until the fly-boys could report. . . .

USASF Reconnaissance Flight
Black Crystal, trans-Lunar orbit
0521 hours GMT

"What the hell is *that*?" Aerospace Force Major Sam Barnes pulled back from the padded double eyepiece and looked at the mission commander, Lieutenant Colonel Jacob DeMitre.

"Whatcha got, Sam?" DeMitre said. Silver-white light flooded the cockpit, dazzling and inexpressibly beautiful. The Sparrowhawk's CO eased himself from his couch and made his way carefully, hand over hand, toward Barnes's console.

There was scarcely room for them to breathe, much less move. For three days, they'd been crammed into a space roughly the size of a small closet, with most of the compartment taken up by acceleration couches and consoles. The SRE-10 Sparrowhawk was a tiny ship, a sleek, black-sheathed lifting body with stubby fins and a rounded nose, designed to be piggybacked for launch to a Zeus II HLV booster. They'd boosted from Vandenberg three days earlier, whipping into a high-speed parabola around the Moon on a recon flight dubbed Black Crystal.

At the moment, they were high above Luna's eastern limb, as viewed from Earth, almost ten thousand kilometers above the Mare Crisium and falling in a long, zero-G curve around toward the Lunar farside. Their primary mission had been to overfly the farside radio-telescope complex at Tsiolkovsky, but a last-minute add-on to their orders directed them to scope out Picard Crater in particular, and to check for UN activity in the Crisium region as well.

DeMitre pulled himself up alongside Barnes, rotating his body enough to peer into the eyepiece. "Damfino," he said. "Never seen anything like it. Where is it?"

"Computer," Barnes said. "Optics display, monitor three."

The monitor flicked on, allowing them both to watch. They were looking down into a highly magnified view of the Moon's surface, all bright silver-white light and black shadow. "Magnify and enhance."

The view zeroed in on a tiny black shape . . . a sleek triangle just edging out of the shadows and into the brilliant light of the Lunar sunrise.

"Crossing the Mare Crisium, east to west," Barnes said. "Looks like it might be headed for Picard."

"Stealth surfacing," DeMitre observed. "On that heading, he could be coming from Tsiolkovsky. Okay. I'll phone it in."

A warning chime sounded, electronic and urgent. "Uh-oh," Barnes said, turning. "We're being painted! Looks like target-lock radar."

"S'okay. We're stealthy, too. But I wonder who's curious . . . and why. Recorders going?"

"Affirmative. The paint's at two-nine-zero and rising." The best stealth materials and geometries in the world couldn't absorb or misdirect *that* strong a pulse. "Damn! It's strong. *Real* strong! I think they may have made us, stealth or no stealth."

"Yeah. I got that feeling. Who's 'they'?"

"Shit! I think it's from Tsiolkovsky." He brought up a graphics display showing the Moon's principal features. Tsiolkovsky was still deep within the Lunar night, but it was above the Sparrowhawk's horizon, in direct line of sight. A red light showed on the graphics, at the top of Tsiolkovsky's central peak, marking the radar source.

"But radar that strong?" DeMitre hesitated, then groaned. "Ah! The old Big-T radio telescope. That could put out one hell of a tight beam."

"Roger that. And they've got us right in their—"

The positron beam struck the Sparrowhawk in that instant, searing through the hull of the reconnaissance spacecraft like a blowtorch through paper, antimatter and matter combining in a brief, unholy alliance of mutual annihilation, generating an intense burst of high-energy radiation . . . heat, light, X rays, and gamma rays.

The burst was instantly lethal to both Barnes and DeMitre. Although they never had a chance to radio a warning to Space Command Headquarters, the high-energy shriek of their disintegrating spacecraft was picked up by Aerospace Force sensors in Low Earth Orbit just over a second later.

THREE

LSCP-44, The Moon
0553 hours GMT

Sergeant Frank Kaminski stood in line with the other members of his squad, waiting to file aboard the spindle-legged, insect-shaped bulk of LSCP-44. The ugly little transport, a Landing Space Craft, Personnel in official nomenclature, but a ferry bug in normal usage or, more often yet, simply a bug, had been designed twenty years earlier to haul personnel and cargo from Earth orbit to the Moon and back in reliable, if less than lavish, efficiency. The Marines had bought eight of the rugged little transports during the last fiscal year and adapted them to the impromptu role of Lunar assault craft.

In Kaminski's opinion, that was roughly on a par with sticking a popgun on a garbage scow and calling the thing a battleship. The old hull number 44 had been left painted below its faceted cockpit sponson, at least partly as a bit of false intelligence, but he wondered if the UN could possibly be concerned about the appearance of forty-some bugs that looked more like child's snap-together toys than Marine assault craft.

"Hey, Ski," Lance Corporal Roger Liddel called over the squad channel. "So what's the word on the skipper? Is she really 'Sands of Mars' Garroway's kid?"

"That's ay-firmative."

"Yeah," Sergeant Timothy Papaloupolis added. "And

Ski, here, has a straight shot at her, 'cause he was with her dad on Mars!''

"No shit, Sarge?" PFC Jordy Rawlins asked. He was new to the unit, one of five newbies who'd transferred in two days before launch. "The guys said you was on the Valles March, but I didn't believe it."

"I was there." Funny. He felt a little reluctant to talk about it now, even with his squadmates. "Wasn't as big a deal as the news downloads make out."

"Huh." Rawlins sounded impressed. "You see any alien shit while you were there?"

"A little. Most of it was too damned big to think of it as alien stuff, though. More like . . . I dunno. Big, funny-shaped mountains."

"Yeah, but you got to see the Cave of Wonders, didn't you?" Lance Corporal Michael Klinginsmith asked. "All the Net DLs've been full of that stuff."

"Television, live from the stars," Pap said, laughing.

"I . . . saw it." Yeah, but he didn't like thinking about it. Some of those . . . *things* he'd seen in the big, spherical chamber had turned his stomach and set the skin on the back of his neck crawling. Even now, some he could remember with crystalline clarity. Others had been so strange he remembered little at all, save a vague impression of color or texture. There'd been nothing about them that the human mind could recognize and seize as its own.

If that first brief and tentative glimpse had been anything to go by, extraterrestrials were . . . *alien*, nothing at all like the prosthesis-clad actors and humanoid digital constructs so popular on the science-fiction channels.

"Can the chatter, people," Lieutenant Garroway's voice said, cutting in on the channel. Ski flushed inside his helmet, wondering if she'd been listening in long enough to have overheard Pap's "straight shot" crack. "First Squad's turn next. Mount up!"

The LSCP's cargo lock was just barely big enough for twelve men and their gear to pass through at one time, so boarding was by squads. The line of armor-suited Marines started forward, each man carrying his assault rifle slung muzzle down, and at least one other weapon or load. Kaminski was lugging a two-round reload case of twelve-centimeter rockets for Sergeant Payne's Wyvern. The bulky container only weighed five kilograms on the Moon, but it *acted* like it weighed thirty. You had to be careful manhandling gear and heavy loads here; a missed step and the load would keep going while you fell flat on your ass. Or your faceplate, which could be worse.

The squad filed into the airlock, then stood packed in shoulder-to-shoulder as the outer door closed and the whine of air vents slowly rose from the vacuum-clad silence. That, Kaminski reflected, was a real problem in using these personnel landing craft for assaults: It just took too damned long to cycle through the airlock . . . especially if unpleasant locals were shooting at you.

The clear light flashed green, and the inner hatch sighed open. The squad shuffled through into cool green light, joining Second Platoon's Second Squad, already aboard, and began stowing their rifles and carry-on gear in the secure lockers. "First Squad, sound off!" Gunnery Sergeant Tom Yates barked. "Ahearn!"

"Yo!"

"Anders!"

"Here!"

As Yates ran down the roster, Kaminski backed his way up against one of the slanting, thinly padded shelves lining the sides of the cylindrical compartment, lowering himself carefully onto his backpack PLSS. Yates reached his name with a sharp "Kaminski!"

"Short!" he replied, but Yates ignored the play and kept reciting. In point of fact, he wasn't short anymore, not after re-upping; that was a joke that was quickly losing its savor. Sometimes he wondered what had possessed him to reenlist during that long, cycler-coast home from Mars. Re-upping had not only restored his former rank of corporal—a rank lost on Mars during that incident with the beer—but guaranteed his promotion to sergeant as soon as the shuttle deposited him and the other Mars veterans once again on the runway at Vandenberg.

But he sure as hell hadn't signed on for six more years in the Corps for the joy of wearing three stripes above the

crossed rifles on his sleeve instead of two. Nor had he
joined for the dubious pleasure of being sealed inside an
aluminum can for a sardine's-eye view of a trip to the
Moon.

To tell the truth, he wasn't sure why he'd re-upped, and
the not-knowing bothered him. Hell, the first thing he'd
learned when he joined the Corps was never volunteer. . . .

The roll call came to an end. "All aboard and squared
away, Gunny?" Lieutenant Garroway asked Yates.

"Affirmative, Lieutenant. All present and accounted for,
sir."

"So what's the word, Lieutenant?" Kaminski called
out. "The brass hear from the Aerospace Force, yet?"

"Negative," Kaitlin replied. "But they must be figuring
no news is good news, because the mission is *go*."

"Ooh-rah!" a chorus of radioed voices sounded over
the channel, in the half-shouted, half-growled Corps battle
cry.

"All right, people, listen up!" the lieutenant went on.
"Flight time will be approximately three hours. You will
stay buttoned up, helmets *and* gloves."

The chorus this time consisted of groans and a few
choice expletives. "Jesus *shit*, L-T!" one voice called
above the rest. "That's inhuman!"

"Who is that?" Kaitlin asked. "Nardelli? Just what
makes you think you can lay claim to being *human*?"
When the guffaws and laughter had died down, she continued. "You should all have your plissers topped off, but
we don't know how long we're going to be on the beach,
so all of you lash down and plug into your umbilicals."

Another moment of shuffling and bumping ensued in
the narrow cargo space, as the twenty-two Marines, all
save Gunny Yates and the lieutenant, took their places,
made all too familiar by the long and deadly boring journey out from Earth. Kaminski backed up against one of
the craft's outward-sloping bulkheads and used the harnesses welded there to strap himself in tight. Hoses
dragged down from overhead racks snap-locked onto con-
nectors on the sides of his PLSS unit, letting him breathe
off the bug's life support instead of his own. Yates went

down the narrow passageway between the Marines, checking the equipment and PLSS connections on each man and woman in turn.

"So, what now, Gunny?" Papaloupoulis called.

"We wait, Marines," Yates growled in reply. "We wait for the word."

As far as Kaminski was concerned, the waiting was always the hardest part.

*US Joint Chiefs' Command/
Control Bunker, Arlington,
Virginia
0610 hours GMT (0110 hours
EDT)*

The place was a fortress, hollowed out of bedrock two hundred meters beneath the maze of offices and corridors still called the Pentagon, despite changes to its architecture and geometry over the years. Though called the Bunker by the thousands of personnel, military and civilian, who worked there, it was more of a city than a refuge, a very comfortable and high-tech fortress with cool air, pleasant background music, and the latest in AI neural-link processing to link the place with the World Above.

In two years of war, there'd been frequent calls to abandon this site, so close to the vulnerable and tempting target just across the river that was the nation's capital, but even in the early months of the war, when the continental United States had come under sustained and brutal cruise-missile bombardment, those calls had never been seriously considered. Even if the war—God forbid!—went NBC, the Pentagon's underground warrens were well shielded, well supplied, and capable of maintaining communications with the nation's far-flung military assets, and no matter if the city above was reduced to radioactive slag. The Bunker was, above all else, *secure.*

Colonel David Walker, USAF, was not feeling particularly secure, however, as he stood up in the cool-lit, thick-carpeted briefing room on Sublevel 20, with its

waiting circle of generals, aides, and politicians, and
walked to the head of the room with its slab of a podium
and the array of wall screens behind him and to his right.
The US had managed to hold its own during the past two
years, since the beginning of what was now being called
the UN war, but the news was rarely good. It was the
United States, the Russian Federation, and Japan against
almost all of the rest of the world, now, and for months
they'd been able to do little but hold their own . . . and in
many cases, not even that. The early successes on Mars
and in Earth orbit had buoyed hopes, of course, and a lot
was riding now on the current Marine op on the Moon,
but in most cases, in most places, US forces were just
barely hanging on.

The worse the war news got, the edgier the Joint Chiefs
and the JCS staff became. This place had a nasty tendency
to shoot the messengers bringing bad news, and the news
he carried to this middle-of-the-night special meeting was
decidedly less than career-enhancing.

"Gentlemen," Walker said, "and ladies. This report has
just come through from Cheyenne. Black Crystal has been
destroyed."

A low murmur of voices sounded around the circular
table. He was no more than confirming the rumor that had
been spreading throughout the underground complex for
the past twenty minutes, he knew, but the shock in that
room as he made the announcement was sudden, almost
palpable, nonetheless.

Admiral Charles Jordan Gray, head of the Joint Chiefs,
fixed Walker with a hard glare. "Who destroyed it?
How?"

"We're . . . Cheyenne, I mean, is still looking at that,
sir. The spacecraft was on the outward leg of its circum-
lunar parabola, approximately ten thousand kilometers
above the Mare Crisium, and about to loop around the
farside. We were tracking it, of course, from the ISS. This
is what we picked up."

A flatscreen on the wall behind him switched on, bringing up several windows, each with its own display. The
image showing the target in visible light gave little infor-

mation, a speck of light all but lost in the glare from the
nearby silver curve of the Moon. Other windows showed
the same picture, but at different wavelengths. The infrared
view was clearest. Alphanumerics scrolled up the screen
and wrote themselves across various windows, displaying
times, camera data and wavelength, magnification factors
and uncounted other informational elaborations.

Walker pointed to the IR image, where Black Crystal
was visible as a red sliver against background blues and
blacks. "We were tracking their IR signature with the big
Humasen telescope at the ISS. Watch this, now. Time fac-
tor slowed, twenty to one. . . ."

The window expanded, magnifying the red sliver. As a
dwindling readout of tenths of seconds reached zero, a
white spot flared brilliant against the sliver's side; the spot
grew brighter, expanded . . . and then engulfed the sliver
in a roiling fireball of orange and yellow, a bright disk
that expanded, thinned, and faded. Red and orange fragments drifted apart in ragged, frame-by-frame silence.

"My God," the Aerospace Force JCS member, General
Grace Sidney, said. Like Walker, she was wearing the
new-style USAF dress uniform, a two-tone pattern in black
and light blue, for space and sky. "What have they *got*
up there?"

"Spectral analysis of the radiation showed a sharp spike
at 115 keV," Walker continued, "which is the characteristic signature of positronium annihilation."

"Would you care to try that again in English, son?"
The tall and soft-spoken black man was Louis Carlton
Harrel, the president's national security advisor.

"Antimatter," Admiral Gray said. "The sons of bitches
have an antimatter weapon!"

"Yes, sir," Walker said. "Specifically, we think
they've developed a weapon that directs a stream of positrons—antielectrons—at the target. When positrons inter-
act with ordinary matter, the two annihilate each other,
releasing a very great deal of energy. That 115 keV spike
in the gamma range is the giveaway. We've known how
to build *electron*-beam weapons for years, but we can't
begin to generate that much antimatter that quickly."

"Was it another spacecraft?" General Lamar Turner, the Army chief of staff, wanted to know. "One hidden behind the Moon?"

"Almost certainly not, sir. The power requirements for this kind of weapon are . . . considerable. Cheyenne thinks it more likely we're dealing with a ground base, one with a large fusion reactor."

"A ground base?" Harrel said.

"How the hell did the UNdies get a ground base on the backside of the frigging Moon?" Turner asked.

"We've known for some time that they were working at something major back there, sir," Walker replied. "The transport launches from Kourou and Xichang have been regular as clockwork. And . . . nothing much has been coming back to Earth. Whatever they've been sending up there has been *staying* there."

"Tsiolkovsky," General Sidney said. She closed her eyes. "What would they be building out of our SETI base? What benefit could they—"

"Power, General," Admiral Gray snapped. "Power from the fusion plant at the site, and Tsiolkovsky's manufactory."

"But SETI was shut down," Turner said, protesting. "Everybody said, with the discoveries on Mars—"

"SETI was shut down," General Sidney said. "And the UN grabbed the radio-telescope facility in . . . I think it was '35, maybe '36? I'd bet they're using the factory to turn out something other than telescope components now."

"Makes sense," Admiral Gray said, thoughtful. "If they wanted to keep something hidden from us, something big they were building, the Lunar farside would be the place to do it, wouldn't it?"

"And the SETI facility's fusion reactor would certainly be big enough to power a weapon like that," Sidney added.

"The president is going to want to know just what it is they're building back there," Harrel said. "He's also going to want to know how the hell they saw our Sparrowhawk! That thing's supposed to be the best we have in stealth technology!''

"Even the best stealth technology," General Sidney said, "has trouble masking IR. Especially in space, where a ship *has* to radiate the heat that builds up inside, from power plants and life support.''

"Was that how the enemy tracked them?'' General Turner asked. He looked at Walker. "Colonel? What is Cheyenne's analysis?''

Walker gestured at the IR image on the flatscreen, now frozen in time. "If we could track them by IR, so could the enemy. Now, we knew exactly where to look, of course. Broad-sky IR sweeps can be tricky. CCDs—the charged coupling devices used in such scans—tend to have a very narrow field of view, so you have to know just where to point them. And the Sparrowhawk's flight profile was designed to keep any radiating surfaces blocked from UN observation by the body of the spacecraft itself. But heat does leak through. Also, to be frank, even a stealth spacecraft with a radar cross section the size of my thumbnail can be picked up by a strong enough radar emitter, and the Tsiolkovsky facility can transmit an *extremely* powerful signal. Our best guess is that the UN forces at the SETI facility were carrying out periodic short-term scans of their horizons, concentrating on probable orbital paths of incoming spacecraft. Once they had a target, they would know exactly where to aim their IR CCDs.''

"But why would they have constructed something as powerful as an antimatter beam weapon on the Lunar farside?'' Harrel wanted to know.

Walker clasped his hands behind his back. This was the *real* bad news, the news he'd feared delivering. There was no way to do it but to be blunt. "There is one other possibility that we need to consider, ladies and gentlemen. An alternative to a major Lunar base with a weapons system with a dedicated fusion plant. There is the possibility that the UN is working on their own version of *Ranger*. And that they're using the SETI facilities as a construction site.''

This time, there was no conversation. The room grew

so silent that Walker could easily hear the faint, shrill ringing in his ears that told him his blood pressure was rising. Absently, almost automatically, he reached into his blue and black jacket's inside pocket, extracting the small plastic box with its dose of a single small, blue pill.

"How likely is that?" Archibald Severin, the secretary of defense, wanted to know. "We've been getting reports for months, I know, but there's been no hard data."

Ignoring the cold stares from his audience, Walker slipped the pill under his tongue, feeling it dwindle and dissolve. Like nitroglycerin, the vasorelaxant absorbed directly into his bloodstream. "So far, we've had very little information to work with, sir. And no means at all of gaining confirmation, short of a reconnaissance overflight— which, of course, is what we were trying to do with Black Crystal."

"If the UN forces are working on a *Ranger* project of their own . . ." Gray said. His fist clenched, relaxed, clenched once more. He turned to Marine General Warhurst, seated across the table from him. "Warhurst? Your people are up there now. Any chance they could manage a look-see for us at Tsiolkovsky?"

"My people," Warhurst replied, "are at Fra Mauro, with orders to conduct a snap raid at Picard. That's twenty-five hundred kilometers away from Tsiolkovsky, across some of the roughest, most mountainous terrain on the Moon."

"They have lobbers. Landing modules," the SECDEF pointed out. "If the enemy is developing their own AM craft, then we are in a race. We *must* know."

"Well, having the Marines trek across twenty-five hundred kilometers of Lunar wilderness seems to me to be out of the question," Turner said. "But they may find some intel that'll help us at Picard. Billaud might know what's happening on the farside."

"Long shot, General," Admiral Gray said.

"Hell, long shots are all we have, right now."

"The big question is whether the enemy's waiting for my people at Picard with something they can't handle." Warhurst cocked his head, nailing Walker with a look.

"Colonel? Anything at all about UN forces in Crisium? Ship landings? Transports from other Lunar bases?"

"None, General," Walker replied. "We assume the Sparrowhawk crew was making their observations of the area when the laser took them out."

"Then they're going in blind."

"We're *all* blind on this one, General Warhurst," Turner replied. "I'd say all we can do is send them in and see what they find at Picard."

"What if the Sparrowhawk was shot down to cover UN deployments at Picard?" Admiral Gray said. "They could be walking into a trap."

"We at least should warn them," Warhurst said, "that Black Crystal was shot down."

"I would strongly recommend against that," Arthur Kinsley, the director of Central Intelligence said. "The Marines *must* reach Picard if we're to have a chance of capturing Billaud. What can we tell them? To be careful? I'm sure they know enough to keep their heads down! And we do not want to tip our hand to the UN, to let them know how much we know . . . or guess."

Harrel rapped the tabletop, commanding attention. "You will tell them, General Warhurst, that they are clear to proceed."

"But, sir. We don't know—"

"You *will* tell them, General. We need that information. And we need Billaud. The possibility that the UN is running an AM project of their own merely makes the acquisition of that information even more imperative. I'm sorry, but I see no way around it."

As the debate continued, Walker dithered for a moment over whether to stay at the podium or return to his seat. He decided on the latter, quietly walking around the table and resuming his seat. There was nothing more in the way of hard information to convey, and it was clear that the discussion had swept well beyond the parameters of his report.

He wondered, though, what the Marines would think about being sent into their objective blind . . . sent in without even knowing that they *were* blind.

LSCP-44, The Moon
0643 hours GMT

Kaitlin climbed up the ladder from the LSCP's cockpit. It had been over an hour now since they'd filed aboard, and the mounting tension within the craft's steel bulkheads was as thick as week-old bottled air. The cockpit was a cramped and claustrophobic space, wedged in among instrument consoles and all but filled by the side-by-side couches for the module's pilot and the mission commander.

The right-hand seat was empty, and Kaitlin pulled herself into it. Lieutenant Chris Dow sat in the other seat, completing the prelaunch checklist.

"We've got clearance, Garry," Dow told her. "We're go for immediate liftoff."

"About damned time! What did they say about the target?"

"Not a thing. Just, 'Proceed with op.' "

"That's it? Proceed with op? Nothing else?"

"Not a word. I guess we can assume the recon didn't spot anything noteworthy."

"Some updated images of the target would've been nice. Okay. How long to boost?"

"Ten minutes." He flipped a row of switches on his main console. "Reactor is on-line, and I'm warming up the main thrusters now. He gestured out the narrow forward window, where a second LSCP was visible on the dusty regolith outside. "Gotta coordinate with Becky, of course. She's on track for liftoff two minutes after us."

"I'll pass the word, then."

He tapped the commo console. "You can plug in from here."

"Thanks. I'd rather do it in person."

Not that "in person" meant very much, when every Marine in her platoon was suited up anyway, with all orders and announcements coming in through the platoon ops channel. Still, she wanted her people to know her as a person, someone with them, and not as a disembodied voice on the IC.

Stepping off the ladder, she turned and faced the double row of waiting, space-suited Marines. "Ten minutes, people. The mission is *go*."

"*Ooh-rah!*" sounded over her helmet headset. "We're gonna kick some UNdie ass!"

"Let's get it *on*!"

"So how about it, Lieutenant?" That was Kaminski's voice. "They sending us after alien shit?"

"You have the same set of orders DLed on your PAD as I do, Kaminski," she replied. "We're looking for Dr. Billaud. And the suits are gonna want to see what we find at Picard. Any other questions?"

"Yeah, Lieutenant. Is it true this place is named after a spaceship captain in that old flat-TV epic?"

"As far as I know, Picard was a seventeenth-century astronomer," she replied, laughing. "Accurately calculated the length of one degree of meridian on Earth, among other things. Anything else? Okay. Next stop, Picard!"

Eight minutes later, in a silent spray of billowing, Lunar dust, the LSCP bug lifted into the black Lunar sky.

FOUR

LSCP-44, Call sign Raven
Mare Crisium, The Moon
0905 hours GMT

A lobber hop on the Moon was nowhere near as violent
as the liftoff from Vandenberg had been—or even the
mildly bone-rattling three-G boost from LEO into trans-
Lunar injection. The LSCP's main engine was a
Westinghouse-Lockheed NTR that superheated water into
a high-speed plasma. Thin and sun-hot, the plasma was
invisible—no rocket blasts or licking flames—and constant, providing a slow but steady shove that lofted the
bug into a low, Lunar suborbital path. Precisely controlled
in short bursts, the jets allowed the bugs to skim the cratered, gray landscape at an altitude of less than three kilometers, terrain-hugging to avoid enemy radar. The
acceleration was gentle, punctuated from time to time by
another nudge from the main thrusters, or the slighter,
more unpredictable bumps from the attitude-control jets.

Kaitlin stood in the meter-wide space just behind and
to the right of the pilot's acceleration couch, stooping to
watch the smoothly sculpted landscape unfold ahead
through the bug's angular, greenhouse canopy, comparing
the view from time to time with the various computer
graphics and schematics displayed on the main console's
monitors. At Fra Mauro, the sun had been almost overhead, and the terrain had been silver-gray. Here, with the

48

sun just above the western horizon at their backs, the regolith had taken on a redder, warmer appearance, one where
long shadows made every hollow and depression, every
rock and boulder and cliff face stand out in diamond-hard
relief.

"We're coming up on the Crisium Ringwall," Dow
said. "Over the top, and then we'll see if they're watching
for us." He reached out and tapped a readout on a console
on the right side of the cockpit with a forefinger. "You
might keep your eye on this one. Threat warning."

"Roger that," Kaitlin replied. Half an hour before,
they'd drifted silently through the skies of the Mare Tranquillitatus, just north of Tranquillity Base, the old Apollo
11 landing site. Someday, she imagined, the place would
be a museum, but there was nothing there now but the
LEM's descent module, some scientific instruments and
mission castoffs, and a launch-toppled American flag.

Now, they'd reached the eastern shores of the Sea of
Tranquillity, and the rugged highlands separating the Mare
Tranquillitatus from the Mare Crisium rose ahead, brilliant
in the long-setting sun. If the UN had established a radar
watch from Picard, it would pick them up as they cleared
the mountaintops.

"So, your dad ever talk much about what he saw out
on Mars?" Dow asked. He turned his head inside his helmet, to peer up at her through the side of the visor. The
question seemed purely conversational, but there was an
edge behind the words that Kaitlin had come to recognize.

"Quite a bit, actually," she said. "But I don't think he
saw anything you haven't heard about already on the
newsnet."

"Well, I was just wondering if there was anything else.
You know, stuff the government was covering up."

"If there was, I could hardly tell you about it now,
could I?" She let the reply dangle a bit of mystery for
Dow. "Or, if I did—"

He finished the old joke's punch line for her. "You
would have to kill me, yeah, yeah."

She laughed. The LSCP pilot was fun, smart, and pleasant, and she enjoyed flirting with him. They'd talked about

alien artifacts on the trip out from Earth a couple of times, and he'd been so curious about what her father had seen at Cydonia that she'd started having entirely too much fun teasing him.

"I guess the two things everyone's talking about back on Earth are the war and the Builders," he said, using the popular term coined to describe the unknown beings who'd carved the immense and still enigmatic monuments on the Cydonian plain on Mars and, apparently, tampered to some extent with the genetic makeup of an unprepossessing hominid known to modern scientists as *Homo erectus*. An archaic *Homo sapiens*—whose freeze-dried corpses had been found at Cydonia now by the thousands—had been the result.

"Uh-huh. Digging up the Builders on Mars helped start the war in the first place. And there were all those ancient human bodies. And the Display Chamber, under the Face. I guess people are bound to be curious."

He snorted, the noise a startling hiss over the helmet com system. "Curious? Yeah, I guess that's one word for it. My family back home, my mom and both dads and my sister, they've all been after me about nothing but the Builders for weeks now. And when word leaked that there might be Builder stuff on the Moon, and that that was where I was going, well."

"They members of any of these new religions popping up?"

"Nah. At least, I don't think so. Did . . . did your dad get to see the Display Chamber?"

"Yes," she said. "He went inside once with David Alexander—that's one of the archeologists who was with him at the site. He hasn't talked about it much, though. Wish I could see it in person. They say the tapes they've been playing over the Net don't do the real thing justice."

"Yeah. Well, maybe we'll find another Chamber at Picard. This Billaud character must be working on something pretty big."

The mountains were rising rapidly to meet the bug, their shadow now a misshapen black spider rippling up the slope ahead as though to escape them. The hillsides facing the sun were so bright; Kaitlin had heard somewhere that the actual color of moonrock and regolith was dark, darker, in fact, than coal . . . but that it appeared bright in contrast to the empty sky around it. She found such facts counterintuitive, however. It *looked* as bright as any white beach sand she'd ever seen. Dow gave another gentle tap to the thrusters, and the bug drifted higher, easily clearing the age-eroded crest of the slope.

The threat warning LED lit up in a flashing constellation of red.

"We're being painted," she said. The words were calm, unemotional, but suddenly her heart was pounding inside her chest. "Looks like traffic-control radar."

"I see it. Maybe they'll lose us against the mountains."

The bug was dropping again, falling abruptly into shadow as it descended the inner face of the Crisium Ringwall. Ahead, the Mare Crisium stretched away clear to the black shadow of the terminator, flat and nearly featureless, the surface far darker than the sun-dazzled highlands had been. A large crater, flattened into a deeply shadowed oval by perspective, lay almost directly ahead.

"Picard," Dow said, checking his displays. "Bang on target."

The warning LEDs continued to show a strong radar signal coming from the crater ahead, though the mountains behind them might well be masking them from detection. Dow gentled the controls, smoothing and slowing the bug's descent with several rapid-fire bursts from the attitude-control thrusters.

"Better let your Marines know we're almost there," he said. The oval of Picard was growing larger second by second, and also flatter, until all that was visible was a sunlit smear of smooth-shaped mountains, the crater's ringwall extending above the surface of the darker basaltic sea. The LSCP had descended to within two hundred meters of the mare's surface, below the top of the crater rim. Kaitlin approved. If the radar was coming from a grounded ship or lobber inside the crater basin, they should have just dropped below its horizon.

The threat indicator stayed on, however. That suggested

that someone was watching them from the crater rim. It also suggested that that someone was waiting for them, waiting and ready for their arrival.

"Heads up, Marines," she called over the platoon channel. "Target in sight. It looks like they see us coming, so be ready to unstrap and bounce as soon as I give the word."

Dow hit the main thrusters again, dropping the craft's nose to accelerate toward the target. Kaitlin found herself twisting her body so that she could peer up through her helmet visor at the rimwall mountains as they filled the cockpit's forward window. She knew she ought to be watching the graphic displays instead—those carried more information than the naked-eye view out the bow of the LSCP—but she found herself wrestling with the terribly human urge to see the threat directly, instead of as it was implied by the craft's electronics. Additional red LED readouts were winking on now, indicating other radar transmitters joining the first.

"I think—" she said, then stopped. A dazzling star appeared on the mountaintop, winking on, then off with the suddenness of a camera's strobe.

"Did you see that?" Dow asked. Apparently, he preferred looking with his eyes instead of electronics as well.

"Sure did. There . . . to the right a bit."

"Your call. Pass it by, or have a look?"

"We look," she decided. "Definitely. We're supposed to land up there to cover First Platoon. I think we'd better check that flash out."

"Roger that." The bug banked right and Dow cut in the main thrusters, clawing for altitude. Kaitlin watched for a second flash, but saw nothing. It had been about *there* . . . between those two rounded peaks at the crest of the crater rim. It might have been sun reflecting from a cast-off bit of space junk from the UN arky team at the crater, but she was betting that a flash that bright had come from something pretty large—as large, say, as the cockpit windows of a Lunar hopper or a ground crawler.

"Gimme a channel to 30."

He keyed in some numbers on the commo console. "Plug in there."

Kaitlin pulled a commo jack from the connector box on her suit's belt, plugging it into the console receptacle. "Eagle," she called. "Eagle, this is Raven."

"Raven, Eagle," Carmen Fuentes's voice came back almost at once. "Go."

Kaitlin checked the time readout inside her helmet. If LSCP-30 was on its mission profile, it would still be over the Mare Tranquillitatus, shielded from UN radar by the Crisium Ringwall. A military communications satellite at L-2 allowed the two bugs to stay in tight-beamed, scrambled contact despite the mountains between them. "We've got a possible hostile OP on the Picard Crater rim," she said. "TC radar and transient visual. We'll try to take it down before you clear the Crisium wall and get painted."

"Copy that, Raven. We'll relay to Falcon. If you run into trouble, give him a yell." Falcon was the call sign for LSCP-38, bringing up the rear with Captain Lee and Alfa Company's Second Platoon. Good luck!"

"Thank you, Eagle. Luck to you. Raven out."

In another moment, LSCP-44 crested the Picard Crater rim, angling between the two peaks Kaitlin had identified seconds before. The crater was a vast bowl stretching clear to the horizon and beyond; she couldn't even see the far crater wall. The bowl's floor, five kilometers below the rim, was shrouded in impenetrable black shadow, but a cluster of lights in the near distance marked the UN's Picard Base.

And then, on the sunlit crest ahead, she saw it, an enclosed Lunar hopper with pale blue UN markings, just rising above a swirling cloud of gray dust. Sunlight flashed again from the facets of its greenhouse windows. The spindly-legged craft was quite similar to the LSCP, though designed around a square base, instead of a rectangular one. It looked a lot like a larger version of the old LEMs, the Lunar Excursion Modules that NASA had used for the first landings over seventy years before, but the resemblance was one of design specifications rather than descent. Spacecraft didn't need streamlining on the Moon, so efficiency and low mass were the key words. Hoppers, like the LSCPs, flew on fission-fired plasma thrusters; they weren't rated for flights between the Moon and LEO, but they could reach Lunar orbit, easily enough, and could use short bursts to hop on suborbital vectors to any spot on the Moon.

"He's making for the base," Kaitlin said. "He's probably already warned them."

"I'm more worried about him getting above us," Dow replied. The UN hopper slewed left, rotating, slowing sharply as it hovered on its invisible jet of hot plasma and rising toward the LSCP's height.

"Why?" Kaitlin asked. Then the answer hit her. "Oh . . ."

Neither hopper nor LSCP carried anything like armor. The hopper's aluminum hull was so thin in places that a clumsily dropped tool could puncture it . . . and the more massively constructed LSCP wasn't that much better. If one of the two craft could maneuver above the other, the jet of hot, charged particles from its ventral thrusters would become a formidable short-range weapon.

The UN hopper was climbing fast now, rising above the bug as the bug descended. As the range closed to within thirty meters, Kaitlin could see the airlock door on the hopper just beneath its cockpit windows; the door was open and a space-suited figure was leaning out, a figure wearing a bright blue UN helmet and aiming a rifle. She didn't see a muzzle flash, but she thought she felt a vibration, a dull thud from somewhere beneath her feet.

"We're under fire," she warned.

"I see him." Dow hit the main ventral thruster for a two-second burst, and Kaitlin felt her knees sag with the acceleration. The bug gained the altitude advantage on the hopper. A moment later, Dow angled the LSCP over, nose down, and fired again, banking slightly with the port thrusters to send the ungainly bug drifting across and above the UN hopper's flight path.

There was no time for calculations or pulling up numbers or scenarios on the computer. The entire maneuver was strictly seat-of-the-pants, executed within the space of five seconds. As the bug passed ten meters above the hopper, Dow brought the ungainly craft's nose up and fired the main thrusters again.

They couldn't see whether the invisible burst of hot plasma was on target or not, but as the bug rotated slowly at Dow's practiced touch, the other vehicle came into view a second later. Together, wordlessly, they watched as the hopper continued drifting down toward the surface, rushing to meet its own shadow . . . and then the two merged in a sudden, silent burst of Lunar dust. The hopper crumpled and rolled, cartwheeling in slow-motion bounds low across the surface, hurling up great, arcing jets of dust with each impact. As it came to rest, a blurring cloud of dust enveloped the wreckage, settling with agonizing slowness.

Kaitlin dropped a gloved hand on Lieutenant Dow's shoulder. "Congratulations, Lieutenant. I think you just scored the first shoot-down of an enemy craft on the Moon."

"Four more and I'm an ace," Dow replied. He shook his head. "Don't think I'd care to try that again, though." Holding the stick in his left hand, he punched in a series of commands with his right, firing port and starboard attitude jets that thumped and bumped through the hull and against Kaitlin's boots. The bug descended swiftly, narrowly missing a tumble of huge, gray boulders before the view was obscured by a cloud of rising dust, and the landing pads settled with a bump and a jar into the hard-packed regolith.

"Contact light!" Dow called, reaching out to flip down a row of switches. "Thrusters off and safed. Reactor to standby. You're clear to debark."

"Right." She keyed the platoon channel. "Gunny Yates? We're down. Move 'em out!"

"Copy that, Lieutenant. All right, Marines, you heard the lieutenant! We're moving!"

LSCP-44, Call sign Raven
Picard Ringwall, The Moon
0914 hours GMT

Frank Kaminski brought his ATAR to his chest, waiting in the dark and close-packed confines of the airlock as the chamber's atmosphere bled away. A winking red light flicked green, then the outer door swung slowly open, flooding the airlock with silvery light.

"Hit the beach, Marines!" Yates shouted over the platoon channel. "Go! Go! Go!"

He crowded ahead close behind Lance Corporal Nardelli, feeling the vibrations through his boots as the file pounded down the metal grating that served as a debarkation ramp. The regolith gave beneath his feet with a crunch felt rather than heard, like thin, crusty snow; directly ahead, the sun blazed above the shadowed western cliffs of Crisium, beneath the slender, just-visible blue-and-silver bow of a crescent Earth.

As at Fra Mauro, he felt again the mingled feelings of awe and desolation. There were no stars visible in the side of the sky near the sun, but if he turned away and looked up, an icy scattering of stars was just visible above the eastern horizon. The crater rim stretched away to either side, to north and south; with nothing but black sky and red-gray hills as smooth as earthly sand dunes as measures of scale, he felt bug-small, tiny and exposed, as he followed the other Marines across the surface.

"Jeez, what happened there?" someone called. "Got a crashed bug, here. South, fifty meters."

"That's a UN hopper, and we just shot it down," the lieutenant's voice replied. "Watch it. They may have left troops on the ground."

"We'll check it, Lieutenant," Yates replied. "Okay! First Squad, check the hopper. Second Squad, deploy in defense perimeter. Let's *move* it, Marines!"

Trotting easily in long, bounding strides that quickly slid into a kind of kangaroo hop-and-skip, Kaminski and the others in his squad scuffed and bounced their way up a shallow slope to the spot where the UN hopper, its thin hull crumpled and torn, lay upside down. A space-suited body, a man in a blue UN helmet, lay sprawled in his back nearby. His face, just visible through a blackened, chipped visor, was horribly blistered, as though his skin had been hit by a blowtorch. The name stenciled on a strip of cloth attached to his suit read LECLERC. Kaminski wondered who the man was . . . and if he had a family waiting for him back on Earth.

"What happened to *him*?" Ahearn asked.

"Didn't you feel us bouncing around before we landed?" Kaminski replied. "I think the lieutenant fried 'em by hitting 'em with the bug's main jets."

"Yeah? Man, that's doin' it the hard way!"

He didn't answer. He was thinking about something he'd read once, as a kid, about how air-to-air combat had begun when pilots on both sides, flying cloth-and-wood-frame biplanes over France in the First World War, had begun carrying pistols with them on reconnaissance flights and exchanging shots with enemy fliers. Pistols had led to machine guns . . . and ultimately radar-homing missiles and airborne lasers. He wondered if they were witness to a dawn of a new and similar type of warfare.

There wasn't time to think much about history, though. A squad sweep through the area turned up bits of scrap and wreckage knocked from the UN hopper, and a portable radar unit mounted on a tripod at the top of a low hill. The footprints scuffed and stamped into the dust showed where UN troops had set the radar up only moments earlier. After a careful check for booby traps, two of the Marines began dismantling the unit; Kaminski took the moment's respite to turn his back on Earth and the sun and stare down into the crater bowl below them.

The bottom of the crater was night black, but enough light was scattering off the crater rim to provide a little illumination. In fact, though, the lights of the UN base shone like a tightly packed constellation of brilliant stars on the crater's floor, only a few kilometers away. Yates was standing on the hill crest a few meters away, pressing the rubber-ringed facepiece of a photomultiplier magnifier to his visor. He was studying the layout of the UN base, the bulky length of his Wyvern resting in the dust by his feet.

Kaminski dropped the reload case he was humping in the dust nearby. "Hey, Gunny. Can I have a look?"

Yates handed him the electronic imager. Kaminski raised the facepiece, positioning the small, rectangular screen against his visor. A tiny IR laser built into the optics gave the range to target as 8.34 kilometers; in the pale green glow of the photomultiplier optics, he could penetrate the night shadows easily.

The Picard base consisted of several squat, upright, cylindrical habs and not much more besides the worklights and a scattering of vacuum-rigged bulldozers and trench-diggers. Not far away were several more lobbers, plus a larger, sleeker shape, an arrowhead of stealth-jet black, sitting erect on quad-frame landing jacks.

Closer, between the habs and the crater's western slope, the ground had been carved and plowed in a rectilinear patchwork of trenches connecting several deep, square-sided pits. It was, Kaminski thought, obviously an archeological dig of some kind. The arky teams on Mars had used similar techniques to carve trenches into the Martian regolith, sampling the layers they cut through for artifacts and cast-off bits of debris.

All the scene below was missing was people. Funny. The UN personnel obviously had had plenty of warning that the Marines were on their way. They'd had time to dispatch the lobber and set up a portable radar unit. They'd probably been warned by the garrison at Fra Mauro the moment the Marines had first appeared

Were they all inside, huddled up in their suits, waiting to see if the Marines would come in with can openers at the ready?

"Seems a bit too quiet, Gunny," he said to Yates. "Don't see a damned thing moving down there. Ah! Wait a sec!"

"Whatcha got?"

"That black ship grounded down there. It's lifting!" There was no flame, but the arrowhead shape was silently rising now above a swirl of lunar dust.

"Gimme the imager."

Kaminsky surrendered the device. Without it, he could just see the UN ship vanishing into the night beyond the base.

"Shit," Yates said. "They're bugging out. Wonder if they're evacuating the place? Or . . ."

"Or what, Gunny?"

"Or if they just stopped long enough to haul in some reinforcements. I don't like the looks of this." He lowered the imager again and handed it to Kaminsky. "They gotta know we're here, all right. But . . . uh-oh. Here comes Eagle."

Kaminski turned, following Yates's pointing arm. Another bug was coming in out of the sun, floating high, passing above Picard's rim by at least two hundred meters. Silently, it drifted overhead and a bit to the north, descending rapidly as it cleared the rim, floating on unseen jets of plasma toward the brilliantly lit base below. Halfway down, the ungainly looking craft switched on its landing lights, casting bright circles of illumination across the habs and trenches.

Kaminski watched a moment . . . then lifted the magnifier to his visor again, staring down into the base. There was something . . .

He saw movement . . . a trio of blue helmets raised above the rim of one of the trenches . . . and the stubby, metallic cylinder of a shoulder-launched missile. "Missile on the ground!" he shouted. "This is Kaminski, I have a slam, in the trenches fifty meters from the base habs!"

Yates jerked the imager from Kaminski's glove, lifting it one-handed to his own visor. "This is Yates! Confirmed! Shoulder-launched missile, in the trenches! They're targeting Eagle!"

"Get the slaw on them!" Garroway's voice called. "Yates! Get the Wyvern in action!"

Yates had already stooped, snatched up the Wyvern, and hoisted it to his shoulder, dropping the sighting display into place in front of his visor. "Clear aft!" he called.

"You're clear!" Kaminski shot back, then slapped Yates's shoulder for emphasis. "Go!"

Yates fired, loosing a silent gout of burning gas and strips of plastic packaging from the rear of the man-portable launcher. The Wyvern missile, kicked clear of the weapon's muzzle by an explosive charge, shot twenty meters toward the edge of the crater rim before its engine switched on, a tiny, white-hot point of light dwindling rapidly toward the UN base.

Long before the Wyvern could cross the distance to its target, however, the UN troops hiding in the trenches fired their own missile. The slam's back-flash was bright enough to be seen with the naked eye from eight kilometers away; the missile streaked skyward, scratching out a needle of white fire against the night as it arrowed into First Platoon's LSCP.

The detonation was a strobe of light banishing the stars, dazzling against the night.

FIVE

LSCP-30, Call sign Eagle
Picard Crater, The Moon
0916 hours GMT

The missile struck the LSCP from the right and from
below, the explosion a hammerblow that sent the frail
craft lurching hard to the left, nose high, then dropped it
into a spin. Captain Carmen Fuentes was standing behind
the pilot, Lieutenant Kenneth Booth, when the blast
slammed her against the back of the pilot's couch.

Booth screamed, the sound shrill over Carmen's headset.

"Ken!"

"I'm hit! I'm hit, damn it!" He clawed at the side of
his suit, where a thumb-sized hole in the tough, layered
plastic matched a larger hole punched through his acceleration couch, and another in the deck centimeters from
Carmen's left foot. Air whistled from the puncture, as a
cold fog condensed above it in a tiny, spinning whirlwind.
The craft continued its roll sluggishly to the left, almost
tipping all the way over, but at the last instant, it wallowed
back, spilling Carmen against the side of the cockpit as
the deck dropped away beneath her and took her stomach
with it.

"Take the controls, damn it!" she shouted at the pilot.
"Get us back under control!"

Booth nodded inside his helmet visor, which was al-

61

ready starting to fog up, and fumbled with the paired joysticks that controlled main thrust and attitude. She felt several hard bumps as he triggered the ACTs; both spin and descent slowed, but didn't stop.

"Machuga!" she called over the platoon channel.

"This is Jaclovic, ma'am. The lieutenant's dead."

"Okay! Hang on! We're hit and going down. You're in charge! Get both squads out as soon as we hit!"

"Copy that! Okay, gyrines! You heard! Brace for impact!"

Booth fired the main thruster; Carmen nearly dropped to her knees with the sudden acceleration, and she heard a grinding shriek somewhere aft, like metal tearing.

Then the bug crumpled into the Lunar surface, almost upright, with the shock taken up by the folding of its six, splayed legs. This time, Carmen did hit her knees as the deck slammed up against her legs. The cockpit tilted heavily back to the right, and she had to cling to the acceleration couch to hold her place.

"The Eagle has damned well landed," she muttered. They were down, at least more or less in one piece. She felt shaken, but unhurt. The tiny whirlwind of escaping air at her feet had become a hurricane, but a short-lived one as the last of the bug's air shrilled out into space. Carmen was already fumbling at one of the pouches attached to her suit harness, pulling out a self-sealing vacuum patch which she slapped over the hole in the side of Booth's suit. There was not a lot else she could offer in the way of first aid. The inside of his visor was smeared with blood and a bright, pink foam, and she could barely see his face. *Damn!* Why didn't these Marine-issue armored suits come with external life-support readouts? She couldn't tell if the man was alive or dead.

Light flared silently outside . . . another shoulder-launched missile strike somewhere close by, she thought. The people who'd shot down LSCP-30 would be closing in pretty quickly now.

"Captain!" Jaclovic's voice called. "Captain! Are you okay?"

"I'm in one piece. Get the platoon out of here, Gunny! Perimeter defense. *On the double!*"

One of the square-paned windows of the cockpit's greenhouse canopy suddenly bore a small, round hole surrounded by a frosting of tiny white cracks. She wondered why she hadn't heard the shot or the impact—then remembered that she was in vacuum now. No sound. Over her helmet radio, though, she could hear shouted orders, calls, and the hiss and puff of heavy breathing as the platoon scrambled clear of the grounded craft.

The bug must be under attack by UN troops outside. They *had* to get out and get clear of the wreckage, or risk being trapped inside. The best thing she could do for Booth, she decided, was leave him where he was. If he was dead, there was nothing more she could do; if he was wounded, there still wasn't much she could do, except arrange to get him inside one of those habs out there as quickly as possible, where his suit could be removed and his wounds treated.

"I'll be back for you, Ken," she said, not knowing if he heard her or not. "Just sit tight!"

The deck had folded enough in the crash that she almost didn't make it, suit, PLSS, and all, through the circular hatch that lead down to the forward end of the bug's main compartment. There, deck had risen to meet a descending overhead, and she had to crouch low to make her way aft through cramped, near-total darkness, groping for the entrance to the airlock. She switched on the light mounted on the right shoulder of her suit and let the pale circle of illumination it cast flicker along both sides of the compartment. Several still, space-suited bodies lay there, two on the deck, three more still strapped to their bulkhead supports up forward. Lieutenant Machuga was one of those still strapped to his bulkhead support, the front of his suit peeled open in jagged leaves to expose pale bone, glistening black blood already freezing, and a fist-sized hole going clear through the platform at his back and the deck underneath. Next to him was HMC Strigel, the company's corpsman, his visor shattered. Shrapnel from the missile strike must have sleeted through the forward end of the compartment.

Stopping only to retrieve an ATAR from a bulkhead storage rack, she kept moving aft, squeezing through the misshapen airlock hatch, then through the lock and out onto the still, vast quiet of the Lunar surface, crawling on hands and knees to squeeze through the outer door.

The bug had come down at the edge of the crisscross of trenches and excavated pits, the spider's legs twisted and snapped by the impact, the frame crumpled badly on one side. Clouds of vapor jetted from a dozen holes in the reaction-mass tanks; as the water escaped into space, it froze, creating clouds of glittering ice particles that gradually settled toward the ground. In the shadows of the crater floor, quite a bit of ice had built up, where water reaction mass had escaped the tanks and frozen almost immediately.

She rose unsteadily to her feet, breathing hard, then leaped for the nearest trench as silently blossoming puffs of dust stitched across the regolith a few meters to her left and black holes appeared as if by magic in the LSCP's hull metal.

She landed almost on top of three Marines, their reactive camo armor black in the blackness of the ditch. "Shit! Watch what the fuck you're doing!" one of the Marines barked as she hit his leg. Then he did a clumsy double take, reading name or rank tabs. "Uh, sorry, Captain."

She ignored the outburst. "Where's Gunny Jack?"

A black figure crouched farther along the trench raised an arm, signaling. "Over here, Captain."

"I'm coming to you."

"Watch your head, ma'am! They've got an MG over there somewhere!"

"Roger that!"

She squeezed past the three Marines and moved toward Jaclovic's position. The trench was a meter deep and only about a meter wide; to stay concealed, she had to crawl on her hands and knees, and even so she wondered if the back of her PLSS was showing enough to make an inviting target.

As she neared Jaclovic, the NCO raised himself above the lip of the trench, aiming his ATAR from the shoulder. The Advanced Technology Assault Rifle employed electronic optics in the sighting mechanism to place a crosshair on the firer's visor, targeting whatever it was aimed at, but long habit had Jaclovic firing from a perfect kneeling stance, even if his suit and helmet didn't allow him to sight his weapon directly. He loosed a quick burst of triplet shots, then dropped back behind the cover of the trench as the enemy's machine gun returned the fire in silent puffs of dust.

"H'lo, Captain," he said as she dropped to the floor of the trench beside him. "Ain't we got fun?"

She twisted about, raising her helmet above the rim of the trench. "Where's the fire coming from? I can't see."

"Stay down! Uh, ma'am." He made a slicing motion with one hand, pointing. "That tall radio mast, call it twelve o'clock. We got a machine gun at about one o'clock, near the big bulldozer, and a slaw in the dirt pile at about eleven. The hab at ten o'clock, I think there's a guy on top of it spotting. There's also troops, maybe ten, maybe twelve, covering in the trenches over closer to the habs."

"Trench warfare!" she said. The thought was almost funny.

"Yeah. Lasers. Spaceships." He raised himself up again and loosed another silent burst toward the habs. "And we're back to shootin' each other from the trenches."

Carmen unslung the ATAR she'd picked up in the bug, flicked on the optic sight, plugged in her suit connector to get an HUD link, pulled the bolt to chamber a round, and flicked the selector to three-round burst. As Jaclovic took cover again, she rose to her knees, swinging the assault rifle toward the bulldozer where he'd said the machine gun was hidden. A bright green crosshair tracked across her helmet's visor, showing where she was aimed at the moment. She adjusted the weapon until the crosshairs were centered on the bulldozer. Carmen waited, watching for movement . . . and then a puff of gray dust exploded across her visor as a round plowed into regolith a few centimeters away. She jerked back down under cover, without having taken the shot.

"Touchy, aren't they?" she said.

"Gotta watch yourself, Captain. They got us covered six ways from—"

"Incoming!" someone shouted over the channel, and a second later a bright light blossomed from the direction of the grounded LSCP. Bits and pieces of rock and metallic debris showered over the trenches.

"Forgot to tell you, ma'am," Jaclovic added. "They got slams out there, too."

"This is fun. Can we work some people over that way, try to get behind them?"

"I sent Second Squad that way soon as we got clear, ma'am. They got pinned . . . about there. We salvaged one Wyvern from the crash, and both squad lasers, but we haven't been able to see a target long enough to hit it. Somethin' else, too."

"What?"

"From the volume of fire we've been taking, I'd say we're facing more than a handful of troops out there. They've got, I don't know . . . dozens, hidden in the trenches all along from there . . . to there, and I wouldn't be surprised if they had more people positioned to move in from the flanks or behind. These guys have it organized, and right now, I'd say they have us just about where they want us."

She rose again, this time simply pointing her assault rifle in the general direction of the bulldozer and clamping her gloved forefinger down on the trigger. The gunfire was silent, of course, but the butt gave a reassuring triple-thump to her shoulder before she dropped behind cover once more. She couldn't possibly have actually hit anything, but at least the gesture *felt* good.

"Communications?"

"No problem there. We've got an open channel with Second Platoon, on the crater rim about eight klicks *that* way. And an L-2 satlink to Fra Mauro. But I don't think either of those are gonna help us."

"Why not?"

He jerked a gauntleted thumb over his shoulder, toward the habs and the concealed UN soldiers. "Because *they're* getting in position to rush us, and there's not one damned thing we can do about it."

LSCP-44, Call sign Raven
Picard Ringwall, The Moon
0919 hours GMT

Kaitlin Garroway held the viewer of her electronic imager against her visor, pressing the button that zoomed the view in to maximum magnification. With light enhancement, she could peer right down inside the trenches below, where a large number of black-helmeted figures were massing in huddled-down groups, weapons very much in evidence. Scanning slowly, she noted the main enemy groupings, the gun positions, and even a pair of suited figures atop one of the habs—probably an OP.

"What do you think, Gunny?" she asked. "Forty . . . fifty of them?"

"At least, ma'am" was Yates's radioed response. "Looks like they came in on that black transport that just bugged out."

"Yeah, but from where? Earth? The bastards could've warned us!" She shifted back to the trenches, then pivoted slowly, zeroing in on the enemy OP atop one of the habs. "Pap! You on the slaw?"

"Hot and ready, Captain."

"Target. Two UN spotters on top of the hab at one-one-three-zero o'clock." The lack of a Lunar magnetic field was proving to be a nuisance. Giving firing coordinates by arbitrary clock-face references, instead of by compass degrees, was considerably less than precise. "Take 'em down!"

Fortunately, the targets stood out like blue-headed bugs on an empty white dinner plate. "I'm on 'em, Skipper."

Both UN troops were studying the Marine positions in the trenches, using electronic imagers like Kaitlin's own. One suddenly spun around, the imager flying from his grasp, a silvery cloud of vapor enveloping his chest. The second UN soldier turned, reaching out . . . then he, too, toppled, his blue helmet spraying a white jet of fast-freezing vapor.

"Nice shooting, Paps. Two up, two down."

"Thanks, Lieutenant. Like they say, reach out and touch someone." The expression was a very old one, still common among Marine snipers and slaw gunners. Like so many other favorite expressions in the Corps, no one knew where it had come from or who'd said it first.

A bright point of light streaked through the darkness from the crater rim, slamming with a flash into the bulldozer that seemed to be providing shelter for a number of enemy troops. Seconds later, another missile was skyborne, this one zigzagging up from the crater floor and slamming into the hilltop, a hundred meters to Kaitlin's right. A second enemy missile followed the first, this from a different position. The explosion flashed just short of LSCP-44. The landing craft was shielded from direct line of sight from the base, but a smart missile—or a lucky shot—would find that particularly vulnerable target before long.

"Man down!" someone yelled over the platoon channel. "Man down! Corpsman!"

"We can't slug it out with them for long," Kaitlin said. "They've got too much firepower." She pressed the button on the left forearm of her suit, opening the com channel to Alfa's Second Platoon. "Falcon! Falcon! This is Raven. Do you copy, over?"

"Raven, this is Falcon," Captain Lee's voice came back immediately. "Go ahead."

"We've got a situation here, Captain. Bravo First is pinned down at the base under heavy fire, their bug shot to hell. We're on the crater rim eight klicks to the west, also taking heavy fire. Enemy is present in force, repeat, in force."

She realized that her voice had been steadily climbing in pitch as she spoke. She stopped, drew a deep breath, and tried to bring her voice back under control. Another shoulder-launched missile streaked up out of the crater, angling almost straight toward her before it whipped low overhead. She crouched low as the blast went off somewhere at her back.

"It looks as though the enemy is preparing to rush First Platoon," she continued. "We need help, fast. Can you comply, over?"

"Raven, Falcon. We're about five minutes out, still over the Mare Tranquillitatus. Can you hold that long, over?"

"Falcon, Raven. Looks like we'll have to, doesn't it? Come as fast as you can. Raven out."

"On our way, Raven. Falcon out."

Five minutes . . . an eternity in combat.

The UN troops were concentrating their fire on First Platoon, and, despite the fire they were taking from the crater rim, it was clear they were going to try a charge, probably within the next minute or two. Kaitlin knew that she had just two choices . . . to sit up here on her ass and watch half of her rifle company be overrun, or . . .

She changed channels on her com. "Listen up, everybody! This is Garroway! Second Squad! Hold your positions. Maintain fire on the enemy. First Squad! Back to the bug, on the double! Get into the airlock, and stay there! Lieutenant Dow! Are you on the line?"

"Affirmative, Lieutenant. I'm here."

"Warm up the fire and stand by to boost. We're going on a little hop."

"Reactor coming up. Pressure okay. We can bounce in two minutes."

"Make it a minute thirty."

"Whatcha got in mind, Lieutenant?" Yates asked.

"Making it all or nothing, Gunny. The captain is going to get wiped off the map if we don't break the UNdies' attack."

"Roger that, Lieutenant. Okay, Marines! Hustle! Hustle! I wanna see nothing but amphibious green blurs!" They started trotting back toward the LSCP, as other Marines closed in from different directions, crowding up the debarkation ramp and into the craft's airlock.

"If I may suggest, ma'am," Yates said, pausing at the

foot of the ramp, "you should stay here and direct the covering fire."

"Negative, Gunny. If I'm about to pull something stupid, I want to be there to take the blame."

She heard the grin. "Understood, Lieutenant. Understood."

Together, they hurried up the ramp and squeezed through into the airlock, where First Squad was waiting.

Seventy seconds later, Dow radioed a crisp warning, then Kaitlin's knees almost gave way as the LSCP boosted skyward from the crater rim.

Forza di Intervento Rapido
Picard Base, The Moon
0921 hours GMT

Capitano Arnaldo Tessitore, of the FIR's *Forza Spazia* rose from behind the shelter of the excavation he'd been crouching in, holding his imager to his visor. The second enemy landing craft was rising from its hiding place, a clear and easy target less than eight and a half kilometers away. "Zhang!" he shouted. "Target . . . above the crater rim!"

"I have, Captain," the PRC lieutenant replied in his thickly accented Italian. Tessitore listened as Zhang sing-songed a barrage of orders in Mandarin to the Chinese soldiers who'd just arrived at Picard aboard the *Millénium*, and wished again the mission planners back in Geneva had made up their Lunar Expeditionary Force out of troops from a single country. Too many nationalities, too many languages might have been great for the public image of a truly *United* Nations, but it guaranteed confusion and misunderstanding.

Two PRC troops shouldering massive Type 80 launchers rose to their feet, loosing their missiles in almost the same silent instant of flame. One of the men pitched backward a second later, freezing vapor spilling from a black-ringed hole low and in the center of his suit's cuirass, a victim of the all-too-deadly and accurate laser fire from the nearby trenches; the shot was too late to stop the launch, however. Twin stars, bright as worklights, zig-zagged away toward the rising spacecraft.

Long before the missiles could hit their target, however, the American craft had vanished below the crater rim, moving under full thrust back toward the west.

Tessitore blinked, lowering the imager. They were *re-treating*, flying back the way they'd come! The missiles, their radar lock broken, detonated in a pair of flashes against the crater rim.

Had that last laser shot really come from the trenches near the crashed ship? Or had it come from higher up and to the left, from the crater rim? No . . . it must have been from the crashed vehicle. The enemy wouldn't have abandoned a laser team up on that ridge, with only their back-pack PLSS units to keep them breathing.

"Captain. We should use chance! Hit enemy now!"

"*Affermativo, Tenente.*" He'd been holding off, hoping to break the enemy with the sheer overwhelming force of massed firepower from prepared positions, or wait for their air supplies to give out while his own troops recharged, a few at a time, in the habs, or, at worst, to work forward through the labyrinth of trenches . . . but Zhang was right. Enemy reinforcements might be on the way, and they had to strike *now*, before the battle spread out of his control. The bombardment of the past several minutes must have the enemy troops dazed and completely disorganized. One quick, sudden rush, and it would all be over. "Go! Go!"

"*Zou! Zou!*" Zhang yelled. "*Kuai! Qianjin!*"

To either side of Tessitore's position, dozens of suited figures rose from the trenches and the shelter of heavy equipment scattered across the crater-floor site; all wore black space helmets, instead of the usual UN light blue, and each wore the bright red arm patch marking them as members of the *Hangkong Tuji Budui*, the PRC's elite Air/Space Assault Force. "San Marcos!" Tessitore called, summoning his own FIR troops by the name of their parent regiment, the San Marco Marines. "Forward!"

He scrambled up out of the excavation, then hesitated as his own troops rose from hiding all about him. He drew in a deep breath, then waved his Beretta M-31 assault rifle above his head. "*Il più forte!*" he shouted. That battle cry of the San Marco Marines had first been spoken by Gabriele D'Annunzio, speaking of the regiment's defense of the Cortelazzo Bridgehead in 1917. "The strongest!"

Still waving the rifle, he started lumbering toward the enemy position, marked by the crumpled, ice-and-vapor-wreathed shape of their crashed lander a hundred meters away. His suit was clumsy and made running difficult, but once he got moving, it was mostly a matter of guiding himself under its inertia. He reached a trench and sailed across, skimming above a surface of fine, gray powder; a Chinese soldier to his right suddenly folded over but kept drifting forward for several meters before he finally hit the ground in an explosion of dust and cartwheeling legs and arms. Things—*people*—fell *slowly* in the Moon's one-sixth gravity, and the wild charge held the slow-motion quality of a dream.

His heart pounding with exertion and fear, Tessitore kept bounding ahead, unable to swerve left or right or to stop, moving on sheer inertia, though the terror that at any moment his suit or—far worse!—his helmet visor would be breached, emptying his air into space, hammered at his brain. Enemy troops were rising ahead, aiming their assault rifles, and more UN troops were falling. Perhaps it would have been better, after all, to have tried working ahead through the trenches . . . but, no, that would have taken too long and raised the risk of having his troops pinned down as badly as the enemy was now. No, this was better. *One quick rush . . . One quick rush . . .*

And then still more Chinese and Italian troops were falling; one of his men, the red-and-gold emblem of the San Marco Marines displayed on his arm, suddenly stumbled as his backpack PLSS exploded in whirling fragments and fast-freezing vapor. That shot had come from *behind. . . .*

He bounced to a stop, taking several long, dust-plowing steps to slow, turning in place as he came to a halt. Behind them, almost directly over the point where he'd started the charge, an American spacecraft, an ugly, angular, spindle-legged contraption, was drifting out of a black sky, descending gently toward a landing. A space-suited figure was visible in the open airlock; dust blasted from beneath the settling lander as plasma thrusters chewed into regolith.

"San Marcos!" he shouted over the regiment's channel. "Take cover! Take cover!"

Other UN troops were noticing the incoming spacecraft now, stopping in their tracks, jumping into nearby trenches. A few dropped their weapons and raised their hands, surrendering.

The Chinese troops, Tessitore noted, continuing their blind charge, were almost to the American lines now, but there were far fewer of them than before. Zhang had started the battle with thirty-two men; fewer than ten were still on their feet as they sprinted the last few meters to grapple with the enemy.

The landing craft settled to the Lunar surface with a gentle bobbing motion of its suspension. Americans were leaping from the already open airlock, some rushing toward the shattered knot of UN troops, others moving toward the habs.

That last decided Tessitore. If the Americans seized the habitats—and there was nothing at all now standing in their way—the UN troops outside would either have to surrender or face death by suffocation as their air supplies gave out. He tossed his Beretta aside and raised his hands.

An American was approaching him, ATAR leveled, suit reflecting the grays and blacks of his surroundings in oddly shifting patterns of light and dark. As the soldier came closer, Tessitore was rocked by two startling revelations. The first was that the suited figure approaching him was a *girl* . . . her blond hair closely framing her face behind her visor. The second was the emblem painted next to the name tag affixed to the front of her suit. The name tag spelled GARROWAY in stenciled letters, but it was the emblem that startled Tessitore more: a globe and anchor, the badge of the United States Marine Corps.

His hands went up higher. "Lebanon!" he shouted, even though he knew she could not hear. "Sudan! Brazil!"

LSCP-44, Call sign Raven
Picard Base, The Moon
0924 hours GMT

Kaitlin held her ATAR pointed at the man's chest, her eyes widening as she saw the crest affixed to his left breast and his sleeve—a gold lion on a distinctive red backing. Until this moment, she'd not known that the enemy included elements of the San Marco Marines. His mouth was moving; he was trying to tell her something.

With one hand, she stabbed the key on her common controls that set up a channel search. A moment later, she heard a burst of Italian, and the words "Lebanon! Sudan! Brazil!"

"San Marco," she said. "The Strongest." What was the Italian phrase? She'd learned it in OCS. *"Il più forte!"*

Part of every Marine officer's training was a survey of the other Marine forces of the world, of the actions they'd taken part in, of the traditions and battle honors they carried. The San Marcos were no exception. The Italian Marines had served together with the US Marines on three separate occasions: in the Lebanon peacekeeping operation of 1983, in the Sudan in 1992 to 1993, and in the Brazilian Incursion of 2029.

"Sì," she said, straining her grasp of Italian to the limit. *"Bene."*

Her prisoner straightened up, then rendered a crisp salute. Kaitlin returned the honor. Elsewhere across the desolate and dusty field, other troops, Chinese and Italian—but so very few!—were dropping their weapons and raising their hands as the US Marines came out of the trenches and began herding them together. She watched, thoughtful, as a Marine lance corporal arrived to take her prisoner away, leading him back toward the habs. They'd fought hard, these Italian Marines. The battle here had been a close-run thing.

Something caught her eye in the dusty floor of a trench close by. Lightly, she hopped into the excavation, reached down, and brushed away at something protruding from the hard-packed powder.

It looked like . . . gold.

It *was* gold, gold worked into a smooth and highly polished figurine perhaps ten centimeters tall . . . a standing human woman with arms outstretched, nude save for bracelets, anklets, and a necklace of some kind. And . . . was that *writing* on the base?

Standing, the figurine in her gloved hands, Kaitlin raised her eyes to the plain around her, seeing it, really seeing it for the first time. Until this moment, the Picard base had been a tactical exercise; even when she'd given the orders to Dow to fly away from the crater, descend, then skim the surface back and around to approach the base from another direction, she'd been thinking of this as a problem in tactics, of ground and cover and fields of fire. But now that the battle was over, what, exactly, had they won?

Archeologists had laid out these trenches; the larger excavations had been marked off into large grids with pegs and white string—most of which had been trampled in the fighting. An archeological dig . . . with golden statues of human women . . . on the Moon.

"This is too weird for the Marines," she said aloud.

"*Non capisco, Signora,*" a voice replied in her helmet set, and she realized that she was still tuned to the Italian Marine frequency.

"That's okay, San Marco," she said, musing. "I don't understand either."

SIX

Institute for Exoarcheological
Studies
Chicago, Illinois
1440 hours CDT

"So, David," the other archeologist said, cuddling close in his arms, "is it true what Ed Pohl told me the other day? That you're now a member of the Three Dolphin Club?"

"And what do you know about the Three Dolphin Club, Teri?" David asked.

"That it's the same as the Mile-High Club, but for zero G. What I don't understand is where the name comes from."

David grinned at her. Dr. Theresa Sullivan might be a colleague, and a highly respected one at that, but sometimes it was hard to get any serious work done with her around. Especially during the past couple of weeks. What had started as a fling at an archeology conference in Los Angeles had swiftly turned into something more.

A *lot* more.

"Ah. Well, back in the late twentieth century, I guess it must have been, the old space agency, NASA, was awfully nervous about any hint of impropriety. Their astronauts were *professionals* and would never consider experimenting with things like sex in zero gravity. Bad public image, you know."

76

"I thought zero-G sex would attract interest."

Slowly, he began unbuttoning her blouse. "Maybe they thought it would be the wrong sort of interest. Anyway, the story goes that some highly dedicated researchers and technicians at the Marshall Spaceflight Center, at Huntsville, decided to experiment on their own, using the big swimming pool at Marshall where they simulated weightless conditions. They sneaked in and used the tank after hours, of course, because if NASA had found out what they were doing, they would've all been fired. But they found out that a couple *could* have sex in weightlessness, even though there was a tendency for them to, ah, come undocked at a critical moment. Your motions, yours and your partner's, tend to pull you apart unless you hold *real* tight and close."

"Where did you learn all of this?"

"One of the officers on the cycler told me, on the trip back from Mars. He was a Three-Dolphins member. Even had a little pin to show me."

"Okay, okay. I've got to know! Why three dolphins?"

"Well, those researchers at Huntsville found that a couple could stay together, but that it worked *lots* better if a third party was present, someone who could kind of give a push to key portions of the anatomy at the right times, y'know? And, as they studied the problem, they learned that when dolphins have sex, there's always a third dolphin standing by, nudging the happy couple with his nose, and for the same reason."

"You're kidding!"

"Nope. It's true! Three dolphins."

"So . . . are you a member?"

He grinned. "Well . . . I don't have the Three Dolphin pin . . ."

"I knew it! And how many were in the room?"

"Just two of us, I'm afraid. But we managed okay."

"How conventional! So, was it true what they say about zero-G sex?"

"Gee, Teri, I don't know. What do they say?"

"Oh, that it's a *really* shib experience. Better than anything on Earth.'' She giggled. ''That you can both be on top at once.''

Dr. David Alexander pulled her a bit closer with his left hand, while roving about slowly beneath her opened blouse with his right. ''It's really just like here,'' he told her, giving her breast a playful squeeze. ''It depends on who you do it with.''

''Mmm. I *would* like to try it, sometime.''

''It's kind of messy. All the sweat and, ah, other fluids tend to form little droplets that just float around in the air. It can be interesting trying to chase them all down with a rag, afterward. And even on a Mars cycler, it can be damned hard finding any privacy!'' He kissed her, then shifted a bit, trying to get more comfortable on his half-seated perch against the corner of his desk. ''All things considered, it's usually a lot more convenient to do it in a plain, ordinary, Earth-bound bed, with a nice steady pull of one G to keep things in place.''

''Like, maybe, a gel-bed? They say that's the closest thing there is to zero G on Earth. If you don't count giant swimming pools.''

''That would work. Like a waterbed without the sloshing.''

''At my place? Tonight?''

He kissed her again. ''That sounds just about perfect. Dinner first?''

''Sure. You have to tell your wife you're working late?''

He winced inwardly at the mention of Liana. Things had not been good between them for a long, long time, not since the very early days of their marriage, in fact. Liana's stubborn refusal to consider a divorce hadn't really bothered him before. He'd always managed to keep his affairs discreet. But now, with Teri, he found himself wishing there was something he could do to overthrow Liana's religious convictions and make her see that their relationship wasn't salvageable. The thought of being able to come home at night to a woman who shared his passions, who wasn't enmired in senseless garbage like Liana's cosmic astronuts, a woman who was intelligent and competent and endlessly fascinating . . .

He shook his head, dispelling the fantasy. "Actually, she's out of town. In Pennsylvania, visiting her sister."

"Great. Then you could spend the night."

David's workscreen chirped. Without letting Teri go, he reached behind his back and touched a key on his desk, opening the channel without turning on the visual. "Yes, Larry."

"Sir, there are two people here to see you from the Department of Science? They say they need to talk to you."

He pulled back from Teri's moist lips long enough to say, "Do they have an appointment? I'm busy right now."

"Uh, nossir. No appointment. But they said their business with you is, uh, Clearance Blue."

Damn. "Wait a minute." He looked down at Teri. "Sorry. . . ."

For answer, she slid her hand down to his crotch and gave him a final, breath-catching squeeze. "Business first," she said, licking her lips, then giving him a last, quick kiss. "I've got work to do, too. I can wait till tonight."

She stepped away from him and busied herself with rebuttoning her blouse and tucking it in. David stood, straightened his clothing, then walked over to the large, corner-office window overlooking Lake Shore Drive and the Burnham Harbor Marina.

The crowd at Soldier's Field, he saw, was still there, larger and more agitated than ever. Many of the protesters held signs. DON'T COVER UP OUR GOD, read one. THE BUILDERS MADE US IN THEIR IMAGE, said another, alongside a photograph of the Cydonian Face. A few had glued flatscreens to their signboards, to display animated clips or video—most of the Face or of some of the released images from the Cave of Wonders. Someone was haranguing the crowd with a microphone and amplifiers from a makeshift tower on Waldon Drive, but the soundproofing in the new IES building was too efficient for him to hear what was being said. Not that it mattered. Scuzzy-headed nonsense, all of it.

Well, not entirely scuzzy-headed. He could understand where the public—long prepared by wild stories of ETs and UFOs, of alien abductions and ancient astronauts— might have picked up misinformation enough to go off on these tangents. But the freestyle mingling of science fact, speculation, and outright fantasy had disturbed him since his earliest days as an archeology undergraduate.

It didn't help at all that some, at least, of the long-running stories about extraterrestrials visiting primitive human cultures in the remote past were turning out to be true, at least in some aspects. *Someone* had transported early humans to Mars half a million years ago . . . and might even have been responsible for some genetic tampering at the time as well. There were still some nasty unanswered questions about the evolutionary transition from *Homo erectus* to *Homo sapiens*, and after a long, rearguard battle even longtime conservatives in anthropological and paleontological circles were now seriously considering ET intervention as a distinct, even a likely, possibility. The timing of the artifacts on Mars and of the poorly understood transition of *Homo erectus* to archaic *Homo sapiens* were too close to believably be coincidence.

David Alexander was now the closest thing there was to an expert on the whole question. The fifteen months he'd spent on Mars had made him a celebrity of sorts, as well as *the* authority on extraterrestrial intelligence within the solar system.

One of the protesters on the street below, a young woman wearing briefs and nothing else in the steamy Chicago-summer heat, was jumping up and down with a large sign held above her head. YOU CAN TELL US, DR. A! it read.

He snorted, turning away from the window. Being a celebrity wasn't so bad—it certainly had enlivened his sex life since his return to Earth two months ago. If only celebrity status didn't attract so many kooks.

And unpleasant responsibilities. Teri, her clothing ordered once again, flashed a smile and a wink filled with promise, and strolled out the door.

"Okay, Larry. Have them come in."

His visitors were Sarah Mackler and Roger Flores, both in conservative orange-and-green business smartsuits, with scancards identifying them as agents of the US Department of Science. "Dr. Alexander!" the woman said. Her costume was accented by a brightly colored Ashanti headband. "How are we doing today?"

"I have no idea how the corporate *we* is doing, Ms. Mackler," he said. "*I* am doing well, although I have a feeling you're about to change all of that. Again."

Sarah smiled pleasantly, a flash of bright teeth against dark chocolate skin, as though she was determined to ignore his moodiness. "Good to hear it, Doctor. We have an assignment for you."

"An *urgent* assignment," her companion added.

David slumped into his chair. "Look. I appreciate the attention. And I certainly appreciate the position you people seem to have carved out for me here. But when are you going to get it through your bureaucratic heads that I am a scientist? A *field* man, not a damned desk pilot!"

"The desk work getting you down?" Sarah asked, taking a chair for herself.

"No. I'll *tell* you what's getting me down." He gestured at his desk's flatscreen. "In the past three weeks, I've been requested by either your department or the administration to speak at no fewer than seven dinners, luncheons, or other functions, from Great LA to Washington, DC! I've been in the air or in one hotel or other more than I've been here! Damn it, the work I'm doing is *important*. And I can't do it when you people are sub-Oing me back and forth across the continent all the time!"

"Now, Dr. Alexander—" Roger Flores began.

"No! You listen to me, for a change! Ever since I got back from Mars, you people have had me on the go. Public-relations appearances. Consciousness-raising talks. Press conferences. Net recordings. Even fund-raisers! I'm sick of shaking hands and making nice to people who don't *understand* what this is all about anyway! I'm sick

of overpriced chicken dinners! I'm sick of not being able
to go home to my wife!'' That wasn't particularly true,
but it never hurt to throw a little extra guilt in a discussion
like this one. ''And I'm especially sick of being pulled
away from my work to serve as some kind of glad-handing
front man for the Department of Science, when I ought to
be *here* studying the data we brought back from Cydonia!''

''I might point out,'' Flores said stiffly, ''that you were
the one to upload such, um, controversial findings to the
Earthnet, while you were on Mars.''

''I did what I thought was right!''

''Of course! No one's blaming you. You rightly judged
that releasing that information would pull the UN's fangs,
when they wanted to cover up your finds . . . but you also
caused quite a few troubles for your own government.''
He gestured toward the corner window. ''Have you seen
your fan club out there? They have the traffic tied up all
the way from McCormack Place to the Field Museum!''

''Worse than a big game at Soldier Field,'' Sarah added.

He sighed. ''I've seen it. And I don't care how many
dinners I attend, how many college speeches I make, how
many reporters I talk to, it's not going to change the minds
of people who have their minds made up already! What
these pop-culture, garbage-science hooligans believe or
don't believe is *not* my responsibility.''

''Isn't it, Doctor?'' Sarah asked him. ''You know, when
you accepted this post, it was with the understanding that
you would work closely with the department. With us.
Between the war and your, um, sudden release of, shall
we say, sensitive information, our society is rather delicately balanced right now. The peace movement is growing, getting more powerful, and it's feeding off this
ancient-astronaut craze. A craze *you* triggered by telling
the world about those human bodies you found on Mars!''

''Well, I'm sorry people are such idiots! But I happen
to be a firm believer in the essential freedom of science.
You can't smother newfound facts just because they're
inconvenient!''

''Nonsense,'' Roger snapped. ''All of history is one big

session of spin control and public-relations management after another!''

"That's an unpleasantly cynical outlook.''

"And yours is unpleasantly naive!''

"Gentlemen, please!'' Sarah said. "Doctor, we appreciate your sentiment in the matter. By and large, I agree with you, and, more to the point, so does the president. We do still live in a democracy, for what that's worth, and total censorship is incompatible with democratic principles. I'm sure you can accept, though, that where there is a danger to the country or to national security, the government has the right, has the responsibility to exercise judgment.'' When David didn't immediately reply, she shrugged and went on. "In any case, Doctor, I'm afraid you jumped the gun on us. As it happens, we don't want to send you out to another college speech.''

"Eh? Why didn't you say so!''

"You didn't give us the chance!'' Roger replied.

Sarah gave her comrade a sharp look, then smiled at David. "Actually, we do want you to go on a trip for us. A rather long trip. But I think you'll agree that it qualifies as fieldwork. And . . . I can promise you, no bad chicken dinners!''

"Where do you want me to go?''

"To the Moon, Dr. Alexander. We need you to go to the Moon as quickly as we can get you there.''

"The . . . the Moon!''

"We have transport waiting for you to take you to O'Hare. We can have you in orbit in two hours, and by tonight you'll be on your way!''

"That . . . is quite impossible!''

"You have another appointment?'' Roger asked.

He thought about his date with Teri—obviously *that* wouldn't be a valid excuse. Besides, he was intrigued now.

"Why would you want me on the Moon?''

"Dr. Alexander,'' Sarah told him, "what we have to say to you now is classified. Classified, do you understand? You are not to discuss it with anyone, including the people working for you in this building.''

"I understand.''

"Several hours ago, US Marines captured a small UN base on the Moon. They were looking for a Professor Marc Billaud. You know him?"

David nodded. "I've met him several times. Last time was at a conference on ET archeology in Athens, before the war. A good man."

"The UN Space Command had him at the Lunar site. Apparently, he and a team were in the process of doing some extensive archeological excavations."

David's eyes widened. He felt his heart pound. Excavations? On the Moon? "The Builders? . . ."

"That's part of what we want you to tell us. Billaud's notes suggest that there was an ET presence on the Moon, a fairly extensive one . . . but that it occurred during historical times."

"How recent?"

"He thinks a few thousand years," Sarah told him. "There are . . . artifacts."

"What was he excavating? A building? A city?"

"Actually," Sarah told him, "the evidence suggests that it was a spaceship of some kind. A ship that crashed on the Lunar surface something like eight or ten thousand years ago. And that is what makes this investigation so vitally important. . . ."

As she talked, David thought about Mars . . . and the Ship.

The Face on Mars had been carved by someone half a million years ago, someone who'd built a number of cyclopean structures in the area and apparently used humans imported from Earth to help with the construction. There was even evidence that some sort of massive terraforming project had been under way at the time; most surface features had been damaged or destroyed by a savage flood of liquid water. Many of the human bodies found so far showed evidence of having suffocated as their atmosphere—possibly contained in some sort of field or bubble—bled suddenly away. There was also evidence—lots of it—of a battle, an attack that had ripped open mile-wide pyramids and left the site in ruins. The Face itself was almost unrecognizable as an artifact carved by intelligence, though the general form and the neatly carved geometries were still visible beneath the rubble.

One of the more enigmatic sites at Cydonia was the hill known as the Fortress. Once, probably, it had been a pyramidal structure like some of the others in the area, but something more powerful than a thermonuclear bomb had sheared off the top, wrecked the inside, and reduced much of it to rubble. Later, a ship of some kind, a vessel over a kilometer long, had toppled onto the ruins, wracked by internal explosions. The wreckage, exposed to the sandblasting of half a million years of Martian weather, was so poorly preserved it was impossible to learn much.

But the ruins—and especially the promise of the wrecked ship—had been responsible for the revitalization of the on-again, off-again vagaries of the US space program, and of the Russian Space Agency as well. Whoever had built the Cydonian complex had possessed the secret of traveling among the *stars*; a careful study of the ruins might bring that secret home to Earth.

And more than that. The Builders had been engaged in terraforming on a planetary scale; the ongoing deterioration of Earth's environment, the coastal flooding and rising global temperatures, had been growing slowly but steadily worse for the past fifty years. The secret of planetary climate control might well prove to be more important, at least insofar as Earth's continued habitability was concerned, than the secret of traveling to the stars.

And so the infant science of exoarcheology, and its bastard half brother, exotecharcheology, had been born.

On Mars, the problem had been the sheer scale of things, coupled with how damnably difficult it was to get there in the first place. By using a system of space stations, called cyclers, that alternately touched the orbits of Earth and Mars, it had been possible to get a few hundred people out to the Red Planet over the past decade or so to study the site; the trouble was, it would take thousands of people, working for years, simply to carry out a decent survey of the Martian ruins. It might well be centuries, yet, before Cydonia yielded the last of its long-held secrets.

But if some of those secrets also lay hidden on the

Moon, just three or four days away, instead of the six to nine months required for a cycler passage to Mars . . .

"We can't tell you everything that's going on right now," Sarah was saying. "Suffice to say that it has become an issue of national security. We need a trained archeologist's assessment of the wreckage, and we need to have an idea of just what the UN scientists might have learned from it."

"But why me?"

Roger shrugged. "That should be evident. You've been to Cydonia. You know as much about the Builders, about exotech, as anyone, and more than most. You are probably the field authority on ET artifacts and technologies."

And, he thought with a touch of bitterness, *I'm here, in your institute, bought and paid for*. The other scientists who'd been to Mars—Kettering, Pohl, Vandemeer, and the others—had returned to their old positions, to promotions, to careers made more secure by their fifteen months on Mars. But David had had no place to go but . . . here. The Cydonian Research Foundation, a government-sponsored organization, had funded the Exoarcheological Institute to study the finds being uncovered on Mars.

And, perhaps, on the Moon as well.

The problem was that David's reputation as something of a maverick in established archeological circles had made him the ideal candidate for exoarcheologist-in-residence here at the institute.

And it was damned hard to say no to a government-backed request.

"You're also already rated for a pressure suit and pliss," Sarah told him.

True enough. In fact, he'd already been to the Moon, briefly, as part of his astronautics training in preparation for his flight to Mars. He'd spent three days at Fra Mauro and been bored most of the time, even with a crowded training schedule.

"Can I take anyone along? Dr. Sullivan has been working with me on . . ."

"I'm sorry, Doctor. Space is limited, and there's no time for training."

Teri was going to be disappointed. Hell, *he* was disappointed . . . but the thought of getting into the field again—and on the Moon!—was too much to resist.

Besides, he knew what LEO–Lunar transports were like. There'd have been no privacy, no opportunity to give Teri a chance to join the Three Dolphin Club.

Later, after his visitors had left, David stood at the window looking down at the demonstrators outside, thoughtful. There was someone he needed to talk to just now.

Someone he wasn't supposed to talk to at all. . . .

EU Science Research Vessel
Pierre-Simon Laplace
Co-orbit with Asteroid 2034L
2235 hours GMT

Dr. Jean-Etienne Cheseaux floated alongside the *Laplace*'s tiny observation port, slipping his dark glasses into place as sunlight flooded into the compartment. Outside, the sun was just clearing the edge of the Rock as the ship's slow drift brought her clear of the small planetoid's shadow. He still wondered why the Académie des Sciences had insisted that he come here.

Cheseaux was an astronomer; his primary specialization was selenology, the geology of the Moon, but the Academy had asked him to serve as payload specialist aboard the *Laplace*. Not that he was complaining, necessarily—he liked it in space, enjoyed the sensations of free fall and the spectacular purity of the sunlight—but the measurements he was taking of 2034L's mass and spin and precise orbit could have been made by any competent technician. It was, he supposed, an indication of the importance the Academy attached to this mission. The knowledge stirred his professional pride, and his ego; there was talk, he'd heard, of naming this particular rock Cheseaux. Of course, the astronomical society frowned on using the names of living people, but there were precedents.

Asteroid 2034L had been discovered eight years ago, one of the fast-growing number of near-Earth asteroids

whose orbits carried them periodically inside the orbit of
Earth. This one was particularly disturbing; as carbonaceous chondrite, like the majority of asteroids, it had an
extremely low albedo, rendering its surface as black as the
blackest coal. It was also small, less than a hundred meters
across.

That combination of orbit, albedo, and small size made
2034L particularly dangerous, a prime target for the Phaeton Project. In Greek mythology, Phaeton was the boy
who'd lost control of Apollo's sun-chariot, bringing it too
near the Earth and nearly destroying humanity in fire.
Since the 1980s, the particular danger Earth-crossing asteroids and comets represented to the Earth had been well
understood; the lesson of the dinosaurs, exterminated by
the ten-mile body that had smashed into the Yucatán sixty-
five million years ago, could not be ignored. By the early
2000s, several skywatch operations were in place, identifying and charting the flying mountains that might someday pose a direct threat to Earth and her inhabitants.

Phaeton, one of the most comprehensive of the skywatch programs, had been begun in 2029, a collaboration
between the European Union, Japan, and the United States.
The UN had assumed financial responsibility five years
later, the same year in which 2034L had been discovered.
The war, of course, had interfered to the extent that neither
the United States nor Japan was participating any longer,
but the work was vital enough that the EU Space Agency
had continued the program, war or no war.

Cheseaux was now confident that this rock, at least,
posed no immediate threat to humanity. With precise measurements now complete, he could confidently report that
2034L would pass within a million kilometers of the Earth
in another five months. That was twice the distance from
Earth to the Moon, a cat's whisker when you looked at
the sheer size of the whole solar system, but comfortable
enough as a margin of safety. He would need to run his
figures through the supercomputer center at the Sorbonne
to be sure, but back-of-the-envelope calculations suggested
that 2034L would again pass close by the Earth in another

forty-five years. That passage would be a near miss of perhaps one hundred thousand kilometers that would slingshot the body in toward the sun . . . which in turn would either destroy the asteroid in celestial flame or send it careening out into the thin, cold dark of the outer system.

Either way, this particular Earth-crosser posed no threat.

"Upload complete, Doctor," *Laplace*'s commander, Colonel Denis Armand, announced, drifting alongside of Cheseaux in a head-down position relative to him. "They have asked us to hold our position, however, until another vessel can rendezvous with us."

"Another craft? What other craft?"

Armand gave a Gallic, inverted shrug, then reached out to brace himself against the bulkhead before he started turning. "They didn't say. The war, after all . . ."

Cheseaux gave a soft grunt of understanding. It was *always* the war. Abject foolishness! The European Union needed to be working with the Americans and the Japanese and even the Russians, now . . . not fighting them. The Americans had already slammed the door to Mars shut in the UN's face rather decisively; the UN risked losing access to the Moon as well, if they persisted in this insanity. It was time to end this, declare a truce, and find out how best to get all of humankind working on the problems of recovering and learning from the newly discovered alien technology.

Squinting against the sunlight, Cheseaux looked for and found a pair of tiny crescents, one silver, one gray, well beyond the horizon of 2034L and bowed away from the sun. Earth was now less than ten million kilometers away, its attendant moon somewhat farther. Both seemed transcendently delicate, ethereal, and small. The war that had wracked the world for the past two years, the burning political questions of Aztlan independence and control of ancient alien technologies all seemed so completely insignificant from this vantage point. It was true, what they said: Looking back at the Earth from space gave one an entirely new perspective, a new outlook.

Perhaps it was Earth's politicians who should be

shipped up here, the lot of them, and not her scientists and soldiers. Let them work out their differences bathed in heavenly radiance, with the Earth nothing more than a frail, silver sliver in the night.

"Well, I think I'll turn in," he told the commander. "Let me know if there's a call from Earth."

"Of course."

Laplace was neither large nor luxurious, even as spacecraft went. Her hab module and laboratory together were ten meters long and five wide, small enough to have fit easily inside the living and working area of the old Skylab, and she carried twice as many people, three crew and three payload specialists. Cheseaux's cabin was a closet-sized space in the aft of the hab module with thin plastic walls and a sleeping bag attached to the bulkhead. His "desk" pulled out from one of the walls, a plastic board with Velcro surfaces, to which his laptop was attached.

Pulling the folding panel shut behind him—the only concession to the human need for privacy aboard—he peeled his computer from the desk and wiggled into the sleeping bag so that he didn't have to think about *not* floating about. Outside his cabin, the bumps and thumps, the conversations, the smells of ready-heat meals and men in close confinement continued to permeate his world. As much as he'd been enjoying this mission, he was going to be glad to get back to Paris. He'd actually felt, he realized now, a pang of disappointment a few minutes ago when he'd learned *Laplace* would not be immediately returning home.

He logged onto Spacenet.

Everyone in *Laplace*'s little crew had his own Net account; the best defense against the feelings of isolation and depression common on long missions in space was the ability to log onto the Net and have immediate access to news, to books or music, to v-mail and e-mail that let the astronauts keep in close touch with people and events back home. As his browser came up, the new-mail icon flashed cheerfully on the menu bar.

Twenty-seven messages, including five requests for real-time v-chats. One from Annette that he'd been looking forward to . . . the rest from sources as varied as the Académie des Sciences and the Cousteau Foundation, and a British UFO e-mag looking for an interview on ancient aliens. Maybe instant communications through the Net weren't such an all-encompassing and unalloyed blessing after all.

One e-mail was flagged as confidential and encrypted, from a masked address. He knew immediately who *that* was from, and it worried him.

He accessed the message. It was in text only, to make the multilevel encryptions it employed simpler . . . as well as making them less obvious to anyone who might be monitoring e-mail packet transmissions.

The immediate address was a remailing service in Finland; he knew, though, that its author was in the United States. It was hard to decide who would get into more trouble if this correspondence was ever discovered—David Alexander for writing it, or Cheseaux for reading it and not reporting it at once to UN officials.

Not that he would even consider reporting it. David was a good friend, had been a friend and close correspondent ever since the two of them had met at a symposium on the Cydonian ruins held in Athens in 2037. It had been one of those relationships that sparks from the first meeting, as though they'd known one another for years, a reflection of what the Latinos called *simpatico*.

His screen went dark as the encryption software began chewing through columns of numbers and letters. There were several such software packages available, none guaranteed a hundred percent secure . . . but the sheer volume of encoded messages routing their way through the Spacenet nowadays meant their correspondence was probably safe, even though such traffic was actively discouraged by both sides in the war.

The words decryption complete appeared, followed a moment later by the complete text of the message.

JEAN-ETIENNE:

THEY'RE SENDING ME TO THE MOON TO INVES-
TIGATE ARTIFACTS YOUR PEOPLE FOUND THERE. I

GATHER OUR MUTUAL FRIEND MARC BILLAUD IS
THERE ALREADY. WHAT GIVES WITH THE INCREDI-
BLE SECRECY SURROUNDING THIS THING? THEY
TELL ME THAT MARC FOUND AN ET SHIP, WHICH IS
FANTASTIC NEWS, IF TRUE. IT MIGHT EVEN BE THE
SORT OF THING THAT WOULD GET OUR GOVERN-
MENTS TO BURY THE HATCHET AND DECLARE PEACE.

IT SOUNDS LIKE YOUR PEOPLE ARE OUT AND MINE
CONTROL THE SITE NOW. IS THERE SOMETHING I
SHOULD KNOW GOING IN? DO YOU HAVE ACCESS TO
ANY OF MARC'S REPORTS ON THE SITE, THERE IN
PARIS, OR DO YOU KNOW ANYTHING ABOUT HIS
FINDS THAT WOULD BE USEFUL ON THIS END? I'LL
PASS ON WHAT I CAN LEARN AS I GET THE CHANCE.

CORDIALLY,
DAVID A.

Cheseaux smiled. A charming letter, and so utterly naive . . . but then, the Americans were a naive people. As
much as he liked, admired, and respected young Alexander, he was not about to give the American military secrets. There was a war on, after all! And as for ending
hostilities—he assumed that that was the meaning of the
enigmatic phrase ''bury the hatchet''—he surely didn't
think that the UN Authority was about to surrender its
claim to the wreckage discovered recently at Picard, did
he?

Except . . .

Cheseaux sighed. How much of what David wanted was
classified for honest reasons of legitimate state security,
and how much was due to the shortsighted scrabblings of
small-minded and paranoid UN bureaucrats?

Just what was it that had divided the world for these
past two years, anyway? The United States refusal to hold
a UN-mandated plebiscite on the question of independence
for some of its Southwestern states. Cheseaux snorted. He
scarcely blamed Washington for refusing that one, especially since the vote was to be limited to the American
states involved and would have included the populations

of Mexico's northwestern states—a stacked deck if ever there'd been one. That wasn't even worth a decent riot or two, to say nothing of the war!

What else? Russia's refusal to back down to China's demands for parts of Siberia; those land claims went way back and could have been settled in other ways. The fear that the United States and Russia were using their superiority in spaceflight technology to grab the newly discovered archeological discoveries and exotechnologies for themselves. The willingness of the United States to actually publish some of those discoveries prematurely, without weighing the impact they would have on religious, political, and social systems worldwide.

Those last two, Cheseaux thought, were rarely trumpeted as reasons for the continued crusade against the US and Russia, but he suspected that they were the *real* reason for the hostilities.

If so, however, it was possible that his friend was headed into considerable danger. He hadn't heard anything about an American attack on the Picard site, but that was implied by David's letter. He doubted that the UN forces at Tsiolkovsky would let the Americans stay without a damned stiff challenge.

He hoped David knew enough to keep his head down when the shooting started.

SEVEN

USASF Tug Clarke
Nearing the Moon
0740 hours GMT

The Moon filled the black sky, half-full from this vantage point, the terminator line a crinkled, ragged lacework of silver-gray, brown, and black, the rest of the visible face as dazzling in the sunlight as new snow. David Alexander struggled to orient himself but found an excess of map detail too confusing. "So . . . where is it we're going?"

The tug's pilot was a US Aerospace Force captain named Heyerson. He pointed beyond the sunset terminator, into darkness.

"About there," he said. Sunlight flashed off the dark glasses he wore inside his comset helmet. "The Mare Crisium is well past sunset, now. You guys are gettin' dropped off at Picard Crater, just inside Crisium's wall."

The third man in the tug's cramped cockpit clung to the back of the pilot's couch, trying to see. He was a Navy man, HM1 Robert Thornton. "What I wanna know," he said, "is where Tranquillity Base is."

"Ah." Heyerson pointed again, this time toward a dark, smooth plain bisected by the terminator. "Up that way. Almost to the horizon. You won't be able to see it naked-eye, though, if that's what you were expecting."

"I just want to see the place, man," Thornton replied. "Where it started."

94

The Aerospace man chuckled. "Whatever." He glanced at Thornton. "Y'know, I still don't know what the *Navy's* doing up here. The Marines, I can understand, kinda. The Army, no problem. Civilian scientists, all in a day's work. But the Navy? . . ."

"Read your briefing, Captain," David said. "The Marines don't have medics, like the Army. They rely on Navy corpsmen instead."

"Bravo Company's corpsman was killed in the assault," Thornton said. He was black, his skin so dark in the instrumentation-lit cockpit that it was difficult to make out any expression at all. "I'm the replacement."

"Yeah, well, the jarheads are all goin' home as soon as I get this lot settled in," Heyerson said, jerking a thumb over his shoulder to indicate the forty US Army Special Forces troops crammed into the tug's cargo bay aft. "Don't know why you bothered to make the trip when you're just gonna have to turn around and go back again!"

"Yeah, well, it's the government's dime," Thornton said. "They say 'Go,' I go."

"The Navy likes to take good care of the Marines," David added. "It's tradition."

"Nah," Thornton said. "The leathernecks just need someone to ride herd on 'em. Us corpsmen, we control their health records, see? Any of 'em get out of line, we lose their shot card, and they have to get every shot all over again. They know better than to make trouble with *us* around."

"How about you, Doc?" Heyerson said, turning to look at David. "Why'd they send you out?"

"First of all," David said, nodding at Thornton, "*he's* 'Doc,' not me. Second, you really should've looked at your briefing."

"I did . . . sir. Didn't say much, except that I was to deliver forty soldiers, one Navy corpsman, and one civilian scientist to Picard Crater."

"Maybe they didn't want you to know, then."

"Screw 'em." His gaze dropped to the garish cloth patch sewn to David's leather flight jacket. "How about that? Is that classified?"

He touched the patch. "What, this?"

"Yeah. I been wonderin' about that since we boosted from LEO. T'tell you the truth, I didn't know at first whether you were civilian or military, wearin' that rig."

Temperatures aboard a spacecraft, no matter how good the life-support systems, could vary swiftly from too warm to chilly, depending on the craft's attitude of the moment with respect to the sun. David was wearing Marine-issue slacks, deck shoes, and orange T-shirt—garb he'd become comfortable with during his long cycler passage back from Mars. Since it was a bit on the chilly side aboard the *Clarke* now, he'd pulled a flight jacket on over the T-shirt—again, Marine-issue, but with a highly unofficial patch sewn to the left breast.

The stitching was a bit crude, but the elements were all clearly recognizable. The badge was shield-shaped, dark blue with a black border. Two black Advanced Tech Assault Rifles were crossed over a red disk representing Mars; a gold, white, and gray cylinder—a fair representation of a beer can—was superimposed over the ATARs. The legend, gold against dark blue at the top of the device, was HOPS VINCET. Curving all the way across the bottom of the badge, in tiny, carefully stitched gold letters, was the unwieldy line of characters: ATWTMATMUTATB.

" 'Hops vincet?' " Heyerson said, mispronouncing the last word.

"Hops *winkit*," David replied, stressing the proper pronunciation. "Latin, sort of. It means 'beer conquers.' "

"Yeah? Well, I'll buy that." Heyerson shook his head. "Some kind of fraternity?"

"You could say that."

Thornton grinned. " 'Hops' ain't the Latin word for 'beer.' "

"Don't tell the Marines," David replied with a chuckle. "It would disillusion them. The poor dears."

"You two better strap down," Heyerson warned. "We're coming up on our final thrust phase, here. I'd hate to deliver the jarheads' new corpsman with two busted legs."

Space, of course, was at a claustrophobic premium aboard the *Clarke*. The ugly little tug had been designed to haul construction materials, fuel, and personnel from LEO to higher orbits—especially to geosynch, and to the construction shacks at L-3, L-4, and L-5. With the addition of a spidery set of landing legs, it could carry heavy cargoes to the Lunar surface; the USAF Transport Command had requisitioned *Clarke* and three sisters, *Asimov, Ecklar,* and *Viglione* for hauling high-priority cargoes to the Moon and back. In fact, the *Viglione*, with forty more soldiers, was trailing behind the *Clarke* by a few thousand kilometers, preparing for her own landing maneuvers at Fra Mauro.

Because of the crowding, and his VIP status of *Clarke's* sole civilian aboard, David had been allowed to make the trip in one of the cockpit couches; his service with the Marines on Mars had almost automatically meant that he and Thornton had found each other on the first day out from LEO, and the permission had been extended to the Navy man, too.

Cramped as the tug's cockpit was, it was a lot roomier than the cargo bay, with space-suited soldiers packed into narrow bucket seats like armored eggs in a carton. David hadn't been at all shy about taking advantage of Heyerson's offer.

And he found he was enjoying his status as an honorary Marine.

As he strapped himself in, listening to Heyerson warning the troops aft of a delta-*v* maneuver in another minute, David thought about that. He'd received his patch at a party on Earth, just a month after his return from Mars. Gunnery Sergeant Harold Knox, one of the Marines on the March, had had a source in San Diego make up enough of the unauthorized patches for every Marine who'd been to Mars, with one left over for the civilian who'd endured the grueling, three-week march from Heinlein Station to Mars Prime . . . and then been on hand to snap the famous flag-raising at Cydonia.

The beer can represented an in joke among the men and women who'd been with the MMEF. "Sands of Mars"

Garroway, in the true improvise-adapt-overcome spirit of the Marines, had converted cans of contraband beer into weapons, showering them on UN troops at Cydonia from a hovering Mars lander. The aluminum cans had burst on impact in the thin Martian air, spraying suits and helmet visors with a fast-congealing foam that had immediately frozen, leaving the enemy confused, frightened, and largely blind.

The ponderous acronym across the bottom of the patch stood for "All The Way To Mars And They Made Us Throw Away The Beer."

"Our honorary Marine," Knox had called him when he'd presented the badge. After the shared hardships and dangers of Garroway's March, after the wild firefight—and the *literal* beer bust—with UN Foreign Legion troops at the Cydonian base, David Alexander had been . . . changed.

It was hard to put into words, even now. David had been a Navy brat, and as a kid had dreamed of being an aviator, like his father. After losing his aviator father to an equipment failure aboard the USS *Reagan*, though, he'd developed a deep-seated loathing for the military, coupled with a pacifist's hatred for war in all its forms.

But now? He still hated war and thought that *this* war, in particular, was suicidally stupid. But for the men he'd been forced to serve with, struggle with, fight beside on Mars, he felt nothing but admiration and respect.

Acceleration slammed at him through the couch, its hand unpleasantly heavy across his chest after three days of free fall. The pressure went on and on for a long time, too. Normally, a Moon-bound craft would decelerate first into Lunar orbit, followed by a second deceleration to drop into a landing approach, and the final burst as it gentled in for a landing. *Clarke* was combining all three delta-v maneuvers in one, however; no one had said anything definite, but David had heard rumors that the Aerospace Force had already lost a spacecraft passing over the Lunar farside. Coming in straight this way, without an initial orbit, was risky . . . but it avoided the possibility of being shot down by the rumored UN forces on the side of the Moon always hidden from the Earth.

And as the *Clarke* plunged from dazzling, white sunlight into the Moon's shadow, David decided that he was all in favor of that. . . .

Hab One, Picard Base
Mare Crisium, the Moon
0758 hours GMT

"Kaminski!"

"Yeah, Gunny?"

Yates jerked a thumb at the ladder leading to the upper deck of the hab. "Get your sorry butt topside, Sergeant. The captain wants to see ya."

"Christ, Ski!" Corporal Ahearn shook her head. "What the fuck did you do now?"

"Dunno, Hern," he said, throwing down his cards. Jesus, always something. It had been a good hand, too. "I ain't been in trouble for, hell, two or three hours, it seems like."

Padding across the steel deck in his socks, he hesitated at the ladder. None of the Marines had their boondockers because they'd all arrived in pressure suits, and their shoes were still with the rest of their personal gear, back at Fra Mauro. It seemed . . . *wrong*, somehow, to be going up to see the skipper in BDUs and padded green socks.

"Get movin', Ski," Yates warned. "She didn't say tomorrow."

"Aye, aye, Gunnery Sergeant Yates, *sir*!" he snapped, and started up the ladder.

Captain Fuentes was seated at the desk that until a few days ago had belonged to the commander of UN forces at Picard, Arnaldo Tessitore of the San Marco Marines. Lieutenant Garroway was perched on the corner of the desk, also in greens and socks. "Sergeant Kaminski, reporting as ordered, ma'am," he announced, centering himself in front of the desk and coming to attention.

"At ease, Sergeant," Fuentes said. "According to your

records, you were with Major Garroway on Mars.''

Kaminski flicked a quick glance at the lieutenant. ''Yes, ma'am.''

''Then you knew one of the scientists on the expedition, Dr. Alexander.''

''Huh? Sure!''

''My father told me that you and Alexander were pretty friendly,'' Lieutenant Garroway said. ''You were with him inside the Cave of Wonders, helped him out, that sort of thing.''

''Uh, yes, ma'am. I guess I was pretty interested in what he was doin'. He let me help out some. And, yeah. He let me come inside the cave with him.'' Kaminski suppressed a shudder. ''Didn't like it, though.''

''Why not?''

''Some of those, uh, *things* on the things like TV screens were pretty, well, they gave me the creeps, ma'am.''

''But you got on well with Alexander?''

''Huh? Yeah! The Professor, he was okay.'' Kaminski drew himself up a little straighter. ''Th' way I see it, any-one on the March with us was okay! And the Prof, he did just great, for a civilian.''

''Excellent, Sergeant,'' Fuentes said, making a notation with a stylus on the screen of her PAD. ''Thank you for volunteering.''

''Volunteering!'' He stopped himself, swallowed, and licked his lips. ''Uh, if the captain doesn't mind telling me, what did the sergeant just volunteer for?''

''We have a guest, Sergeant,'' Fuentes replied. ''Dr. Alexander. He's just arrived to investigate the UN archeo-logical dig outside. And you just volunteered to be his assistant.''

Kaminski sagged just the slightest bit with relief. *That* ought to be easy enough. A real skylark detail. He'd seen the new arrivals filing from their bug transport, of course, but had had no idea that Alexander was aboard. ''Uh, yes, ma'am. Thank you, ma'am.''

''He's in Hab Three, with Dr. Billaud and the other UN

scientists we captured. Suit up, hotfoot on over there, and make yourself useful. That is all."

"Aye, aye, Captain!"

He came to attention again, whirled in place, and dived for the ladder. Hot damn! If they had to roust him from a friendly game with his squadmates, at least it was for an assignment that ought to be interesting.

The last few days, since the Marine assault on Picard, had been downright boring.

He had a happy feeling that that was about to change.

Hab Three, Picard Base
Mare Crisium, the Moon
0815 hours GMT

They'd been shouting at the prisoners when David had walked into the hab compartment, moments before. "You had damned well better cooperate, mister," the Army colonel bellowed, his voice ringing off the metal walls as he leaned over the prisoner. "I'm losing my patience! It is one hell of a long walk back to Earth, and right now, we are your *only* hope of a ride!"

Dr. Marc Billaud stared past his tormentor with an icy indifference. "*Je ne comprends pas,*" he said.

"He's lying," the Army captain at the colonel's side said. "His record says—"

"Ah, Colonel," David said, interrupting, "I really don't think you're going to get anything out of them this way. Do you think I could have a few moments with them?"

The interrogators—three Army officers who'd made the trip out aboard the *Clarke*—stared at David for a moment. The senior officer, Colonel Thomas R. Whitworth, opened his mouth, then closed it again, as though fearful of appearing foolish. The other two, Major Dahlgren and Captain Slizak, glanced at one another, but said nothing.

Stiffly, then, hands clasped behind his back, the colonel glared at David. "For your information, Doctor, these . . . *people*," he replied, "have information that we need. They speak English . . . or at least this one does. But they're not cooperating.''

"I understand all that. I also *know* Marc Billaud."

"Eh? How's that?''

"He's a friend of mine.''

"Dr. Alexander, how the hell is it you're friends with this *UNdie*?"

"I met him before the war, Colonel. There was such a time, you know. It only *seems* like the war's been going on forever.''

"Hmpf. My orders—''

"Are these people prisoners of war, Colonel?''

"Technically, no, Doctor," Dahlgren said. "They are civilians, and unless we can prove that they've borne arms against American military forces, they must be treated as civilians according to the terms of the Geneva Convention." The major was staring at Whitworth as he spoke, and David had the feeling there was no lost love between the two.

Well, being cooped up in a tin can with thirty-some other troops for the three-day coast up from Earth could do that to people. David was glad once again that he'd been able to spend much of the voyage up forward with the pilot.

"I am *well* aware of the legalities of this situation," Whitworth huffed. "But these people know things that are vital to our operation here. I will not see this mission jeopardized by—"

"Give me a few moments with them alone, and perhaps I can get him to talk to you. *Without* the histrionics.''

Whitworth's eyes narrowed with an expression hovering between disbelief and outright suspicion while Major Dahlgren looked carefully noncommittal. The major, it turned out, was fluent in French and had been serving as interpreter . . . though Whitworth appeared dedicated to the age-old linguistic theory that speaking very loud and waving the arms about would hurdle all language barriers.

As though suddenly arriving at a decision, the colonel cocked his head, shrugged, and exchanged a glance with the other officers. "Well, of course. This isn't a formal interrogation. Not *yet*, anyway.'' He gestured at the French scientists. ''Go ahead. Knock yourself out. I'll be back . . . later.''

''A friend of yours?'' Billaud asked in English, rolling his eyes toward the doorway through which the colonel and his entourage had vanished.

''A friend? No, my God. An acquaintance only. I met him on the transport bringing me here. I think the major, the one with the mustache, is Army Intelligence.''

''*Oui*. He has the look. So, my friend. What did you hope to accomplish with that little show, just now?''

''I thought it would be more pleasant in here without the shouting.''

Billaud shook his head with a wry chuckle. ''Thank you for that, David. We appreciate the quiet. But . . . you must know, I will not betray my country.''

''Of course not. But . . . well, damn it, Marc, what *can* you give me?'' When Billaud did not immediately answer, David spread his hands. ''Look, it's all just a big, ugly game, right? Give me something, *anything,* to make the bloodhounds happy, and maybe we can get 'em to leave you alone for a while.''

Billaud sighed. ''You have, no doubt, read my notes. The ones I left at Fra Mauro? Your people, I'm sure, picked them up when they captured our base there.''

''No, actually. I came straight here, from Earth.''

''Ah. Well, your people already have those notes. I can only tell you what is in them . . . and nothing more.''

''At least it gets Whitworth off your back.''

''*Oui*.'' Billaud hesitated, as though wondering where to begin, then pursed his lips. ''You are in for a surprise, my friend, when you examine our dig outside.''

''I've been wondering about that. I was told it was a ship.''

Billaud nodded. ''A ship, *oui*. Or rather, a piece of a ship. A piece of a very large ship that . . . ah . . . suffered an accident, we think, six thousand years ago.''

''I saw the trenches outside. How is it that the ship was buried?''

Unlike Mars, where winds blew, dust accumulated, and

sand dunes migrated across the landscape in million-year marches, the Moon was not a place you associated with changes in the terrain. A crash thousands of years ago, even millions of years ago, should still be on the surface, where it fell. The slow infall of meteoric dust was not enough to bury something as large as a spacecraft, even after millions of years.

Billaud exchanged a quick glance with the other scientists—there were three, two men and a woman. Then he sighed. "There *was* some wreckage on the surface. Most of that is . . . gone now. Salvaged."

"Salvaged! What do you mean?"

"I'd rather not say more. But . . . you Americans are interested in the technology of these aliens, no?"

"Of course." David nodded. Then he slapped his knee. "Of course! You found a power plant . . . or an engine assembly! Good for you!"

"Good for us, yes," the woman said. "Perhaps not so good for you!"

"Estelle!" one of the other scientists warned.

But David already understood . . . enough, at least, to know in general what was going on.

"There really wasn't that much to salvage," Billaud went on, as though he'd not been interrupted. "In fact, it appears the vessel was torn open some distance above the ground. The contents spilled out . . . here. Much of the wreckage was scattered across most of the floor of this crater."

"There have been TLPs associated with Picard," David said. "Transient Lunar Phenomena."

"Yes. That was our first clue, in fact, to look here. Large chunks and scraps of highly polished metal. When it catches the light just right, it can look like unusual clusters of lights, here on the crater floor. Observers on Earth have seen unusual lights and effects here for some time."

TLPs had been seen for almost two hundred years at many different sites on the Moon. They appeared only rarely and were usually dismissed as volcanic phenomena. David wondered if those sites now warranted a closer look by xenoarcheologists.

"The largest fragment was a kind of module or capsule containing the ship's power generator," Billaud continued. "When it struck, most of it was buried. It took six weeks to dig it free. Many of the smaller, heavier fragments were buried on impact as well, which is why we have been digging the trenches."

David found a chair by the compartment's one small table and sat down. "Tell me more," he said.

One of the other men said something sharply, in French.

"Ah," Billaud said. "Jean-Paul thinks I've already said too much."

"Not really. We'd guessed that you'd found something important at Picard. And that you'd already moved it to your base on the Lunar farside."

None of them said anything, either in confirmation or in denial.

"What can you tell me about the aliens? They had a base here?"

Billaud leaned forward, his eyes bright. "Oh, my friend! I wish I could tell you what I've seen, what I've learned! Things wonderful . . . and things terrifying, as well."

"Where? Here? Or at your base? You're at Tsiolkovsky, right?"

Billaud sighed. "Your people must know that by now. Yes. And thousands of years ago, another race, another civilization, was there as well. Until they were attacked by *les Chasseurs de l'Aube.*"

"The . . . what?"

" 'Hunters of the Dawn' is how we have translated the name. There appears to have been a terrible war fought, here . . . and elsewhere."

"I think you need to tell me more. Everything you can. Please."

Twenty minutes later, he walked out of the compartment. The three Army officers were there, seated at a table. The Marine guard posted outside the room with the UN scientists stood by the door, and another Marine was leaning against one wall. He straightened as David entered the room. "Hey, Professor!"

"Kaminski!" David said, startled. "What are *you* doing here?"

"Waitin' for you. They told me you needed an assistant."

David nodded absently. "That's . . . good. . . ."

"Well?" Whitworth demanded. "Did they tell you anything?"

"Yes," David replied. "They told me quite a bit."

Whitworth's leathery face creased in an unexpected grin. "Excellent, Doctor! You had the routine down just perfect!"

"Routine? What routine?"

"Good cop–bad cop, of course. I had 'em rattled and worried. Then you stepped in and sweet-talked 'em. Works every time!"

The major gave David a sour look. "What did you learn?"

David resented Whitworth's implication that he'd been playing some sort of game. How little could he get away with telling the bastard and still have it sound convincing? "I'm not sure you're going to want to hear this," he replied. And then he told them.

But not everything . . . especially what Billaud had said about the place he called Gab-Kur-Ra. The alien base uncovered at Tsiolkovsky he decided to keep to himself. He was damned if he would let the military fight over the treasures Billaud had hinted at, as they had the archeological treasure house at Cydonia.

Hab One, Picard Base
Mare Crisium, the Moon
1038 hours GMT

"Why just you?" Kaitlin wanted to know. "The Army's here. We should all pull back to Fra Mauro."

Captain Fuentes shrugged. "God knows, Garroway," she replied. "His message just said he needed to consult with the company commanders. He's a major, Lee and I are captains, so we'll go consult. We'll take Bug Thirty-eight.''

"It's damned idiocy, if you ask me. Why do you think God invented radios and scrambled channels?''

"Here, now, Lieutenant Garroway!'' Captain Rob Lee replied with a wry grin. "Are you actually implying that Battalion has something in its ditty bag masquerading as common sense?''

She smiled. Captain Rob Lee, Alfa Company's CO, was young, smart, and good-looking, with that sense of rough give-a-damn that she normally associated with fighter jocks. His penchant for scathing one-liners was legendary in 1-SAG.

"That's asking too much, huh?'' she asked. "I *have* noted a tendency in Major Avery to slip back into his childhood, counting beans and shuffling files.''

Rob closed his eyes. "The major,'' he said quietly, but with great seriousness, "is a good man, means well, and works hard. Unfortunately, he would not be able to get a clue if he went out into a field full of horny clues during clue mating season, smeared his naked body with clue musk, and danced the ritual clue mating dance.''

Kaitlin groaned. "Now *there's* an image I'd really have preferred you'd kept to yourself.''

"There shouldn't be a problem, Lieutenant,'' Fuentes told her. "You're senior to Palmer, so you're in charge of both companies while we're gone. Colonel Whitworth, of course, will be in overall command of this station, but that shouldn't affect the regular routine.''

"The routine's not what's bothering me, Captain,'' Kaitlin said. "It's the *non*-routine. If the UNdies are going to counterattack, it'll be in the next day or two, before we have a chance to get dug in.''

"We should be back by 2200 hours tonight,'' Rob told her. He folded his arms. "I imagine the major just wants to go over routine joint-op protocol with us. IFF freaks, pass codes, and so on.''

"Which ought to already be set up,'' Fuentes said. "Garroway's right. If the bad guys hit us anytime soon, we're screwed, and it won't help things a bit if we're attending a fragging staff meeting at Fra Mauro. *Damn*!''

"I *do* have an idea," Kaitlin told them. "If we could set things up this way . . .''

EIGHT

The Dig, Picard Base
Mare Crisium, the Moon
1438 hours GMT

"So, anyway," Kaminksi said, "I was wonderin' if we could, well, trade e-mails or something. I really enjoyed learning that stuff you were telling me about on Mars, and I keep wanting to ask you questions about it. And it looks like you've got a lot more to learn here." They were standing on the Lunar surface, among the crisscrossing trenches of the French excavation. It seemed like a huge area for two men to search.

"That," David said, grinning inside his helmet, "is an understatement! I'd be delighted to correspond with you, Ski. You're not afraid to ask questions, and you have a knack for asking the right ones."

"Thanks! I'll try not to be a pest with it, but, well, the news, Triple-N, and all, they always seem to get the facts tangled up, at least from what you were saying."

"Sometimes they do."

"So, anyway, you was sayin' that the aliens who built the Face, and all that stuff on Mars, they're different from the aliens who were here on the Moon?"

"That's right, Ski," David replied. "The Cave of Wonders, the Face, all of that is about half a million years old. Whatever crashed here was a lot more recent. Eight thousand years, six thousand years, something like that."

Kaminski turned slowly, surveying the harshly illuminated patch of the crater floor, trying to imagine what must
have happened here. This part of the Moon was now completely dark. Only the worklights cast any light at all, and
they made this one tiny corner of the Lunar surface seem
very small and isolated. Even the stars were banished by
their glare, though the Earth, a blue-and-white first quarter,
still hung in its unvarying spot in the western sky.

"Quite a mess, isn't it, Ski?" David asked, misinterpreting Kaminski's silent gaze.

"What do you mean?"

David, swaddled and clumsy in his government-issue
space suit, turned to face Kaminski. "In proper archeology," David told him, "we're interested in the layers, the
strata, of debris, of how things are laid down one on top
of another. We're also very interested in the precise lo-
cations in which artifacts are found, relative to one another, and to the terrain. We're very careful about such
things, laying out precisely numbered grids, taking photographs of everything in situ, making sure we understand
everything there is to know about an object's position before we remove it."

"You were tellin' me about all that on Mars, sir," Kaminski said.

"So I did. The problem there, of course, was far too
much in the way of buildings, artifacts, and debris to explore and catalog, with far, far too few people to do the
work. It's different here." Turning again, David waved
one arm, taking in the entire black panorama of the crater
floor, the trenches and excavated pits beneath the worklights, the mounds of debris piled nearby. "We archeologists have a technical term for this sort of site," David
told him. "We call it fubaritic strata."

"Yeah?"

"As in fubar."

"Ah! As in 'Situation Normal, All Fucked Up.'"

"Exactly. See? We'll make an archeologist out of you
yet." David started to walk. Kaminski followed, shouldering the massive canvas satchel he'd been packing for
Alexander since they'd left the hab. It didn't weigh very

much in the Lunar gravity, but its inertia made it a chore to move or to stop.

With the satchel, his PLSS, and his slung ATAR, Kaminski was beginning to feel like a caddie following a VIP around a golf course. A golf course with grays instead of greens that was one big sand trap from tee to hole.

"So, how's it screwed up?" Kaminski asked.

"We just had two small armies tramping back and forth through these trenches the other day, Ski. What else *would* it be?" They arrived at the edge of a large, shallow pit. David jumped in, followed a moment later by Kaminski. The floor was covered by treaded-boot prints, with tangles of white string scattered about seemingly at random. "Looks like they had that area laid out in a proper grid for photography and cataloging, with string and posts, but so many people stampeded through that the grid lines are all torn down. I don't know if we'll ever be able to recreate Dr. Billaud's survey work here."

"Maybe you could get him to help? I mean, back in the hab this morning, you were tellin' those Army guys that he was cooperatin' with you. He told you all that stuff about Sumeria."

"Hmm. An attractive idea, Ski. Unfortunately, the government frowns on close collaborations with the enemy. I imagine they'll be shipping Dr. Billaud and his colleagues back to Earth on the first available transport."

"What'll happen to them then? They're not gonna get sent back to France."

"No. I'm afraid that's most unlikely. Especially considering what they know."

"Is what they found here really that important? I mean, it's just more alien shit, like we found on Mars, right?"

Kaminski heard David's sigh, a blast of air across his helmet microphone. "What we're finding on Mars—and here—is completely changing everything we thought we understood about human origins, about who and what we are. The artifacts, the bodies and so on we found on Mars suggests that someone was tinkering with our DNA half a million years back. That's momentous enough. But what Billaud and his people have found here on the Moon is a lot closer to our *historical* origins. It tells us, not about our biology, but about our culture, our civilization. I'm afraid this is going to upset people even more than the news from Mars did.''

"You mean the ancient-astronaut stuff? The stuff we found on Mars is already really stirring people up. All those cults and things.''

"Yes." That one word sounded almost sad.

" 'Course, doesn't this all just go to show the ancient-alien people are right?''

"Not the part about the ETs being God, or us being created in their image, or any of that. No.''

"You were telling the Army guys about what Billaud told you. Something about the Sumerians?''

"Sumer was one of Earth's earliest true civilizations. Dates back to about 4,000 B.C., though they probably had their start well before that. They established quite a remarkable culture at the head of the Persian Gulf, one that literally seemed to spring up overnight, out of nowhere.''

"The Fertile Crescent? Tigris and Euphrates Rivers?''

"That's right, Ski! Very good!''

He shrugged inside his suit. "Okay, so I *did* remember something from high-school history class. And you guys think these aliens got the Sumerians off to a civilized start, is that it?''

"The amusing thing is that the Sumerians themselves claimed—in their myths and legends—that the gods were people much like themselves who came down from the heavens and taught them everything they needed to know, agriculture, writing, building cities, working gold, numbers, medicine . . .'' He stopped, then bent over, hands on knees, as he intently studied a patch of boot-trammeled Lunar soil.

"Yeah, but don't *all* those ancient civilizations claim they got their start from the gods? Kind of like a good public-relations campaign, y'know? My civilization is better than your civilization, 'cause it was started by the gods. I'm king, 'cause God said that's the way it is.''

"You're absolutely right. Still, that doesn't mean that the first people to claim that distinction weren't telling the exact and literal truth.'' He stooped and began scraping at the ground with his gloved hands. The regolith was soft and powdery, but firmly packed, with the consistency of damp beach sand.

"So . . . what were they doin' here?'' Kaminski asked after a long moment. "The aliens, I mean. Why would they come all the way here to give us writing and stuff. What was in it for them?''

"Excellent question. Let me have that bag, will you?''

Kaminski let the massive satchel slide from his shoulder, and David unsnapped the cover and opened it up. Inside was a variety of tools, including hammers, a whisk broom, mirrors with handles, small shovels, and numerous pry bars, from a half-meter-long crowbar down to probes the size of a nutpick. The archeologist selected one of the latter, picking it up clumsily in his heavy gloves.

"According to Dr. Billaud," David went on, scraping at the ground with the tool, "there was an alien ship flying over Picard a few thousand years ago. It . . . well, it didn't explode. But it apparently tore open, just like a seagoing ship getting ripped open by an iceberg. The loot inside spilled out.''

"Loot?''

"Statues. Gold plates or tablets with writing on them. *Objets d'art.* A lot of the stuff landed here, inside this crater, in an enormous footprint. The heavier pieces were moving fast enough to plow down into the regolith a ways, like bullets. The lighter, flimsier stuff ended up on the surface.''

"I don't see nothing like that up here.''

"Our UN counterparts have already cleaned the area out pretty well, Ski.'' He began prying something shiny up out of the clinging dust. "They were in the process of sinking these trenches to try to find and recover the heavier things. Like . . . this.''

David straightened up again, holding something in both hands. Kaminski stepped closer, his eyes widening. It was a statue, perhaps ten inches long . . . and it gleamed in the worklights like pure gold. At first, Kaminski thought the figure was human . . . but then, as David turned it in his hands, he got a better look at the face . . . roughly human, with mouth and nose and eyes in about the right place, but with eyes that looked like enormous goggles or bubbles, with deeply incised, horizontal lines instead of pupils. In one clenched fist it held a kind of staff or scepter; in the other, it clutched five ropes or leashes that ran down the front of the statue to the necks of five delicately sculpted figures, grouped waist high in front of the main figure. These smaller images were clearly human, with almond-shaped but human-looking eyes—three men and two women, nude, with their hands tied and their heads bowed.

"I wonder," David said slowly, "if this might be our answer to your question."

"If it is," Kaminski replied, "a lot of these ancient-astronaut worshipers back home are in for one hell of a shock. That big guy there doesn't exactly look like their idea of a happy, loving, creator god, like they've been saying."

"You're right there, Ski. This is going to upset a *lot* of folks back home. . . ."

"Heads up, Marines, this is Bravo-six" cut in on their suit-to-suit channel. The voice was that of Lieutenant Garroway. Bravo-6 was the company's radio code for Marine C-cubed. "We have bogies inbound, presumed hostile! All Marines outside, take cover and look sharp." There was a pause. "Kaminski! You copy?"

"Six, Kaminski. I copy."

"You have the package?"

Alexander. "That's affirmative. Right here beside me."

"Get him back inside, stat! We don't want him wandering outside when . . . shit!"

A babble of radio voices sounded over Kaminski's headset.

"Bravo-six, OP-two! Bogies in sight, repeat, bogies in sight, bearing two degrees north of Marker East Three. They're coming in low and tight!"

"Six! OP-one! I have them! Incoming, by East Three!"

"Bravo-six! Bravo-six! Perimeter Green One! We are taking fire! We are taking—"

Static hissed over the radio channel. Kaminski crouched in the pit, staring toward the blackness of the eastern horizon, but his night vision, burned by the worklights, was gone. He *thought* he saw—

Gray dust exploded in a silent, deadly blossom the size of a small tree in the airless void twenty meters to Kaminski's right. David was standing, staring in the wrong direction, his back to the explosion, and didn't even see the danger. Swiftly, Kaminski reached up, grabbed Alexander's PLSS harness, and yanked, hard, toppling the big man in a slow-motion tumble to the ground, the gold statue spinning in a gentle descent from the archeologist's hands.

"What the? . . ."

"Get down, sir!" Kaminski snapped, peeling the ATAR off his shoulder and slapping the charging lever to chamber the first round. "We got problems!"

He could see the first of the UN hoppers now, an ungainly flying bug shape dropping out of the glare of the lights fifty meters away, almost directly between the two of them and the HQ hab. "Ooh-rah!" he shouted over the radio. "Target acquired!"

He brought the assault rifle to his shoulder, switched on HUD targeting, and dragged the muzzle until the crosshairs on his visor aligned with a hatch in the hopper's side, already gaping open.

"All units!" Kaitlin's voice called. "We're under attack! Fire at will!"

Kaminski had already squeezed the firing button.

Hab One, Picard Base
Mare Crisium, the Moon
1455 hours GMT

Kaitlin looked up as a voice crackled from an overhead speaker. "Bravo-six! Bravo-six! Enemy troops in sight. They're not blue-tops. Repeat, negative blue-tops!"

"Chinese," she said.

Gunnery Sergeant Yates, at her side, nodded. "Almost certainly."

"Blue-tops" was slang for the light, UN-blue helmets worn by European troops. The Chinese forces encountered so far tended to wear olive-drab and black space suits, with either olive or black helmets.

The door to the Battle Management Center clanged open, and Colonel Whitworth stormed in, with Major Dahlgren and Captain Slizak in close tow. "What the devil is going on?" he bellowed. Kaitlin looked up from the map table and looked him in the eye.

"We are under attack, Colonel," she said, her voice cool.

"I *know* that! By who, goddammit?"

Yates pointed at the map table, which had been set to display input from a small computer operated by one of the Marines at the communications console. It now showed the various buildings and trenches at Picard, together with a scattering of green and red symbols. "UN forces, Colonel. Probably dispatched from the UN base on the farside, unless they had the foresight to set up a ready reserve someplace a little closer than Tsiolkovsky. They're not wearing European Union space suits, so we suspect that they may be members of the *Hangkong Tuji Budui*."

"Chinks, eh?" Whitworth said, nodding. "Right. As senior officer present, I am officially taking charge of this action." He stared down at the map table for a moment. "Where . . . where are my troops on this thing?"

"There, Colonel," Kaitlin said, pointing to two of the blue symbols denoting Habs Two and Four. "Those are the quarters they've been assigned to. But, with all due respect, I think you should—"

"Young lady!" Whitworth barked. "Are you presuming to tell *me* how to run a battle? Or are you simply telling me what to do with my troops?"

Kaitlin fought down a burst of anger. "No, sir. But you should know—"

But Whitworth was not listening. He turned to the communications personnel. "You, there! Get me an open channel to Captain Bladen, in Hab Two!"

"Aye, aye, sir," one of the technicians said, his face carefully expressionless.

"These UNdies can't know that the Green Berets are here, in force! We'll goddamn teach the bastards a lesson!"

"Sir!" the Marine at the radio called. "Captain Bladen."

"About goddamn time!" He strode to the com console, snatched the mike from the Marine's hand, and began talking.

Kaitlin exchanged a long look with Gunny Yates. "I don't like this, Lieutenant," he said, keeping his voice low. "It's going to get damned sticky out there!"

"Granted, Gunny. But he *is* senior officer aboard. Pass the word to your people to be careful about IDing their targets."

"Roger that. But it's not going to be easy!"

"What'd you expect, Gunny? A goddamn walk in the park?" She stared at the map table, where small green squares were spilling across the contour-marked terrain. Red squares—the enemy—appeared and vanished as trackers identified them and fed the data into the Marine battle-management system. Most of the red symbols were ghosted, indicating probable positions based on last confirmed reports.

There'd been six Marines outside when the alert had first been sounded, in three widely separated two-man OPs. No ... make that seven, counting Kaminski, who was supposed to be hustling his civilian charge back inside. A ready force of Second Platoon Marines had been waiting, however, already suited up and ready to go except for gloves and helmets, on the lower decks of Habs Three and Five, and they were spilling out through the airlocks and onto the lunar surface right now. Every Marine had an IFF transponder mounted in his or her suit; the coded signal from each IFF was picked up by the antenna arrays atop Hab One and fed into the battle-management system. The BMS, in turn, displayed the positions and identities of all of the Marines in the action. Ranging data picked up from the Marines' laser sighting systems on their ATARs located the unidentifeds—the probable UN troops.

The problem was that Whitworth was now giving orders to some forty Army Special Forces troops to join the battle. There'd been no time yet to set their IFF transponders to frequencies recognized by the BMS; hell, she didn't even know yet if the Army suits *had* transponders. When those troops stormed out onto the crater floor, there would be no way at all to separate them from the enemy.

Yates was right. This could be *real* sticky.

The Dig, Picard Base
Mare Crisium, the Moon
1456 hours GMT

David started to pull himself to his feet once more, but Kaminski was lying across his legs. "Stay down, dammit!" the Marine shouted, before adding a perfunctory "*Sir!*"

"But I can't see!" Try as he might to lever the front part of his suit higher, David could not find a position that would let him see what was happening. Kaminski seemed to be shooting at something; David could feel the jarring against the legs of his suit as the Marine's ATAR recoiled.

A battle. He was smack in the middle of a battle once again, though the eerie silence, the lack of crackling gunfire and explosions, gave a surreal, almost dreamlike feeling to the engagement. He could hear distinct voices over his radio, though for the most part they were all but unintelligible. They might have been kids playing some backyard game utterly beyond the ken of listening adults.

"*Delta-one, this is Five! Heads up, on your six!*"

"*Copy, Five, I see 'em!*"

"*Clear! I gotta lock! That's fox!*"

"*Ooh-rah! Hey, UNdie! Special delivery from the Corps!*"

Those voices sounded so young.

War might arise from the failings of old politicians, but always it was the young who paid war's price. The average age of the SAG Marines, he'd heard during his trip out from Earth, was twenty-two—a little over half David's age—and it was as old as that only because SAG included a higher-than-usual proportion of seasoned NCOs than the typical Marine rifle company back on Earth.

He wondered if war had been the same the last time this crater had been illuminated by fire from the black Lunar sky, a drawn-out game between elders, with brave youngsters as the playing pieces, the expendable pawns. That was the most disturbing bit of intelligence that Marc Billaud had passed on that morning—the knowledge that thousands of years ago, at the very dawn of human civilization, the aliens worshiped as gods by those humans had been destroying themselves in a cataclysmic war; the wreckage of the cargo ship that had fallen here within this crater allowed no other interpretation. The vessel had been destroyed by powerful weapons . . . almost certainly a positron beam, a bolt of antielectrons that had annihilated the target in a deadly flash of hard radiation.

Similar weapons had been employed half a million years earlier, on the Cydonian plains of Mars.

Was war the inevitable fruit of all civilization, of all so-called intelligence?

"We got another UNdie bug, comin' in from East One!"

"Lauden! Can you tag him with your Wyvern?"

"That's negative! I'm foxed out!"

Damn! he thought. *I wish I could see.* Unable to rise to watch the unfolding battle, David looked instead at the marvelously delicate and expressive figurine he held cradled in his arms. The back, he saw, was flat, as though a three-dimensional statue had been sliced cleanly in two from top to bottom . . . then heavily inscribed all over the back with tiny, crisply incised marks. The entire lower half, he saw, was covered with tiny pictographs, the top half with something like writing, with repetitive symbols that . . .

With an ice-shocked jar that literally drove the breath from his body, David understood just what it was he was holding. Rolling suddenly out from beneath Kaminski's legs, he sat up, holding the statuette in both hands, staring at it as though it had just come alive.

Which in a very real sense, it had.

"Goddammit, sir," Kaminski screamed, lurching toward him. *"Get the fuck down!"*

Dazedly, he looked around, becoming aware of running shapes, bright and silent flashes against the darkness, and Kaminski's wide-eyed face behind his visor. "The Rosetta stone!" he said, more to himself than to the frantic Marine.

"Whatever!" Kaminski hit him, hard, with one outstretched hand, knocking him back to the ground. "Hit the dirt!"

David lay on his side, continuing to stare at the inscriptions on the back of the gold statue. They had a machine-precise look about them, as though they'd been stamped into the metal, rather than carved out by artisans. Those on the bottom half were almost shockingly familiar; David couldn't read it, but he was quite familiar with the pictographs known as Proto-Sumerian, the antecedent of Mesopotamian cuneiform writing.

And as for the stranger, more fluid writing at the top . . .

He clutched the artifact more closely against the front of his suit. Suddenly, it was vitally important that he survive this firefight, vital that he return with the golden statue and its paired texts to the institute in Chicago.

The statue he was holding was more important than his life.

The Dig, Picard Base
Mare Crisium, the Moon
1457 hours GMT

Kaminski was aware of Alexander curling himself up around the odd gold statue, but didn't think any more about it. The important thing was to keep the civilian alive, and if the idiot would just keep his head down, there was at least a chance of that happening.

The battle, from Kaminski's point of view, at least, was a confusing, night-cloaked collision. Alexander's complaint a moment ago about not being able to see struck him as hilarious. All Kaminski could see was the pitch-blackness surrounding the base, the glare of worklights illuminating the central area, and various large and vaguely defined shapes—the habs and the insect-legged hoppers the UNdies were arriving in. Occasionally, a space-suited form would dash across the light, moving from shadow to shadow. When he kicked in the IR overlay of his helmet's heads-up display system, he could see the wavering, red-yellow man-shapes of other figures concealed by the dark. To sort friend from foe, he had to rely on the radioed commentary from C-cubed.

"Heads up, Marines! We have four Marines coming out of Hab Three, crossing toward Marker South Five."

He turned to look at the indicated hab, spotted three . . . no, four heat-shapes moving on the double. Superimposed on each was a small, bright green symbol, marking them as IFF-IDed friendlies. Good enough. He raised his ATAR and painted another target, a glowing mass crouched in the blackness beneath the first grounded hopper, perhaps ninety meters away. He couldn't see an IFF tag. "Six! This is Ski! I got a paint! What's my target?"

"Kaminski, Six. That's a hostile!"

"Roger that! Takin' 'im down!"

His selector switch was already set to a three-round burst. Holding the crosshairs on his helmet HUD steady on the red-glowing shape, he squeezed the trigger, felt the soft triplet of recoils as the 4.5mm caseless rounds snapped toward the target. The red mass suddenly split apart—there'd been *two* space-suited figures there—and started to move in opposite directions. He picked the one on the right and fired again. He *thought* he'd hit it; the figure wasn't moving anymore, at any rate. The one to the left . . . was gone by the time he tracked back to reacquire it. *Damn!* . . .

"All Marines! Heads up! We have ten Army troops coming out of Hab Four! They don't have IFFs, so watch what you're shooting at!"

He glanced toward Hab Four and saw moving shadows against the light. About time the damned doggies made it to the party. He wondered just what the odds were. There were three UN hopper transports, but they were *big* sons of bitches, bigger than the Marine bugs, big enough to carry a *lot* of troops. At the moment, the Marines were theoretically mustering fifty-three men in three companies—the fight three days ago at Picard had killed seventeen men and women, fifteen of them in Bravo's First Platoon. Three hours ago, though, just after the departure of Captain Fuentes and Captain Lee, all twenty-three Marines in Alfa Company's Second Platoon had boarded LSCP-44 and boosted skyward in a silent swirl of moon dust. Scuttlebutt had it that they were reconning off south of Picard somewhere, or even that they were scouting the approaches to a UN base hidden on the farside of the Moon, but no one was saying for sure. That left just Bravo's Second Platoon and the remnants of First—thirty people against possibly three times that number . . . unless the Army's Green Beanies entered the fight.

Two of the UN hoppers were on the ground; the third was still aloft, landing lights glaring against black space and the crisscross of steel struts. A streak of flame angled down from the hovering craft, striking a ditch digger in a soundless blossoming of white light that toppled Marines sheltered in the vehicle's shadow. Shit! The bastards had jury-rigged a missile launcher to the outer hull of the hopper and were using it for close air support.

Behind the glare of its landing lights, Kaminski could see a UN trooper leaning out of an open hatch, struggling to reload the now-empty launch tube. Taking careful aim, he squeezed off four fast triplets, and the loader jerked back inside, lost from view. Kaminski didn't know if he'd hit the guy or simply managed to scare him. Flicking the selector switch to full auto, he shifted his aim to the hopper's angular cockpit as the hovering craft slowly rotated in the sky. He wasn't sure how much 4.5-mm rounds would do to the ungainly thing, but he could sure let the UNdie bastards know that their presence above the battlefield was *not* appreciated.

God . . . was it falling?

It was spinning faster now, and settling, nose high.

Other Marines, and Whitworth's troops as well, were firing now at the hovering craft; Kaminski could see the sparks as rounds struck the craft's lightly armored hull. It struck the crater floor two hundred meters from Hab One, one of its landing legs crumpling beneath it as it set down hard in a high-flying billow of Lunar dust, pitching it sideways at a steep angle. By the harsh illumination of its landing lights, still on, Kaminski could see shadowy, space-suited figures tumbling from the wreckage. He took aim and opened up on full rock-and-roll, holding down the ATAR's firing button until the hundred-round stock magazine ran dry.

"*Ooh*-rah!" Kaminski shouted, holding his ATAR above his helmet in triumph. He was standing—and didn't even remember getting to his feet. He fumbled at his vest harness for a fresh box of caseless rounds, dropping the empty mag and snapping home the fresh one. A soundless explosion detonated forty meters away, and he heard the clatter of flying gravel rattling lightly from his helmet.

"Maybe *you* should be the one to get the fuck down, Kaminski," David called from his part of the excavation. "It's getting damned hot out here!"

He dropped back to his knees. "I think you're right. C'mon. Let's see if we can find better cover over that way." As they started to crawl, Kaminski looked back and noticed that Alexander was still carrying the statue he'd found. "Drop it, Professor," he said. "Won't do you no good if you get killed."

"No way, Ski. You just keep crawling. I'll keep up."

Kaminski hesitated. Damn it, Alexander was a civilian, and short of knocking him out and dragging him, Kaminski couldn't think of a way to enforce the order. He gave a mental shrug and kept crawling.

"Heads up, Marines and Berets!" the lieutenant's voice called. "We have incoming friendlies, coming in near South Two! Hold your fire to ground targets!"

Friendlies! Kaminski stopped crawling and searched the sky toward the southern direction markers. He couldn't see a thing . . . and then the bug switched on its landing lights, a quad of dazzling stars casting moving circles of illumination across the crater floor. Dust swirled as the vehicle gentled in for a landing not far from the wreckage of the downed UN hopper. The troops that came spilling out of the open cargo bay all bore green pips on Kaminski's HUD display, and he felt a surge of sheer joy. Someone— the company commanders, or maybe Lieutenant Garroway—had come up with one hell of an idea, sending Alfa Company's Second Platoon off to some nearby hidey hole beyond the crater rim as a strategic reserve. Once the UN forces had committed themselves to the counterattack, the reserves had come in, and now, suddenly the UN deployment was dissolving, their attack teams breaking into small groups of men, most of them now breaking for their remaining two hopper transports.

"Ski!" David called out suddenly. "On your left!"

Kaminski turned and saw a group of five or six red-orange heat images loping toward him. They were running in the general direction of one of the unloaded UN hoppers, and he and Alexander were squarely in their path.

He raised his ATAR, checked for green pips . . . and when he saw none he squeezed the firing button, sending a stream of 4.5mm rounds slashing into the running troops at a range of less than fifty meters. Two of the space-suited figures went down . . . then a third, his visor exploding in a spray of plastic shards and pink mist that froze instantly into an icy cloud as it blossomed from the helmet. The two survivors dropped prone, and puffs of dust exploded from the rim of the excavation as they returned fire.

"Hold your fire!" Kaitlin's voice cried over the general combat channel. "Damn it, hold your fire! Kaminski! Hold fire! *Those are friendlies*!"

Oh, *God.* . . .

NINE

*Parris Island Recruit Training
Center
0725 hours EDT*

Jack Ramsey—*Private* Jack Ramsey, US Marine Corps—
stood at a rigid, fair approximation of attention on the recruit battalion grinder, gaze focused on the tops of the
palmetto palms in the distance. Parris Island, they said,
was slowly sinking as the world's sea levels continued to
rise. Scuttlebutt had it that the whole island was already
beneath sea level, like Holland, and the only thing holding
the Atlantic at bay were the rings of seawalls, dikes, and
tide barriers erected by the Army Corps of Engineers and
a few thousand Marines.

Jack was less interested at the moment in the possibility
of a storm's fury sweeping over the low-lying island than
he was in the fury of another force of nature. Moments
before, Recruit Platoon 4239 had met their drill instructors, and, in an old and venerable tradition of the Corps,
they were enduring their first inspection and their welcom-
ing speech, delivered by the platoon's senior DI, Gunnery
Sergeant Harold Knox.

"Never, *never* in my entire military career," Knox was
saying as he stalked along the solitary line of recruits,
"have I seen such sorry specimens!" The expression on
his leathery face gave every appearance of a man appalled
by what he had just had the misfortune of witnessing. His

voice, crackling with the authority known throughout the Marine Corps as the *Command Voice*, bore the punch and edge necessary to carry above a howling storm . . . or a pitched battle. The stress he laid on certain words gave his oration an almost singsong, mesmerizing quality, holding the recruits spellbound. "It makes me *sick* to think that my beloved Corps could someday be in *your* pale, flabby hands!"

The Voice went on, and Jack swayed slightly on his feet. He was exhausted . . . running about ten hours minus on sleep at the moment. It felt like he'd been here for days already, and yet he'd only arrived at Parris Island that morning. Somehow, confusion and sleep deprivation had conspired to keep him from clicking in with the routine.

Every waking moment for the past month had been geared toward this moment, from his last on-line discussion with the recruiter, Staff Sergeant Henson, to his physical in Pittsburgh, to his swearing in at the recruiter's office. The maglev bringing him down from Pittsburgh had arrived in Charleston late on the previous afternoon, but the bus to take them the final short leg to the Parris Island Marine Recruit Depot—a clattering wreck with a gasoline engine, no less—had been mysteriously delayed. They'd not arrived at the base until 2:00 A.M.—0200 hours, in Marine parlance—a bit of disorganization that Jack was convinced had been done on purpose. Arriving in the middle of the night, told to "hit the beach" by screaming Marine NCOs and made to line up on yellow-painted footprints on the pavement, bullied, harassed, and screamed at some more, had resulted in the forty-three men and women aboard the bus feeling as cut off from their former lives as they might have been on the farside of the Moon.

After an initial orientation lecture, the female recruits had been called off and marched away into the night; the Marines alone of the four major services continued to maintain separate training battalions for its male and female recruits. There'd followed a nightmare, sleep-deprived blur of standing in line, of running, of standing in *more* lines, and of listening to bellowed lectures that extended throughout the rest of the night hours and well into the dawn of the morning. After breakfast, they'd been officially mustered into Recruit Platoon 4239 with a number of men already there in a holding company, bringing their numbers up to an even eighty. After that, they'd been checked into a recruit barracks, issued uniforms, and herded through a thirty-second haircut that left each recruit "high and tight."

And then there'd been more lectures, where they learned to start and finish every sentence with the word "sir," where they learned to come to attention at a shouted "attention on deck," where they learned not to speak in ranks unless spoken to, and where they learned that an order was to be answered by a shouted "aye, aye, sir," a hoary phrase meaning "I understand, and I *will* obey." High-running tension, shock, and lack of sleep had them all stumbling by the time they were marched to supper; the midday meal was never referred to as "lunch," a term strictly for civilians.

They'd mustered here on the grinder this afternoon to meet their company DIs.

Gunnery Sergeant Harold Knox was their senior drill instructor; Jack had felt in awe of the man from the moment he strode into their presence, crisp, immaculate, his traditional "Smoky Bear" hat precisely straight. Most of the other recruits, Jack knew, couldn't read the colorful splash of ribbons that started high on the left breast of the man's creaseless khaki shirt and extended halfway down to the black web belt that marked him as a senior DI. Silver Star. Bronze Star with cluster. Purple Heart. Presidential Unit Citation. Andhra Pradesh Intervention Ribbon. Colombian Civil War Ribbon.

And, for Jack, the most stunning campaign ribbon of them all, the gold-and-ocher rectangle of the Mars Marine Expeditionary Force. Gunny Knox had been *out* there, on the same mission as his uncle!

They stood in their long line, sweating in the steamy, April heat, stiffly at attention as Gunny Knox paced down the line, giving each recruit a look razor-edged enough to count their individual vertebrae and spot-check the contents of their stomachs.

He stopped, finally, in front of one Marine six down the line from where Jack was standing. "What in the *hell* do you think you are?"

"Sir! I'm a Marine! Sir!"

Knox's control was masterful. "I beg your pardon," he replied, his voice dropping in volume without losing any of its command, "but you are not. You are a *recruit*, and in future, when you are referring to your sorry-assed selves, you will *not* say 'I' or 'me,' but you will speak in the third person, saying 'this recruit.' There are no 'I's' here, except for the eyes in your head! Do you understand me?"

"Sir, yes, sir!"

"Furthermore, you do not have the *right* to refer to yourself in the first person! And you do not have the right to call yourself Marines! I have been making Marines out of sorry, slime-bucket maggots like you for twenty years, now, and I promise you that I *do* know what a Marine is! Trust me! You ain't it!"

Knox moved to the next man in line. "Good God in heaven! *What*, may I ask, is that *thing* on your face?"

Jack couldn't see from his current vantage point, staring across the grinder at the distant palmettos, but he knew who the DI must be talking to. Lonnie Costantino had been on the bus with Jack out from Charleston. He had a subdural implant under the skin of his forehead, a glow-tattoo powered by his body heat. It cast an illuminated, inner tattoo of an eight-pointed star centered by an alien-looking symbol, glowing in eerie yellow-and-red light clearly visible right through his skin. Jack had seen that symbol before, he was pretty sure—something from one of the alien scenes discovered in the Cave of Wonders on Mars.

"Uh . . . I mean, sir, that's my mark, sir. I'm, uh, like, a member of the Alien Astronauts Church, y'know? Freedom of religion! Uh, sir."

There was a long silence, and Jack wondered if Knox was about to explode. His eyes grew large, and a vein in his temple popped out, throbbing. Jack had the feeling that it was an act . . . but if it was, it was masterful, an Academy-Award performance.

Jack's breath caught in his throat. Lonnie had seemed like a nice enough guy, in a Pittsburgh tough-kid kind of way, but he wasn't, well, *Marine* material.

"The Corps will not interfere with the practice of your religion, son," Knox said, and he sounded almost fatherly. Then the edge came back, sharp and hard. "*However*, I will not stand by and watch some dink sniper drill you a new puckered asshole smack between your eyes—or between the eyes of one of the young men or women who end up in your squad—because you're wearing that damned glow-in-the-dark tattoo. You, therefore, have two options. I'll write you out a chit and you can go see the regimental chaplain. He'll arrange for your immediate discharge on the grounds of religious conscience. *Or* you can report to sick bay and have them remove your . . . mark. There is no place in the Corps for a man with his own luminous head-shot target. What'll it be?"

"Uh . . . I'll stay, sir."

"Report to sick bay. You know where it is?"

"Uh . . ."

"Bryce!"

"*Yes*, Gunnery Sergeant!" One of the junior DIs following Knox down the line rasped out.

"Escort our religious friend to sick bay."

"Aye, aye, Gunnery Sergeant!"

"But *first*, recruit, drop down and give me fifty! That's for being stupid enough to show up here with a headlight!"

"Uh, aye, aye, sir!"

"And then give me twenty-five more after that for not using the third person, *as* you were instructed! You are not an 'I'! You are not a 'me'! You are a recruit, and by God you will *act* like one and you will *talk* like one, because you do not have the *faintest* idea of how a Marine should act and talk! Hit it!"

"Aye, aye, sir!"

As Lonnie began counting off his push-ups, Knox continued his walk. "You, you *civilians* are disgusting! You are *not* Marines. At this moment I have grave doubts that any of you can ever *become* Marines, and you will *not* sully the name of my beloved Corps by claiming that you are! Right now, each and every one of you is too low to ever even think about becoming a United States Marine. You are *so low* that whale shit looks like shootin' stars to you! *You!* Are you smiling at me?"

The object of Knox's sudden attention, three to Jack's left, paled.

"S-sir! No, sir!"

"Do you find me amusing?"

"Sir! No, sir!"

"Hit the deck! Gimme twenty-five!"

"Aye, aye, sir!"

"And sing out!"

"One! . . . Two! . . ."

"You!" Knox said, stopping in front of the recruit to Jack's left, his voice strong above the first recruit's cadence. "Why the *hell* are you here in *my* squad bay pretending you're good enough to join *my* Corps?"

"Sir! This recruit will fight and die for my—uh—his country, sir!" The words came out with a crack and a squeak.

"Then you are no good to me, or to my Corps," Knox said, with overtones that were almost sorrowful. "General Patton said it best, and he knew what he was talking about, even if he was a doggie. The idea, ladies, is to get some *other* poor dumb bastard to die for his country. When we are done with you, you will be *Marines*, you will be *killers*, you will be America's fighting elite, *fully* capable of making that poor dumb bastard die for his country. To accomplish this, you will use the ATAR, you will use the Wyvern shoulder-fired missile system, you will use your Marine-issue K-Bar knife, you will use rocks, you will use your bare hands, you will use your teeth if you have to, because you *will* be Marines, and you *will* be trained to kill! *Do* you understand me?"

"Sir! Yes, sir!"

"But you are not Marines yet. You do not *look* like

Marines. You do not *sound* like Marines. The battle cry of the US Marine is *ooh-rah*! Let me hear you ladies wrap your throats around that!"

"Ooh-rah!"

Knox surveyed the line of recruits, fists on hips. "Pathetic! Again!"

"*Ooh*-rah!"

"Again!"

"*OOH-RAH!*"

"*You!*" Knox bellowed into Jack's face, as suddenly, as unexpected as an explosion. "Why are *you* here? What do you plan to make of yourself in this man's Marine Corps?"

Jack thought he knew what would impress the man. "Sir! This recruit intends to become a Space Marine, sir!"

Knox stared for a half a heartbeat, then startled Jack with an explosion of laughter. "A *Space* Marine! Well, what do you know about that? We've got Flash Gordon, here, ladies! Or is it Buck Rogers?" He laughed again, with a contortion of muscles about his eyes and mouth that threatened to crack his lean face. "I've got some hot intel for you, Flash. There are, as of this moment, three hundred ninety-five thousand men and women in the US Marine Corps. Of those, approximately twelve hundred are currently serving in the Space Assault Group, on space deployment, or in various support units.

"Now, since I know that you could not count to twenty-one *even* if you were barefoot *and* you removed your pants, I'll make it simple for you. The odds are something like three hundred thirty to one against you, son. Six months from now, you are *far* more likely to be serving in Siberia or some dink country you've never heard of and couldn't spell if you had, than you are to be playing *space* he-ro!"

Jack flushed, suddenly angry. "But my recruiter said—"

"WHAT DID YOU JUST SAY?"

Cold fear clawed up the back of Jack's neck. "Sir! I'm sorry, I mean, this recruit is sorry, sir!"

"I *know* what you *are*, recruit! What I *don't* know is

what you were just doing with that constipated, *sorry*-assed turd you call a brain! While in ranks, you will *not* speak unless I demand a response from you! Do I make myself *clear*, Flash?''

"Sir, yes, sir!"

"Hit the deck! Gimme one hundred! *Move!*"

"Aye, aye, sir!" He dropped to a push-up position and began doing push-ups.

"*And* you will sound off with each one!"

"Sir, yes, sir! Three! . . . four! . . .''

"I *did* not hear one and two, recruit! I must have *missed* them! Start over!''

"One! . . . Two! . . .''

Knox dropped into a crouch next to Jack, speaking softly now, but still with that whipcrack of command in his voice. "And as for what your recruiter may or may not have promised you, maggot, perhaps you would like to take that up with the regimental chaplain. Or maybe you'd like to run home to your momma! *She* might feel sorry for you. But *I* do not!" Straightening suddenly, he walked on down the line of men.

"And while Recruit Flash is demonstrating the proper technique for push-ups, the rest of your sorry-assed wannabes might consider this! *Every* Marine, and I don't care if he's a fighter jock joystickin' a Valkyrie, a space Marine on the Moon, a guard at an embassy or a goddamned *cook*, he is, first and foremost, forever and always, a Marine *rifleman*! You people will learn that lesson, and you will learn it well, because if you don't, some goddamn dink is gonna pop you a new asshole right between your eyes!''

He walked on down the line, and Jack kept pumping, calling off the numbers. "Eighteen! . . . Nineteen! . . .''

He had to concentrate, because the other recruits were calling off the numbers of their push-ups and were a bit ahead. By the time Knox had reached the end of the line and started making his way back, half a dozen other recruits were pumping and counting as well. And yet, over the cacophony, Gunny Knox's Voice of Command cracked and badgered, pushed, snapped, and berated. "I don't think any of you will ever have what it takes to be a United States Marine, but by *God* in heaven I am going to try! I am going to personally break every last one of you miserable lowlife worms, and in the process I guarantee each and every one of you that you will wish that you have never been born! And then we will take what's left and begin molding it into something that *might, perhaps*, begin to resemble a Marine!''

Jack's arms gave out at sixty-four. He kept trying, struggling to raise himself, but by that time the DI had decided that the entire platoon needed to report to their racks inside the barracks to learn something about how to properly stow gear. And after that . . . perhaps a little run to warm them all up for the afternoon's activities. . . .

"Give it up, Ramsey!" he bellowed. "That is *pathetic*! On your feet! And you have the unspeakable *gall* to think you can become a Marine? Move out! All of you, move out! I want to see nothing on this grinder but amphibious green blurs! On the double, move-it-move-it-move-it!''

The most humiliating part of the whole sorry affair was the sudden realization that his mother might have been right about his chances to get to space by joining the Corps.

Alexander Residence
Arlington Heights, Illinois
0810 hours CDT

Liana Alexander slammed the door behind her as she stalked into the house. Damn the man! Damn, *damn* the man! How he could be so insufferably arrogant, so cold, so . . . so *heartless*! . . .

Such a simple request, and he'd refused her, point-blank!

She walked into the E-room and dropped onto the sunken couch facing the wall screen. Picking up the remote, she thumbed through several menu selections, calling up her Earthnet access. David must have some files in here, things he was working on now, preliminary reports, something that would be useful!

David didn't know that she knew his private file-access code: Sphinx. Not that he'd ever tried very hard to hide it from her. In fact, he seemed to assume that she simply didn't have the brains to work *any* electronic equipment. Well, it was true that she had trouble recording more than one program at a time off the entertainment feeds without getting hopelessly lost in all of the menu selections and information trees. And she had trouble with some of the interactive Net services. So many choices!

But she could handle files and recorded messages just fine, thank you, and she knew how to use access codes. She'd been looking over his shoulder once when he'd keyed in the word "Sphinx" to get a locked file. He'd *known* she was there at the time, but in his usual arrogant way, he'd probably thought that she had no idea what he was doing.

She'd done this a number of times in the past, and it always gave her a small, guilty flush of excitement, the feeling she imagined a spy must have breaking into the enemy's computer database.

Well, she *was* a spy, in a sense. It was the only way she had to get at the truth, the only way she knew of finding the ammunition the Church needed. Reverend Blaine had told her last Sunday that what she was doing . . . what was it he'd said? It "transcends mere human law, in the eternal service of the Ancient Divine Masters of the Cosmos!"

So *there*, David!

Anyway, whatever it was she was doing, David had it coming!

She'd first started taking sneak peeks at David's files and correspondence several weeks after his return from Mars. He'd been gone one day, she couldn't get him on his PAD because he was busy in a meeting and refused the call, and she'd needed to find his government disbursal number for the tax forms she was filling out. Armed with the password she'd seen him type in once—Sphinx—she opened his private files and almost by accident discovered a saved vidcast.

It was one of the people at his new office—what was her name? Teri, she thought. Teri something-or-other. "Hiya, good-lookin'," the woman had said, leaning forward and smiling into her E-room's vid pickup. She was naked.

Well, the old taboo against public nudity was one of those aspects of modern society that was changing fast, had *been* changing since the turn of the century. Lots of people went nude these days, at home or when gathered with a few friends. It didn't mean anything, she knew. Even in public, on hot days lots of people wore shoes and UV block and nothing else but a wallet strap; with global warming and all it was just more comfortable that way.

But the way that Teri person had smiled and moved and said "Hiya, good-lookin' " had rankled. Damn it, it was inappropriate, it just wasn't *proper* for her to act and talk that way to a married man, especially when that man was her boss!

"Hey, Teri!" David's voice had answered. "What's up?"

"Oh, *lots* of things, I'm sure. What I'm calling for, though, is to find out about the trip to LA."

Liana had watched the whole sordid recording, wondering all the while if David was sleeping with that woman. The rest of the message was innocuous enough—her asking about details on the speech he was scheduled to give in LA, and his voice replying matter-of-factly, without any leering or flirting or innuendo. But the way, at the end, she'd stood up and slinked closer to the pickup, closing out with the words, "Okay, honey. See you . . . *later* . . ." had shocked her. At that moment, she was certain that David had had sex with Teri, was having sex with her on a regular basis. The fact that David had saved that damned message instead of deleting it was proof enough.

She wondered how often he played it back, with HER up there two times larger than life on that damned big wall screen. Yuck.

Liana sighed. Nudity taboos weren't the only aspects of

society that had been changing lately. Marriage, for instance. Nowadays, the institution was pretty much whatever people said that it was. There were so many new kinds of marriage and social groupings now that simply hadn't been around when she was younger . . . or at least, no one had talked about them, things like line marriages with several men and women all married to one another.

That sort of thing had never been for *her*, not the way she'd been raised!

And . . . and divorce was so easy, now! All you needed was for both parties to agree that it was over, and that was it, unless the initial contract specified something more enduring.

The thought made her uncomfortable. She knew that David wanted a divorce; they'd talked about it several times, but she'd simply not been brought up that way. Stacy might be able to shake off the way they'd been raised . . . but not her. "What God has brought together, let no man put asunder" her mother had always said, and while Liana had lost much of her once fiery Baptist faith during the past few years, especially since she'd started going to Reverend Blaine's church, she hadn't lost the upbringing that had come with it. If marriage vows meant anything, they were holy vows to be kept, and kept forever!

Even if she now believed that Jesus had been the genetically manipulated child of a woman artificially inseminated by extraterrestrial visitors. Her mother, dead now for six years, would have thrown a fit if she'd known.

Every time David had brought the subject of divorce up, she'd managed to change the subject . . . or else throw a crying fit emotional enough to make him back off. The law, at least, was on her side. If he walked out on her, she would get the house and half of their joint bank account, and that seemed to be holding him back.

As for her divorcing him, well, she wasn't about to let him off the hook easily. She was certain that he was cheating on her—probably had been for a long time—and that was grounds for a divorce if she wanted one. The point was that she didn't.

She sighed. The very word "cheating," she knew, was a holdover from an earlier age of more formal and binding marriage contracts, but she simply couldn't help that. For her, as for her mother, marriage was *forever*.

Besides, if she and David separated, she wouldn't find things like . . . *this*!

A folder marked "Picard/Sumeria" opened to a scrolling page of notes, including some PAD-scanned images of what looked like gold or silver statues. She squinted at the pictures, trying to make sense of them, but there was little sense to be made. The figures were so stiff and cartoonish, somehow . . . and did not resemble her notion of the ancient astronaut-gods very closely.

Nonetheless, she made a copy of everything, transferring the duplicates to her own private files. Later she would uplink them to Pastor Blaine's Net address, and the Church elders could make of them what they could.

Guilt nagged at her, but she angrily pushed the feeling aside. She'd given David his chance, just a short while ago when she'd driven him to the maglev station. Every morning she drove him to the Arlington Heights station so he could take the commuter maglev into town; every evening she picked him up again . . . at least on those days when he wasn't gallivanting off around the country somewhere, giving talks, giving lectures. Did he have time for her and her church and her friends? No!

He could sleep with his goddamned secretary or assistant or whatever she was, but he couldn't tell his own wife about what he'd discovered on the Moon, even if he knew how important the subject was to her.

This morning had been the worst. She'd asked him, yet again, if he could tell her about what he'd found on the Moon that obviously had him so concerned, asked him if there was anything there that she could share with the people at her church. "What, that bunch of idiots?" was what he'd said.

And, by implication, that was what he thought of her. There'd been more. A lot more, none of it pleasant. The part about "a bunch of losers who think God was a spaceman, and that he's going to come down and rescue them all from the evils of the world," that had hurt, a lot.

Maybe because there was some truth in it. The First Church of the Divine Masters of the Cosmos did hold that there would be a final reckoning, when the Divine Masters returned—any day now!—and demanded an accounting for Man's stewardship of the planet. And on that day, the faithful would board the great mother ships, to be carried in rapture into heaven, abandoning a world corrupted by greed and sin and Adam's fallen nature, a wicked world already under judgment by global warming, a world about to face the nuclear destruction levied by the Masters on Sodom and Gomorrah. . . .

And David simply couldn't *see*. . . .

She'd been skimming the material on the screen, looking for key words or phrases that might pop out at her, and finding nothing. Some of the sub files were cryptically named: Gab-Kur-Ra, Shu-Ha-Da-Ku, Shar-Tar-Bak. What in the Name of the Divine Masters were *those*?

She copied them faithfully, nonetheless.

Then, however, her eyes landed on a pair of concluding paragraphs, and she read them carefully.

"It seems obvious that the aliens, tentatively identified as 'An' or 'Anu,' and which from admittedly preliminary and scanty evidence quite possibly can be identified with Species Eighty-four, from the Cydonian visual data, did indeed have considerable direct contact with humans living at the head of the Persian Gulf, the peoples we know today as Sumerians. That contact, however, does not appear to have been a friendly one from the human perspective. The accounts translated so far speak of enslaving the 'lu,' a term used in ancient Sumerian to mean "human," but which includes the connotation of 'something herded,' 'something taken care of.' Humans appear to have been useful to the An primarily in working mines, raising crops, forming military units for further conquests, and for attending the masters as personal servants.

"It remains to be seen whether human civilization was something bestowed on human slaves by the masters, or whether it was developed independently by primitive cul-

tures attempting to emulate the godlike visitors in their midst.''

She read the paragraphs again, her eyes tearing, her head making little, involuntary no-no motions. He had it all wrong! The Divine Masters hadn't been like that, couldn't have been like that at all! He was misinterpreting the data; he *had* to be!

No matter. Pastor Blaine would know what to do. He always did. He never admitted it, but she was certain he was somehow inspired by the Masters themselves, as they orbited the Earth in their invisible mother ships, watching over their people below.

She completed her final copy and uploaded it to the pastor's address. Then she checked through David's files once more, this time—with a painful curiosity that burned like the picking of an old scab—looking for any more of those saved vid recordings or other files that might have been sent by *that* woman.

She was almost disappointed when she failed to find any more.

TEN

*Institute for Exoarcheological
Studies
Chicago, Illinois
1610 hours CDT*

There were no marching crowds today, for a change,
no ancient-astronut mobs calling for revelation, no
church groups denouncing him as inspired by Satan. Traffic flowed along Lake Shore Drive, building toward the
afternoon rush, and, for once, Chicago was ignoring him.

It was still a little startling to David to stand at his office
window, looking past Soldier's Field and the Adler Planetarium causeway out to the cold, flat, gray horizon of
Lake Michigan, and realize that he'd actually been out
there, on the surface of the Moon. He was now one of
that handful of men and women who'd stood on the surface of three separate planetary bodies. A most exclusive
club indeed.

And the place to which he'd returned, the real world of
work and politics and deadlines, seemed so . . . ordinary.

"David?" Teri called from his desk. "Is something
wrong?"

Fixing a smile in place, he turned. "No. Not a thing.
Just woolgathering."

She smiled and stroked the copy, cast in resin, of one
of the artifacts he'd brought back from Picard. "Howard
agrees completely with your analysis of P-3, right down
the list, word for word. Congratulations!"

"Good," he replied absently. "Uh, *very* good. Sorry. I just wish I had a little more confidence in that thing."

"That thing" was the Expert System Program running in the Institute's local network, one of the new AIs that offered encyclopedic knowledge within its expert purview, combined with an almost human flexibility and reasoning power.

Almost human.

Privately, he'd named this one after Howard Vyse, the nineteenth-century adventurer and soldier of fortune who'd done so much damage to the science of archeology in his ham-fisted and outright criminal explorations of the three main pyramids at the Giza Complex, in Egypt. Vyse, it was now nearly certain, had perpetrated several incredible hoaxes in order to establish that the Great Pyramids had been built as tombs by three particular Fourth Dynasty pharaohs—Khufu, Khephren, and Menkaure—all three within a period of eighty years, from about 2550 to 2470 B.C. So much of the modern understanding of history and historical timetables had been built upon Vyse's claims, so much professional literature published, so many reputations established and doctorates awarded and names secured, that even now, two centuries later, there were firmly entrenched adherents to the "traditional" views of Egyptology. Vyse might have been a charlatan, the conservatives insisted, but he was still *right*. His conclusions were valid even if his proofs were faked. To claim otherwise would unravel two centuries of carefully interwoven dates and meticulously constructed historical comprehension.

By calling the Institute's archeological ESP Howard, David reminded himself not to take what it said as gospel.

"I still don't understand why you're so paranoid about expert systems," Teri said with a laugh. "They give us access to more information than we could absorb in a decade or three of solid study, and without the human politics you're always railing about." She patted the desk's open display screen fondly. "Howard wouldn't lie to us! The way you talk, you'd think we had your friend Kettering locked up in here!"

David snorted. Craig Kettering was a professional rival—an enemy, really—who'd been on the expedition to Mars. They'd parted ways when Kettering had gone along with the UN plan to hush up the Cydonian findings. Now that they were back on Earth, the man was happily publishing with the data David had made available, acting as though nothing at all had happened between them.

"Actually," he said, "I think my problem is that Howard isn't political enough. He agrees with *everything* I say, and that's scary."

"Well, if you can't trust the machine, can you trust *me*? I hope you don't keep me around here just because I'm good in bed!"

"Of course not!" Technically, Teri was on loan to the Institute from the Field Museum's Oriental Department. The Cydonian Research Foundation had paid a lot of money to hire her general archeological expertise, but when the Lunar tablets turned out to be partly written in ancient Sumerian, she'd proven herself absolutely invaluable.

"Your translations have all agreed with Howard's *and* mine." She made a face. "Admit it, David. You're good, and that's all there is to it."

"Maybe. But that's not going to be enough for . . . them."

" 'Them'?"

"This could be Egypt all over again," he told her. "*Worse* than Egypt. And here I'm just on the point of gaining my reputation back."

She knew that story, of course. He'd told her about it the first time they'd slept together, in a hotel in Los Angeles during one of his public-relations appearances for the government upon his return from Mars. David Alexander had been an authority on Egypt before the war, an expert in sonic-imaging tomography, an expertise that had landed him that billet in a cycler to Mars. His discovery of confirmation that the Sphinx went back long before the Fourth Dynasty had ended with him being evicted from Egypt and his reputation being called into question; some lies, he'd discovered, were too well established—and too important politically—to be challenged. The Egyptian government had a vested interest in maintaining the myth that *Egyptians* had raised the Great Pyramids, not some unknown civilization from eight thousand years before.

Things were far worse, with the dawning realization that extraterrestrials had been responsible for shaping human culture millennia ago. With the discoveries on Mars and, now, on the Moon, there could be no doubting their reality, or the fact that they'd visited Earth more than once and for long periods of time. The argument came down to how much, if at all, they'd actually interacted with humanity.

Belief was fast polarizing into absolute and unshakable opposites. On the one side were the ancient astronuts, with their cosmic-awareness sessions, their churches of universal life, and the conviction that ETs had done everything notable in human history, from building the pyramids to establishing each of the world's major religions. On the other side were the diehard conservatives within the archeological, anthropological, and historical-academic communities, who admitted—most of them, anyway—that, yes, extraterrestrials might have visited Earth, Mars, and the Moon in the remote past, but who stated point-blank that even open contact could have affected no more than a handful of individual humans . . . and human culture not at all.

The truth, as usual, lay somewhere between the two extremes. Establishing exactly where could well destroy his professional reputation for a second time.

"Are you saying," Teri said carefully, "that you *want* Howard to be prejudiced? As political as Tom Leonard?"

He grimaced at the name. Leonard was one of his most outspoken critics, the author of several prominent papers attacking the cultural-intervention theory.

"It might help." He gestured at the replica on the desk. "Leonard and his bunch are going to be all over this. All over our translations. If there is any possibility that we're missing something, missing some nuance or shade of meaning, or misinterpreting what was being said, we have to *know*."

"I'd say our identification of this one name alone, *An*,

with the eight-pointed star as their symbol, makes any of their quibbles pretty irrelevant. The Sumerian tie-in is perfect.''

''Which is exactly the problem, Teri. It's *too* perfect. The astronuts are going to grab this and run with it. I . . . I don't think we'll be able to keep a lid on it after this.''

''So . . . what's worrying you? That your work is going to get lost in all the shouting and yelling? Or that people are going to call you dirty names? Damn it, it's the *truth* that's important.''

''I'm beginning to think that there is truth . . . and more important truth. . . .'' He rubbed his eyes. ''I'm not even sure what I believe anymore.''

The reproduction on his desk was a resin faxcasting of the first of the seventeen gold, silver, and electrum artifacts he'd uncovered on the floor of Picard. His desk's computer screen was open, displaying long columns of symbols, Proto-Sumerian characters and English words, the beginning of a translation of the artifact's dual text.

In 1799, a French soldier with Napoléon's army working on the fortifications of Rashid, Egypt—a place Europeans called Rosetta—turned up a flat, polished stone inscribed with Egyptian hieroglyphics, with a kind of cursive hieroglyphic script called demotic, and Greek. The Rosetta stone was the key that allowed Jean-François Champollion to decipher the language of a civilization in some ways as alien to eighteenth-century Europe as the Builders were to humankind.

What he'd found at Picard was a Rosetta stone indeed . . . or, rather, seventeen Rosetta stones that together were slowly but conclusively hammering home a definite link between the Sumerians of ancient Mesopotamia, and another race of extraterrestrials that—if the Proto-Sumerian translations were accurate—called itself the An.

''If our translations are accurate,'' David went on after a moment, ''then we have a race, a civilization that called itself *An*, building colonies on Earth something like six thousand . . . maybe as far back as thirteen thousand years ago. The artistic style definitely ties them in with ancient Sumer.''

"What the natives called Shumer," Teri said. " 'The Land of the Guardians.' The name of their chief god was An or Anu. And the pantheon of Sumerian gods was called the *Anunnaki.* . . ."

" 'Those who came to Earth from the place of An,' " David added, translating. He'd been working on Proto-Sumerian translations now for days, and it was becoming second nature.

"You know," she said, "this has always been one of the biggest mysteries of archeology, as big a question mark as the Sphinx or the pyramids. The Sumerian language is unrelated to any other we know. The people . . . we have no idea where they came from. They were not Semitic, like the Akkadians or the others who built on their culture later. And when they settled in Mesopotamia, well . . . it was almost literally as though civilization sprang into being overnight. They claimed the gods had given them writing, medicine, architecture. The gods domesticated animals and created new kinds of grain and other crops."

"Small wonder some of the astronuts have been claiming the Sumerians themselves were extraterrestrial."

She snorted. "That idea's ludicrous, of course. They were human, which means they shared their DNA with the life evolved here."

"Yeah," he said. "That's the one bit of silliness that gets me most about some of the ancient-astronut crowd. Adam and Eve were *not* shipwrecked visitors from another planet! Not when chimpanzees share something over ninety-eight percent of our DNA!"

"I do wonder, sometimes, if the Sumerians might have come from the human colony on Mars, the one the Builders put there. The bodies you found there?"

He grunted. "Hard to see how that would fit. The Builders were on Mars half a million years ago. That's a long time, between whoever built the Face and the rise of Sumeria. No, there's more to this. A *lot* more." He shook his head. "Anyway, what we found on the Moon is going to upset *everybody*. The ancient-astronaut cults, established religions, the archeological community. The government. Historians. It's hard to think of someone I'm *not* going to piss off when I release this stuff."

"I still think you're being too sensitive. I can understand the problem with the conservative archeologists. But the cults? And the churches?"

"Remember all of those places in the Bible, in Genesis, where God says things like, 'Let *us* make Man in *our* image? . . .' Holdovers from the Sumerian texts that those passages were based on. Hell, ever since George Smith translated the *Epic of Gilgamesh,* back in 1872, we've known that a lot of Genesis came to us from Sumerian myths and writings. The Garden of Eden, the Flood, the Tower of Babel, all of that." He chuckled, but the sound was grim. "Don't you think the Vatican is going to be a bit upset if we produce proof that the Yahweh of the Old Testament was an Anunnaki, straight out of Sumerian myths?

"As for the ancient-astronaut churches, they all see the ET 'gods' as saviors. Protectors. Angels and divine guides. Nice people who might turn up again someday to help Mankind out of its current mess."

She made a sour face. "It would help if the An were the savior type."

He reached out and lightly stroked the faxcast, with its row of five humans, bound and leashed. "Kind of puts the whole idea of worshiping God in a new light, doesn't it?"

What he'd translated so far seemed to match certain aspects of the Sumerian myths; humans had been slaves under the An, working in their mines and agricultural colonies and even as janissary armies, conquering "uncivilized" neighbors under the direction of their godlike masters. Most of the translations he'd worked out so far, with Howard's help, spoke of primitive tribes rounded up and "civilized" by troops under the command of *Sharu-Gaz,* a term literally meaning "Supreme Leaders of the Killers," but which both David and Howard had translated as "war-Leaders." They listed cattle, sheep, and crops taken, gathered, and counted; tributes offered; enemies killed; villages burned; precious metals—the Sumerian word was *zu-ab*—gathered for transport to "Heaven"; and vast numbers of slaves captured, penned, and sold. The An, whoever they'd been, appeared to share human biochemistry, with left-handed amino acids and a preference for right-handed sugars. They'd been able to eat crops and animals native to Earth, and they'd forced the natives to raise those crops and herds. For them.

There was even the extraordinarily disturbing possibility that large numbers of humans had been taken away . . . as food. He was beginning to wonder if *that*, in fact, was the root of the worldwide primitive practice of sacrifice.

Each of the artifacts recovered at Picard appeared to be a different list of tribute and conquest. Seventeen dual inscriptions, in Proto-Sumerian and in a totally unknown language that David assumed was the native language of the An colonizers, had opened a crack in the door to an entirely new and previously unguessed-at chapter in human history, one reaching back far before the known, historical beginnings of civilization three to four thousand years earlier.

A chapter in which humanity had been enslaved by warlike invaders with a technology vastly superior to their spears and bows.

The discussion had left David feeling depressed. Lonely. The universe was not the small and comfortable place it had been back when he'd written his doctoral thesis . . . or when he'd married Liana.

Teri seemed to sense his mood. She leaned forward, touching his arm. "So," she said, "not to change the subject . . . but what are you doing tonight? That new gel-bed of mine could use a real workout. I might even be able to rent a dolphin, just for the evening."

He stared into her eyes for a moment and into the promise behind them. Then he looked away. "Damn. I'm sorry, Teri, no. I wish I could . . ."

She gave his arm a squeeze. "That's all right, love. We'll just have to be patient."

He laughed, a harsh and bitter sound. Patient? He was fed up with being patient! Liana almost certainly knew about his relationship with Teri, even if she wasn't aware of the depth of his feelings for her, but *still* she refused to talk about getting a divorce or even a legal separation.

The truth was that he and Liana simply weren't well matched with each other. They'd married when he was twenty-nine and she was nineteen; lust, he'd long since decided, had a nasty tendency to cover up a person's character flaws.

Well . . . not *flaws*, exactly, unless you called having the brains of a box full of facial tissue a flaw. And there'd been some good times, especially early on. But damn it all, how could he stay with someone as enamored of these weird cults and bizarre religions as she was, especially when those same groups seemed to be feeding off the information he'd uncovered? Sometimes, it seemed like distorted versions of his discoveries were being bandied about on the Earthnet talk shows before he'd even released them to the director of the institute. It was eerie how quickly the news was spreading through the religious underground out there.

Liana kept pestering him for information about his discoveries. Damn, but he hated that. Sometimes, he wondered if he hated *her*. He didn't want to; he really simply wanted the two of them to agree that they'd made a mistake, that they weren't well matched, and that they should go their separate ways. But the way she was clinging to him, his disdain for her was going to turn to hatred pretty soon.

He was, he realized, unhappy with his life, and that wasn't Liana's fault. Working jaunts to Mars and the Moon were a wonderful perk—at least, they were when he wasn't being shot at—and the chance at making discoveries destined to change humankind's understanding of history went a long way toward guaranteeing that he would never be bored . . . but there was still a bitter restlessness within. He wasn't even sure it had anything to do with Liana. Maybe it had more to do with the constant uphill battle against entrenched academia.

Damn it all, he needed to be sure of these translations. Self-doubt, that was the big weakness. If he could confirm this connection between the An and the Sumerian Anu, *prove* his discovery despite the unsavory connections with ancient astronuts and all that that entailed, maybe he could still get the last laugh on Tom Leonard and all of the rest.

After that, all he would have to do was prove to his wife and the other crackpot astronuts that he wasn't some kind of reluctant messiah. That was what he hated most about the church groups his wife was involved with. They looked to him as some kind of prophet, and he simply wasn't willing to fill that role.

And then there was the problem with the government.

They'd sent him to the Moon to investigate the UN's discoveries there, and he'd turned up more than anyone had expected. Still, discoveries involving ancient Sumeria and alien slave-raiders were pretty remote . . . things that might upset astronut churches, the Vatican, and mobs in the streets but didn't have much to do with the war at all. The government had been far more interested in that piece of an ancient spacecraft that had already been salvaged at Picard than in any of the engraved artifacts he'd found.

He was still keeping secret the information Marc Billaud had given him about an ancient alien base at Tsiolkovsky. There was too much he was still unsure of, too many questions about the exact translations of some of what he'd found.

Before he could go much farther, he needed to be certain of his translations—and he needed something more reassuring than Howard's cheerfully matter-of-fact pronouncements.

Shesh-Ki, which he translated as "Guardian of the Earth," and which seemed, by context, to refer somehow, to the Moon.

Gab-Kur-Ra, "In the Chest of the Mountains" or "In the Hiding Place of the Mountains." The phrase seemed to refer to some sort of secret cavern or base, again, from the context, located on the Moon. That was the secret place Billaud had talked about . . . on the Lunar farside, at Tsiolkovsky.

Shu-Ha-Da-Ku. "Supremely Strong, Goes Bright" was the exact translation, but it sounded ominously like a reference to a weapon.

And, perhaps most worrisome of all, was the repeated

mention of a terrible threat, an enemy that threatened the An, and Earth itself, with Tar-Tar, with utter destruction. The name of this enemy was variously rendered Gaz-Bakar or Ur-Bakar, sometimes with the preface "Shar," which meant great or the ultimate. Gaz-Bakar—David was guessing, here—must mean something like "Killers" or "Smiters of the Dawn." Ur-Bakar, then, could be translated two ways, as "Foundations of the Dawn," or as the far more ominous "Hunters of the Dawn."

Marc had mentioned that phrase first, on the Moon, when he'd named the nemesis of the An.

The phrase sent an icy shiver down David's spine. Such phrases, ever since the first decipherings of ancient Sumerian pictographs and the later cuneiform, had been assumed to be poetic references, figurative language only. Now he knew that some, at least, of the allusions were to something all too real.

What *had* so completely destroyed that An ship above Picard? What had happened to the An colony on Earth, a complex of several dozen high-tech settlements scattered from Egypt to the Indus Valley? He *had* to know, had to know his translations were right. Confirmation. He needed confirmation.

"Teri, who would you say is the best Sumerian linguist?"

"Hmm. I'd have to say François Villeret at the Sorbonne."

David nodded thoughtfully. "That would have been my call, too." He picked up the cast and tucked it under his arm. "Excuse me a moment, Teri," he said, walking to the door.

"What are you doing, David?"

"Trust me. You don't want to know. I'll be back in a few minutes."

It would be better if he could keep her out of what he was about to do.

In the larger room outside of his office was a faxcaster, a table-sized piece of business-telecommunications equipment. He opened the bin, placed the artifact inside, engravings down, and closed the lid. At the keyboard, he

typed in his Earthnet access and two addresses—that of
the ultimate destination, and that of his blind remailer address in Finland. With a hum and a leaking of brilliant
light from around the seal of the bin's lid, lasers scanned
the cast, as a computer converted each detail in three dimensions into a string of data, uploaded to the Net.

That data would wait in Villeret's server thousands of
kilometers away, until it was used to recast and carve an
exact duplicate.

The fact that some people would consider him to be
committing treason by sending this data to a French national was worrisome, of course . . . but David Alexander
had no patience with the blinkered authorities and idiot
politicians who were running this ridiculous war.

If François confirmed the translations he and Teri had
made, he'd be a lot happier about publishing.

And the hell with what anyone else had to say about it.

ELEVEN

Administration Complex
Vandenberg Space Command
Base
1635 hours PDT

"It is the finding of this court that Sergeant Frank Kaminski was not at fault for the friendly-fire incident that took place on Wednesday, 15 April 2042, at the former UN base at Picard Crater in the Mare Crisium, resulting in the deaths of three American soldiers attached to the US Army Special Forces Space Command.

"This court further finds that said friendly-fire incident occurred because the IFF codes that might have prevented the incident had not been programmed into the space suits worn by the victims. The threat to which they were responding developed before Army and Marine personnel at the site could coordinate the necessary codes and other protocols necessary for smooth joint action. Tasked with protecting the civilian in his care, Sergeant Kaminski responded properly to what he perceived as a direct and immediate threat when the Army personnel moved toward his position. In the chaos of battle, with no IFF codes registering on his helmet HUD and no easy way to clearly discriminate between the outward appearance of the space suits worn by newly arrived Army personnel and attacking Chinese troops, Sergeant Kaminski responded as he'd been trained and in full accord with his duties and orders as a United States Marine.

"This court of inquiry finds the cause of the incident leading to the soldiers' deaths to be human error but can assign no specific blame or responsibility in the matter.

"We hereby declare this case to be closed, with no further recommendations." A gavel cracked on the wooden strike pad. "Case dismissed!"

"Attention on deck!" the bailiff cried, and everyone in the chamber rose as the panel of three Marine and two Army officers stood behind the bench, gathered their papers, then filed out of the room. Kaitlin watched Kaminski's back as the young man, who'd been standing at attention to hear the court's verdict, swayed a little on his feet. *This is going to hit him hard*, she thought.

She walked forward and touched his shoulder. He jumped.

"You going to be okay, Frank?" she asked.

"Uh, yes, ma'am! I'm fine."

"You understand, don't you, that you didn't have to go through all of this because anyone thought you'd killed those men on purpose, or even because they thought you screwed up. The Corps *has* to go through the motions, to find out what really happened, and to try to make sure that accidents like this one don't happen again."

"Yes, ma'am. I understand all that. Mostly, well, I'm just sorry for those three guys I . . . that I killed."

She nodded, patting his shoulder. "It was an accident. There *is* a difference between an accident and a screwup, Frank. It just happens that accidents tend to be especially deadly in an environment like space."

"Doesn't make it easier for their wives and families, does it, ma'am?"

"Sure doesn't. But people get killed in war, and sometimes people get killed by accident. It wasn't your fault, Marine. Remember that."

"Aye, aye, ma'am." But he didn't sound convinced.

As Kaminski's commanding officer, of course, Kaitlin had had to testify at the inquiry. She'd emphasized the lack of coordination between the Marine and Army components of the US force at Picard and tried to assume responsibility for the IFF gaffe herself. If she'd just tried to force the issue with Colonel Whitworth. There simply hadn't been time. . . .

Her testimony had been accepted; her attempt at taking the blame had been rejected: likely, she thought, because both the Army and Corps wanted to keep the incident as low-profile as possible.

Even so, she'd been very much afraid that someone intended to throw Frank Kaminski to the wolves, a sacrifice to appease the media gods who'd been writing about the friendly-fire incident at Picard ever since the unit's return to Earth.

The Second Battle of Picard Crater had been a complete victory for the American forces. Kaitlin's ploy, holding a platoon in reserve south of the crater until the Chinese attack, had been a triumphant vindication of the long-standing Marine tactical dogma of fighting with two lead elements, and keeping a third in reserve. Casualties had been light: eight killed, including the three killed by friendly fire. Twenty-eight UN troops, all members of the seventy-fourth People's Army of the Republic of North China, had been killed, and fifteen captured. Those prisoners, when added to the Italian POWs taken in the first battle, had posed a real problem, stretching American logistics and the ability to feed them and keep them breathing to the limit. The mining shuttle captured at Picard had been kept busy making runs to and from the Moon's north pole, bringing in loads of polar ice for the base's O_2 converters. Even at that, by the time a relief expedition, including twelve more tugs, had arrived from Earth five days later, everyone had been on short rations, and off-duty personnel were kept in their racks, sleeping, to conserve oxygen.

One-SAG had returned to Earth and to a heroes' welcome; maybe that was why the powers-that-were hadn't pushed the court of inquiry thing further.

"You look mad," a voice said in her ear.

She turned, looking up at Captain Rob Lee, trim and sharp in his razor-creased khakis. "Damn it, if anyone had to face an official court of inquiry," she said, "it should have been me."

"If anyone had to face a court," he corrected her, "it should have been that idiot Whitworth. You done good, Kate."

"Wish I could believe you."

"You got the duty tonight, Marine?"

"No. . . ."

He drew a deep breath. "Then I'll tell you what. Ol' Doc Lee prescribes dinner out tonight. Followed by a drive down to Gaviota and a moonlight walk on the beach. Say . . . I pick you up at nineteen hundred?"

"A moonlight walk?" She smiled. "Not as good as a walk on the Moon itself."

"But a damn sight more romantic. You ever try necking while sealed up inside one of those tin suits? Not my idea of a good time."

"Well, I guess you'll have to show me what your idea of a good time is. Nineteen hundred it is. Where do you want to eat?"

"I was kind of thinking of the Menkoi."

Her eyebrows went up. " 'Love noodles'?"

"Is that what it means?" The scalp beneath his short-cropped Marine haircut flushed darker, and he looked uncomfortable.

"More or less."

"It's the name of a new Japanese restaurant in Las Cruces."

"I know. It sounds great. I'm looking forward to it."

It wouldn't be their first date since their return from the Moon. In fact, they'd been seeing rather a lot of one another lately. She hadn't known Rob all that well before the mission, but since then, she'd discovered that they had a lot in common besides a passionate love of the Corps. Both loved long discussions and longer walks; both were outspoken and not afraid to express an opinion. Both were well-read, enjoyed programming, and loved science fiction. Both were taking cram courses in French, in the spirit of know-your-enemy. And they both loved Japanese food.

Dinner was, for Kaitlin, a blissful escape from the stress she'd been under for the past week, during the official inquiry. The chefs all knew her—she'd been to the Menkoi more than once and startled the Japanese manager by bowing and greeting him in fluent Nihongo—and they made a fuss over the two Marines, so much so that Rob was embarrassed. "I keep forgetting you're half-Japanese yourself," he said with a wry grin.

"Only in the heart," she replied. "Living there as long as I did will do that to you."

"And that's why you're so good at French, right? Because you speak Japanese?"

"Any second language makes the third easier," she told him.

While the Menkoi had a Western section in the front, there were rooms in the back reserved for traditional dining, where shoes were left outside the door, and the rice was served *after* the various side dishes that made up the meal, to fill the belly and cleanse the palate. They ate seated on the floor, using *o-hashi*; Kaitlin had to help Rob get his fingers properly positioned for the exercise and to reassure him that it was okay to lift the soup bowl to his chin in order to get at the solid bits of meat and vegetable afloat inside. Their conversation ranged from the alien images and information discovered on Mars to the future of humankind in space.

By tacit consent, they both steered well clear of anything about the inquiry, or the friendly-fire incident at Picard.

"Mark my words, Kate," Rob told her as they ate. "The military is taking us back into space. And it's the Marines who are leading the way."

" 'Sfunny," she said around a mouthful of bamboo and mushroom. "I thought it was all the alien stuff we've been finding out there. *That* was what revitalized the space program, back when we'd all but given up on space."

"Sure. I guess that got things rolling." He chewed for a moment, thoughtful. "But if you think about it, it was the need to get lots of people out to Mars, and provide 'em with air and power, that got us on track with the cycler spacecraft and the big bases at Mars Prime and Cydonia. And most of the people we ended up sending were Marines. To protect our national interests . . . meaning the ET technology and stuff we were finding out there. And now, the same is happening on the Moon.''

The conversation had veered perilously close to a dangerous area. She decided to try steering the subject clear of the Marine missions to Fra Mauro and Picard. ''It's the technology we need,'' she told him. ''The things we can learn from the ancient ETs. *Everyone* knows that!''

''Think about history,'' he told her. ''Think about what happened in the American West. Sure, settlers started heading west looking for gold or farmland or whatever, and they built covered wagons and, later, transcontinental railroad lines to get 'em there. But it was the *soldiers* who went along who spread civilization to that whole empty stretch of the continent, from Missouri to California. It was the soldiers who built the forts at Laramie and Fort Collins and Leavenworth and Dodge and Lincoln and how many other lonely outposts across the West that later became towns and cities.''

''Well, the Native Americans might quibble with your use of the word *civilization*,'' she replied, ''but I guess I see your point.''

''The Army opened the West in a way the mountain men and the gold rushers never could,'' he insisted. ''Without those forts stretched clear across the continent, we would have ended up with two countries, the US and California, with nothing but wilderness and mountains between the two.''

''And the Mormons,'' Kaitlin said. She knew enough history to hold her own against Rob, usually, and she enjoyed a good debate. ''Don't forget the Mormons.''

''Finicky details,'' he said, with a dismissive flutter of his hand. ''In the grand scheme of things, it was the soldiers who built those outposts, then brought their wives along and started the towns. The settlers moved in to feed the Army. The railroads came through and connected the new towns. The soldiers retired and took up farming cheap land in the area. And that's what's going to happen in space.''

''I'm not sure there'll ever be 'cheap land' in space.''

''C'mon, Kate. You see what I mean.''

"Sure. And you might have a point. . . ."

"*Might* have?"

"What was our biggest problem on the Moon?"

He gave her a weary smile. "You mean, besides the Army?" She nodded, and he shrugged. "Logistics, I guess. Especially water and air."

"Right. We had working parties at the Lunar north pole the whole time, digging up ice and hauling it back to Picard. Most places in the solar system, it won't even be that easy."

"Actually, it might. Y'know, probably the only place in the whole solar system that doesn't have readily available water somewhere close by is Venus."

"Mercury?"

"There's polar ice there, too."

"Yeah, that's right," she said, remembering an article she'd read on the subject.

"And wherever we can find ice, we can make oxygen, drinking water, and rocket fuel. And what I picture, see, is the Army having to set up outposts, like those frontier forts, to guard the water holes."

"By 'Army,' I'm assuming you really mean 'Marines.' "

He laughed and lifted his cup of *o-sake*, as if in a toast. "Semper fi, do or die!" he cried. "The Marines will go in first to stake out the beachhead, just like always. As soon as it's safe, the doggies move in and claim the credit!"

"Okay, okay, I'll go along with all that. Still, you've gotta admit that if it hadn't been for all the alien stuff we've found out there, the space program would be dead on arrival, right now."

He shrugged. "It still might be, too, if the ET tech doesn't deliver something pretty spectacular."

"Like what?"

"Hell, I don't know. A cure for global warming?"

"That's a good one."

"Has to be something more than these crazy new religions. Maybe a new kind of space drive, or a new power source. Anyway, I think we're going to keep looking now, now that we have a presence out there."

"So do I," she told him.

And then she told him her lifelong dream, about how she was going to be among the first to go to the stars. . . .

After dinner, Rob drove them down out of the mountains to Gaviota State Park. As with every other beach in the world, the steady rise of sea levels was slowly devouring the sandy shelf, and the increase in violent storms and El Niño years frequently scoured the surviving sand away to bare rock.

But storms also returned the sand, sometimes, and current beach conditions were posted as fair to good. If the shelf, even at low tide, wasn't as broad as it had been fifty, or even twenty years ago, it still offered a glimpse of what the wild and spray-drenched interface between land and sea had once been like.

The Moon was well up in the southeast, just past full and gleaming silver in a cloudless sky, when Kaitlin and Rob left his car at the lot and started down the long flight of steps leading to the beach below. Waves crashed and hissed, each incoming roller shattering the dancing pillar of reflected moonlight in the water up the beach.

By day, the park, like all of the state beaches, tended to be jammed with refugees from the city enjoying a spray-laden taste of clothing-optional nature. After sunset, though, the crowds had thinned to a scattering of couples and small family groups, gathered around fires or discreetly making out on blankets scattered among dunes and rocks. The stars were as brilliant as they ever got this close to Los Angeles, which even this far up the coast flooded most of the eastern horizon with warm light.

"So, what've you heard about Operation Swift Victory?" Kaitlin asked Rob. They'd talked a little about it during the drive. Lately, Kaitlin had been thinking a lot about the rumored upcoming assault but hadn't talked to anyone who knew any more about it than she did. Security was extraordinarily tight.

Stopping suddenly, she slipped her shoes off and let her bare feet sink into wet sand. Rob crouched and untied his shoes, pulled off his socks, and rolled up the cuffs of his jeans. He'd brought a towel along, which he kept slung over his shoulder. The air was still hot after a day that had hit thirty degrees, but the sea breeze was refreshingly cool, almost chilly. As always, weather this warm in April made Kaitlin wonder how bad the summer was going to be. Each year, somehow, seemed a bit hotter, a bit stormier, than the last.

"Don't know," he said at last. "But I got a bad feeling. You know who's in command?"

"General Richardson, I heard."

"Overall, yeah. But he won't be leaving the Pentagon. No, the CO on-site. The guy up front, leading the charge."

"Not . . ."

" 'Fraid so. Your old friend, Colonel Whitworth." He chuckled. "Someone figured he was *the* man, because he's had experience with vac-combat."

"God help us."

"I heard there was quite a row during the planning. Seems like all of the services wanted a crack at the UN-dies."

"What happened?"

"The Army won. The Marines lost out, because someone pointed out that they'd already had a shot at Moon-glory."

She laughed. "Is that what they call it?"

"Well, it makes great copy on the vidcasts. Anyway, I imagine Aerospace Force transports will take 'em in. Don't know what they're planning, but my guess would be a quick, one-step thrust, straight from Earth to orbit to Moon. Come in low, mountain-skimming, to avoid the De-mon." The Demon was the currently circulating slang for whatever it was that had nailed Black Crystal, variously rumored to be a powerful laser, an antimatter beam, or an entirely new type of weapon unlike anything known be-fore.

"Think it'll work?"

"Damfino. I hope so, but . . ."

"But?"

"Shoot. It just feels all wrong, you know? I don't think

anybody has any decent intel. No one knows what's going on back there, on the back side of the Moon. The Army could be walking into six different kinds of hell.''

They'd walked a fair distance east from the steps, and were on an almost deserted stretch of beach. A few fires flickered in the distance behind them, but they were alone here, save for crashing surf and glittering stars and Moon.

"How about a swim?'' he asked.

She had to consider that cheerful suggestion for a moment. She hadn't brought a swimsuit, and she suddenly wished she'd worn something more appropriate under her slacks than filmy panties, even a thong-G. Oh, she'd been nude in public plenty of times, on the beach and elsewhere, but she'd never stripped down in front of *Rob*. Kaitlin was suddenly aware of feelings, unsettled feelings that made her state of dress or undress more important than if he'd been an anonymous stranger in a crowd at the beach.

"Sure,'' she said, deciding suddenly. She began shucking her clothing and dropping it on the sand. "Why not?'' She felt daring . . . and a bit giddy. They left their clothing piled on the beach next to the towel. Holding hands, then, they started jogging down the narrow shelf toward the breakers.

Before they reached the waves, however, thunder tolled, a distant, muffled drumroll. Both of them stopped and turned, looking up into the northwestern sky, but the stars were still sharp and clear, with no hint of an approaching storm.

Then a dazzling flare of light appeared, rising slowly above the Santa Ynez Mountains, brighter than the streetlamps over the parking lot and trailing a long, wavering tail of white flame. It rose high toward the zenith, its path curving slightly, until it passed almost directly overhead, moving out over the ocean now, traveling rapidly south. The sound, which lagged far behind the moving flare's visual position, faded a bit to a ragged, thuttering chain of cracks and claps chasing the flare toward orbit.

"Zeus II,'' Kaitlin said, as the noise faded. The flare vanished into the distance, but the contrail, illuminated by the moonlight, remained hanging in the sky like a scratch across heaven.

"Heavy lifter," Rob added, in needless elaboration. "Jeez. Doesn't seem possible that we rode one of those things to space, does it?"

Thunder tolled again, and another flare heaved into view above the mountains to the northwest. "There goes another," Kaitlin said.

The second was followed by a third, then a fourth and a fifth, each one almost seeming to crawl up along the path of the last, their gleaming contrails appearing to tangle and merge in their vast arc across the star-dotted zenith.

Kaitlin didn't know how it had happened, didn't remember it happening, but she and Rob were standing together now, their arms tight around one another as they stared up into the sky. The incoming tide brought a sudden rush of cold seawater surging past their ankles, and she let out a little gasp. Letting go of Rob, she jumped back, splashing back onto dry sand, the spell broken.

"Go Army," Rob said, still looking up. "And Godspeed."

"Think that's Swift Victory?"

"Gotta be," Rob replied. "Five HLVs in as many minutes? I doubt that they'll even change orbits. They'll probably rendezvous with some tugs already parked in a polar orbit, then boost straight for Luna."

Launches from Vandenberg were always aimed toward the south, over open ocean and into a polar or near-polar orbit. It would never do to have the fragments of a failed launch coming down in a fiery footprint stretching across Greater Los Angeles. The tight clustering of the launches suggested that they were aiming for an unusually small launch window, which in turn suggested a rendezvous with a fleet of LEO-to-Luna transports already in orbit.

Dropping his gaze from the heavens, he gave her a long and appraising look in the moonlight. Then he shrugged. "I . . . guess maybe we'd best be getting back to the base, huh?"

She had to give that one some thought as well. There

were regulations aplenty regarding sexual liaisons within military service, especially when there was a difference in rank involved that might be seen either as an abuse of power or as sex-for-privileges. Still, the practical implementation of those regs tended toward the assumption that men and women were going to do what was natural for them, and to turn a blind eye . . . unless the couple was flagrant in their play or the relationship involved ''conduct prejudicial to good order and discipline,'' as Article 134 of the Uniform Code of Military Justice so succinctly phrased it.

The question wasn't what the Marine Corps had to say about a lieutenant sleeping with a captain. It was what she was ready for. She hadn't had a sexual relationship with anyone since Yukio's death, and that was two years ago now.

She knew she couldn't put her life on hold forever.

''We don't *have* to go back yet,'' she told him. ''Do you have the duty this weekend?''

He shook his head no.

''Me neither. We don't *have* to report in until oh seven hundred Monday morning, right?'' She stepped back into the surf, moving close, letting her hands lightly caress his body. ''So . . . whatcha want to do about it, huh?''

''This,'' he replied, reaching for her.

The kiss lasted for a long, long time.

TWELVE

Recruit Platoon 4239
Parris Island Recruit Training
Center
1345 hours EDT

"Okay, ladies," Gunnery Sergeant Knox said, grinning. He was holding a lump of something that looked like heavy, gray clay. He tossed it a few centimeters into the air and caught it again in the same hand several times, the soft slap of each catch emphasizing his words. "I wanna show you all somethin' here. Somethin' important."

It was a sweltering, humid May afternoon beneath a brassy, overcast sky. Week Three of recruit training for Platoon 4239 had brought them face-to-face with a number of firsts as they settled into the boot-camp routine. Early in the week they'd run the obstacle course for the first time, a run through obstacles, over walls, and hand over hand along a rope above a mud pit in a routine euphemistically known as the "confidence course." The recruits had also faced their first written exam, their first physical evaluation since the admission physicals, their first inspection, and their first parade to demonstrate their growing command of close-order drill.

Training had been grueling, an exhausting regime deliberately orchestrated to spring one surprise after another on the recruits as they struggled to overcome each new challenge. Head knowledge was emphasized as much as physical training, on the theory, as Knox expressed it, that "a smart Marine is a live Marine." Because of the incessant heat, physical training, calisthenics, long runs, and close-order drill tended to be held in the morning or late in the afternoon; midday, before and after noon chow, was reserved for lectures and demonstrations, such as this one.

Of course, that often meant that the recruits ended up sitting in mud-drenched utilities after a late-morning romp in the mud pit or getting drenched in sweat running the confidence course, trying to stay alert while they listened to the lecture.

As he sat cross-legged on the ground, watching Knox work the clay a bit more, Jack realized that he'd really accomplished something just making it this far. In three weeks, attrition had whittled an eighty-man platoon down to sixty-one—reducing it by almost a quarter. There'd been that kid from Tennessee who'd pleaded with the DI one evening to be allowed to go home, tears streaming down his face; there'd been that sharp, smart-mouthed kid from New York named Doud who'd snapped in the mess hall and actually taken a swing at Knox . . . a swing that hadn't connected but *had* resulted Doud's being hustled away and never seen again. There'd been Martelli—one of the platoon's "fat trays," or overweight recruits—who'd washed out when he couldn't pass the physical quals earlier in the week.

There'd also been those six or eight guys who'd hurt themselves—a couple of them badly enough to end up in the hospital with broken bones—and the word was they'd all have to pick up their training in a later platoon. *That* sucked, in Jack's expert opinion. Having to come into a platoon full of strangers partway through, knowing no one, no one knowing you . . .

Jack lived in dread of that happening to *him*. He knew these guys, was bonded with them, molded with them, become a part of them in a way that he'd never been a part of anything else in his life. After three weeks, Gunnery Sergeant Knox and his assistant DIs had broken everyone about as low as it was possible to break them.

Now they were in the process of building them back up.

As something *new*. . . .

Turning away from the watching recruits, Knox walked ten meters across the open ground of the training field to the two lifelike mannequins standing next to one another, plastic faces showing no emotion. Both dummies wore Marine-issue Class-Three armor breastplates, over OD utilities.

Reaching the dummy on the left, Knox slapped the clay against its breastplate, high up, just below the throat, kneading it with his thumb to make it stick, then inserting a small, black object the size and shape of a domino.

Returning to the recruits, waiting in a semicircle in their soggy, mud-covered utilities, Knox jerked a thumb over his shoulder, indicating the waiting dummy. "That, ladies, which I just placed on our volunteer out there, is two hundred grams of C-320 plastic explosives. That's less than half a pound." Taking a position next to the table set behind the firing line, he picked up a small controller. "Sergeant Bayerly?"

"Range clear, Gunnery Sergeant Knox!"

Smiling, Knox entered a code into the controller, flipped off a safety, then mashed his thumb down on the firing button without even turning to watch the display.

There was a sharp, ringing crack, and the dummy on the left was kicked backward in a flurry of plastic limbs. Several of the recruits jumped. One said, "Oh, God!"

"God's not going to help the poor son of a bitch now, recruit," Knox said, replacing the controller. "Let's go see."

Together, the recruits followed Knox across the open field to see the effects of the blast up close. The explosion had punched a hole big enough to admit three fingers straight through the breastplate, through the dummy, and out the rear of the breastplate as well, though the exit hole was smaller than the width of a pencil. Bright red gelatin, the semiliquid stuffing inside the dummy's chest, was splattered across the ground in a realistic display of human gore.

Jack heard a retching sound from one of his fellow recruits but couldn't see who it was. *God, if he gets sick seeing a damned dummy get holed!* . . .

"Two hundred grams of high explosives, ladies," Knox said in his best lecturing tone, "releases one million joules of energy upon detonation. That is enough, as you can see, to penetrate standard Marine-issue armor and blast a very nasty hole clear through your giblets! One megajoule. Remember that! Okay, back to the firing line!"

When the recruits were seated once again, Knox walked over to the table and picked up a long and complex-looking weapon. With its bipod and pistol grip, it had the look of an old-fashioned squad light machine gun, but it was connected to a foil-encased backpack resting on the ground by a segmented cable as thick as a man's forefinger. Knox hefted the bulky weapon easily with one hand, while he reached down and flipped a switch on the backpack with the other. A tiny, high-pitched whine spooled up from the power pack, and a red light began winking on the weapon's receiver assembly.

When the red light stopped blinking and glowed steadily, Knox brought the weapon's stock to his shoulder with a crisp, efficient motion straight out of the Marine Corps manual and squeezed the trigger. There was no flash, no beam, or other outward sign, but downrange, the second target dummy leaped backward with a sharp crack, leaving a faint, hazy blur of vaporized metal hanging in the air. As Knox lowered the weapon, the recruits could hear the power pack spooling up again, until he reached down and switched it off. He replaced the laser weapon on the table, muzzle pointed carefully away from both the students and the range.

"Time to compare," he told them.

The two dummies lay on their backs, side by side. The second now sported a hole in its breastplate in exactly the same place as the first. The entry hole was a bit smaller . . . but the exit hole was larger, *much* larger, with a *lot* more red goo spattered on the grass.

"One megajoule," Knox repeated, speaking slowly and patiently, as if for the slowest of students. "One million joules. Watkins! What is one joule?"

"*Sir*! One joule is one watt of power applied for one second, *sir*!" It was one of the thousands of isolated facts and bits of information that had been hammered into them all during the past three weeks, like the serial numbers of their ATARs or the names of the ten people in the chain of command above them, from Gunnery Sergeant Harold Knox all the way up to President Roger Markham.

"Correct. Since it's damned hard to get an uncooperative target to stand still for one whole second, we use a ten-million-watt laser to release a pulse that lasts one-tenth of a second. One million watts for one second equals *ten* million watts for one-tenth second. The result is the same. One million joules, delivered on-target. That is enough to punch through the best personal armor we know. It's enough to chew though your guts, charbroil them, and spit them out your backsides. Flash!"

Jack gritted his teeth. "Flash" had become his nickname, his handle in the platoon, a jeering reference to Flash Gordon and his desire to be a space Marine.

"What is the effective range of the Sunbeam M228 Squad Laser Weapon?"

"*Sir!*" Jack shouted as hard and as loud as he could, reciting the relevant textbook paragraph. "The effective range of the Sunbeam M228 Squad Laser Weapon is approximately eighteen hundred to twenty-two hundred meters, but that range may be sharply restricted by attenuation or by adverse atmospheric conditions, *sir*!"

"Correct! And what is the maximum range in hard vacuum?"

"Sir! In vacuum, the maximum range of the Sunbeam M228 Squad Laser Weapon is theoretically infinite, *sir*!"

"*Theoretically?* You gonna trust your life, or the life of your buddy in the hole with you, to *theory?*"

That sounded like one of Knox's frequent rhetorical questions, so Jack remained silent. It turned out to be the right response.

"The important thing to remember about the slaw," Knox went on, "is that if you can see your target, you can hit it.

"And the important thing to remember about *energy*, is

that energy is energy, whether it comes from a lump of plastic explosives, or the muzzle of M228 Squad Laser Weapon, or your fist. All *any* weapon is is a means of delivering energy on target. And delivering a hell of a lot of energy on-target, accurately and lethally, is what being a Marine is all about. With an M228 ten-megawatt Squad Laser Weapon. With an ATAR standard personal weapon. With an entrenching tool. With a rock. With your fist. With your teeth. *You* are the weapon! *You,* the men of the United States Marine Corps! *Do* you read me?"

"Sir! Yes, sir!" the recruits chorused.

"A US Marine is far more deadly than a ten-megawatt M-228 Squad Laser Weapon! And that is because a ten-megawatt M-228 Squad Laser Weapon cannot *think*. It cannot *plan*. And most of all, it does not possess the courage, fortitude, adaptability, willpower, or sheer, mean grit of a US Marine! *Do* you read me?"

"Sir, yes, sir!"

"I can't hear you!"

"SIR, YES, SIR!"

"What does a US Marine *do*?"

"Kill! Kill! *Marine Corps!*"

Jack shouted with the others, yelling past the harsh rasp in his throat, overriding the chill, the discomfort, the bone-tired ache, the chattering of his teeth.

Still, it was impossible not to look down at those two, drilled-through dummies and not imagine himself lying there. *My God*, he thought, and not for the first time since he'd come aboard at Parris Island. *What have I gotten myself into?*

Assault Shuttle 06, Army Space
Force Assault Group
Approaching Lunar South Pole
2035 hours GMT

The K-440 Space Transport Cargo pod was the size and roughly the shape of a boxcar, a no-frills pressurized module capable of transporting up to fifteen tons with a Zeus

II HLV to provide the initial kick. With Aerospace Force modifications allowing for air and temperature control, it could carry fifty men to orbit, or thirty as far as the Moon.

Colonel Thomas R. Whitworth floated in the two-man cockpit between the commander's and pilot's seats, peering through the narrow slit windows at the rugged terrain ahead. Sunlight, reflected from silver-white mountains, flooded the cockpit and warmed his face; he preferred spending the travel time aft with his men—a good leader never separated himself from his men or their discomfort— but he'd asked Major Jones, the Aerospace Force mission commander, to call him forward for the final approach. It always helped to be able to actually *see* the terrain you were supposed to assault, using your God-given Mark I eyeballs instead of watching a computer simulation. He'd not had a good feel for the terrain the last time he'd led his men into this desolate waste, and he thought that that was why they'd made a relatively poor showing when the enemy counterattacked.

They would do better this time. The damned Marines weren't here to get in the way, for one thing . . . or to inflict casualties with so-called friendly fire. Whitworth had a soldier's native distrust for joint operations, and a dislike in particular for the Marines. Like Truman a century earlier, he thought they served well enough as the Navy's police force, but the needs of the military as a whole would be best served if there was *one* aerospace arm, and *one* ground assault force. So-called elites like the Marines simply pulled good men and women away from the service that could best use them—the Army, and, in particular, Army Special Forces.

Today we'll see what the Army Space Force can really *do*, he thought. *This one could end the goddamned war!*

Everything hinged on the Moon's reserves of frozen water.

Water ice had been discovered on the Moon over forty years ago, first by a Defense Department Lunar probe, with confirmation a few years later by Lunar Prospector, a NASA satellite. When humans had again walked on the face of the Moon after the half century hiatus following

Apollo, long-term explorations had been launched and permanent bases had been built with the knowledge that large reserves of water—locked up in ice mixed with the Lunar regolith—existed within the deep, eternal night of crater floors at both the north and south poles of the Moon. Theory held that cometary impacts over the past few billions of years had scattered droplets of water all over the Lunar surface—but only deep inside the craters at the poles where the sun literally never shone could it accumulate as ice, droplet piling upon frozen droplet for four billion lightless years.

It was estimated that some hundreds of millions of tons of water ice now lay buried in the regolith at each pole. Transports like the K-440 had originally been designed in the late 2020s to haul ice from the poles to places like Fra Mauro and Tsiolkovsky, where it could provide drinking water, oxygen, and the fuel for fuel cells or for chemical-fuel launch systems, so that more pounds of payload boosted from Earth could be devoted to food, nonconsumables, and people.

Lunar ice was, arguably, *the* most important natural resource discovered so far in near-Earth space. With all mass expensive in terms of having to drag it out of Earth's gravity well, having a local source of drinking water, oxygen, and fuel—both the hydrogen and oxygen employed by chemical thrusters, and the water used as reaction mass in nuclear-plasma main engines—meant the difference between viable long-term settlements and what was euphemistically referred to as a fingernail op, fingernail as in hanging on by a.

Operation Swift Victory had been conceived as just that—a means of stabbing straight through to the heart of the UN's Lunar operations, rendering them untenable. With the UN blocked from both the Moon and Mars, the war could indeed be brought to a swift and victorious end; after all, it was control of the ancient-alien artifacts out here that was the principal cause of the war . . . even if the folks back home were being told that issues like independence for the Southwest US or sovereignty under United Nations rule were the *real* cause of the fighting. Whoever controlled the technology still locked up in those old ruins and archeological digs would ultimately make *all* of the rules, no questions asked.

Mars had been brought under US control by grabbing both ends of the cycler transport system to and from the Red Planet—the former International Space Station in Earth orbit, and the Mars Shuttle Lander bases on Mars.

The best way to control the Moon, however, was to control the water.

He watched the landscape unfolding below and ahead with an intent eagerness. The terrain appeared impossibly rugged, but that was an illusion brought on by the extreme contrast between light and shadow, day and night. The sun was very low on the horizon behind them, now, and every bump, every ridge and boulder, each crevasse and hill and crater rim cast shadows far longer than might have been expected. A screen on the pilot's console showed the same view, rendered through the far less ominous-looking medium of a graphic radar display.

"Acceleration, sir," the transport's pilot warned. "Maybe you should grab a seat."

"I'm fine." Whitworth swung his feet around until they were in contact with the deck plating. A moment later, a tug of returning weight dragged at him, hard enough to make him sag a bit at the knees.

A green light began winking rapidly on the console. "Contact light!" the pilot said.

"Okay," Major Jones added. "That's our come-ahead."

"Excellent!" Whitworth said. He grinned, adding in deliberate imitation of an old Marine Corps expression, "The Green Berets have landed and have the situation well in hand!"

The first troops down at Objective Sierra Peter had been a detachment of Special Forces tasked with securing the landing zone; had there been an overwhelmingly powerful occupation force or a trap of some kind, they would have uncovered it and flashed the incoming transports a warn-off. The come-ahead meant the LZ was clear and nonhostile.

"How far?" Whitworth asked.

"Another two kilometers," Jones said. He pointed. "Just beyond that crater rim up ahead. Um, maybe you should seal up, sir? Helmet and gloves in the locker back there."

"I'm okay." He wanted to *see*. The transport was dropping lower now, skimming the Lunar mountains at an altitude of barely a hundred meters. The ground canted up as they swept across the crater ringwall; the floor beyond was lost in black shadow. On the screen, several glowing green triangles came into view—the IFF codes of the Rangers already on the ground. A flashing X marked the LZ beacon.

"Here we go," Jones said. "Take us in."

"Roger that," the pilot said. "I'll set us down over—"

The green flashing come-ahead went out. Two seconds later, a different light winked on, a baleful red.

"Shit!" Jones snapped.

"What's happening?" Whitworth demanded.

"Wave off!" The landing zone beacon snapped off. "They're waving us off!"

"Give me a direct channel!"

"You're on the air."

"Advance Delta!" Whitworth shouted into his needle mike, using the Army team's call sign. "Advance Delta, this is Capstone! What the hell is going on?"

"Capstone, Advance Delta," a voice called back, tinny and strained in Whitworth's earphone. "Wave off! Hot LZ! Repeat, hot—"

The transmission ended in a burst of static.

The transport's pilot hauled back on both of his armrest joysticks, and a sudden surge of acceleration dragged at Whitworth, slamming both feet against the deck. Struggling to stay up, he managed to lever himself down into the cockpit's jump seat and strap himself in.

"I've got laser fire," Jones announced, his voice maddeningly calm. "Someone down there is painting us."

"Where?" Whitworth demanded, leaning against his harness, trying to see. "I don't see anything!" There was no answer, and Whitworth cursed himself for speaking without thinking, a sure way to look stupid in front of subordinates. Of course! In a vacuum, with no dust to illuminate or air molecules to ionize, laser beams would be invisible. The flashing beams and eye-popping bolts of colorful radiance so popular in the entertainment vids had no basis in reality.

A hard thump, like some giant kicking the transport from beneath, sounded through the thin metal hull. "What was that?" Whitworth demanded.

"Number three O-two tank just went," the pilot shouted. "Hang on! We're losing it!"

A flash as brilliant as sunlight shone briefly through the cockpit windows, so bright that Whitworth thought they'd turned to face the sun. Then the light faded, and he realized he'd just seen an explosion—one of the other transports disintegrating in a violent, soundless detonation.

"Brace for impact!" Jones shouted over the transport's IC system. "Everyone brace for impact!" Then black-shadowed mountains swept past the cockpit window at an impossible angle, and Whitworth felt the deck slamming up against his feet and the mounting of his chair. A shrill scream—unmistakably the howl of atmosphere venting into hard vacuum—rang in his ears . . . which began to hurt intolerably as the cabin pressure dropped. Fumbling with the latches of his harness, he managed to get shakily to his feet, then accepted a helmet and gloves from Jones, who'd broken them out of an emergency locker at the rear of the cockpit. He clamped the helmet down over his head, seating it in the locking ring of his suit and giving it a hard quarter-twist to lock it. Jones, who seemed a lot more adept at garbing fast in an emergency, helped him with the gloves.

The pilot wouldn't need to suit up; he was slumped forward in his seat, his head twisted at an impossible angle. Whitworth wondered how many of his men in the main cargo bay had survived. At least they should have all been suited up for the approach.

As he should have been.

Still unsteady on trembling legs, he made his way back

through the cockpit hatch and into the cargo bay, where vac-suited troops struggled to get clear of cases of supplies that had shifted and broken free in the crash. The company radio channel was clogged with moans and a few screams; Lieutenant Hastings was shouting orders, trying to get a team to clear the airlock hatch of a spilled tangle of debris and electrical wiring. A number of men were trapped in their seats yet, some struggling feebly, but all too many lying as limp and as still as the transport's pilot. Ice— frozen out of the evacuating air as it thinned—coated many of the surfaces, gleaming eerily as handheld emergency lights flashed and swung and touched it.

Whitworth tried to think of something to say, some order to give . . . and couldn't. The situation was now completely out of his control, and all he could do was stand by helplessly and watch as Hastings and three others finally cleared the hatch and pried it open. A few moments later, he stood in the midnight shadow of the crater pole, looking up at hard, bright stars and an encircling rim of mountains, with only the highest peaks silvered by bright sunlight. The regolith crunched under his boots as he moved, and he could feel the crumbly texture of ice mixed with Lunar dust. The scene was utterly peaceful; other transports lay scattered across the crater floor where they'd landed, marked by the bobbing and moving emergency lights of other survivors. All three transports had been downed, probably in as many minutes.

"Colonel Whitworth?"

He turned. A soldier in black-and-gray vac-suit armor with Special Forces patches on left chest and shoulder, came toward him.

"Here. I'm Whitworth."

The figure saluted. "Sergeant Canady, sir. Ranger LZ assault team. We, sir, are in a world of shit."

"What the hell happened?" He wanted to lash out at someone, *anyone*, for this disaster. "Why didn't you pick the bastards up with your IR scans?"

He heard the blast of air across a mike as the Ranger sighed. "Sir, I don't think there were any bastards! The fire was coming from up there." He pointed, indicating the crater rim. "I think they have some kind of robot or teleoperated defense system. When we came in, we overflew and scanned for infrared leakage. If there were people, habitats, a ship, anything with operating life support, we would have seen the heat signature. But there was *nothing*!"

The words hit Whitworth like hammerblows. He'd been expecting some sort of token guard force or garrison . . . but not lasers aimed and triggered by men thousands of kilometers away. When had they set up the defense grid? After Picard, certainly, since the Navy had been making regular runs down here to collect ice for Picard's life support. Maybe the UNdies had even planted the things before the US invasion, sitting here quietly, letting individual transports come and go, while waiting for the transports that obviously meant an all-out assault on their farside fortress.

With a cold, hard, sinking sensation in the pit of his stomach, Whitworth realized he'd been guilty of the worst sin possible for a military commander.

He'd completely underestimated the enemy.

An hour later, he knew the worst. Out of 160 men in the South Polar assault force, 98 were dead, killed by the initial laser fire, or the crash of their transport seconds later. When contact was at last established with the North Polar group, his worst fears were confirmed. An identical ambush there had killed 82 out of 105; the survivors were in communication with UN forces and had decided to surrender.

There was, really, no alternative. It would be days before a relief force from Earth could arrive, and the tiny Army garrisons at Picard and Fra Mauro could offer no help. Their suit PLSS units would keep them breathing another twelve hours, or so, and they might scavenge more oxygen from supplies still aboard the wrecked transports, but they had no food, no water, and no way out save walking . . .

The alternative to an impossibly long and difficult overland trek appeared in the sky overhead two and a half hours after the brief battle that had marooned them. The ship was death black and diamond-shaped, streamlined except for the wire-cage basket housing landing legs, reaction-mass tanks, and a plasma engine mounted on the stern. The only markings visible on the vessel as it drifted toward a vertical landing on invisible jets of high-temperature plasma were a small, blue, UN flag painted on each of the three fins, and the name, picked out in gray lettering near the prow: *Millénium*.

The mystery ship reported at Picard. The "unknown" that had launched from Earth months before and vanished behind the Moon.

There was no question of fighting the thing. Ball turrets mounted in that sleek, black hull rotated, tracking men on the ground. Oh, they could have opened up with the handful of missile launchers or squad lasers recovered so far from the wrecks, but to do so would have sealed their fate.

He opened Channel 9, the universal emergency frequency. "This is Colonel Thomas R. Whitworth, commanding the US Special Forces Lunar Assault Unit, calling UN ship. We are prepared to lay down our arms and surrender."

There was no other option open.

None at all.

THIRTEEN

*Institute for Exoarcheological
Studies
Chicago, Illinois
0855 hours CDT*

David was whistling as he entered the broad, skylight-illuminated lobby of the Institute for Exoarcheological Studies. They were waiting for him there, next to the faux-stone cast replica of the Sphinx, among fountains, palm trees, and rented vegetation.

"Dr. Alexander?" Both men flashed badges, though David was too startled to read them. "I'm Special Agent Carruthers. This is Special Agent Rodriguez. We have a warrant for your arrest, sir. Please come along quietly."

"My . . . arrest! What charge?"

"Criminal espionage, violation of national security, and electronically consorting with agents of foreign countries with whom we are currently at war." The two closed in on him from opposite sides. Handcuffs flashed. "You have the right to remain silent. You have the right to an attorney. Should you require an attorney . . ."

As Carruthers recited his rights, Rodriguez snapped the handcuffs closed on his wrists, pinning his hands at his back. Passersby in the lobby stopped, watching curiously. Helplessly, stunned by the suddenness of the arrest, he stared up at the enigmatic and secretive face of the Sphinx. The replica was only a fraction of the size of the original, of course, crouched in one corner of the lobby among palms and tinkling fountain pools, but it was still large enough that David had to look up to stare into sightlessly farseeing eyes.

There was a rustle of fabric at his back as the recitation ended. Teri walked over, her PAD case slung over her shoulder. "David! What's going on?"

"Nothing to see here, Miss," Rodriguez said. "Go on about your business, please."

"David? . . ."

"Call my lawyer," David told her. "Julia Dutton. Her number's on my v-mail address list in the office."

"C'mon, Dr. Alexander," Rodriguez said, tugging at his elbow. "You'll have lots of time to discuss things with your girlfriend later."

"Go on, Teri," David told her, as they led him toward the front door. "Call her! I need help!"

"That's for sure," Rodriguez told him as they stepped outside. "Treason's not so hot as a career choice, you know what I mean?"

"Treason! What the hell are you talking about?" *Damn!* They must have found out about the fax.

"There's a war on, fella," Carruthers said. "Maybe you hadn't heard. Sharing classified information with foreign nationals is—"

"*Look*, damn it!" David interrupted him. "I *know* we're at war. But there's a, a fellowship within the scientific community that transcends national borders. The people I was communicating with are friends of mine. There was no spying involved!"

"That's not for us to decide, sir," Rodriguez replied. "You'll get your chance to explain it all in court."

"But, you know, Dr. Alexander," Carruthers added, "we've been keeping a close eye on you for some time now. What was happening here was sufficient grounds for us to get a court order to access your home network. Seems you've been electronically passing confidential files to the, ah, what is it? The First Church of the Divine Masters of the Cosmos."

"What, those nutcases! You've got to be kidding!"

"You've been feeding them classified documents for the past couple of months, and we've got the records to prove it."

Still protesting, David was hustled into a black Lancer Electra waiting outside.

Recruit Platoon 4239
Parris Island Recruit Training
Center
1120 hours EDT

"Listen up, now, recruits. You're about to meet the best friend you have in this world besides your rifle!"

Jack sat cross-legged on the deck at the forward end of the squad bay, listening attentively as Gunnery Sergeant Knox addressed them. The platoon was leaner now, after four weeks. Attrition had continued, though at a slower pace now that the deadwood and ballast had been jettisoned. Platoon 4239 was down to fifty-six men. They were still tired nearly all of the time from the grueling schedule of up to seventeen hours a day of drill, exercise, and training, but at least now they acted less like a herd of sheep chivvied along by screaming DIs. Now, they moved with purpose.

And a common goal.

Knox held up a pouch that was obviously designed to clip to a Marine's combat web gear. Each of the recruits, minutes before, had been issued an identical pouch before being mustered to the squad bay for a training session.

"Each of you will now remove the device you've just been issued from its holster," Knox said.

Jack did as he was told, sliding a small but massive black case from his pouch. It looked like a computer of some sort, a PAD folded closed to protect screen and keyboard, of course, but a computer nonetheless. Folded, the device was about the size and shape of a paperback book, though it was considerably heavier. He could see a line of data jacks and power ports along one end.

Jack felt a surge of excitement, closely followed by an

almost reverent nostalgia. He'd been so busy for this past month that he'd not realized how much he missed his computer at home.

"The device you are holding," Knox continued, "is the Marine-issue HP-9800 Mark III Personal Access Device, or PAD. Do not open it until I give you the word to do so." Knox held up the PAD in his hand. "Two hundred years ago, a combat rifleman was expected to be able to march and drill in close formation, stand shoulder to shoulder with his fellows in the battle line, and give fire and reload while taking fire from the enemy. Combat has changed in two centuries. Not only the weapons and the techniques have changed, but there has been a profound change in the way riflemen are expected to operate in combat. To stand shoulder to shoulder with your buddies while you loaded and fired your musket took bravery, but you didn't have to be smart. Today, we expect you to be smart, because being smart spells the difference between victory and defeat, between you scoring a kill and what's left of you coming home in a body bag.

"The PAD will help you be smart. To *fight* smart." He pointed to a catch on one of the long ends. "Press here to open your PADs. Now! Open them, but do *not* touch the ON switch until I give you the word!"

It opened just like a book, too, revealing two screens of dark, high-impact plastic. A single small button, inscribed ON/OFF, was recessed into the case at the lower right; a tiny camera lens was set into the plastic just above the top screen.

"The HP-9800 Mark III Personal Access Device is a computer," Knox said, "two and one-half gigahertz, one hundred twenty-eight gigabytes of one-hundred-fifty-picosecond RAM, and onboard laser-read quantum-state crystal storage with a capacity of three hundred terabytes. The built-in gallium-selenide-arsenide dense-charge battery provides power for eighteen to twenty-four hours of continuous operation and can be recharged in one hour from either AC or DC sources, including your pliss converters or the power pack for your standard Sunbeam M228 Squad Laser Weapon."

Jack felt a patronizing amusement as Knox ran through the PAD's stats, though he'd learned by now to keep his face impassively neutral with the smile well hidden inside. The device was impressive, yes—especially in its rugged construction, theoretically allowing it to be carried, jarred, dragged, dropped, bumped, kicked, and stepped on in hard vacuum, desert sand, thick mud, ice, or seawater at temperatures ranging from minus one hundred to plus seventy degrees Celsius and keep on working. By civilian standards, though, it was almost laughably primitive. His own home system, running at 4 gigahertz with almost a terb of 80ps RAM and 650 terbs of storage, was far superior.

It was a lot bigger, too, and not nearly as robust. The manufacturers of these devices had outdone themselves in making Marine-issue PADs as indestructible and idiot-proof as possible.

"Your PADs will function as computers in their own right, of course," Knox continued, "but their true power lies in their ability to tap into either the Earthnet or a special Marine tactical network, or tacnet. To accomplish this, they use a radio-connect onboard modem at 98K baud, fast enough to allow the transfer of high-resolution, full-color video. By connecting with the local network, you will be able to use your PADs as full-capability vidcom units; to download orders, tactical information, and updates; to use your PAD as a full-featured mapping and autolocation device; or to access other computers in order to extend your PAD's computational power or to retrieve or to uplink data. Tactical range for the radio modem varies with the signal strength of local Net repeaters but is typically on the order of one to two kilometers. By connecting your PAD to any uplink station and antenna, however, you can access any Net system or data base required through available communications satellites, which gives you essentially unlimited range.

"You may now press the ON switch. Do nothing else, *touch* nothing else, until I give you the word."

Obediently, Jack pressed the button, and the double screen came to life. The lower half showed a graphic representation of a keyboard and was obviously configured as a touch-sensitive screen. The upper half showed the Marine globe-and-anchor, the single phrase "ENTER PASSWORD": and a winking cursor.

"Your PAD is password protected. This is to prevent the enemy from accessing our communications codes and protocols in the event your device falls into their hands. Further, there are certain special passwords which you will memorize. If you are captured and forced to divulge your password, one of these special passwords will not only scrub your PAD's memory, it will release enough energy from the battery pack to render the device unusable.

"For now, you will all use the password 'recruit' to access your machines. You may do so now."

There followed an inevitable period of confusion, as several of the recruit PADs refused to function. Several might have been genuine faults, though in at least three cases, it turned out that the operators were trying to access their devices with either "recrute" or "recroot." Recruit Kirkpatrick was still having trouble getting the case open and needed help, accompanied by a suitable chewing-out from Knox, to work the catch.

Eventually, though, all of them had operating PADs, and all were tuned into the Parris Island Recruit Training Command tacnet. Knox led them all through the basic operations of the device, using it as a calculator, as a data bank with range and ballistics information for various ATAR rounds, and as a vid-com. They learned that, so long as they were recruits, they would only have access to a single specific and very narrow channel on the local tacnet—this, Knox patiently explained, to keep some ham-fisted idiot-brained recruit from tapping into Earthnet or the Pentagon and causing a disaster of global proportions.

They also met AIDE—the Marine Corp's Artificially Intelligent Dedicated Executive, a decidedly masculine and somewhat narrow-minded version of Sam, without the pictures.

"AIDE is your friend," Knox told them. "Your advisor and your mentor. He will act as your on-line agent. Tell him what information you need, and he will get it for you, either on a general search or by searching databases that you specify. He can communicate with you audibly through the PAD's speakers, through your helmet radio headset, or—if you require silence to avoid giving away your position to the enemy—by printed words on your screen or relayed to your combat helmet's HUD. For those of you used to those high-powered civilian AIs, with artificial personalities and full-vid presentation and all the rest, AIDE will seem a bit spartan, definitely a stripped-down version of those slick-chassis jobs. But, believe me, it will do the job.''

Jack suppressed another smile at Knox's description of the AIDE as stripped-down. He much preferred Sam when she was stripped down . . . and he suspected that she could do just about any agent work better, faster, and with a more efficient use of onboard memory than the military-issue AIDE. And this thing didn't even have a visual component.

Funny. He hadn't thought about Sam during the past month, even in his dreams. He'd been too tired and too stressed lately, he supposed, to waste any energy on a fantasy simulation. That part of his life, he realized with a small, inner start, seemed very distant now, almost like the life and memories of someone else entirely.

He might not be a Marine yet, but, by God, he was no longer a civilian either.

Knox led them through several routines involving their AIDEs, retrieving specific pieces of information from the recruit tacnet, including their drill and training schedules for the next week, and the menu for evening chow. The AIDEs' voices, male, deep, and with the precision and decidedly artificial inflection of low-grade, no-personality AIs, turned into a male a cappella chorus as all fifty-six of them responded to recruit queries together.

It didn't take Jack long to get the hang of either the PAD or his AIDE. The PAD was slow and clumsy compared with his computer at home, and the AIDE had all of the simulated intelligence of a doorknob, but he knew he was going to be able to work with them just fine. He wondered how he could get at the AIDE's source code, however. He'd done enough tinkering with Sam to have a good idea how basic artificial-intelligence programs worked—the non-self-aware ones, at least—and he thought he knew three or four tricks at least that might put a bit more zip in the thing's operation.

At least he could find a way to give it some personality, some inflection in its voice and speech patterns! Somehow he doubted that the Corps in general or Gunnery Sergeant Knox in particular would appreciate his tinkering with the standard, Marine-issue AIDE. Still, he knew he was going to *have* to try, sooner or later. It was a challenge.

"From now on out, ladies," Knox said with that now-familiar and almost pleasant menace in his voice, "the vacation is over! If you thought the first four weeks of recruit training were hard, you soon will learn that they were a freaking *vacation* compared to what you're about to hit! Your physical training and drill will be continued and escalated, of course. But your classroom training, your *knowledge* skills, will be sharply accelerated. You will be expected to learn how to use your PADs and your AIDEs to full advantage in order to master the information you must acquire if you are to pass your qualifying exams. They will serve as notebooks, as learning devices, as research tools, as *brains* as you continue your studies, because you have not yet been issued with Marine-quality organic brains!"

Strange, how the slightly grainy texture of that black case gave Jack a sharp, electric thrill. *A Marine-issue PAD!* he thought. *They wouldn't pass these out until they knew most of us were going to stick! I'm actually gonna make it! I'm gonna be a Marine!*

He felt better now, more sure, more confident, prouder than at any time since he'd raised his hand for his swearing in.

Maybe he would make the Space Marines. Maybe not. *But he was going to be a Marine. . . .*

FOURTEEN

Le Édifice de la Monde Uni
Geneva, Switzerland
1540 hours GMT

"We have a problem," the tall man said. "And an unparalleled chance to rectify it. With this one decision, this one act, we can end the war once and for all. To ignore this opportunity would be . . . criminal."

His name was Marie-Claude Balmont, and he, with the fourteen other people gathered about the large, round table with him, was the closest thing the Earth had ever had to a world ruler. Not Alexander, not the Caesars, not Kublai Khan or Adolph Hitler or Josef Stalin had ever commanded the allegiance of so vast a sweep of territory, peoples, and forces. Alexander the Great might have wept when he believed he had no more worlds to conquer, but his empire stretched across barely a fifth of the lands now under United Nations control.

To say nothing of the various UN orbital stations and facilities . . . or the Moon, for that matter, now again solidly under UN control.

Officially, perhaps, it was Dr. José Luís Lozoya who might be said to be the true ruler of the world . . . but the title of Secretary General of the United Nations was nowadays largely an empty title, one reserved for ceremonies, speeches, and the signings of treaties, not for the real work of consolidating global power and authority. The same could be said for the UN General Assembly, which still argued and voted on a variety of issues but more and more was simply a rubber-stamp body for the Security Council.

No, it was definitely the United Nations Security Council, with five permanent members and the representatives of ten other nations elected every two years, that represented the world government's true authority. For the past year and a half, the Security Council had been largely responsible for the planning and the execution of the war, at least in terms of broad strategy.

"You cannot possibly be serious, Monsieur Balmont," George Sinclair, the British representative said. "What you are proposing is sheer madness!"

"You might consider voting for a change, then, George," Balmont replied, speaking fluent English with a grin. "Instead of carrying on with this perpetual sulk."

Sinclair scowled as several others at the table chuckled. "The stand my nation is taking in regard to the prosecution of this illicit war—"

"Is well-known to us all, yes."

"I, for one," Zhao Dinghua, the North China representative said, his Mandarin translated emotionlessly over the delegates' ear clips, "would like to hear more of this proposal by the European Union. We believe it has considerable merit." Several of the other members, permanent and elected, nodded agreement.

"We've not been able to say much about it thus far," Balmont said, "for reasons of security." He glanced at Sinclair, the weakest of several weak links now on the Council. Something would have to be done about that one.

Standing, Balmont gestured at the huge, electronic world map that filled the upper half of one of the chamber's curving walls. UN member states were shown in blue, the neutral or antiwar states—Great Britain, Sweden, Korea, Belarus, Australia, Canton, Quebec, and a handful of others—in gray. The enemy nations—Russia, Japan, and the United States, glowed red. All of the major fronts were shown as well in brighter red, from the largely static battle lines in northern Mexico, to the broad Russian fronts along the Ukraine, Kazakh, and Chinese borders.

"The war," Balmont said, "has ground to a standstill. With Quebec's withdrawal from the war in the first year, we have only been able to keep up direct pressure against the United States through cruise-missile attacks, and along the Mexican front. I needn't add that we are making little headway."

"Are you suggesting that Mexico is not doing its part?" Ramón Suarez, the Mexican representative, demanded. "If the rest of the member states would give us sufficient munitions, men, supplies, and weapons, we could perhaps drive the *yanquis* back across our border, and liberate sovereign Aztlan! *That*, I remind you, is the reason we are fighting this conflict!"

Well, that might have been why Mexico was in it. "No one is questioning the valiant effort and valuable martial contribution of Mexico in the prosecution of the war," Balmont said. He managed to keep a straight face as he said the words, too, despite the fact that Mexico's performance so far had been little short of comical. If the Americans hadn't already been so drastically overextended with their expeditionary forces in Russia, if they hadn't been holding back massive reserves against the possibility of major UN landings on their coasts, they would have captured Ciudad de México long ago, in all probability knocking Mexico out of the war as decisively as they'd done to Quebec early in the fighting. "And it is regrettable that the member nations have not been able to afford more in the way of men and materiel on the Mexican front. That should, we expect, change in the very near future. *After* the implementation of Operation Damocles.

"However, the fact remains that for now, our primary military effort has been against the Russian Federation. Russia has the largest border, is most vulnerable to invasion, and thus far has offered the greatest strategic reward."

"The best chance for plunder and rape, you mean," Suarez exclaimed, ignoring the council's speaker protocol. "Who gets that reward you mention? Ukraine! Kazakh and the Shiite Union! And, of *course*, our good friends in North China!" He bowed sardonically toward Zhao, who watched impassively. "These people are enriching themselves at Russia's expense, while we in Mexico stand at the edge of total defeat! Meanwhile, you talk of asteroids and orbits and magical plans for ending the war. What we need, my countrymen, is sufficient military assistance and reinforcements to punch through the *yanquis* lines." He slammed the table with an open hand. "Fast! Hard! We do not need these circular and complex plans of yours, Señor Balmont."

"*If* I may continue," Balmont said coldly, "we will address your complaints, Señor Suarez. As I was saying, the front lines have been largely static for well over a year, now. Ukraine forces are stalled at Voronezh. Russian forces have counterinvaded Kazakh and even retaken their former launch facilities at Baykonyr. And China, while making substantial gains past the Amur, and even managing to cut the Trans-Siberian Railway at Belogorsk and Khabarovsk, has after two years been unable to crack the Russian and American lines near Vladivostok." He glanced at Zhao, wondering if the Chinese representative was going to interrupt or protest as Suarez had done, but the man was as silent, and as unreadable, as ever. "It is time to try something new, something daring and bold, to break the stalemate once and for all and end this bloody, unfortunate conflict. And Damocles is the way to do it."

"If I may ask," Shekar Rikhye, the North Indian representative, said in his quietly formal, diffident manner, hand raised, "about *Millénium*? I thought that the antimatter warship was considered the key to UN success."

"True," Balmont said. "It *was*. But we can no longer depend on the one ship, however powerful, as a guarantee for victory. The Americans have learned far too much in recent months. And their own work on an antimatter-powered warship appears to be proceeding rapidly. The well-known American proficiency with things technological could easily put them in the lead of this particular race, despite our recovery of the ancient ET wreckage at Picard."

The representative for one of the ten elected members, Abdel-Malek of Egypt and the Islamic Union, raised a hand. "Sir! The plan as you have described it seems to me to risk ecological catastrophe. I speak as the citizen of a nation that has for thousands of years lived balanced on the slender line between plenty and starvation! To wield such powers as you suggest, to risk such devastating and wholesale destruction—" He stopped, then shook his head. "Perhaps an all-out attack against the American antimatter ship instead?"

"The Security Council's Military Advisory Committee has worked out the plan for Damocles in considerable detail, with extensive computer simulation. General Brunmuller and his staff believe it offers us the best chance for complete and immediate victory. With the United States decisively knocked out of the war, both Japan and Russia will capitulate swiftly, especially if they are told a similar judgment will be unleashed upon them if they do not. The Advisory Committee did look at the possibility of a raid or even a nuclear strike against the Americans' L-3 shipyard. That facility is so remote, however, and so closely screened by detection webs and sensors, that there is no hope of approaching undetected, even with the stealthiest vehicles." He gave a Gallic shrug. "And even if we should succeed in knocking out their AM vessel, what then? A counterstrike against *Millénium*? Or the discovery that they have other such vessels under construction elsewhere, perhaps within the continental United States where we have not been able to ferret out their existence? No, no, my friends, the risks are too grave, the prize too important, failure too terrible to contemplate. It is Damocles, or defeat!"

Still standing, he tapped out a series of keystrokes on the touch-sensitive surface at his place at the table. A large display monitor on the wall opposite the world map came to life. Half of the people at the table turned in their chairs to watch.

On the screen was an image a select few in the room had seen before, a dusty, smooth-sided boulder; the girder-and-tin-can assembly of the European Union's Science Research Vessel *Pierre-Simon Laplace* hung in the slow-tumbling boulder's shadow, a measure of its scale.

"Asteroid 2034L," Balmont said. "Currently some three and a half million million kilometers from Earth. We have been pacing it for months now and know its orbit and its mass to the highest precision possible. The nuclear charges have already been placed by the *Sagittaire*, which arrived on-station in May." He tapped out another code, and the image of the asteroid and the trailing research vessel was replaced by a detailed, animated graphic, showing the orbits of the Earth, the Moon, and the asteroid. "At a precisely determined moment, the detonation of those nuclear charges will give Asteroid 2034L a precisely determined nudge, a delta-*v*, as the rocketry engineers say, that will send it into a new course, one that we have computed with complete accuracy." As he spoke, the graphic of the asteroid flashed once, brightly, and shifted to a new orbit, diverging from the old. As a counter marking elapsed days flickered in the lower right corner of the screen, 2034L curved inward, accelerating rapidly, leaping toward the turning blue-and-white globe of Earth, which expanded as the animation's point of view zoomed in close. The asteroid, traveling slightly faster than the Earth, actually missed the planet by a narrow margin, cutting inside its orbit and crossing over the dayside.

Then, under the steady tug of Earth's gravity, it began curving back, entering the slender blur of Earth's atmosphere just as the continental United States rotated smoothly beneath the falling point, as though to catch it.

The endpoint of the asteroid's journey was marked with a flashing red beacon above glowing crosshairs, in the west-central United States just east of the Rockies. The coordinates 105° 33' W, 38° 51' N appeared on the screen.

"The gods of orbital mechanics favored us with 2034L," Balmont said, smiling. "It will need remarkably little in the way of orbit modification to bring it down on target. Our people are confident that the impact will occur on 15 September and within sixty kilometers of these coordinates.

"Greater precision is not necessary. Asteroid 2034L, though trailing Earth as it falls and therefore moving quite slowly relative to the planet, will nonetheless strike with an expected yield of between two hundred and four hundred megatons. Peterson Aerospace Force Base, home of the 46th Aerospace Wing. Falcon Aerospace Force Base, home for the 2nd Space Wing. The North American Defense Command, the Aerospace Defense Command, and the entire Cheyenne Mountain Complex. These last, which are hardened to survive direct nuclear strikes, may not be destroyed, depending on 2034L's exact point of impact, but they will almost certainly be so deeply buried in rubble that they will be knocked out of the war. And a direct or near-direct hit by that large a falling object . . . '' He spread his hands. ''NORAD, the enemy's nerve center, the very heart of his command and control, would be obliterated.''

On the screen, the view drew back, showing now the battle lines in northern Mexico as a violet ring spread out from the impact in Colorado.

''The destruction will not be limited to Colorado, of course. Several dozen major cities from California to the Mississippi River, cities as far away as Great Salt Lake and Albuquerque, will suffer serious damage. Denver, Colorado Springs, Pueblo, Cheyenne, all will be destroyed. The flash will set vast forest areas aflame. We estimate initial civilian casualties to be on the order of three to five million.

''More important, however, military forces throughout the American Southwest and in northern Mexico will be at least temporarily crippled. Their communications knocked out, blinded by a vast pall of dust filling the sky, bombarded by a fiery rain of debris, their morale destroyed, roads and maglev rails cut, supplies lost, their entire rear area overturned in complete chaos and confusion . . . they would not be able to resist that single hard, sharp thrust by your armies, Señor Suarez.''

The Mexican representative looked thunderstruck. ''But . . . but my people would suffer, too . . .''

''There may be earth tremors as far south as Mexico City, true,'' Balmont admitted. ''Your northernmost towns and villages might be hit by quakes and windblown dust. What of it? Your troops would . . . as the Americans say, 'hunker down' before impact. They would know what was coming, know that the enemy had been thrown into turmoil. They would weather the shock, then stride forward in victory. They will find, I think, the entire proposed state of Aztlan, from southern California to Texas to what was left of Colorado, in such bad shape that they would be welcomed as saviors.

"But far more importantly, the ability of the United States to continue prosecuting this war would be ended. Permanently. We will have literally carved the heart from the beast. Their troops would barely be sufficient to maintain order at home, in the face of widespread losses of water, power, transportation, and medical services. And that, of course, is the point."

As Balmont continued talking, continued trying to convince the uncommitted members of the Council, he studied the face of each member in turn. He was, first and foremost, a politician; he'd led the European Union Socialist Party for five years, before being elected chancellor of France, then Secretary General of the Union, before finally being appointed as his country's representative to the UN. In all those years, in all those power struggles, he'd learned how to read the faces of enemies, of friends, and of the people he needed to sway.

The Security Council's makeup had changed a lot in the past decade. Originally the five permanent members were the United States, the Soviet Union, China, Great Britain, and France, but the changing face of the world's major governments had forced the Council's evolution into a more flexible, more powerful form. The United States had been expelled from permanent membership for refusing to accept the UN-sponsored referendum on independence for the proposed new nation of Aztlan. The Russian Federation—heir to the old Soviet state—had been expelled as well for refusing to recognize China's age-old claims on much of Siberia.

To replace the two vacancies, the North Indian Federation and Brazil had been added to permanent-member status. The current problem child was Great Britain, which both continued to refuse to join the European Union—a rebellion ongoing now since the last century—and, worse, insisted on a policy of strict neutrality in what they called the American war. In the face of Britain's stubborn intransigence, the Charter rules had recently been rewritten so that binding resolutions could be passed with only four of the five permanent members voting aye . . . though still with a total of nine necessary for passage. Lately, there'd been talk of a major reorganization of the Security Council, in order to grant permanent status to other nations, such as the Islamic Union, Iran, and Argentina, to better reflect the true balance of power in the world.

It would not be enough, Balmont knew. The tendency these days, more and more, was for superstates to fragment. It had happened to the old Soviet Empire in 1989, to Yugoslavia in the 1990s, and to Canada a decade later. It had happened to both India and to China in the late 2020s, and there was growing fear that the relatively young European Union would not be able to remain united for long.

And the conclusions of the Geneva Report still hung over them all. The year 2050—just eight years away—had been identified as a kind of point of no return. If the world was not united by then, fully united under a United Nations able to set policy and law and enforce them, the future of humankind would be bleak indeed, with a population of ten billion, dwindling reserves of oil and other natural resources, and the prospect of disease, starvation, and cannibalism on a global scale.

The war *had* to be ended, and it had to be ended now, with a decisive UN victory that would give the presumptive world government the teeth it needed to begin the rationing programs that might, *might* save humanity.

The alternative was too dark to contemplate.

And yet, even within the UN Security Council, the bickering, the divisive power plays, the games continued. It was enough to make Balmont sick. Operation Damocles, he was certain, would bring more nations to heel than the US, Japan, and Russia. There were other enemies to be defeated, enemies still nominally members of the United Nations.

Enemies like . . .

George Sinclair stood suddenly, his face flushed. "I find the details of this plan of yours . . . disturbing. Even terrifying. What you propose . . ." He stopped, shaking his head, groping for words. "It is well-known that an asteroid striking the Yucatán Peninsula millions of years ago changed the climate of the entire world and brought the dinosaurs to extinction. You could do the same to us, to all mankind! This, this Damocles of yours is a doomsday weapon!"

"It is genocide!" Abdel-Malek added. "You threaten our entire world!"

Balmont smiled. "Gentlemen, gentlemen, the numbers say it all. The so-called dinosaur-killer asteroid was ten kilometers across and must have had a yield of some tens or even hundreds of thousands of megatons. Asteroid 2034L is barely a kilometer across, and the trajectory it will be following gives it a relatively low-speed impact. This is good, for it ensures that the mass will not explode high up in the atmosphere but will penetrate through to the ground. This will cause far more damage at the impact site, but in a smaller, more contained area."

As he spoke, he typed out a quick message on his PAD, addressed it with the appropriate encryption, and hit the send key.

"I told you we expect the total yield to be between two and four hundred megatons," he continued. "The exact figure depends on how much velocity it sheds during its passage through the atmosphere. This is far greater than any nuclear weapon ever constructed, true . . . but it will be a pinprick compared to the strike that destroyed the dinosaurs."

"And no radioactivity," Zhao observed. "A *clean* destruction in fire and darkness."

"Just so. One that leaves us free, then, to mop up surviving US units in their West and Southwest, then turn our full attention to the Russians and the Japanese."

He was watching Abdel-Malek as he spoke. With widening eyes, the Islamic Union representative was reading

his own PAD now. Reading the message Balmont had just
sent him.

"Indeed," Balmont added, "the mere threat of another
asteroid impact on those countries . . . or, in the case of
Japan, in the sea just offshore, will most likely be sufficient to force their immediate and unconditional surrender."

"Even if we have no more asteroids coming in?"
Abdel-Malek asked. He was typing on his PAD as he
spoke. An instant later, a message appeared on Balmont's
PAD, a single word. *Agreed*.

"They won't know that," Balmont said. "All they will
have is the knowledge of what has happened to the United
States, and the dread that the same fate awaits them."

"What about the dangers of changing the climate?" Da
Cunha, of Brazil, asked.

"That, perhaps, is the best news of all," Balmont replied. "Our simulations suggest that the dust cloud thrown
up by the impact could have a slight but definite effect on
the climate, slowing the global warming trend signifi-
cantly. Our scientists predict that global temperatures
could run between half a degree and two degrees cooler
for the next decade. That could buy us some time with the
Geneva Report, by allowing larger harvests."

"I will have no part of this!" Sinclair declared. Abruptly,
he stood, gathering his papers into a briefcase and closing
it with a snap. "Further, I intend to make a full report
available to the governments of the United States, Japan,
and Russia at the earliest opportunity. This, this callous
toying with genocide, with global catastrophe, is nothing
short of irresponsible, and I and my government will have
no part of it!"

As he turned to leave, Balmont touched a symbol on
the touch surface of the table, and the Security Council's
door slid silently open. Four UN Blue Guards, in full cer-
emonial dress but with unmistakably serviceable H&K
980s at the ready, stepped in.

Sinclair stopped, then turned. "What is the meaning of
this!"

Balmont ignored him. "Escort the former representative

of Great Britain to a holding room and keep him there, please. He is to talk to no one, have no electronic access with the outside.''

''Sir!'' one of the Blues rasped. Both turned their weapons on Sinclair.

''You can't do this!'' Sinclair cried. ''I have diplomatic immunity!''

''And you are being placed under diplomatic protective custody until this matter is settled, George.'' He jerked his head. ''Take him.''

Minutes later, after two of the guards had departed with Sinclair and the explosion of urgent conversation around the table had died down, Balmont resumed his seat. Two of the Blues remained inside the room on either side of the door, in violation of all tradition and precedent, their automatic weapons at port arms. ''I submit, ladies and gentlemen, that the Islamic Union, currently represented by Mr. Abdel-Malek, should be elevated to permanent-member status on this Council. All in favor?''

The motion passed, as he'd known it would. And, though another three hours of debate was necessary, so did the resolution to employ Asteroid 2034L as a weapon against the United States. His message to Abdel-Malek had been, simply, ''Will you support my position if the Islamic Union is given permanent-member status?'' That much of a shift in the balance of power had been enough to ensure a successful vote.

It was, Balmont thought, a satisfying ending to a trying day.

FIFTEEN

Interrogation Room 12
Joliet Federal Prison
1004 hours CDT

"Well, Dr. Alexander," Carruthers said with a smile. "Are you enjoying your stay at Joliet?"

Escorted by a guard, David shuffled into the bare room with its institution-green cinder-block walls and single table and set of chairs. His hands were chained to a locked belt about his waist, his feet hobbled by a short chain that kept his steps crabbed and short. He was wearing blue prison dungarees and soft shoes.

"That's *Joliet*," David replied, giving the name as close to a French pronunciation as he could manage—a softer and more musical *Zhoal-lee-ay* quite different from the harsher Anglicization Carruthers had used. "And I'm beginning to get used to it."

His mispronunciation was, in fact, a small joke. Reputedly, there was a law on the books dating back more than a hundred years which made it a crime to say the name of the town any other way than with a hard "J," short "e," and hard ending "t." Deliberately using the "illegal" form of the name was a tiny, but somehow satisfying bit of rebellion on David's part.

It was the only rebellion he was capable of at the moment. That, and not giving the bastards what they were asking for.

"It's been four weeks, now," Carruthers told him. "It could get a lot longer. And more uncomfortable, too." He nodded to the guard. "Go ahead and unlock him. He won't give me any trouble."

The chains, David had decided, where part of the show, a way to intimidate him, along with chucking him into prison with the threat of no trial. Joliet, he had to admit, was a scary place. Once a state prison in the town of Joliet, sixty kilometers southwest of Chicago, the facility had been converted to a federal prison in 2010 as part of a government prison buyout plan. It was a hot, noisy, and dismal place, a place in which he had no intention of staying.

Even if he didn't yet know how he was going to get out of this.

"You guys are playing pretty fast and loose with the Constitution," David said as the guard unlocked the cuffs and chains. He sat down in the chair opposite Carruthers, who was opening up an executive-model large-screen PAD. "Last I heard even spies had a right to a speedy trial."

"So Ms. Dutton has been telling us. In peacetime, normally, that's true . . . though, you know, the dockets are awfully crowded lately. In wartime, well, even the best court system can fall behind on the paperwork quite a bit."

Julia Dutton was his lawyer. "If you're here to question me," he said, "I think I want Ms. Dutton here with me. I have *that* right, too, even in wartime."

"Jailhouse lawyer, huh?" Carruthers smiled. "Well, we'll have her come on down, if that's what you want. But I'm not here to question you right now. In fact, to tell you the truth I think we have all the evidence we need to put you away for a long, long time. I don't *think* you'll get the death penalty for espionage . . . though these days, with juries the way they are, and all the bad public feeling against the UN, you just never know. . . ."

"And for the hundredth time, at least, I wasn't spying on anybody!"

"You faxed a model to François Villeret at the Sorbonne. You've been communicating with Jean-Etienne

Cheseaux for months. You've been transferring classified electronic documents to this Pastor Blaine kook in Chicago. Now, maybe you don't call that spying, but the Federal government does.''

David sighed. They'd been through this before. "I told you. I admit to communicating with Cheseaux and Villeret, and even a few others. But they're scientists. And friends. My relationship with them has nothing to do with the war.''

"Your *problem*, Doctor, is that you have this *problem* with enemy identification. Those people are working for the European Union. Which means they're working for the United Nations.''

"Maybe. But the information we exchanged had no military value. As for the records sent to the Church of the Divine whatever, that's total nonsense. I never did any such thing.''

Carruthers pursed his lips. "Actually, I think I believe you on that point.''

"Eh? You do?''

"After we started monitoring your home system, we checked the times of the transmissions to Blaine against your whereabouts. You weren't at home when the transmissions were made.''

"Then what . . . ah! Liana.''

"Now, we *could* assume that your wife was making those transmissions at your orders. I mean, the files in question were passcode protected, weren't they?''

"Of course.''

"Of course. Still, given your wife's, um, extreme religious beliefs, and her connections with Blaine and some other cult leaders, we'd probably have trouble proving in court that you had anything to do with it.''

"I'm relieved to here it.'' Liana! How the hell had she gotten at his files? The woman couldn't program a toaster without getting into trouble. He didn't think she could handle any part of the home system except the entertainment channels. Maybe he'd been underestimating her; in an odd, almost perverse way, he found he was proud of her.

"But we could still nail you just for not keeping con-

fidential material safe on your home system. And we're
for sure going to run your ass up the flagpole for passing
confidential information to the UNdies.''

"Look. I'll say it again, as clearly and monosyllabically
as I can. I did not violate any security regulations by talking to Dr. Cheseaux or any of the others. Yes, I faxed a
copy of a plaque I found at Picard to Dr. Villeret at the
Sorbonne. As far as I was aware, the thing was not even
classified. Certainly, there was no information on it that
would have compromised security! No plans for super-
bombs. No maps to hidden fortifications. Nothing that
would have hurt the United States!''

"For your information, everything that came back from
the Moon with your expedition was classified! You'd have
known that if you'd read your debriefing forms! As for
the plaque's message being harmless, who the hell appointed *you* as a judge of American security? What makes
you think you can say what might be important to the
enemy, and what isn't? Maybe just the fact that we have
the thing is important, you ever stop to consider that? You
damned scientists are all alike, talking about global scientific communities, but you're not able to see past your
next government grant! Well, I've got news for you, Alexander. You are in violation of some very heavy regulations. In fact, you are in one hurtin' world of trouble.
Unless you decide to cooperate with us.''

"By selling out my friends.''

"By helping your country! Look, I'm not a hard guy.
And I'm not hard to get along with. All we're asking is
that you do just what you've been doing with these, ah,
backdoor contacts of yours. Talk to them. Maybe ask them
some questions. Maybe pass along some select information that we'll provide you with, from time to time.''

"No.''

"Don't be hasty, now.''

"I said no! These people are my friends. They trust me,
and I trust them. I won't have anything to do with this!''

"Ah. Your final word?''

"Absolutely.''

"Well, if you say so, then that's the way it'll be.'' He

stood, then stretched. "So, you say you're getting used to this place? That's good. That's real good." He turned and started to leave, then appeared to think better of it. Turning again, he gave David a twisted smile. "So, you been taking your TBEs lately?"

The question was so unexpected—and such a non sequitur—that David blinked, unsure of the FBI agent's point. TBEs—Telemere Binding Enzymes—had been available to the general public for a number of years now. The tablets were expensive, and no one could yet say how well they worked, but David had always figured the chance they offered was worth the cost. But how had Carruthers known? "Uh . . . yeah. . . ."

"Thought so. You look pretty young. Younger than your forties, that's for sure. Figured you must be on the regime. Those things are supposed to add . . . what? A hundred years to your life? A hundred fifty?"

David shrugged. "No one knows." What the hell was Carruthers getting at? TBEs were one step up from the popular fad drugs and herbal remedies available in health stores; supposedly, they bound up the telemeres—the protein caps on the ends of DNA molecules that became unraveled with age—and helped stop or slow the aging process itself. The stuff hadn't been sanctioned by the FDA, yet, but millions of people took daily TBE tabs in the hope that they held the key to long and youthful life.

"No one knows," Carruthers repeated. "I'll tell you, I always figured TBEs were a crock. Like some of the claims the cultists make for their ancient astronauts, y'know? The claims people make sound pretty wild, and there's no good way to test them. I mean, people haven't been taking them long enough yet to see if they work as well as advertised. They might not do anything at all."

"What's your point, Carruthers?"

"Oh, nothing much. I was just wondering, though, what it must feel like knowing you could be in here for another, oh, century and a half. You're forty-one, according to your record, right? That's not too old, but, still, without your TBEs, you might be in here another thirty, maybe forty years before you finally kicked off. That's a long, long time. Especially for a bright guy like you. But another century or two? Man, that's a hell of a stretch. A guy could go mad, being locked up in here for a couple of centuries, nothing to do, no way out, no friends except the guards and the other inmates. And, you know what? The food here just isn't that good. . . .''

David swayed a bit in his chair, a roaring in his ears, a dryness in his throat. He'd tolerated life at Joliet for these past few weeks knowing that he wouldn't be there much longer; the charges against him were ridiculous . . . trivial, even. He'd given nothing of political or military value to "the enemy"; at worst he was guilty of bad judgment.

But for the very first time, now, he teetered at the edge of an abyss, knowing that these people had the power to take away his freedom for the rest of his life, however long that might be. The prospect was terrifying.

"Maybe I'll stop taking them." Somehow, he kept his voice from shaking. "Just to spite you."

"Yeah? And maybe I'll leave orders for the dietary staff to mix 'em in with your food. I'm that kind of guy, you know?" He sounded cheerful about it.

"You can't keep me here for the rest of my life, damn it! Go ahead! Put me on trial! The worst I could get is a few years, And I didn't get any money for this supposed espionage of mine. The case'll be thrown out. Hell, I might sue you for false arrest!"

"Well, we'll worry about that when the time comes. It'll only happen, though, if your case actually comes to trial. You see, what lots of folks don't know is that the government has certain powers it can exercise in wartime. Suspension of *habeas corpus* is one of 'em. Your right to a speedy trial, well, things slow down in wartime. And people get lost in the cracks." He folded his arms, leaning back in his chair. "Not many people know this, but ever since 1933 the United States has essentially been operating under an ongoing declared presidential state of emergency. All it takes is the stroke of a pen to revoke a lot of 'rights' Americans take for granted. They can be arrested for saying the wrong things. They can be relocated to special camps. Held without trial. 'National security' is a very large blanket that can cover a hell of a lot of pretty nasty stuff. Why, you'd be amazed—''

''You can't keep me locked up in here forever, goddammit!''

''Just try me, Dr. Alexander. Just try me! You could simply disappear in here, and no one would ever know! You could lose any right you have to access the Net, so you wouldn't even know what others were doing with your research. You'd be cut off from your career, from everyone you know and love, from everything you've done and hoped for, as completely as if you were dead!'' He smiled. ''But, as I was saying earlier, I'm a reasonable kind of guy. If you make me happy, why, I just can't do enough for you. But, man, if you piss me off, I'll just go out of my way to make life as miserable for you as I possibly can. And if that means seeing to it that you don't see daylight for two hundred years, that's *exactly* what I'll do.''

Something thumped against the door to the interrogation room, and David heard muffled shouts outside. A moment later, the door banged open, and Julia Dutton walked in, a tall, slender black woman with steel in her jaw and fire in her eye. A guard hurried after her.

''Damn it, I said we weren't to be disturbed!'' Carruthers shouted at the guard.

''Tough!'' Dutton said. ''Just what the hell do you think you're doing, Carruthers, questioning my client in my absence?''

''Just offering him the best deal he's going to hear. I'd advise him to take it, if I were you.'' He gave them both a satisfied smile, then left them alone in the room.

She dropped her briefcase on the table. She wore a conservative suit; the only jewelry David noticed was a quiet subdermal pattern of yellow stars and moons flashing on and off around the outer corner of her left eye.

''Haven't you learned yet, David?'' she said. ''Don't you talk to any of these sons of bitches, don't you even give them the *time* unless I'm here with you!''

David found his heart was pounding hard and fast after the encounter. He was sweating, and it had nothing to do with the temperature of the room. "I didn't agree to anything."

"What did he want?"

"I think they want to use me to plant disinformation in the enemy camp. Maybe spy on some friends of mine." He shook his head. "I won't do it, counselor."

She didn't look at him for a long moment. "You may not have much choice. Not if you want out of here before the war ends."

He looked up at her sharply. "He told me he could make me . . . disappear. He said they could keep me from going to trial and just keep me locked away for the rest for my life! Julia, they *can't* just keep me locked up in here, can they?"

She took too long to answer. "David, I'm afraid you've made some people mad. Powerful people. This ancient-alien gods garbage is getting out of hand, with its end-times melodrama and its message that our real allegiance is to angelic beings or whatever on some other planet. Some people, high up, think it could undermine the war effort. And they see you at the center of this thing."

"I don't have anything to do with those lunatic cults!"

"Guess again. You found those human skeletons on Mars and uploaded the news to the whole world. You found the Cave of Wonders in the Cydonian Face, with all those weird aliens on TV, including some that look like they might be the folks who were visiting this part of the galactic neighborhood just a few thousand years ago. And you found those tablets on the Moon, with information that got passed on to the churches almost before it was deciphered."

"I didn't—"

She raised a slim hand. "I know. You didn't. But you *did* broadcast that stuff from Mars all over the Net for everyone to see and download."

"They—the UN—were trying to suppress it!"

"And you kept them from doing that, yes. Kept them from suppressing *your* discovery. Your little news flash from Mars probably caused the UN a lot of domestic problems, just when they didn't need them. But it also caused

Washington some similar problems. And that wasn't appreciated.''

''So . . . what? I betray these people, and that makes it better?''

''It makes you some friends in high places. And, believe me, David. You need some right now.''

''Just whose side are you on, anyway?''

''Yours,'' she snapped. ''And don't you forget that! Now . . . I've got some things to go over with you, here. . . .''

She opened her briefcase and began laying out papers for his inspection. He couldn't really focus on them, though. Though he hated to admit it, even to himself, Carruthers had found a deadly, weak chink in his armor. David was an archeologist, but that didn't mean he was suited to the academic, indoor life. He was, above all, a *digger*, a man who lived for getting out in the field and conducting his own excavations, who still felt that spine-tingling thrill each time he picked up a coin or a pottery shard or a graven bone tool and knew that he was the *first*, in some thousands of years, to see and touch that bit of human ingenuity, industry, and artistic skill. He needed the sun on his face . . . the dirt under his fingernails.

His love of fieldwork had taken him as far as Mars and the Moon. How could he possibly cut himself off from that?

But how could he buy his freedom by betraying his friends? An impossible dilemma. Worse was the growing fear that he was on the *wrong side*, that somehow, when he'd not been looking, the so-called land of the free, home of the brave had acquired some of the blood-encrusted patina of a police state.

War could bring out the worst in people and in governments. Just as, occasionally, it brought out the best.

He found himself thinking of the Marine, Kaminski. The man had little education, but a good mind, a kind heart . . . and absolutely unimpeachable loyalty to his buddies and to the Corps.

What David admired most about the Marines, he thought, was the way they looked out for one another.

He'd been with Garroway on the March from Heinlein Station to Mars Prime; the esprit, the camaraderie, the sense of belonging during that cramped, uncomfortable, and desperate three-week trek through a portion of the Valles Marineris had been downright magical. Powerful. Throughout that time, there'd been a sense of us-against-the-world, a do-or-die flame that could not be quenched.

Marines never left their own behind. *Never*. They didn't turn on their own. They *belonged* to one another in a way civilians could never quite comprehend.

The scientific community was hardly the same as the United States Marine Corps. Still, David wondered if he'd somehow assimilated Marine values after being locked up with them for three weeks on that grueling march.

Semper fi!

Recruit Platoon 4239
Parris Island Recruit Training
Center
1510 hours EDT

"Move it, move it, *move* it, recruits!" Gunnery Sergeant Knox yelled. "*Hit* that wall! *Up* and over! We don't have all freakin' day!"

Jack ran down the path, taking the muddy stretch in two steps, then leaping, high and hard, slamming against the wooden barrier, his outstretched arms snagging the log at the top three meters above the ground. He chinned himself, dragging his body up and over. *Couldn't have done* that *ten weeks ago*, he thought, a little wildly. As he straddled the barrier, the next recruit behind him leaped and slammed; Lonnie Costantino's hands were muddy from an earlier fall, and he nearly lost his precarious handhold. Without thinking, Jack reached down with a hard, forearm grip, helping the other recruit over the top.

"Thanks, man!" Lonnie gasped.

"Semper fi, man," Jack repeated, dropping down the farside of the wall. Technically, each recruit was being timed on this run, with the results entered in his final record. In fact, the average time of the entire platoon was what counted toward the awards and honors ceremonies at graduation next week. It was one small part of the not-so-subtle process of indoctrination here. You could run the obstacle course as fast as you could and get the best personal time possible. *Or* you could help your platoon win.

By this time, the recruits scarcely needed to think about that. They were a unit, a team. The good of the platoon came before the good of any individual.

Knox was still shouting as more recruits came over the wall. "What're you ladies *waiting* for? I don't wanna see *nothing* here but amphibious green blurs! . . ."

Amphibious green Marines. It was an old concept, dating back at least to Vietnam. There were no black Marines, the saying went. No white or yellow or red Marines. Only amphibious green Marines. Recruit Platoon 4239 was down to fifty-one men now, and they made up a fair cross section of American society. Twelve were African-American, seven were Asian, fifteen were Latino. One, John Horse, was Lakota, while Gary Lim was Polynesian. Such distinctions, though, had been lost on the recruits a long time ago, lost in their step-by-step metamorphosis from civilians to Marines.

Another hard, quick run, a leap, a grab. Jack snatched hold of the Cable, a massive rope, stretched at an angle across the mud pit, which bounced and swung dizzyingly as he gripped it with hands and legs and began working his way along it, head down. If he slipped and fell, tradition demanded that he emerge from the mud singing the "Marine Corps Hymn" at the top of his voice; he'd done that a time or two in weeks past and knew it would knock precious seconds from his score.

He didn't slip, not this time. He hit the ground running, as Knox made a notation on a PAD and kept on shouting. "Go-go-go-*go*!"

Jack attacked the final line of obstacles with a second wind that was more of the spirit than in his lungs. Flat on his back in the mud, he slithered forward beneath tangles of barbed wire, as an old-fashioned machine gun yammered somewhere close by, live bullets snapping and hissing a meter or two above his body.

One more week, and he would be a Marine. A *Marine*, not a recruit. Even now it was hard to credit; boot camp had been his whole life for so long he scarcely gave a thought anymore to what was going on outside the narrow, isolated, sandbagged and leveed world of Parris Island.

It was hard to imagine being free of the mud and the aching muscles, of the night firewatches and the sand fleas, of the drills and Gunny Knox.

Damned if I'm not going to miss this. The thought made him laugh. Somewhere along the line, he'd gone over that infamous hump that every recruit faced.

Gung ho! All together . . .

EU Science Research Vessel
Pierre-Simon Laplace
In Trans-Lunar Space
2150 hours GMT

Laplace was eight thousand kilometers from 2034L, falling toward the distant twin-star pair of Earth and Moon, when Jean-Etienne Cheseaux saw the flash. It was small, an unremarkable pulse of light partially blocked by the body of the asteroid itself, but his instruments registered hard radiation—gamma and a flux of high-speed neutrons—together with the electromagnetic pulse that was the characteristic fingerprint of a nuclear detonation.

"Damn them!" Cheseaux exclaimed, pulling back from the eyepiece on his broad-spectrum analyzer. He checked the readouts again, to be sure there was no mistake. "*Damn* them! What do they think they're doing?"

The second EU ship, the *Sagittaire*, had rendezvoused with *Laplace* and 2034L over a month before. Two weeks ago, *Laplace* had been ordered to return to Earth.

Cheseaux had liked no part of the arrangement. *Sagittaire* was unmistakably a military ship, with a dorsally mounted ball turret that he suspected housed a high-energy laser. What possible interest could a military vessel and crew have in an asteroid orbiting the sun in deep space?

He could think of only one possible reason, and the mere possibility chilled him to the core. *They couldn't be thinking of . . . that!*

Colonel Armand and the rest of *Laplace*'s small crew were eager to leave the desolate boulder in space and return to the Moon, but Cheseaux had found a pretext to stay—a broken spectrometer and the urgent need for some additional data on 2034L's chemical composition.

A message had arrived from Earth a few days later. *Laplace* had until the twenty-third and then she *must* burn for the return trajectory. Food and water would soon be a problem, and the crew of the *Laplace* were obviously angered at Cheseaux's apparent scientific fussiness.

Let them fuss! As *Laplace* had completed her burn, falling into a vector that would carry her to the Moon and then to home, he'd stayed at the science vessel's instrument suite, watching the asteroid and the tiny *Sagittaire* hanging in its shadow.

He wasn't surprised when the nuclear explosion briefly flared against the night, but the horror nearly overwhelmed him. Maybe, *maybe* they were changing the asteroid's orbit for some other purpose than the one he feared, but he couldn't imagine what that purpose might be. A base of some sort? Raw materials for the highly secret construction rumored to be proceeding on the Lunar farside?

As hour followed hour and he continued to watch the change in 2034L's course, the surer he became. Running simulations on his computer suggested that the nuclear blast—which he estimated to be in the fifty- to one-hundred-kiloton range—had nudged the tiny, flying mountain just enough to swing it inward, ever so slightly toward the Earth.

His software wasn't good enough, and his measurements over the course of twenty-some hours weren't precise enough and they didn't cover a long enough span of time, but Cheseaux was now convinced that the European Union government was planning to smash 2034L into the Earth. He wasn't sure of the target; it might be Russia, which would be on the outer, nightside of Earth at impact.

But it might also be aimed at the United States, which would be on the trailing, sunset side of the planet when the asteroid came plunging in from space.

The sheer irresponsibility of the act was staggering; not for the first time, Cheseaux wondered if he was on the right side of this war. He rarely followed politics; politicians were buffoons at best, criminals at worst, and any claims they laid to concern for ordinary people was purely for show. Still, he'd read the Geneva Report and thought that its conclusion—that civilization could collapse across the planet if Earth was not united under one rule within another eight years—was accurate, if unduly pessimistic in the timetable it presented.

But, *mon Dieu*! How serious could they be about their concern for the plight of Earth's billions when they were willing to drop an asteroid on the planet? It was insane!

For the next hour, Cheseaux thought carefully about what he must do. He could talk to Colonel Armand, of course . . . but that didn't seem to be a productive option. What could the man do, save, possibly, join his protest to Cheseaux's? And he certainly wouldn't condone the single other option Cheseaux could think of, the only option possible, under the circumstances.

No, Cheseaux would have to shoulder this particular responsibility alone.

After copying the visual and spectographic records of the explosion and the observations that showed the asteroid's new and deadly orbit to PAD microdisk, he made his way hand over hand through the zero-G complexity of the ship to this quarters.

He had an important call to make. . . .

SIXTEEN

Interrogation Room 12
Joliet Federal Prison
1445 hours CDT

The FBI special agent was different, this time, not Carruthers, but a small, dark-haired man with a worried accountant's expression. He had a large-screen executive PAD open on the table as they led David in. "Dr. Alexander?" He stood, and offered a hand which David refused. "I'm Bill Twiggs. We need to talk."

"Not without my lawyer present," David replied.

Twiggs sighed. "Dr. Alexander . . . *David*, this is not a formal interrogation. We need your help."

"That's what Carruthers has been telling me for the past month. I am not going to use my friends as, as intelligence sources."

"All I want you to do is read this." He turned the PAD so that David could read what was on the screen.

The header was David's own Net address. This was a message sent to him, which someone else had intercepted electronically.

MY DEAR DAVID:

DO YOU REMEMBER OUR CONVERSATION ON THE THIRD NIGHT OF THAT CONFERENCE IN ATHENS? WE WERE AT THE HOTEL POOL, AND YOU WERE WITH

THAT ENTRANCING WOMAN NAMED DANI OR DAN-
IELLE, OR DONNA, I FORGET EXACTLY. WE TALKED,
YOU AND I, ABOUT SOMETHING OF TERRIBLE IM-
PORT.

IT IS IMPERATIVE THAT WE TALK AGAIN, OLD
FRIEND. A DIRECT VID CONNECT WOULD BE BEST,
SCRAMBLED, ENCRYPTED, AND SECURE. SEND IT VIA
THE USUAL ROUTE. I'LL ARRANGE TO HAVE IT RE-
LINKED HERE.

YOUR GOVERNMENT MUST KNOW WHAT I HAVE
SEEN HERE. PLEASE LINK IN PERSONALLY AS
QUICKLY AS POSSIBLE. MOST URGENT!

JEAN-ETIENNE

David read the message through twice, his mind racing.
His first thought was that this was some sort of a trick,
that the FBI was baiting him with this message in an effort
to set up the backdoor intelligence line they wanted him
to establish with Jean-Etienne.

The more he thought about it, though, the less likely
that seemed. The message header proved it had arrived
encoded, so someone had broken that code before delivering the message to him; they didn't need him for that.
The reference to the Athens conference, well, how could
the Feds know that much detail? His attendance at the
conference was a matter of public record, but they
wouldn't know about Donni, unless Donni herself had
been a spy.

Despite himself, he smiled at that small stab of paranoia.
Just because you're paranoid, the old saying went, it didn't
mean they *weren't* out to get you. Still, Donni, a graduate
student spending a year in Greece, had been anything *but*
a government agent. He would stake anything on that, including the nights they'd spent together in bed. Besides,
she'd been in the pool, a nude and gaily playful water
nymph, when he and Jean-Etienne had had that particular
conversation.

He remembered the conversation well, too.

"David, we intercepted this message through our court-

ordered tap on your home-computer system," Twiggs
said. "We know that you have been in communication
with Dr. Cheseaux in the past . . . as recently, in fact, as
the tenth of April, just before your departure for Luna. We
would very much like to know what has Dr. Cheseaux so
worried."

"I'll bet you would," David replied.

"Dr. Alexander, please! We're not trying to get you to
betray anything, or anyone! From the contents of this message, it sounds as though Cheseaux *wants* to tell us something. Specifically, he wants to talk to you, and to tell you
something he thinks Washington needs to know."

How were they using this situation against him? The
message had to be from Jean-Etienne. There was simply
no way they could have gotten that level of detail on his
meeting with Cheseaux in Athens.

"I'll be honest with you, Dr. Alexander," Twiggs went
on. "We are extremely concerned right now about some
sort of weapon the UN is building on the farside of the
Moon, a weapon which they used two months ago to destroy one of our reconnaissance craft. We believe this
weapon is a device that creates, contains, and fires a beam
of positrons. Antimatter. The weapon almost certainly uses
technology acquired from the aliens you've called the An.
In fact, they may have picked up an intact antimatter reactor or generator at Picard, shortly before you visited that
site.

"What we are wondering, quite frankly, is whether Dr.
Cheseaux might have some information on the UN
antimatter-beam project for us. Was that what the two of
you were discussing in Athens? Such a weapon would be
devastatingly powerful, certainly. A spacecraft armed with
such a weapon would be able to obliterate any city on
Earth and would be next to impossible to destroy. Might
he oppose antimatter research on humanitarian grounds?"

"No . . ." David said, softly.

Twiggs looked surprised. "We have quite a dossier on
Cheseaux. While he's not a confirmed pacifist, he doesn't
seem the sort of man who would advocate wholesale destruction of cities."

"Eh? Oh, no. Of course not. He wouldn't. What I was saying no to . . . well, you have the wrong idea. We weren't talking about antimatter weapons that afternoon in Greece."

"Oh? What were you discussing?"

David drew in a deep breath, then let it out slowly. "Asteroids. Specifically, how easy it would be for an irresponsible government to turn one into a weapon."

"Go on."

"Actually, we talked about a lot of things." He smiled, thinking of Donni. "And not all of them had to do with business. But, looking back, I think he must be referring to our discussion about using asteroids to bombard an enemy." He shifted in his seat, suddenly uncomfortable. "This is really Dr. Cheseaux's field, not mine. He's the astronomer. But we got to talking about some unexplained climatic changes in Earth's history, times when the climate grew much colder."

"The ice ages?"

"Oh, no. Nothing that dramatic. There is evidence, though . . . rather vague evidence, in fact, but evidence, that something strange happened in Europe in, oh, about A.D. 500, I think it was. Rome had fallen, but you couldn't say that life was that much worse for the fall. But, well, some of the records of the times hint at unusually cold winters. At crops failing with the long winters. At 'dragons' and other aerial phenomena in the skies. At unusual sunsets and glows in the skies. Some theorists have suggested the Earth was hit by one or even several small asteroids that threw up enough dust into the atmosphere to change the climate. There are other cases like that in the Middle Ages, too."

"I read something once," Twiggs said, "about a . . . a minimum of some sort in the Middle Ages? Making the winters unusually harsh?"

"That would be the Maunder Minimum, and that referred to a decrease in solar activity, not asteroid strikes. We talked about that, too, as I recall. The point was that Earth's climate is really terribly delicate. Volcanic eruptions like Tambora and Krakatoa and Pinatubo have put enough dust in the air to lower global temperatures and cause unusually severe winters for years. Fifty years ago, scientists were discussing 'nuclear winter,' a possible ice age brought on by the exchange of nuclear weapons. And the KT event—the asteroid or comet that struck the Yucatán sixty-five million years ago—must have turned high noon into midnight all over the Earth for a year or more. Something like seventy percent of all of the living species on the planet died off, became extinct.''

"I wonder," Twiggs said. "Now that global warming is accepted, we know the sea levels are rising . . . I wonder if some folks haven't been thinking about dropping mountains on the planet to deliberately stop the temperature rise."

"I can't believe anybody would be that irresponsible," David replied. "I mean, how do you balance a thing like that? How do you know just how many degrees the average temperature is going to drop?" He snorted. "I'd rather go with some of the cultists and a few blue-sky technoarcheologists who claim we're going to find a cure for the warming in the ruins on Mars."

"You think we will?"

"It's possible. They were way ahead of us, whoever they were, and they were certainly trying to alter the Martian climate. We know that much. But it'll take a long time to figure out how they were doing it.

"Anyway, in the past fifty years or so, we've been finding out just how vulnerable Earth is to bombardment by asteroids. Even a small one, a few hundred megatons, say, could conceivably change our climate, bring on a sudden cooling that might last for years. We learned back in the nineties that near misses were frequent, that multimegaton asteroids that exploded high up in the atmosphere—usually well away from inhabited areas—were commonplace, every few years or so. In any given century chosen randomly, it turns out you have a good chance of at least one major impact, somewhere on Earth.

"And that's what we face *naturally*. Now. You get some unscrupulous dictator who has a grudge against the

United States and owns his own spacecraft. He finds a convenient asteroid, ideally one that already passes within a million or two kilometers every few years. He gives it a tiny, tiny nudge . . . just so . . . and a few years or months later, it comes thundering down, dead on target. Bang. Armageddon in a conveniently sized package.''

''And that was what you and Cheseaux were talking about in Athens? You think that's what he's referring to in this message?''

''That would be my guess. We talked about lots of things but . . . yeah, that would have to be it.''

''I see.'' Twiggs was silent for a long time. ''Two days ago, one of our orbital telescopes picked up a flash in space, somewhere out beyond the orbit of the Moon. We weren't able to confirm the flash, and it could have been a strictly deep-space phenomenon, but the spectrum matched that of a small, low-yield nuclear detonation.

''What has some folks worried is the fact that the position of that explosion was quite close to the expected position of a small asteroid, a near-Earth asteroid, one discovered only a few years ago. The coincidence seems a bit too much, here. There's been some speculation in Washington that someone has just . . . as you put it, given that rock a nudge. It sounds as though Cheseaux might have some information about that.''

''I don't see how. He's in Paris.''

Twiggs smiled. ''Apparently your pen pal doesn't tell you everything. See here in his message where he's talking about having your reply relinked 'here'? Cheseaux has been on an EU space mission for the past two months.''

''In space!''

''Intelligence tells us he's the chief science specialist on an asteroid rendezvous mission. With that same damned asteroid.''

''Oh . . . God . . .''

''In light of all this, I wonder if you would consider calling the guy back and getting some clarification? Or confirmation.''

David felt light-headed. This was all happening too fast.

Any thought that this might be some sort of elaborate deception by the government was gone; it felt too . . . *right*. The UN was preparing to drop an asteroid onto the Earth somewhere, and Jean-Etienne—bless the man!—wanted to talk about it, to warn the United States.

"Yes. Of course I will."

"Thank you," Twiggs said. "You know, we do appreciate this. I know you don't have . . . well, any cause to trust us. Or a reason to want to help us, or even talk to me."

David shrugged. "You talk to me like a human being. Carruthers makes threats. There's a difference."

"Will you talk to Cheseaux now?"

"Will you let me go if I do? That was Carruthers's deal, you know. I talk to my French buddies so that our side gets the intel. That's what I'm doing now, isn't it?"

"I'm sorry, Dr. Alexander. I can't promise anything. But I'll certainly talk to my superiors and see what we can arrange."

David considered this. Almost, he decided not to help until there was a more substantial offer. *Hell with it,* he thought. *This is too important.* "Give me the computer."

It didn't take long to establish the connection. Using Twiggs's PAD, David logged into his home system, then linked through the series of anonymous servers that put him in touch with Cheseaux's home system in Paris. There, he left a v-mail stating that he was ready for a real-time link; how soon that was depended on how soon Cheseaux contacted his home system from space, but a flashing "You've got a message" alert on his PAD would let him know that one was waiting.

In fact, just five minutes and twenty seconds passed before Twiggs's PAD shifted to real-time mode and an image built itself up, in rippling clusters of pixels, of his old friend Jean-Etienne Cheseaux.

"Jean-Etienne!" David exclaimed. "*Bon jour!*"

For several long seconds, the face on the PAD's screen showed no reaction. Cheseaux's face looked lined and worn, and he'd not shaved in several days. His head and shoulders were not perfectly aligned up and down on the screen, and David realized that the man must be drifting in zero G. The background was nondescript and fuzzily out of focus, but David was pretty sure he recognized the sort of thin, cubicle partition common aboard manned spacecraft that he'd grown all too familiar with during his months of deep-space voyaging to Mars and back.

Suddenly, Cheseaux's face brightened, and something of the old sparkle returned to those intensely blue eyes. "David! *Allo!* I see your accent has not improved in the past months. And it is evening here. We are on GMT."

"I got your message. I remember that night in Athens. Ah . . . I should tell you, I'm not alone. There are people here who're worried about what you might have to say."

Again there was no response. David silently counted off four seconds before the worn face on the screen reacted to his words. Time delay. He'd forgotten about that. A four-second there-and-back lag time, though, meant that Jean-Etienne must be two light-seconds away. The Moon was about one and a quarter light-seconds away, with a two-and-a-half-second round-trip lag. The UN ship must be something just under twice the Moon's distance from the Earth . . . a million kilometers or so.

"Government people? CIA? Military Intelligence? That is good. What I have to say, they need to hear." He glanced back over his shoulder, then pulled himself closer to his PAD's optical pickup. The encryption algorithms in the comm software at both ends of the conversation should keep their talk secure from electronic eavesdroppers, but he was evidently concerned about being overheard by other members of his ship's crew. "David, they have gone mad, back on Earth. Back in Geneva! I have some data for you. See that the right people see it!"

He pressed some keys, out of sight below the image frame, and the amber light on David's PAD indicating a high-speed data transfer began winking. It took only a few seconds, with most of that time taken up by the decryption process at David's end.

"We shouldn't talk longer, my friend," Cheseaux said.

"It would not be good if I were found out." His eyes narrowed suddenly, and he seemed to be examining David's image on his PAD's screen. David realized Cheseaux must just now be noticing the dungarees he was wearing, and the number stenciled just above the left breast pocket. "Ah," Cheseaux said, nodding sadly. "Perhaps you already know the risks involved."

David glanced at Twiggs, who was sitting nearby, watching intently . . . but who was too far away to interrupt a message, if it was quick. "I do," he replied. "Be sure to tell François and the others. *Au revoir, mon ami.*"

He cut the link with a single quick tap to the touchscreen keyboard. Twiggs had not reacted to his warning to Cheseaux, so either the man really didn't care, or he'd missed it. If the little ring of French and German scientists that David had been communicating with knew that he was in prison, though, it would be a lot harder for the US government to reach them with disinformation transferred through him.

Of course, it was always possible that David's transmission was being intercepted somewhere, edited, and sent on its way. That would explain part of a four-second time delay very nicely as well. He didn't let himself dwell on that, however, because there was nothing at all he could do about it.

"So," he said as Twiggs took the PAD back and began checking on the data transferred from space. "Can I go, now? Home, I mean?"

"I hope so, Dr. Alexander," Twiggs said. "I really do. But I wouldn't get my hopes up. Carruthers is in charge of your case, and, well, let's just say that he's very goal-driven, very one-track. I don't really know what he has in mind for you. All I can do is promise to talk to my superiors, and see what we can do."

"I understand." Carruthers would see a recording of the conversation with Cheseaux, and know that David had warned the other side. He wondered if Carruthers would see his plan as a lost cause and give it up.

Or if he would begin thinking of retribution.

Institute for Exoarcheological
Studies
Chicago, Illinois
1622 hours CDT

"I'd like to speak with Ms. Dutton, please," Teri said, staring up at the big corporate logo for Smithfield, Klein, and Jorgenson, Attorneys-at-Law.

"Julia Dutton is not in the office," the genteel voice of an AI replied. "Will you hold while we relay your call?"

"Yes, I'll hold."

She glanced out the office window as she waited, looking down at the sea of people that by now was a routine part of the afternoon scenery along Lake Shore Drive. The astronut crowds didn't seem to realize yet that David Alexander was no longer here.

Hell, David's on his way to being the astronuts' patron saint, she thought. *You'd think they'd care what happened to him.*

A chirp brought her attention back to the screen, where the corporate logo winked out and was replaced by the face of an attractive black woman with green-and-scarlet-striped hair. A pattern of glowing stars and moons winked next to her eye. "Julia Dutton."

"Ms. Dutton? Dr. Theresa Sullivan. Remember me?"

Dutton's dispassionate mien warmed a bit. "Yes, of course, Dr. Sullivan. Good to see you again."

The camera angle had the face off-center on the screen and was aimed awkwardly up. Teri guessed that the lawyer had her PAD on the seatback tray table of a commuter maglev. "Well? Do you know anything?"

Dutton's eyebrows rose higher on her face. "About what?"

"About David! He's been in prison for a month now! And this past week, they won't even let me in to see him . . . and a letter I wrote was returned with 'Addressee unknown' stamped on the envelope! I can't even get through on PAD-vid or v-mail! And no one at the prison I talk to seems to have any idea what I'm talking about! Just what the hell is going on?"

"Dr. Sullivan . . ."

"Is he dead? Has something happened to him? I want to *know*! . . ."

"Dr. Sullivan!"

"Sorry . . ."

"I know what you've been going through. Believe me, I know. I've been getting the same runaround since last Friday, when I came to consult with him and was told he'd been released."

"Released! Was he?"

"Hell, no. The proper papers hadn't been filed, either here or with the court that issued the original arrest order in Chicago. They were just trying to get rid of me. I can be an *awful* pest when I put my mind to it."

"Well . . . what happened, then? Where is he?"

"Depending on who you talk to in the system, David is: a) a free man, already released; b) transferred to Fort Leavenworth, Kansas; c) dead."

"Dead!"

"You'd at least think the sons of bitches would get their cover stories straight!"

"Well, if he's not dead—"

"He's not, honey. If he were, there'd be a record at the Medical Examiner's Office in Chicago and in the penitentiary records office."

"Okay. Where is he?"

"As near as I can tell, he's still right there in Joliet." Suddenly, Dutton looked very tired. Her face sagged. "I'm coming home on the Joliet commuter mag now. Been out there all day trying to get someone to talk to me. My guess is they're holding him incommunicado. No outside contacts. They may be trying to pressure him into cooperating with them. Tell me. Do you have any idea what they might be after?"

"I'm not even sure I know who you mean by 'they.' "

"God knows. I don't. The government. Some agency with alphabet soup initials. Your friend has made some enemies, you know. Enemies in pretty high places."

"But they can't just arrest him without cause! There's a thing called the Constitution!"

"Yup. There's also a war on, in case you haven't heard. The government has pretty broad powers during wartime. They can censor your newspaper, listen to your v-mail, read your computer files, hold you on suspicion, and draft your ass if they have a mind to. And there's not a whole lot ordinary citizens can do about it."

Tears burned Teri's eyes. It was so damned *unfair*! "I thought this was a free fucking country!"

"Welcome to the real world, lady."

"Look. He was supposed to have sent secret files to foreign nationals, right? They still have to put him on trial!"

"They don't *have* to do anything. Look, if it makes you feel better, I'm pretty sure they're just holding this over him, trying to get him to cooperate. Probably some sort of government sting on his foreign friends. Maybe a heavy-handed attempt to make them help the CIA." Dutton paused, looking thoughtful. "You know, if this is spy stuff, or even if it's just bureaucratic idiocy, we might be able to fight this with publicity."

"What, call the news services?"

"Hell, no. They'd just say a word in the right editorial ear, and the story would dry up. No, I'm thinking about David's friends. The people he knew and worked with, like you. Get enough of you together and asking uncomfortable questions, the government might have to relax a little. Who did David know that might help? Especially anyone powerful, or well connected."

"Jesus, I don't know." Teri sighed. "He's always been so damned apolitical. I don't know if he has *any* friends, outside of the archeological community." *Or the Marines*, she added to herself. The thought of a Marine regiment assaulting the walls of Joliet Penitentiary was quite appealing . . . She sighed. Not very realistic, though.

"Doesn't have to be the president of the United States. Damn it, there's *got* to be a way we can work this! I am sick to death of the government doing what it likes to people, and then blaming them for the mess."

A lawyer with a genuine sense of moral outrage, Teri thought. *No wonder David likes her.*

"So . . . you want me to start calling people he knew?"

"It couldn't hurt. Maybe a petition with a few hundred names. Or if he did know some politicians." Dutton snapped her fingers. "He must have computer files with the names of his business associates, other archeologists, museum directors, whatever. Some of them will be sure to have connections!"

A frightening idea was taking form in Teri's mind. "He does keep pretty extensive files, I know," she said. "But not at the office. At his home."

"That's not good," Dutton said. "I'd have to get a court order to see them. And if I do that, and they decide to charge him with something and take him to court, I'd have to share with the prosecution. If there was anything damaging in there—"

"No. I think I can do it," Teri said. "I can try, anyway. . . ."

"You don't sound to happy about it, hon."

"I'm not. I'm not happy about it at all. . . ."

What she would have to do was going to be the hardest thing she'd ever done in her life.

SEVENTEEN

US Joint Chiefs' Command/
Control Bunker
The Pentagon, Arlington,
Virginia
0947 hours GMT

General Montgomery Warhurst took his seat next to his boss, five-star Admiral Charles Jordan Gray, in the bunker's main briefing room. The chamber was already crowded with both high-ranking military personnel and civilians, so many that while the main players sat around the huge, oval table at the center, perhaps a hundred more, secretaries, assistants, and aides, took seats in a gallery to one side, connected electronically to their bosses through PADs and console touch screens.

Warhurst looked about, not nervously, but with a distinct sense of being a fish out of water. The commandant of the US Marine Corps was not normally an invitee to meetings of the Joint Chiefs, which consisted of the chiefs of staff of the Army, Navy, and Aerospace Force, and their entourages. In that respect, at least, the Marines were still considered to be an appendage of the Navy, though there'd been talk for a long time now about giving them a seat of their own on the JCS.

The big table was so crowded because a number of other high-powered guests were present as well: Louis Carlton Harrel, the national security advisor; Archibald

Severin, the secretary of defense; Arthur Kinsley, the director of Central Intelligence. All looked worried. The tension, the worry, the *fear* in the room all were palpable.

"Big turnout, CJ," Warhurst said *sotto voce* as he opened up his PAD on the table in front of him. "All the VIPs are out."

"Most of 'em. There was talk that President Markham would be here, too," Gray murmured. "Canceled at the last minute. Harrel, over there, will be briefing him later. This whole session is being recorded for his sake, too, so be sure to put on your best camera smile when you say your piece."

"Should I bow and say 'Mr. President'?"

"No, but be sure to keep a rein on that temper of yours. The word is we're going up against the Aerospace Force."

"They developed a counter, too?"

"Yup. And Harrel and the president are going to have to decide which one to use."

"Easy. Deploy both. If number one plan fails, we still have number two, and we double our chances of getting out of this alive."

"We may not have the resources for both."

"Resources! You mean funding? My God, CJ, the UNdies are dropping a goddamn mountain on top of us, and the bean counters are worried about money?"

"Money is always a problem, Monty, even in war, when everyone pretty much prints what he needs. But there are other assets we're going to be scrambling for, too."

Warhurst nodded. "The LSCPs."

"And HLV assets."

"We've both been saying for years that we needed a bigger permanent presence in space," Warhurst said. "An orbital military base with its own booster reserve, and at least one Lunar base and manufacturing and fuel-processing facility."

"And there's always something more urgent on the table," Gray replied. "The word is we're short of prepped Zeus IIs. That's where the bottleneck is, right now."

"Damn. We can't kill asteroids if we can't get off the friggin' planet."

An Aerospace Force colonel called the meeting to order. A moment later, Admiral Gray was standing at his place, addressing the listening personnel.

"Gentlemen and ladies. You've all seen the reports from Langley. The UN has just drastically upped the ante in the war by launching a weapon of unprecedented potential destructive force. Computer simulations confirm that, if nothing is done to alter Asteroid 2034L's present course, it will strike the central United States at precisely 2032 hours EDT on Monday, 15 September. The projectile appears to be aimed at our command/control facilities at Cheyenne Mountain and will strike with an estimated yield of two hundred to three hundred megatons. While we can evacuate the military facilities in the target area well before I-Day, the infrastructures of our NORAD and Space Command centers will be destroyed, along with the entire state of Colorado and a considerable portion of the west-central United States. Evacuation of civilians from an area stretching from Nevada to Missouri and from Wyoming to Texas is, quite frankly, completely beyond our capabilities. We estimate direct civilian casualties in the range of four to six million. We have no way of estimating civilian casualties caused by the starvation and thirst, disease, lack of medical care, and civil unrest that will certainly follow the strike, but they will certainly run into the tens of millions. In short, the effect will be similar to a massive nuclear strike against the continental United States, lacking only the aftereffects of radiation to make the comparison perfect.

"When news of this impending catastrophe was relayed to the Joint Chiefs last week, I directed the other members of the JCS to submit detailed plans by which we might counter the UN threat. Two plans have been submitted, and we will now hear summaries of both." Turning, Gray nodded to General Grace Sidney, the Aerospace Force chief of staff. "General Sidney? Would you care to start us off?"

Sidney stood, tapping out a key combination on her

PAD and bringing up an animated graphic on the big board at her back, and on the PAD screens of all of the people present. The room lights dimmed. "Thank you, Admiral.

"Our approach is straightforward and simple . . . I might even say elegant. On or before Thursday, 24 July—that's just three weeks from tomorrow—a pair of Zeus II heavy-lift boosters will put two SRE-10 Sparrowhawks into deep-space trajectory. That is, they will not be placed into orbit but will be launched essentially straight up, on a high-energy boost that will put them on a direct intercept vector with 2034L. At an altitude of twelve hundred miles, each Sparrowhawk will launch two modified VB-98 Starburst missiles, each carrying a single GB-8020 thermonuclear warhead with a yield of forty megatons apiece. Each Sparrowhawk will also launch three additional VB-98s, each carrying cluster decoy munitions."

On the screen, the mission unfolded in animated graphics, as two delta-winged craft climbed straight out from the Earth, then released a total of eight slender missiles before starting the long fall back home.

"The Sparrowhawks will fall back toward the Earth, reenter, and glide to dead-stick landings. The missiles, which will have been modified with solid-fuel boosters to give them a high sustained delta-v, will proceed toward the target behind the decoys, on a trajectory that will take seven days. The decoys will detonate at precisely determined points to confuse enemy tracking and scanning. They will also disperse clouds of microchaff, which will scatter any antimissile laser fire from the *Sagittaire* and also make radar tracking of the warheads difficult.

"Both missiles will arrive at the target on Thursday, 31 July. They will be precisely targeted and will employ radar altimeters that will detonate them on this side of the asteroid, within ten to thirty meters of the surface. We will launch two warheads to double our chances of success, just in case the enemy is able to get through our masking cloud. Only one needs to get through.

"The explosion's shock wave, imparted by some six kilograms of vaporized material from the warhead, will be negligible in vacuum, of course, but the radiant thermal energy will be enormous, sufficient to convert a thin layer of the asteroid's surface, amounting to some fifty metric tons, to vapor. That vapor will escape the asteroid on that side at a velocity of four kilometers per second, imparting a lateral delta-v to the body of some ten to fifteen centimeters per second.

"Now, ten centimeters per second doesn't sound like much, but in forty-one days that amounts to a change in vector of just over 397 kilometers . . . almost 250 miles. If we were trying to prevent a dead-on, center-of-target impact on the Earth, of course, we wouldn't have a chance, since the radius of the Earth is over six thousand kilometers. But—and this is crucial to this problem—we don't need to change 2034L's path by anything near that much. The asteroid's inbound course, remember, deflected by the Moon's gravity and again by Earth's as it comes up from behind, is delicately balanced. Every computer simulation we've run shows that if we can change the path by as little as 125 kilometers away from Earth as it passes from the nightside to the dayside, there will be absolutely no chance of a collision. The asteroid will continue past the Earth and on in its orbit about the sun. There is a remote chance of a collision on another orbit at some date in the remote future, but plenty of time to deal with the possibility before it becomes a danger.

"If both warheads reach their target and detonate, the asteroid's delta-v is increased to something closer to twenty to twenty-five centimeters per second, with a total displacement over forty-one days of almost eight hundred kilometers. One warhead will do the job. Two will simply ice the cake. We will be attempting to intercept and deflect the body while it is still beyond the Moon, which gives us an excellent chance of completely screwing the UN calculations here." She looked around the table. "That concludes my summary report. Are there any questions?"

Harrel, the national security advisor, tapped his finger rapidly on the tabletop, a quick *tic-tic-tic* of sound in the near-silent chamber. "General Sidney," he said, "if two missiles are good, wouldn't four be better? Or ten? Or fifty?"

"We are looking into the possibility of multiple launches. Unfortunately, our assets are badly limited at the moment, and the best we can do within the next three weeks is two launches, as I've just outlined for you. If we can get additional Zeus II boosters on the pad at Vandenberg or Canaveral, we will certainly see about maximizing our chances with as many additional launches as possible. Of course, the closer the asteroid gets to the Earth, the harder it is to change its course enough to do any good."

When there were no further comments, Admiral Gray stood again. "Thank you, Grace. General Warhurst? What do you have for us?"

"Yes, sir." Warhurst stood at his place, tapping his own combination into his touch pad. The large wall screen lit up with scrolling columns of data, while an inset window showed a graphic animation of a pair of LSCPs intercepting the asteroid as it tumbled toward Earth. "Gentlemen. Ladies. We do not propose to screw around with this thing. One-SAG, of the US Marine Space Tactical Command, is ready to land a special assault force of fifty Marines on Asteroid 2034L. We project a launch from Vandenberg employing two Zeus II HLVs." He glanced at General Sidney and wondered what she was thinking. There would be only two heavy-lift vehicles available until mid-August.

"After engaging and destroying any UN forces stationed on the asteroid or in the immediate vicinity," he continued, "they would land directly on the surface. They would carry with them twelve DS-50 thermonuclear devices, which they would plant . . . in this pattern." On the screen, the graphic showed twelve bright green points embracing the slow-tumbling, roughly potato-shaped body in a dodecahedron. The two LSCPs lifted from the asteroid and swung back toward Earth, moments before the twelve points flared up together in a fireball of incandescent fury. As the fireball dissipated, only an expanding cloud of glowing dust motes remained.

"Our information suggests that 2034L is a carbonaceous chondrite, which means its mass is friable, fairly soft, and not densely packed. Twelve thermonuclear explosions in the five-to-ten-megaton range should serve to vaporize nearly all of the asteroid. Any surviving fragments will be small enough that they will burn up upon entering Earth's atmosphere.''

Kenneth Morrow, the secretary of technology, cleared his throat. ''Ah, General Warhurst. I've reviewed your figures, and must say that your people have worked this out in considerable detail. However, there are a few points I'm not clear on. You say that twelve ten-megaton H-bombs should vaporize nearly all of that thing. Can't you guarantee a clean sweep? Disintegrate it? Maybe by using more bombs. . . .''

''With all due respect, sir, there's no such thing as a disintegration ray. Not yet, anyway. That asteroid masses some hundreds of millions of tons. We can transform a very great deal of that mass into gas or droplets of liquid rock, but the mass doesn't just *go away*. It's still there after the blast, and most of it is still heading our way. What we hope to achieve, here, is to disperse that mass, from one big lump into trillions of grains the size of sand and bits of gravel. A hundred million tons of sand will burn up in the atmosphere. A hundred-million-ton mountain will not.

''The plan calls for twelve thermonuclear devices in order to melt and disrupt *all* of 2034L, right down to its heart. More devices would not do a better job.''

''Might there be a possibility of some of the nuclear devices detonating ahead of the others?'' Secretary of Defense Severin asked. ''Wouldn't that disrupt your dodecahedron?''

''That *is* a possibility, sir. We believe the technology is good enough to guarantee near-simultaneous detonation . . . within a few thousandths of a second. If we're that close on the mark, all of the warheads would detonate before they could be disrupted by a neighbor. But I would be lying if I said it was a sure thing.''

''And yet the survival of the United States may be riding on this operation, General,'' Severin said, thoughtful. ''Possibly the survival of the entire world, if our UNdie friends have miscalculated with this damned thing.''

"How soon could your people be ready to go, General?" Admiral Gray asked.

Warhurst nodded his thanks to his friend. Morrow had interrupted his report and gotten him off the track. Now he was back in the groove. "One-SAG is already on full alert. We need to arrange to borrow a ride to orbit from the Aerospace Force, of course. We would need those two HLVs General Sidney mentioned to boost our LSCPs into an intercept trajectory. We could have the ground-to-orbit transports mated to the boosters by the first week of August. The, ah, Army's setback in May has left us a bit short on deployment vehicles. So we're having to scramble to get the LSCPs.''

"Screw you, Monty," General Turner, the Army chief of staff, said pleasantly.

"However," Warhurst continued, "I'm told we can have two LSCPs fueled and ready by 25 August. Eight days to target, at that point. We could be on 2034L by 2 September. That would, incidentally, allow time for a backup mission to be readied, just in case the first mission had to be scrubbed or met with defeat.''

"I thought the Marines never admitted defeat, General," Severin said, grinning.

It might have been meant as a joke or jibe. Warhurst responded seriously. "Those of us planning the broad strategy always consider that possibility, Mr. Secretary. Always. To do less would be criminal negligence.''

"One last question, General Warhurst," Harrel said. "You mentioned the possibility of combat. Of having to clear the asteroid and the vicinity of enemy forces.''

"According to our intelligence, sir, the French warship *Sagittaire* is tucked in next to the asteroid. We suspect that she's there to protect the UN investment, so to speak. If missiles are fired, if troops are deployed to stop their toy, they have people on-station with whom they can counter our move. They may also be in place to provide last-minute course adjustments, right up to the last moment.''

"A suicide mission?" Severin asked.

"No, sir," Warhurst replied.

"In other words, they're expecting 1-SAG. They'd be ready for them."

"Sir, in every opposed amphibious operation in the Corps' history, the enemy knew we were coming. What they won't be expecting is the ferocity of the assault."

"Maybe," Harrel said. "Maybe. But that ferocity isn't going to do us a damned bit of good if they laser your LSCPs out of the sky before you can deploy."

"If you'll read the full briefing, sir, you'll see that we have anticipated that. An initial strike with low-yield nuclear weapons will blind the *Sagittaire*'s sensors, and convince the enemy that we are trying to use missiles to destroy or deflect the asteroid." He glanced around the table. "So . . . if there are no further questions, that concludes my report."

"I have a question, General," Grace Sidney said, raising her hand.

"General?"

"Your plan seems awfully . . . complicated. And risky. You could lose a lot of men out there."

"There's always that risk. If we don't try, we know we'll lose a lot more here on Earth."

"Is there a threat to Earth from radiation?"

"Negligible. The hot debris would largely be scattered on the solar wind. And we'll still be intercepting the asteroid outside the Moon's orbit."

"Well," Harrel said, folding his hands. "Two alternatives to put on the president's desk. That's two more than we had when this mess began. I will let you know of his decision."

"Sir," Warhurst said, "if I might suggest, we can begin implementing both the Marine and Aerospace Force alternatives, at least up to the point where we have to decide on one plan or the other in order to allocate the booster assets. It will save time."

"Of course, of course. We may well have to rely on both plans, with one serving as backup for the other, as additional HLVs come on-line. You will be informed. Thank you, both of you, for your presentations."

"Nice job, Monty," Gray said later, as the crowd began breaking up. "I think we've got a good chance."

Warhurst shot a hard look at the admiral as he folded up his PAD. "CJ, I don't care who takes the honors with this thing. It's not a *game*, and it's not about next year's budget. Frankly, her idea might be the better one."

"Why is that?"

"If nothing else, she can launch sooner than we can, because of the snafu with the LSCPs. The farther away from Earth that we can intercept this thing, the better."

"Do you really think a couple of missiles launched from near-Earth space can do the job better?"

Warhurst sighed. He felt tired, deflated. "Hell, if I knew that . . ." He ran a hand through his hair. "Admiral, I know what Marines can do, even against impossible odds. I know what having trained men on the site can mean to an op, as opposed to remotes or robots or surveillance cams. My honest-to-God, gut feeling is that it's better to handle this with *men* than with machines. And if you need men, the Marines are ready."

"I think you're right, Monty. We'll just have to see if Markham agrees with you."

Alexander Residence
Arlington Heights, Illinois
1615 hours CDT

"Someone is coming up the walk."

Liana looked away from the E-room wall screen, startled. *Someone?*

The door's recognition software knew all of her friends, all of the neighbors or Church of the Divine Masters acquaintances who might come to call. Delivery people, postal servers, and police all wore small transponders in their clothing, like military IFF beacons, that identified them to smart doors.

So who was coming up the walkway that she didn't know?

Rising from the sofa, she walked to the front door.

"Display," she said, placing a hand on the small flatscreen mounted there.

Her!

Liana heard her door asking the visitor to leave her name and a message. She was tempted not to answer, to pretend she was out, even though the car in the port outside gave the lie to that deception.

What was Teri Sullivan doing here? Didn't she know that David had been arrested?

"Hello," Teri's voice said over the door's messager. "This is Dr. Theresa Sullivan. I work with your husband at the Institute. Ms. Alexander? I need to talk to you." A moment passed. "Please answer the door!"

Liana waited a moment more, trying to decide. Then, abruptly, she jerked the door open. "Excuse me," she said, putting all of the ice she could into the words. "I didn't recognize you with your clothes on."

The other woman closed her eyes, face reddening, but then she opened them again. "Please. May I come in? I need to talk to you."

"I can't imagine about what."

"About David."

"The door didn't recognize you," Liana said. She felt angry, and hurt. What was this woman doing here? What was she *thinking*? "I would have thought David would have keyed it for you. Didn't he bring you here for a fast screw on nights when I was out?"

"No, Ms. Alexander. Never." She drew a deep breath. "Look . . . it's true. I have slept with David. And obviously you've seen some of my v-mail to him. I'm . . . I'm terribly sorry if I've offended you."

"*Offended* me! You bitch! You were trying to take my husband!"

"Ms. Alexander," Teri said softly, "I'm afraid you lost him long before I came on the scene."

Liana trembled on the brink of losing her last shreds of control. *She's right, damn her. Maybe there really isn't any hope for us.* With difficulty, she drew back, took a couple of breaths, and managed to put the ice back in her words. "David is not here. I can't imagine what you and

I could possibly have to talk about. Good-bye.''

"No!" As Liana started to close the door, Teri barged forward, blocking it with her leg. "No, you don't understand! I need your help to get him out of prison!"

That stopped her. "What are you talking about?"

"Look . . . last week I was talking to David's lawyer. She says they're not letting anyone in to see him. She's right. I've been trying."

Liana nodded. "They told me he was in transit, whatever that means. And they're not returning my v-calls and messages anymore."

"Same here. I . . . I've been thinking about this all week. Trying to, well, trying to work up my nerve to come here and talk to you. His lawyer said that we might be able to rally some support from people David knows."

"What, all those archeologists and scientists and things?" She shook her head. "I don't know any of them."

"I do . . . what I was wondering was if we could go through his correspondents' list on your home computer. There might be others on the list who could help. Or people who know people. If you let me copy that list, I could send out a letter, asking for help. Or . . . you could do it from here, but I'm afraid your home connection might be monitored. I have a system that will get the messages out, no matter what."

Liana drew herself up taller. "Maybe you don't understand, Dr. Sullivan. David's and my marriage, well . . . maybe you're right. Maybe it's all over. So why should I want to help him? Or you, for that matter?"

"Because it's the right thing to do? Because the damned government is trying to pull a disappearing act with one of its citizens, and can't be allowed to get away with that shit? Maybe because, even if your marriage is over, you two still loved each other once, cared for each other, and wanted what was best?" When Liana didn't answer, she added, "Look, I know you want to strangle me, and maybe him, too, but there's time for that later. The bastards are magleving David, and we've got to do something about it!"

Liana stared at the woman for a long several seconds, then finally stepped back from the door. "C'mon."

She led the way to the E-room and sat again on the sofa. Reaching out, she tapped away at the touch-screen keyboard, closing the novel she'd been watching and bringing up David's private system. She typed in the word "Sphinx," then navigated with swift, sure strokes on the touch screen to his correspondents' list. "There you go."

Names and v-mail addresses scrolled up the screen . . . perhaps a hundred of them.

"Lots of scientists," Teri said. She pointed. "That name, Kaminski. He's a Marine. David told me once he was exchanging a lot of mail with him."

"I'll make a copy of the list for you."

"Thank you."

"Don't thank me. Just take the thing and get out of here. I don't want to see either of you, ever again." Her mother wouldn't have approved, Liana knew, but she was changing her mind about the whole question of divorce. Some things could never be forgiven, even in the light of the Divine Masters.

EIGHTEEN

Ramsey Residence
Greensburg, Pennsylvania
1635 hours EDT

"I just can't tell you how good it is to have you back home again!" Jack's mother was very much aflutter, now that they were back on her home turf. "I simply can't believe that you're finally home!"

Jack felt uncomfortable with the attention. "Yeah, it's really great to be back. And, uh, thanks again for coming down to see me yesterday."

"Well, I wouldn't have missed your graduation for the world!" It had been something of a surprise. She'd taken the maglev down to Beaufort and come out to Parris Island to watch his graduation ceremony, and that, Jack knew, had been truly and act of devotion above and beyond the call of duty. They didn't have that much money to begin with . . . and South Carolina in July was not exactly a vacation spot anymore, with its global warming–augmented temperatures, high humidity, and enthusiastic insect population.

The graduation, fittingly enough, had been held on the Fourth of July, with one hell of a spectacular fireworks display that evening for both the graduates and the families who'd come to see them. Even the fact that the evening's festivities had been cut an hour short—the rumor that a UN arsenal ship had surfaced offshore and launched a pair

238

of cruise missiles at Charleston proved to be false, fortunately—had failed to curb the partylike atmosphere. Jack and his mother had taken the maglev back to Pittsburgh the next morning; by early Saturday afternoon, he was home . . . and *that* was a concept as alien as anything Uncle David had discovered inside the labyrinthine caverns of Cydonia.

As he stood awkwardly in the E-room, still wearing his summer service "A" khakis, trying to connect with his mother and this house that seemed suddenly so strange and small, he began to realize how much he'd changed in the past three months.

At least he hadn't slipped and lapsed into profanity, yet. Back in boot camp, he'd heard dozens of stories about guys who'd gone back home on leave, sat down to a wonderful home-cooked meal with all of the family, relatives, and friends, and turned the atmosphere to ice with an accidental "This is fucking great, Ma," or, "Hey, would you pass the fucking potatoes, please?"

Most of the vulgar language he'd heard in boot camp, in fact, had come from the other recruits. With only a very few lapses, the DIs had been almost startlingly clean and correct in their language, which he hadn't expected at all. He still chuckled, though, at one of Knox's vulgarities, the one about recruits being so low that whale shit was like shooting stars to them. The imagery was perfect, and all the funnier now that he was no longer a recruit.

In fact, if Jack had any problem with language at all, it was breaking the automatic "this recruit believes . . ." or "this recruit requests . . ." that leaped to his lips every time he opened his mouth.

The story was told at Parris Island of one recruit, many, many years ago, who'd determined to escape the unrelenting hell of boot camp by going over the hill. There was only one way off the island, and that was the Boulevard de France, across the bridge over Archer's Creek and on through the Main Gate. The recruit had worn his PT shorts and T-shirt and stolen a bicycle, and in the dark the Marine guard at the gate had assumed he was the dependent son of someone stationed at the base. "Where are you going this time of night, son?'' the guard had asked pleasantly.

The recruit, just a few meters short of freedom, had leaped off his bike, snapped to attention, and sung out, ''*Sir! This recruit requests*—'' The sentry had immediately restrained him and called the recruit's platoon commander.

''So, what are your plans?'' his mother asked with that characteristic perkiness he thought of as a smoke screen masking darker thoughts. She plopped down into the big lounge chair and picked up some crewel work. ''Come on, sit down! Sit down! Tell me your plans! I mean, you said you had two weeks' vacation, but then where will you be going after that? Have you decided what you're going to do?''

'' 'Leave,' Mom,'' he said, taking a seat at the very edge of a straight-backed chair. It was going to take him a while, he knew, to break himself of always sitting or standing at attention. ''Two weeks leave. And the Corps is going to be making my plans for the next few years.''

''Well, yes . . . to be sure, but you get to tell them what you want, don't you? I know you always talked about Space Camp—''

''Space training, Mom. And, well, I don't think that's going to happen. At least, not right away.''

''But you said your recruiter promised—''

Jack chuckled. The reality no longer burned the way it had once. ''Mom, I'm a Marine. I go where the Corps needs me. There are half a million of us in the Corps, and only a few thousand ever get to go to space.'' He shrugged, completely comfortable now with the knowledge. ''Maybe, someday. If I qualify.'' He brightened. ''In the meantime, though, this rec—I mean, I have to go through the next phase of my training.''

''But . . . wasn't boot camp it? Your training, I mean.''

''Training never stops in the Corps, Mom. Boot camp was where they made me a Marine, yeah, but I still have one month of combat training. I mean, I've learned the basics, how to take care of my rifle, how to shoot, stuff like that. But now I have to learn small-unit tactics. Get to crawl through the boonies with my buddies, playing war games. And after that, well, it looks like I'm shipping out as a replacement for the 5th MarDiv. And that means Siberia.''

He'd been hoping to put off discussing that particular bit of news. He found, to his considerable surprise, that he didn't mind it at all himself. Oh, there was some apprehension, of course, even outright fear, but nothing he faced in Vladivostok would be as terrifying as those first few days in Company 4239. He could handle it.

But his mother, he realized, didn't have the advantages of his training. She was still a *civilian*, and she thought in civilian terms.

"Siberia! Why in God's name would they send you to *Siberia*!"

He shrugged. "Fifth MarDiv has a commitment to help the Russians, Mom. They've been holding the Amur Line now for two years, ever since the Japanese changed sides, keeping the Chinese out. You know, if it hadn't been for Colonel Westlake's defense of Hill 229, outside of Ussuriysk, the Chinese would've broken through and taken Vlad last April! In one week, 515 Marines held off at least eleven human-wave assaults by elements of the 103rd and 140th People's Armies! General Warhurst said it was the most gallant stand by the Corps since Khe Sanh. He said—''

Jack stopped, aware that his mother was staring at him with an unhappy mix of horror and incomprehension in her eyes. At that moment, Jack realized how much he'd changed . . . and how different, no, how *distant* he was now from her.

"I, uh, anyway, I'll be shipping out by the end of August," he said, the words feeling lame. "They've been doing six-month rotations, there, so I should be back by the end of February."

"You . . . you'll be sure to pack lots of warm clothes," his mother said. She looked down at her crewelwork, hands busy. "It's awfully cold in Siberia, I hear. . . .''

He saw no point in explaining that parts of Siberia was as hot in the summer as South Carolina, that, strictly speaking, he wouldn't even be in Siberia, but in a region designated as the Russian Far Eastern Maritime Territory.

Or that the Corps was cycling people through on six-month rotations because the war over there was such a hellish meat grinder.

"Oh! I almost forgot!" his mother said abruptly, in what was clearly a deliberate change of subject. "You probably haven't heard about your Uncle David."

"Uncle David? What about him?" Jack had been missing his occasional e-mail exchanges with his uncle . . . not to mention the steady updates on new aliens from the Cave of Wonders.

"He was arrested! Tossed into jail like a, well, like a criminal! Your Aunt Liana was really upset about it. She seems to think it was her fault, but *I* know better. He got in trouble with the government, talking to spies and UN agents! You know he had all those foreigners he liked to talk with. It looks like he was still talking to them, even though a lot of them were *spies*. . . ."

"Uncle David? I don't believe it!"

"Oh, it's true. And Liana says she doesn't think they're ever going to let him out!"

It didn't seem possible. They didn't lock people up for no reason in the United States . . . at least, not in the United States he'd sworn to defend three months before. What the hell was going on?

"I, uh, gotta use the head, Mom."

"The what?"

"The bathroom."

"Why didn't you say so? I wish you wouldn't use that slang. It's *so* hard to know what you're talking about!"

He left quickly, to escape the look in her eyes. He could tell she was really worried about Siberia.

Upstairs, after a *pro forma* use of the lavatory, he walked into his room, astonished—as he'd been a few hours ago when he'd brought his seabag in and stowed his gear—at how tiny the place seemed. How cluttered. He did still like the Marine posters, though. Especially the one with Uncle David's photo, with the space-suited Marines raising the flag against a pink-orange sky at Cydonia. God!

How could they throw him in jail? The man was an honorary Marine, for Pete's sake, a gesture not extended to many who'd not been through the hell at Parris Island. It had to be some kind of mistake.

Sitting down at his desk, he flicked on his computer, opening up his personal system. A few moments later, Sam smiled her warm and sexy smile at him from the screen. "Hello, Jack! I haven't seen you in simply . . . *ages*!"

"Uh . . . hi, Sam!" His agent had caught him by surprise. It wasn't that he'd forgotten about her, but he hadn't really had the time or the energy in boot camp to fantasize much about her, and he'd somehow gotten out of the habit. She was conservatively dressed this afternoon, in white slacks and a pullover shirt, as she lounged on her poolside patio.

"You have 227 messages waiting for you, Jack. Shall I get them for you?"

"Uh, no. Not right now."

"I've also collected 793 articles that I think you'll be interested in seeing, articles about space exploration, about aliens, with special attention for the aliens being cataloged at the Cydonian archeological site, and about the US Marine Corps. Shall I retrieve them for you?"

"Not right now, Sam." It seemed he had some catching up to do. "Maybe later."

"I was wondering if you would *ever* get back!" In one smooth, languid motion, she peeled her shirt off over her blond head. Her breasts bounced entrancingly as she tossed it aside. Smiling, she reached for the elastic waistband of her slacks. "I was getting *so* lonely!"

"Uh . . . hold on a moment, there, Sam. Don't get undressed."

"Are you sure?" Her eyes twinkled at him from the screen. "It's *awfully* hot today. And *I'm* awfully hot, too. . . ."

"I know you are. But, well, I don't have the time right now." He paused, thinking fast. "Tell me something, Sam. Could I download you to an MD? You know, to install you on another system?"

"Of course, Jack. The microdisk would have to be able to load 2.7 terb if you wanted to capture my full range of behavior, speech patterns . . . as well as the personality of that *other* Sam you have stored in here with me. What other system were you thinking of?"

"My PAD, actually. A military model. I was thinking it might be kind of nice to have you with me where I'm going."

"Ooh, that would be *nice*, Jack. You know, if you have the standard adapters, you could jack your PAD into this system, and download me directly. Or you could use your Earthnet connection to download me through your PAD's modem."

"Well, I don't have the PAD yet." The limited model he'd been issued in boot camp had been strictly for basic training, and he'd had to turn it back in on Thursday. "I'll be having a new one issued to me when I go back. I could load you onto it then."

It was an intriguing thought. He would have to pare back a lot of the extras to get her to fit. Her backgrounds—the pool, her bedroom—those could be replaced by a single, simple, colored backdrop, with no detail. And her clothing. Limit her to one costume—the tight white slacks were nice—and that would save a lot of space. He could eliminate clothing entirely, of course, but he had a feeling that that would be boring after a while.

How much of Sam's personality could he save, though? Not that he had a *personal* relationship with his AI—masturbation was about as lonely and impersonal as things could get—but he had missed Sam while he was at boot camp. At his next duty station, he would have more privacy than there'd been in the recruit barracks. Best of all, he was thinking that he might be able to share Sam with some of his buddies. He was proud of the modifications he'd hacked into the original commercial AI package; Sam was so bright and responsive that it often seemed like she had a mind of her own, that she was genuinely self-aware. And that, of course, was the point.

Besides, he'd seen what military-issue AIs could do, especially with things like writing and debugging quick field programs, and he was not impressed. In boot camp, he'd not been allowed to question the way things were done—as Gunny Knox always said, there were three ways of doing things, the right way, the wrong way, and the Marine way, and so far as the recruits had been concerned, there was *only* the Marine way.

Well, Jack had always preferred Jack's way, and that meant the *right* way, at least when it came to programming AIs.

He knew he might get in trouble if his superiors found Sam; pornography of any kind was actively discouraged, and one recruit had been sent home during the seventh week of training when he'd been caught during an inspection with a three-D vid peeper in his ditty bag, a bottle-cap-sized player with an eyepiece showing a nude couple engaged in an endlessly looped sexual act. Jack was pretty sure the brass would be more lenient with "real" Marines once he reached his first duty assignment, and even if they weren't, Sam would be easy enough to hide. He wondered if he should get her to pull a quick-change act, the way she did now when he said the word "Mom."

Only this time, he would have her change to the dull-as-a-rock issue-AI every time he said the word "Sarge"!

MONDAY, 7 JULY 2042

Platoon Commander's Office
Second Platoon, Bravo Company,
1-SAG
Vandenberg Aerospace Force
Complex
0925 hours EDT

Frank Kaminski rapped three times on the door, hard. "Enter!" his CO's voice called from the other side. "Center yourself on the hatch!"

He palmed the door open and walked in. Lieutenant Garroway was at her desk, staring up at her wall screen, on which was displayed a game of chess. It looked like a camera's eye view from behind the black king, but the spectacular detail in armor and weaponry, in fluttering flags and nervous horses showed that the game was a computer animation. The name "Garroway" appeared at the bottom, by the black pieces; at the top, behind the white, was the name "Warhurst."

"Holy Christ! . . . ." Kaminski blurted out, his eyes widening.

Kaitlin swiveled her chair around to face him. "*What* was that, Sergeant?" she asked sharply. Then she grinned. "Even during working hours I'm allowed to go through my personal v-mail."

Kaminski snapped to attention. "Sorry, ma'am! I meant no disrespect. I was just, uh, startled, is all."

"By what? You find it surprising that your commanding officer plays chess?"

"Uh, no, ma'am. It was who you're playing chess with. That . . . that wouldn't happen to be *General* Warhurst you're playing, would it?"

She blinked, then relaxed a bit and laughed. "You are absolutely correct, Sergeant Kaminski. It would not!"

"Yes, ma'am! It was the name, you see. I thought—"

"It's Jeff Warhurst, the commandant's grandson!"

Somehow, that seemed worse. The commandant of the US Marine Corps had a grandson? That was about like learning that God Almighty had a maiden aunt.

"I met the Warhursts a couple of years ago," Kaitlin explained. "Just before I joined the Corps, in fact. I was in Japan when the war broke out, and it happened that I received some . . . information. Some important information from my father that had to be passed on to Military Intelligence." Something passed behind the lieutenant's gaze. She became distant for a moment, as though she was remembering something, something sad. Then she seemed to shake the thought off. "Anyway, I managed to get out of the country before everything was shut down and contact a friend of my dad's by vid while I was airborne. I was met at the LA airport by some Marines with orders to take me straight to the commandant. He let me stay at his place, with his family, while I was being debriefed."

She smiled. "Jeff is fourteen now, and brilliant. He also plays a hell of a mean game of chess." She jerked her thumb over her shoulder, indicating the wall screen. "We've been playing v-mail chess for a year now. Not real-time, of course. Just sending animés of the moves back and forth. The damned little son of a gunny beats me two times out of five, too. So, what can I do for you?"

"Ma'am, I've got a problem. I don't know who to talk to, so you seemed like the logical place to start."

"If it involves getting off base, the answer is negative."

"I know, ma'am." Kaminski nodded. One-SAG had gone on full alert four days ago, with no sign yet of the order being lifted. Scuttlebutt held that the UN had diverted an asteroid out of orbit and sent it toward the Earth, and that 1-SAG was going to have to go capture the thing and destroy it. It was, Kaminski thought, one of the craziest wild rumors he'd heard in his entire Marine career, and whoever first started it as a joke must be laughing his head off right now. Whatever the *real* story was, though, it had the entire Vandenberg complex sealed off tighter than a vacuum chamber. "I don't need to go ashore. It's, well . . . it's this e-mail I got."

"Something from home?"

"No, ma'am. Uh, do you remember the Prof, uh, Dr. Alexander? Back at Picard?"

"Of course."

"You know he was with your dad, on Mars. And that he was, I mean, he *is* a kind of honorary Marine. Unofficial, but, well, he was one of us on Garroway's March."

"I can certainly understand that. Everyone on the March went through hell, to hear my dad tell it."

"Yes, ma'am. It wasn't that bad, really, but air and food were damned tight, and we couldn't get out of our space suits for three weeks. That meant we were getting pretty ripe by the time we closed on Mars Prime, and the suits and armor were really chafing us, raising blisters and sores and, well, it wasn't real pleasant. But the Prof hung right there with us. He was the one who patched through that information about Cydonia, putting it out over the Net to screw the UNdies. He might have been a civilian, but if he was able to tough it out the way the rest of us did, he was okay. One of us, you know?''

Kaitlin nodded. ''Understood. What's the problem?''

''This, ma'am.'' He reached into his BDU left breast pocket and extracted an MD. ''I just got this e-mail last week, and I haven't been able to figure what to do about it. I downloaded it to disk so you could see.''

She slipped the disk into her desk PAD; the chess game on the display behind her vanished, replaced by the e-mail text, writ large.

Silently, Kaitlin read the message on her PAD's smaller screen. ''Who is this Teri Sullivan?'' She asked, looking up.

''Don't know her, ma'am, but I gather she's another archeologist. And a friend of the Prof's. She explains that further down the letter, ma'am.''

''Got it. Says she worked with him at the Exoarcheological Institute in Chicago.'' She looked up. ''He's been arrested? For spying?''

''Ma'am, I talked to Dr. Alexander a lot. Starting back on Mars, when he let me come into the Cave of Wonders to see the aliens and stuff he was finding on those TV screens. He never had much use for government or bureaucracy or that kind of thing, but he's no enemy spy!''

''She says much the same. She also says his lawyer isn't being allowed to see him, that they're holding him incommunicado at Joliet. God, what's this country coming to!''

''This woman says she's sending this same message out to everyone on Dr. Alexander's v-mail address list, hoping someone can help. Since I exchanged some mail with him, I guess I was on the list. Ma'am, I don't know what I can do, but I do know that the Prof is a good guy, and he's getting the shit-dipped end of the stick, here!''

''If this is a legal matter, Sergeant, there's not a lot I can do. . . .''

''Sure, I understand that, ma'am. But it sounds to me like the Prof is having his rights run over by a Mark II Cataphract, y'know? There's gotta be someone we can tell, someone who can check on this thing, but damn if I know who.''

"Judge Advocate General's out. Alexander's not military." Kaitlin pulled the MD from her PAD. "I'll keep this, if I may. I might know someone after all."

"Sure, ma'am. I knew you'd come up with something."

"I appreciate your confidence. I'll let you know if I hear anything. Anything else?"

"No, ma'am!"

"Dismissed."

"Aye, aye, ma'am!" He turned on his heel and left, and the relief he felt was like an awakening. Kaitlin Garroway was a lot like her father, he thought. Sharp. Determined. Bulldog-stubborn. And always looking out for her people. When she'd testified at his inquiry, she'd damn near had the board ready to give him a promotion instead of a court-martial for that friendly-fire incident. She was a damned good Marine to have on your side.

And God help you if she had you in her sights.

THURSDAY, 31 JULY 2042

EU Spacecraft Sagittaire
Pacing 2034L, on intercept
vector with Earth
2028 hours GMT

She was not a pretty vessel, with a blunt, cylindrical hab section, a cluster of spherical tanks holding water as reaction mass, and the massive, squat ovoid of the heavily shielded main reactor and plasma-drive inducers. She hung in the shadow of the low-tumbling mountain called 2034L, as the Moon grew slowly larger dead ahead.

Sagittaire had started life as a survey vessel, one of the small fleet of ships, like *Laplace*, built at the old International Space Station ten years before to serve as a part of the Phaeton Project, searching out, cataloging, and visiting near-Earth asteroids that might one day pose a threat to the mother planet. There was a special irony in the fact that the *Sagittaire*, outfitted now with an eight-hundred-megajoule gas-pumped laser in a dorsal ball turret, was being used by her UN masters to deliberately divert 2034L into a collision course with Earth.

Colonel Victor Antoine Gallois, formerly of the French Air Force, now a senior officer of the EU Space Force, viewed his orders with a mixture of stoicism and the career military officer's mistrust of bureaucrats and politicians. His orders, delivered to him sealed hours before his launch from Kourou, had been most specific, devoting three full pages to a discussion—unusual in military orders—of just why his mission *must* be carried out precisely as specified. It was clear that if he refused them, his career would be over, and another officer would be found to take his place and see that the job was done.

The explanation had been unnecessary. He would carry out his orders. He just hoped the politicians knew what the hell they were doing. He'd read all about dinosaur-killing comets and nuclear winters, and 2034L was a hell of a big rock to drop in anyone's backyard. This rock wasn't as big as a dinosaur killer, not by several tens of thousands of megatons . . . but it was a serious threat to anything as small as a continent.

"*Monsieur Capitaine?*" Abelard, the ship's chief electronicist, said, turning from his board. A clipboard with a galley stores manifest drifted by, and he snagged it from the air and slapped it against a Velcro pad on the bulkhead. "We may have a problem."

"What is it?" He floated closer, snagging the back of Abelard's seat to see. The radar showed . . . static. That wasn't right. "What the devil is that?"

"I would guess, *Monsieur Capitaine*, that we are being deliberately jammed. Diagnostics indicate our equipment is functioning normally. This interference appeared a few moments ago, from a point source. The way it is expanding, I would have to say it is chaff, probably from a munitions canister of some kind."

"Ah. And the question is, what is being hidden by the chaff cloud? Have you tried a ladar sweep?"

"Yes, Captain." Abelard touched a control, and the display switched to a different kind of snow, clumpy and multicolored. "Chaff . . . and some type of aerosol or powder which scatters the laser beam. Range now 240 kilometers, relative velocity three kilometers per second, in direct approach.''

''Which gives us twelve minutes.'' Pushing off from the back of the electronicist's seat with a practiced shove and half turn, he floated across to the main control center and palmed a flat red button. The harsh bray of general quarters sounded through the ship's hab compartments. He touched the needle mike next to his lips. ''All hands, all hands, this is the captain,'' he said. ''Battle stations! Engineer, prepare for maneuver! Weapons Officer! Ready the laser for firing!''

Sagittaire only carried a complement of eight, but the deck plating and bulkheads carried the rattlings and clatterings of men going to their ready stations so well it sounded like a much larger company. The roll and pitch indicators on the main console's readouts showed the slight but definite change in the big ship's attitude as so much mass shifted position inside the ship so quickly.

''Sir!'' Abelard said. ''I've got a fix on the cloud's central impact point. It's on 2034L, grid coordinates two-five-three by zero-one-nine.''

Gallois called the data up on his primary display, revealing the potato-shaped asteroid as a topo-relief network of green lines in three dimensions, the impact site flashing red, and columns of numbers scrolling up the side of the screen. Impact—now in eight minutes, thirty seconds—would be at a spot just over the horizon from *Sagittaire*'s current station. ''I've got it.'' He keyed some figures into the ship's computer, then watched the result scroll onto the screen. ''It looks like they're attempting a course change on our . . . baby.''

''Sir?''

''An explosion at that point will give 2034L a delta-v along a new vector. The computer can't give me precise figures without data on the warhead's type and size, but my guess is that they're trying to shove our mountain off course, to make it miss the target.''

Major Yvonne Ponet, the ship's senior pilot, slid into her seat at the *Sagittaire*'s thrust controllers, slipping the harness over her shoulders and snugging the belt tight. "Helm ready for orders," she announced.

"Very well. We will need a delta-v of five meters per second, bearing three-two-zero by zero-zero-eight."

"Three-two-zero by zero-zero-eight, delta-v five mps. Initiating." The sound of thrusters firing thumped hollowly through bulkheads, and Gallois felt the slight but definite surge of low acceleration. Slowly, the *Sagittaire* pivoted . . . and then came the stronger nudge of her main engine, firing for just an instant with a bump from behind, as though Gallois had been nudged in the back.

"Captain, Main Gun," the voice of Captain Paul Marichy, the weapons officer, said in Gallois's headset. "I can't find a target! Weapon track-and-lock radar is being blocked!"

"Do it manually, if you have to! My guess is that there's at least one large, chemical warhead behind that chaff cloud, and probably more."

"What if they're throwing something heavier at us, Captain?" Abelard asked. He sounded worried.

"Then the bastards are escalating this war. No one has used nuclear weapons in the fighting yet."

Even so, the question was disquieting. The Americans would be desperate, once they found out that a mountain was about to smash into the heart of their country, with the explosive equivalent of hundreds of megatons of TNT. Such a threat might warrant, in their eyes, a nuclear response. . . .

As an aide to General Bourges, before he'd received his latest command, Colonel Gallois had been privy to some of the EU planning sessions in Brussels and Geneva, and he knew quite a bit about the top-secret ship-construction project at Tsiolkovsky, on the Lunar farside. In his own mind, it would have made far more sense to wait until the *Millénium* was ready for combat than to tempt the gods of war with Operation Damocles. Once *Millénium* was ready, the EU would have a sword of terrible, dazzling power, a weapon that would bring the United States to her knees and guarantee both the Union and France a solid position of leadership within the UN for the next century, at least.

But then, the generals, the bureaucrats, and the politicians rarely seemed to make sense these days. All a soldier could do was keep quiet and follow his orders in the highly risky assumption that the civilians really did know their asses from rabbit holes, even if they gave the impression at times that they did not.

On the main display, the graphic animation representing *Sagittaire* was rising slowly from the asteroid, maneuvering now to bring the oncoming chaff cloud, an irregular and ragged blob of translucent red, well above 2034L's horizon. When the range closed enough, Marichy ought to have a good, clear shot; if he missed, even a chemical explosion could hurl fragments of the asteroid that would sweep through the *Sagittaire* like shrapnel. And if the warhead was a nuke . . .

The red cloud washed over one side of the slowly tumbling asteroid, scouring across grid coordinates two-five-three by zero-one-nine like a blood-hued storm. Gallois could hear a new sound, now, a *tick-tick-ticking* of small particles colliding with the EU vessel's hull. The ticking became a steady hiss, then a roar as bits of aluminized polymer chaff and reflective metallic particles like coarse grit stormed against the hull.

"I have a target!" Marichy called. "Bearing zero-three-zero by minus zero-one-one! It looks like! . . ."

"Fire!" Never mind what it looked like. That could be sorted out later.

On the main display, the target, a fast-moving yellow diamond traveling in the red cloud's wake, flared brightly, pulsed visibly for a moment as metal vaporized in a light-and-radar-reflecting cloud, then winked out. A second diamond was moving in along a slightly different vector. Gallois could feel the humming in the deck as Marichy brought *Sagittaire*'s ball turret to bear. . . .

The second missile's warhead detonated on target, eleven meters from Asteroid 2034L's surface, and less than three hundred meters from the *Sagittaire*. The flash, silent and deadly, briefly touched both the asteroid's dusty surface and the ship's hull with liquid fire and the rippling quicksilver of metal and ceramic flowing like water. Dust vaporized, erupting from 2034L's surface in mute, explosive fury; superheated rock cracked, split, and exploded, hurling multiton chunks into space. One of those chunks struck *Sagittaire* squarely in her propulsion unit, rupturing water tanks and setting her thirty-meter length tumbling in the center of a spiraling cloud of fragments and glittering spray.

That wild tumble scarcely mattered. *Sagittaire*'s entire crew was already dead, strapped in at their duty stations as superheated clouds of smoke and steam from burning wiring and ruptured feed lines filled the radiation-blasted interior of her hab module.

A dead ship now, with dead hands at her lifeless controls, *Sagittaire* continued to fall with the slowly dispersing cloud of debris along much the same path that she'd been traveling before the warhead's detonation. . . .

NINETEEN

Marine Fire Base 125
Near Kirovsky
Russian Far Eastern Maritime
Territory
0800 hours local time

The met-boys were calling for another day with a high of 30° Celsius, humid, with the wind from the southeast . . . a typical summer's day, in other words, in this muddy, godforsaken, global-warmed corner of Asia. It was hard to imagine, Jack thought as he came to attention, that in another three months this place would be a howling, ice- and snowbound wilderness. Across the grinder, canned music began playing the "Star Spangled Banner," and he snapped to a crisp salute as the American flag fluttered up the pole set in front of the sandbagged Quonset hut serving as 3rd Battalion HQ. Right on cue, he heard the sharp but distant *thump-thump-thump* of the NC mortars, but he held his salute as the anthem continued to play.

He knew the game now, and the rules. After two weeks at Marine Fire Base 125—"Ol' Buck and a Quarter" to the old hands—he could play it with the best of them. He still remembered that first Monday, his first at Kirovsky, when he'd come to attention with his entire company at morning colors and heard the thump of the mortars. He'd flinched—hell, he'd been ready to dive headfirst for the nearest slit trench—but Gunnery Sergeant Blandings had been standing nearby. "As you were, Marine," Blandings had growled from the side of his mouth, just loud enough for Jack to hear. The man must've had eyes in the back of his head.

The anthem had finished, Captain Rollins, his company commander, had dropped the salute he'd been holding for the unit, and then, *finally*, Blandings had shouted, "*Incoming!*"

The company had melted away, diving into slit trenches, bunkers, and foxholes. Seconds later, the first savage *crump* of a mortar round had thundered on the grinder where the company had been drawn up for colors, followed by another detonation . . . and a third . . . and a fourth. It had been Jack's first time under hostile fire, and he'd huddled in the bottom of a muddy trench with five other Marines, as gravel, mud, and hot bits of shrapnel rained on them from the startlingly clear, blue sky.

Blandings had explained it to him later. "The NCs always fire a few rounds when they see us raising the colors . . . especially if they see us in formation, like today. But the first rounds don't arrive until ten, maybe fifteen seconds after the anthem ends, so there's plenty of time, see?"

If that had seemed strange, the aftermath was even stranger. The bombardment had lasted only a couple of moments and consisted of perhaps a dozen rounds. After the silence following the last tooth-rattling *whump* of an explosion, Marines all over the camp began jeering, whistling, and catcalling, as though taunting the unseen enemy. Seconds later, another flag had gone up . . . a T-shirt dyed bright red and affixed to a pole so it could be waved back and forth in slow, lazy arcs.

Jack had caught the symbolism immediately. Maggie's drawers . . . the flag waved on the target range that signified that the poor recruit on the firing line had not only missed the bull's-eye, but had, in fact, missed the entire target. He'd laughed out loud, a harsh, nervous bark, when he got the joke.

"Tradition," Blandings had told him. "Marines did the same damned thing at least as far back as Khe Sanh."

After the recording of the national anthem crashed to its home-of-the-brave conclusion, Jack dropped his salute and trotted easily to the nearest sandbagged trench along with several other Marines. There was no formation held this morning—that was reserved for Mondays—but Ol' Buck and a Quarter was heavily populated, and there were always a dozen or two men and women crossing the grinder when Colors sounded. Lazy seconds later, with lots of time to spare, the first detonation erupted from the grinder, spraying dirt, gravel, and smoke skyward.

"One of these days," Jack said, leaning back against a sandbag wall and feeling the ground shudder and buck beneath him, "those people are going to get smart and send a volley of hypes after us." Hypersonic artillery rounds would reach the hilltop target before the sound of their firing had covered five kilometers.

"Nah," PFC Duberand said. He was a big man—a "fat tray" in Company 4239 who'd trimmed down into hard muscle. He was one of fifteen of Jack's boot-camp buddies who'd been deployed to the Vlad theater with him. "They ain't that smart."

"Shows what you know, newbie," Corporal Virginia Casey replied. She was an old Siberian hand, a Marine who'd been at the fire base since late July. "Wait'll you find a company of NC sappers coming through the wire on your watch some night!" Another mortar round thundered, close by, and the Marines hunkered down a bit lower.

"Shit," Lonnie Costantino said, brushing a scattering of gravel from his active-camo body armor. "If they're so freakin' shit-hot, how come we're up *here* looking down at them down *there*?"

"Maybe they don't like this any more than we do," Jack said.

"Fuckin'-A, Flash," Casey said. "If there's one thing we've learned about the NCA, it's that the opposition is as tired, as dirty, as hot, as hungry, and as fucking sick of this fucking war as we are."

"That's right," Corporal Slidell said. "They're just like us, 'cept they talk funny. Hell, they wouldn't want to upset the nice, friendly little balance of power we've worked out here.'' Two more mortar rounds whistled in with a savage *whump-whump*.

Jack looked at Slidell—''call me 'Slider,' ''—with interest. ''You mean they don't want to kick our asses into the Sea of Japan?''

''Oh, sure. They would if they could. But they know that trying it'll buy 'em another Hill 229. The poor SOBs got enough trouble back home across the river without bleedin' themselves dry trying to break our line.''

That seemed true enough. Precious little news had come out of North China since the war had started, but POWs and deserters spoke of street fighting in Beijing and Harbin, and of the possibility of wide-scale civil war. Even so, the Chinese had a well-deserved reputation for being able to field huge armies, inexhaustibly supplied by new levies of peasant troops. Some wit in the company had actually calculated that if the Marines killed one Chinese soldier per second for the next twenty years, the Chinese birthrate would still produce a larger standing army than they had now, and that invading Russia was simply Beijing's way of reaching UN-mandated population controls before the year 2050.

There was a long silence, and then Marines began rising from their shelters. Over in front of the mess hall, the familiar red banner went up, accompanied by shouted jeers and insults. *Maggie's drawers*.

He wondered if the Marines would lie to the enemy and wave the red flag one bright morning when the enemy barrage had actually killed someone. Or if they'd keep waving the flag if the Chinese lobbed a few rounds extra someday, after the red flag had gone up. Hell, maybe the Chinese weren't any more anxious to rock the boat than the Marines were.

Standing, shrugging his torso armor into a more comfortable position and straightening his helmet, Jack walked toward the wall of sandbags and tightly coiled razor wire that made up Fire Base 125's inner bastion. Covered firing positions, carefully camouflaged, housed Marine riflemen and SLWs. Beyond, the ground, which dropped away down a steep hill toward Chancre Valley below, had been churned and blasted into a flat and open killing ground, one heavily laced with claymore and robotic mines, with teleoperated pop-up weapons towers and hopper-poppers, with sensors that could pinpoint a stealthy man's heartbeat and relay targeting data that could nail him with fire from a dozen separate positions.

Far off, down the valley, Chancre Lake—actually the Ozero Khanka or Chanka, depending on which maps you consulted—gleamed silver in the morning light, twenty kilometers to the northwest. The enemy mortars were south of the big lake, between the lake and the fire base. Other enemy positions must be closer . . . perhaps as close as that tree line beyond the outermost ring of the base's robotic defenses. The bad guys were rarely seen, however. Since Jack had arrived at Fire Base 125, he'd been in exactly one firefight. He'd scrambled to his assigned position on the wall and taken his place with the rest of his company, blazing away with his ATAR into a thick middle-of-the-night fog of smoke and dazzling flashes, burning flares, and savage explosions, trying to make sense out of the confused jumble of greens and yellows squirming across his helmet visor's HUD on its IR setting.

Once, during that ten-minute firefight, he thought *maybe* he'd seen someone running out there . . . but it could easily have been a shadow cast by a drifting flare or fast-strobing chain of poppers. He'd fired at the target and not even known if he'd hit anything or not.

So much of his recruit training, and the combat training that had followed, had emphasized *personal* combat. He now knew a dozen different ways to kill a man with his bare hands, could take a man down with a knife or a rock or the butt end of his ATAR, could end any hand-to-hand encounter with a Marine-approved shout and stomp to the head. A lot of that training, he knew, had been designed to overcome civilian sensitivities and squeamishness and to bring out what Knox had called "the native aggressiveness of the US Marine." Somehow, though, he'd never quite picked up on the fact that most combat was at ranges where you never saw the enemy.

From here, he had an impressive view of the entire Chancre Valley. In the distance near the lake, a flight of drone VT-20 hunter-killers banked and darted in the sunlight, seeking out the enemy mortar tubes, as a pair of Marine Valkyries circled watchfully overhead. Closer, a pair of hulking Marine A-25 Cataphracts growled and rumbled as they nosed through the underbrush outside the perimeter. 'Phracs in the distance were always a comforting sight, quad-tracked mobile weapons platforms twice as long and four times more massive than the old Abrams and Schwarzenegger tanks that still served as Marine reserve armor. They were the subject of lively debate at the base, now, with their detractors claiming they were obsolete in an age of smart-AI battlefield HK missiles and pinpoint railgun bombardment from orbit, but most Marines liked having them about.

Just so long as they weren't *too* close by; 'Phracs tended to draw enemy artillery fire like bodies drew flies, and it was generally safer to admire the behemoths from a comfortable distance.

"Hey, Flash!" Slidell called from behind. "Whatcha doing? Admiring the scenery?"

"Hey, Slider," Jack replied. He still wasn't sure how Slider and the others had picked up on the handle he'd earned at boot camp. It almost had to be Lonnie or Dubber or one of the others from his boot company, but he'd thought he'd had them all sworn to silence. "You know what they say. Join the Marines. See exotic, far-off lands. Meet fascinating people. Kill them. . . ."

"Ooh-rah. Listen, buddy. You 'n' me need to talk!"

Jack peeled back the Velcro cover on his watch. "Got a few minutes. I've got honey-bucket detail at zero-eight-thirty."

"This won't take long." Slider gestured at a stack of sandbags and grinned. "Step into my office and pull up a seat!"

Jack grunted and dropped onto a sandbag. Slider pulled another bag a bit closer, sat, and leaned forward, dragging his PAD from its holster. He opened the screen, keyed it

on, and Sam's lovely face appeared, wearing a sultry smile
and nothing else. "Hi, Slider," she said.

"Listen, Flash," Slidell said, ignoring her, "this has got
to be the greatest fucking gimmick since Net-babe downloads! You are a fucking *genius*, man!"

Jack shrugged, embarrassed. "Hey, no big deal. I just
hacked some commercial AI software."

" 'No big deal,' the man says. How'd you crunch her
down to fit on a Marine PAD, anyway?"

"That was pretty easy, actually. The government-issue
AI, well, the source code just isn't that efficiently written,
you know? Loose, redundant, and looking like it was
turned out by a committee. Turned out that Samantha's
source code wasn't that much bigger than the government
program. It just, well, it's tighter. Does more in less space,
and better."

"Better! I'll say!" He eyed Samantha's body apprecia-
tively. "Hey, baby!" he said. "Let's see your ass!"

"Whatever you say, Slider." Standing, she turned
around, spread her legs, and gracefully bent over, grabbing
her ankles to give Slider a good look.

"The color's a bit flat and garish," Jack said. "I had
to go down from millions of colors to two fifty-six. But I
might know a way to get around that. I'm still tweaking
it, you know."

"Well, all I can say is I would love to give *her* a tweak!
Flash, m'boy, you and me are gonna clean up!"

"What do you mean?"

Gently, he patted the screen over Sam's raised bottom.
"Okay, honey. Let's see you dance for us!"

"Whatever you say, Slider." She straightened up and
began a slow, sensuous bump and grind, turning slowly
as she danced to nonexistent music. Frowning, Jack made
a mental note to check her source code, especially the
random sequencing routine. She was falling into that
"Whatever you say" response much too often.

"Flash, do you have any idea what the guys would *pay*
to have their very own naked babe, at their command, right
on their own PADs?"

"Pay? I figured some of the guys would just like to *have* them. . . ."

"Oh, Flash, Flash, Flash, I am so *disappointed* in you! There is *opportunity* here, big-time, and you obviously are in desperate need of someone to show you how to make the most of it! You *gotta* learn how to play the angles, man!"

"But we can't sell it, can we? I mean, I started with this commercial package. It was really pretty lame, a kind of customized do-it-yourself date on your computer, but it was protected by a copyright, you know? And the AI agent came from another package. I just kind of knitted the two together."

"Ah, that stuff is all in a gray area, know what I mean? You probably already technically violated copyright just by rewriting her source code, right?"

"I don't think I—"

"Sure! And with all the stuff you did with her code, you changed her quite a bit, right? Like, you were telling me you worked in that emergency quick-change bit, and got her to respond personally, with your name, and stuff? And obviously you worked in the Net agent stuff, and the government-issue agent, too, right?"

"Yeah, but I still used—"

"You used the store-bought program as a template. Sure. But what we have here is a whole new product! *Trust* me!"

Jack looked at Slider for a moment, letting his gaze flick up to the patch glued to the Marine's helmet. Armor and helmet decorations weren't authorized for the 5th MarDiv, strictly speaking, but none of the brass, up to Major General Holcomb himself, had issued any orders to end the widespread practice. Slider carried his Hops Vincet patch glued to his helmet, right next to the visor drag and above the stenciled name SLIDELL.

All The Way To Mars And They Made Us Throw Away The Beer. . . .

Jack knew all about the beer patch and the story behind it from his uncle, but he'd been startled to find someone who'd been on Garroway's March *here,* in Russia. He'd heard that the Corps was a tight little family, that if you stayed in long enough, you would inevitably run into just about everyone . . . but he'd not really believed it until he'd met Slider.

He was worried about Slider's proposition. It still didn't seem entirely legal . . . and Jack hadn't really planned on *selling* Sam to the other Marines. He'd thought that she might be a good way for him to make friends, but he hadn't thought at all about using her to make money. But the fact that Slider had been there, with the MMEF on Mars went a long, long way toward making Jack want to trust the guy. In point of fact, Slider was a little vague about the details; once he'd claimed to have been at Mars Prime during the march, helping to offload the contraband beer that Garroway had used in his unorthodox attack at Cydonia, but most of the time he claimed to have actually been with "Sands of Mars" Garroway in the long trek up the Valles Marineris.

It hardly mattered. Slider was obviously an operator, as old-hand Marines called them, but he seemed a decent enough guy. And whether he'd actually been on the March or not, he'd been to *Mars* . . .

Jack did wonder, sometimes, why the guy was still only a corporal when he had to have been in damned near forever to have gotten a billet with the MMEF. He'd asked Slider about it once, but the Marine had just shrugged, and said, "Sergeants. Can't live with 'em, and it sure would be nice to live without 'em."

"So what's your idea?" Jack asked.

"I figure we could sell these to the other guys at sixty bucks a pop, maybe seventy-five, see?" He stared at Sam for a moment, watching her silent, writhing dance on the PAD's display. "Hell, I'm gonna have to think about the price, some. Even a hundred wouldn't be too much for one of these baby dolls! Anyway, I figure you and me split the take, fifty-fifty. You do whatever customizing is necessary, you know, to get her to use the customer's name and everything. And I'll see to the sales and marketing end of things. I can make the pitch, close the sale, collect the cash, and then we make the split. Deal?"

"Oh, man," Jack said. "I'm going to have to think about that one."

"Lemme ask you one thing."

"Shoot."

"You think you might wanna go with this idea? I mean, it's a possibility, right?"

"Well, I guess so. . . ."

"Then do us both a big favor, kid. *Stop giving the fucking things away!*"

"Huh?"

"You're gonna kill the market with freebies, man! What's worse, some other techie-type might get ahold of this and do up a product of his own! Man, you gotta go into business with me on this thing just to protect your interests, y'know?"

Jack shrugged. He'd only given Sam to Slider and a couple of others . . . and three or four of the guys like Lonnie who'd come over to the Vlad with him. He didn't suppose it mattered. "Okay, sure. Why not? But I'm still not sure this thing's such a good idea."

"Hey, *trust* me, Flash! I wouldn't steer ya wrong! You 'n' me are gonna clean up big!"

Jack looked at his watch again. "Hey, I gotta get to the honey buckets, Slider. I'll see you later."

"Okay, man. Just remember! No more freebies!"

Honey-bucket duty was one of the less glamorous aspects of service with the Marines, Jack was finding. Each morning, and again in the evening, the cut-down two-hundred-liter fuel cans set beneath the latrine benches had to be hauled out into the open, the contents doused with diesel fuel or kerosene, and burned. It was filthy, back-breaking, stinking, stomach-turning work, the sort traditionally reserved for the newbies and the replacements who either hadn't yet proven themselves, or who hadn't been aboard long enough for anyone newer to come along and get picked for shit detail instead.

"So, anyone hear any more about that asteroid the UN-dies are supposed to've launched at the US?" Lonnie wanted to know. There were four of them on the detail—Jack, Lonnie Costantino, Duberand, and PFC Alan Kale, another alumnus from Platoon 4239. They'd dragged out the first three honey pots and set them ablaze. Oily, foul-smelling smoke boiled above the barren hillside.

Kale leaned on his shovel. "I still think it's all bullshit. The UNdies'd never launch an asteroid at us! I mean, they gotta live on this planet, too!"

"I dunno," Duberand said. "My sister's in the Air Force, stationed at V-berg, and she said they already launched missiles to knock the thing off course. She swore it was true."

"You're too ugly to have a sister, Dub. How come they didn't tell the whole country, huh?"

"Maybe because they didn't want a panic," Jack said. "Or because they want to wait and make sure it's going to miss."

"Man," Kale said. "You think they'd let something like that go down without warning folks? Without trying to evac 'em or something? That's cold, man."

"If they can't move everybody," Jack said, "maybe they opted not to move anybody, just because of the panic and stuff."

"You know," Duberand said, "there's a story goin' around that it wasn't the UN that moved that asteroid. It was aliens."

"No way," Costantino said. "Uh-uh, no way it was aliens."

"What makes you an authority, Lonnie?" Kale wanted to know. "You talk to 'em?"

"As a matter of fact, yeah." Lonnie pointed at his forehead, where four months earlier he'd worn the star emblem of the An. "I'm still Alien Astronauts, y'know. The Masters don't want to harm the Earth. They want to save it."

"I don't know what scares me more," Kale said. "The idea of the UN dropping rocks on us, or you telling me that the aliens won't."

"Some churches back home are saying the aliens are the Antichrist's forces," Jack pointed out. "Others say they're angels, here to save us. They *both* can't be right!"

"What do you say?" Duberand wanted to know.

He shrugged. "I don't think they're gods or devils. I think right now they're telling us more about humans, from the way people react to them, than they are telling us about themselves."

"Yeah, so you think the UN has been changing asteroid orbits?"

"Wouldn't put it past them. A small enough rock might just be enough to cripple us, without hurting the rest of the world. It'd be a hell of a weapon. Of course, that's why the Marines are going to need more of a presence in space."

"Uh-oh," Kale said. "Flash is gonna do his speech again!"

"Fuck you too, Kale. No speeches. But if any two-bit dictator or terrorist with even minor space capability can bump a fair-sized rock into an Earth-intercept orbit, we're going to *have* to set up some sort of regular patrol out there, just to make sure no one tries that shit! What I want to know is, if that rock is on the way, how come they didn't scramble the Marines to go get it?"

"Would you have gone on a mission like that?" Lonnie asked.

"Hell, yeah. Wouldn't you?"

"Hell, no. I don't mind joining the Marines and getting shot at by unfriendly natives. But getting stuffed into a tin can and fired into space, man, a guy could get killed that way. No thanks!" Costantino stirred the bubbling, smoking mess in one of the burn bins with his shovel. "I think we're ready for another load, here."

"I'll get it," Jack said. Turning, he started down the hill toward the latrines. Lonnie followed him.

The move—all of four meters—saved their lives.

A Chinese railgun located well inside Manchuria had fired a hypervelocity fléchette cluster moments before; the depleted uranium fléchettes, traveling at nearly eight times the speed of sound, slammed into the hilltop occupied by Ol' Buck and a Quarter with a release of kinetic energy equivalent to a kiloton pocket nuke.

Kale was sliced cleanly in two. Duberand was lucky; he only lost his leg. The thunderclap of the impact was deafening, as buildings, sandbag walls, artillery pieces, and one of the Cataphract MWPs were either shredded, flattened, or enveloped in flame. When Jack was able to raise his head again, he was fifteen meters from where he'd been, half-buried in mud and gravel. The air was choked with clouds of smoke, and the shrill screams of the wounded went on and on and on above the crackle of flames in nightmare choruses of agony and terror.

This time, no one bothered with the Maggie's-drawers joke.

TWENTY

HQ, Marine Firebase 125
Near Kirovsky
Russian Far Eastern Maritime
Territory
1540 hours local time

Jack stood at rigid attention in front of Captain Thomas Rollins, his company commander, with Slider to his right. His left arm was still in a sling to immobilize the shoulder wrenched by the hyper-V attack, and he'd been on light duty for the past five days. They'd both been summoned by Gunny Blandings, whose sorrowful mien was all Jack needed to convince him that the two of them were headed for nothing less than a court-martial. "The Old Man is freaking *pissed*" was all Blandings would tell them.

When they knocked at his door, they were admitted with a brusque "Center yourselves on the hatch!" Inside, Rollins was seated at his desk, his PAD open and an expression on his features that managed to merge astonishment with both sadness and anger.

"Corporal Slidell, Private First Class Ramsey, reporting as ordered, *sir*!" Slidell rapped out. He could sound every inch the Mr. Clean Marine when he wanted to.

"Would either of you gentlemen care to explain . . . this?" Rollins said, turning his PAD so that they both could see the screen, with Sam enticingly displaying herself, and Jack knew that the worst had happened.

Or, more accurately, perhaps, the worst was just about to happen.

"Why, ah . . . sir," Slidell said. "That's just a little skin program that Flash here picked up Stateside. No one's ever said anything about not being able to bring in a skin book or magazines, so what's wrong with—"

"This," Rollins said, shaking his head dangerously, "is considerably more than a skin mag, Corporal. I've had Gunny and a couple of the tech people from Battalion look at this."

God! Jack thought, now terrified. *This has gone all the way up the line to Battalion?*

"They tell me," Rollins went on, "that you've somehow dropped a new agent program on top of the government-issue AIDE, actually recoded the thing so it works better, smarter, and faster. And this new program, they tell me, is probably cobbled together from at least two other programs, though they can't tell for sure. Very slick stuff, I'm told. Very professional work."

Jack had to clamp down on himself to keep from blurting out a pleased "Thank you, sir!" He doubted very much that the Old Man had hauled him in to admire his programming prowess. He remained at attention, his eyes focused on a spot on the green-painted wall above and behind Rollins's left shoulder.

"Slidell, according to your records, you have all of the programming skills and cybernetic savvy of wet spaghetti. But you do have a penchant for con jobs, scams, dealing, and selling just about anything you can lay your hands on. You're the best scrounger in the company, but you're just a little bit too greedy. My guess is that you've been, um, marketing Ramsey's little toy here." He turned his cold gaze on Jack. "As for you, Ramsey, you're brand-new to this outfit, and I don't know you that well. You have a good boot-camp record, though, and your quals tell me you have an unusual aptitude for programming and computers. I'm surprised as hell they didn't put you in for a 4069 MOS and send you to nerd school." The 4069 Military Occupation Specialty code designated a systems programmer. "I'm guessing that this young lady is your doing. Am I right?"

"Yes, sir!"

"Are you aware that you're probably in violation of half a dozen different copyright laws with this little gem?"

He started to tell the captain that copyrights and programs were still a gray area in law but immediately thought better of it. "Yes, sir." He swallowed, then added, "It, ah, didn't start off as something to sell, sir. But, well, things kind of got out of hand."

"I'm much more concerned about the alterations you introduced into the mil-issue PAD agent. Tampering with that is about as smart as tampering with the pin on a hand grenade. Suppose your alterations left it unable to perform some vital task, like calling up the right tactical data, or providing you with the correct map?"

"Sir, I made very sure that that didn't happen."

"Normally, I would put a statement like that down to damned-fool arrogance. However, I am told by Battalion's technical team that you are correct. Your revisions not only allow AIDE to do everything it was designed to do, they let it operate faster, more efficiently, and *smarter*. In effect, you've managed to upgrade the damned thing to a level-two AI and done it in a smaller and more efficient package. Battalion is still shaking their collective heads over that one.

"As a result, Ramsey, you are going to luck out. This time. My first instinct was to hit you with mast. Deliberate misappropriation and alteration of government property. Endangerment of yourself and your fellow Marines. Even taking into account the fact that you seem to have fallen in with bad company and been led astray, you would've been in deep trouble. Those charges *could* have ended in a general court-martial. Believe me, son, this is some serious shit you've stepped in.

"However, Major General Holcomb has reviewed the case, including the recommendations by the tech team. He has directed me to put through your transfer, effective immediately. You will be put on the first transport back to the States, where you will report to the Space Combat

Training Command at Quantico, Virginia. There, you will be given a course in space operations.

"It seems, Ramsey, that the Corps is in desperate need right now for people with talents such as yours. You are headed for 1-SAG. Now get the hell out of here."

"Aye, aye, sir!"

Dazed, ears ringing, Jack all but stumbled from the captain's office. As he left, though, he heard Rollins turning his full attention to Slider. "You know, Slidell, I'm beginning to think you *like* being a private! So. I'll tell you what I'm going to do. . . ."

The thundering, numbing shock of what had just happened didn't really hit home until fifteen minutes later.

He was going to space after all. . . .

FRIDAY, 12 SEPTEMBER 2042

*Vandenberg Aerospace Force
Base
0740 hours PDT*

They both showed their passes to the Aerospace Force guard at the front gate, who looked at them carefully before waving them through and saluting. Security at Vandenberg was unusually tight now . . . a decided case of locking the barn door after the horse had already galloped off. Rob swung the rented blue-and-silver Samurai onto Oceanview Drive with a thin, electric whine and steered for the old Visitor's Complex, which for several years now had housed the Marine enclave on the base.

"What a mess," Kaitlin said, as the hydrogen-fueled vehicle passed a burned-over stretch of scrub brush and the charred-forest remains of an H_2 tank farm. The smoldering, skeletal remains of a K-120, its blue UN flag still visible on one upthrust wing, sprouted from the center of the farm like some obscenely alien, flame-scorched tree. "Looks like that one pulled a kamikaze smack into the hydrogen tanks."

"Might've just been a lucky hit," Rob replied.

"Unlucky for the pilot. That's not one he's going to walk away from."

She shivered. She and Rob had been lucky as well, lucky they'd not been on base when the sneak attack had come. The orders confining 1-SAG to base had been lifted three days before, and the next evening, she and Rob, seeking privacy, had gone to a motel off-base to spend the night together.

Their play had been interrupted by the thunder of explosions. By the time they'd gotten back to the base, the attack was over.

A second sentry, a Marine this time, waved them through at the Visitor's Complex gate. Smoke still stained the morning sky above the airfield and the assembly hangars in the distance; the pall was especially thick above Pad 4B, where it was expected that the fires, fed by ruptured underground feed lines, would continue burning for days more. A Marine Valkyrie rested tail high in the scrub just outside the complex, where its pilot had brought it in for a none-too-gentle emergency touchdown.

The UN raiders had struck late in the evening two days before, a flight of German stealth K-120s coming in off the Pacific at wave-skimming altitude, minutes behind an initial wave of cruise missiles. The aircraft had been launched by a UN submarine aircraft carrier that had crept to within twelve hundred kilometers of the California coast. The cruise missiles had been launched from a pair of French arsenal subs lurking eight hundred kilometers farther north.

Both UN squadrons had been hit by US retaliatory strikes; one of the arsenal ships, the *Pluton*, had been sunk by Aerospace Force A-40 Wasps vectored out of Travis by a spotter aboard a US military orbital recon station. The German carrier, believed to be the *Seeadler*, had been heavily damaged by the *Lakota*, a US strike sub, and was still being hunted in the dark, cold waters beyond the Jasper Seamount. None of the six attacking K-120s had made it back to their carrier.

Still, the raid had to be chalked up on the big board as a UN success. The stealth attack had left twenty-one Wasp and Defender Aerospace Force fighters destroyed or crippled on the ground. Worse, far worse, a Zeus II being readied on Pad 4B had been destroyed in a titanic fireball that had lit up the western night skies for all of Los Angeles, and six precious SRE-10s being readied in the assembly hangars had been badly damaged. Those Sparrowhawks had been on the prep line, being fitted with missiles to bump those surviving fragments of 2034L that still posed a threat to the Earth; there would be no more counter-asteroid launches now, and the techies still weren't confident that the oncoming fragment cloud was going to leave the Earth unscathed.

Rob pulled the Samurai into the parking lot outside Building 12. The two of them stopped in the lot and saluted as morning colors sounded, then walked up to the entrance, returned the salutes of the two Marine sentries posted there, and went inside.

Room 310, on the third floor down from ground level, was the Marine enclave's main briefing room in a building devoted to the planning of the missions that were extending the reach of the US Marine Corps from the surface of sea and land into the empty reaches of space. Several dozen men and women were already in the room when Kaitlin and Rob checked through the last security station and walked in, but they were still early. A buffet table to one side provided doughnuts and coffee, and they helped themselves as the crowd quietly milled about, ate, and talked.

Captain Fuentes approached them, coffee cup in hand. "Action briefings the civilized way," she told them. "Complete with breakfast."

"Don't want to get into a firefight on an empty stomach," Rob said.

"So, what's the word?" Kaitlin asked, pouring herself a Styrofoam cup of coffee. "Are we going to get clobbered or not?"

"I imagine we'll hear today," Fuentes said. "The astronomers'll have a precise vector for it, and any splinters that got bumped off." She shook her head. "I still find it

hard to believe that we have the power to change the orbit
of something like that!''

"Who was it who said, 'Give me a lever long enough
and I'll move the Earth'?" Rob wanted to know. "Eurip-
ides?"

"You rippa-dese, you pay for 'em," Kaitlin shot back.
"Actually, he wrote plays. Archimedes played around
with moving the Earth." She frowned at the thought. What
was it about humans, what was it about *her* that cracked
jokes three days before the greatest catastrophe on Earth
since the ice ages? Life went inexorably on; maybe people
simply weren't able to face disaster on such a scale
squarely.

"I still like the first idea that was floating around the
base for a while," Rob said. He chose a doughnut from a
plate, broke off a piece, and ate it—leaning forward carefully to avoid getting powdered sugar on his uniform.
"Send in the Marines and blast the thing out of the sky."

"Not an option now," Fuentes said. "I heard we won't
have any more Zeus IIs on the ready-pad for a couple of
weeks, now. That leaves 1-SAG sitting in the mud, all
dressed up with no way to get there.''

"A permanent Marine presence in space," Rob said.
"That's what we need, and we needed it a year ago."

"You want to be stationed in space?" Kaitlin asked,
smiling. "I hear the liberty is awful. No bars, no cat-
houses, no tattoo parlors, no girlie reviews or skin flicks.
I mean, what's a Marine supposed to do with his free
time?"

"Well, this special-launch-for-every-mission business
stinks," Rob replied. "If we had SAG teams stationed up
there all the time, they'd be in a position to do something
right away if some nut-case decides to drop rocks on
Earth. The farther away we intercept an incoming rock,
the smaller that lever needs to be."

"No argument there," Fuentes said.

"I'd like to know why we can't use the *Ranger* against
those fragments," Kaitlin wanted to know. "From what
I've been reading, the hardest part about rendezvousing
with an oncoming asteroid is matching vectors with the

thing. You've got to fly past it, stop, and accelerate back to match course and speed. That takes time, and a hell of a lot of reaction mass. But if *Ranger*'s specs are anything close to what I've seen published, she could match vectors with the rock easy enough.''

Rob grunted. "She could . . . and then the UN would know all about her. Maybe even rush through the completion of their own antimatter drive. Besides, she's not ready yet, is she? I know they don't have her weapons installed yet.''

Fuentes shrugged. "I heard her drives were operational. They could've used her to plant Marines on the asteroid, if they'd gone that route instead of trying to nudge it with nukes. But that would've given the game away, y'know?''

"National security,'' Rob added.

"Yeah. The UN would know we had a working antimatter-drive vessel. Maybe they're close enough with their AM ship that they could rush it through to completion, confront us with an armed supership. We lose the edge . . . maybe lose the war.''

"Somehow, that's a worrisome thought,'' Kaitlin said. "Sacrifice five million civilians in the name of national security.''

"We'll only have one shot with the *Ranger*,'' Fuentes pointed out. "She has to work, and she has to work perfectly, first time. If we lose her, if something goes wrong on her first mission, we don't have anything on hand when the UN unveils their AM supership. And scuttlebutt says they *are* armed, with something that makes lasers look like flashlights.''

"What's *Ranger* supposed to be packing,'' Rob asked. "You know?''

"Lasers. Probably in the hundred-gig range. Probably missiles. I don't know. Everyone's being pretty tight-lipped about it.''

"All things considered, that's good,'' Kaitlin said. "If we don't know, maybe the UN doesn't either!''

The door at the far end of the room opened and Major Avery stride in, accompanied by Captain White and a base photographer. "Attention on deck!'' someone yelled, and the Marines already seated in the briefing room came to their feet.

"As you were, as you were," Avery said, waving them down. He made his way to the podium at the head of the room, taking his place there with his hands braced on the sides as though he were conning the thing through a storm. His photographer crouched nearby, taking shots as the rest of the Marines in the room filed through the aisles to take their seats.

"Good morning, Marines," he said as the room went quiet. "First item on the agenda. The Deep Space Tracking Net at Colorado Springs has just issued an all-clear for Earth, which they now say is safe from Asteroid 2034L. Apparently, the vector change introduced by the Aerospace Force strike a month ago *was* sufficient to deflect the body. They report that, while we may be in for some shooting-star fireworks on Monday evening, the main body has definitely changed vector sufficiently to easily clear the Earth as it passes us." Several of the Marines in the room broke out into cheers and applause at the news. Avery waited, frowning, until the noise had died down before continuing. "Of course, this means that the One-SAG alert is canceled. It now appears that our services will *not* be necessary in dealing with this threat."

He almost seems disappointed, Kaitlin thought, bemused. She wondered how much career capital Avery had had riding on the possibility of a Marine-SAG mission to disintegrate 2034L. It was possible. Of course, after the UN strike against Vandenberg, it would have been impossible to launch any kind of space intercept mission at all, which was probably why the UN had launched it in the first place. The sub-carrier air strike must have been planned months ago, before 2034L's course had been changed in the first place.

"We can, therefore, turn to the second item on the agenda, which we are now calling Operation Dark Star. Gentlemen, ladies, we are now assured that the USS *Ranger* will be fully operational within two weeks. We have authorization from President Markham himself to use her in a combined-arms sky-and-ground assault against the enemy forces dug in at Tsiolkovsky, what the Army tried to do last May, and failed. We now anticipate being able to mount a major op against the enemy within the next two months.''

That caused a stir in the audience. Avery tapped out something on his podium's touch pad, darkening the room lights and opening the wall at his back to reveal a large display screen. Another few taps, and the screen lit with an image, a high-orbit view of a portion of the Moon's surface.

It was a particularly rugged and forbidding stretch of terrain, heavily cratered and broken. The only flat area at all was a flattened oval that stood out as much darker than the surrounding highlands, a large, deep bowl of a crater with an off-center central peak and steep walls.

''This is the crater Tsiolkovsky,'' Avery told them. ''As you can see, it's one of the very few flat places on the entire Lunar farside. The near side is characterized by the flat-plain maria, with some highlands. On the farside, there are no true maria at all, except for the Mare Moscoviense, farther north, and the Mare Ingenii to the southeast, and those, properly speaking, are just large craters with lava-plain floors, a little larger, a little less steep than Tsiolkovsky, here. On the whole farside, there are no seas at all even as large as the Mare Crisium. Very rugged territory. Very hard to traverse on the ground.

''The crater Tsiolkovsky was originally chosen as the primary site for the joint US–Russian SETI radio telescope project back in the '20s. The Mars landings and the discovery of alien artifacts at Cydonia resulted in the funding for the project being cut. After all, if we had an actual alien civilization to study, even a dead one, we wouldn't need to spend hundreds of millions of dollars on an antenna to listen in on their equivalent of *Monday Night Football*.''

Polite chuckles rose from the audience. Avery smiled and continued. ''In any case, the facility was mothballed and came under UN control in 2036. Since the beginning of the war, we've known they were up to something back there, but intelligence has been damned hard to come by.

This series of intel photos, unfortunately, is almost two years old. We have nothing more recent, and attempts to send recon spacecraft around the Lunar farside have all met with disaster."

He touched a key, and the photo on the screen expanded sharply, zooming in until the oblong, dark gray plain of Tsiolkovsky filled the screen. The shot was oblique, taken from the north at an altitude of under one hundred kilometers; the three-dimensional nature of the terrain was plainly visible, with the crater clearly a deep, steep-sided bowl, with the central peak a prominent cluster of smoothly rounded mountains closer to the north rim than to the south. A cluster of lights was just visible in the shadows at the base of the central peak.

"Those lights," Avery went on, "are at the site of the old SETI base. We believe the UN has simply added to the facilities there. The amount of space transport traffic we've tracked going around the back side of the Moon suggests they've expanded the port facilities there. They've probably built containment tanks of some sort for water hauled in from the Lunar south pole. They probably also have a large nuclear reactor. The creation of antimatter, I needn't remind you all, requires a *very* large expenditure of energy, so we expect a small fusion plant on-site, at the very least."

The scene expanded again, this time zooming in on the central peak. The lights at the base were more numerous now and seemed to sketch out short lines and geometric figures. The base, obviously, was a big one. At the rounded top of the highest mountain, a slender silver tower extended high into space. It would have been almost impossible to see if not for the telltale shadow it cast, a long, black scratch across the sunlit mountaintop.

"That tower was part of the original SETI project. The idea was to raise the tower as the focus for incoming signals. A thin mesh of very fine wires would have extended from the mast clear to the crater rim, kind of like the old RT built in a round valley at Arecibo, in Puerto Rico. That would have resulted in a radio telescope dish 185 kilometers across, big enough to eavesdrop on a private, short-range radio conversation clear across the galaxy.

"What we believe the UN has done is fit that central mast, which was already in place, as a transmitter instead of as a receiver. Easy enough to do, technically. In 1974, scientists used the radio telescope at Arecibo to send a symbolic radio message into space. The UN techies have probably done the same sort of thing, setting it up as a powerful radar station.

"Somewhere in this crater, the UN has also erected a powerful weapon designed to fire bursts of antimatter . . . specifically, positrons. Antielectrons. Such a burst destroyed a recon Sparrowhawk last April, at a range of some tens of thousands of kilometers. We think, but don't know, that they would have constructed their weapon somewhere at the top of the central peak, to give it a good field of fire, without raising the horizon by firing out of the bottom of this bowl. It's also possible, of course, that the weapon is sited somewhere along the crater rim.

"Somewhere inside the crater, we don't know where, the UN has assembled some sort of shipfitting or shipbuilding complex and is busily working on their version of our *Ranger,* an antimatter-powered spacecraft of tremendous range, power, and maneuverability. We believe, but don't know, that this spacecraft is a heavily modified Dauphin-class transport." A diagram and accompanying photograph appeared in windows inset over the view of Tsiolkovsky, showing a black, diamond-shaped craft, streamlined for atmospheric flight. "We believe her to be the *Millénium,* launched early this year from Kourou, the ship some of you reported seeing at Picard. Also, fragmentary reports from the Army expedition at the Lunar south pole suggests that she was there as well, though this has not been confirmed. Intelligence believes that the *Millénium* is being refitted with both an antimatter drive and an antielectron cannon. It is possible—though we cannot count on this—that they have only one antimatter cannon, which was set up on the ground at Tsiolkovsky in April but is now being mounted, or else has been mounted already, aboard the ship."

"If we knew any less about the objective," Carmen

whispered at Kaitlin's side, "we'd be going in completely blind."

The sentiment echoed Kaitlin's own thoughts. How did you plan an attack on an objective that you hadn't reconned, that you hadn't even *seen* for two years?

"We have been working on a plan of battle," Avery went on, "one that will allow us to approach Tsiolkovsky with a fair chance of success. The operation, as we see it so far, will require a two-pronged attack, beginning with an assault on these perimeter defenses . . . incapacitating the enemy's long-range radar.

"Three gets you five he had nothing to do with the planning," Rob whispered at her side. "This had to come from the very top."

Kaitlin shushed him, then leaned forward, trying to capture every word. He was now describing a new vehicle, which he called the new and improved LAV, and how it would be used for the initial phase of the Tsiolkovsky attack.

The plan, she thought, was nothing short of brilliant. Risky . . . even dangerous, but brilliant nonetheless. . . .

Discharge Office
Joliet Federal Prison
1543 hours CDT

"Sign here, sir . . . and here."

David Alexander signed the release forms on the indicated lines. He'd already had his personal effects returned to him . . . the suit he'd been wearing the day he'd been arrested, his digital Rolex, his Sony PAD, his wallet with eighty-five dollars, pocket change of three dollar coins and a quarter, and a small globe-and-anchor pin one of the Marines had given him as a keepsake after the return from Mars; he liked to carry it as a good-luck piece.

"Thank you, sir," the prison clerk said, checking the form over inside his cage. "That'll do it."

"It certainly will," David replied.

"Is it, ah, true what they've been saying? That you're

gonna sue the government for false arrest?''

He considered a sharp answer and discarded it. The clerk was a part of the system, but he wasn't the system and certainly had had no part in David's arrest and illegal imprisonment. He smiled. ''My lawyer recommended that I reply to that question with a firm and definite 'no comment,' '' he replied. ''But damn it, you people stole almost four months of my life, maybe even derailed my whole career. You can bet that pretty blue uniform of yours I'm at least *thinking* about the idea!''

''Well, that's your business, of course.'' The clerk looked uncomfortable as he countersigned the papers, then typed something into the computer on his counter. ''I'll bet you're looking forward to getting to sleep in your own bed tonight! Here ya go.''

The clerk slid the prison-release form through the slot in the cage front, and David pocketed it. Julia Dutton had told him that morning to be damned sure he kept all of the paperwork they gave him; it would all be evidence at the trial when they sued for wrongful arrest and imprisonment.

He still wasn't sure what had happened, exactly. His lawyer had seen him in the prison's visitor center that morning, ecstatic with the news that he was to be released. Apparently, he'd had some pretty big guns on his side and not even realized it. If Dutton had her facts straight—and she always seemed to—then General Warhurst himself, with a small army of JAG lawyers in tow, had dismantled at least part of the Justice Department in Washington, DC, threatening all-out war if David Alexander's case was not investigated, reviewed, and brought out into the open. The investigation had taken weeks; according to Dutton, there'd been some deeply entrenched political powers behind the scenes trying to delay or derail the process, but Warhurst and his legal legions had triumphed in the end.

David had met Montgomery Warhurst several times, both before and after the MMEF expedition to Mars, and been impressed with the man's sharp intelligence, determination, and sheer guts. What David didn't know yet was why the commandant of the US Marine Corps had gone

on the warpath for *him*. Sure, sure, he was an honorary
Marine, and all of that, but the way Dutton told the story,
Warhurst had been *that* close to declaring war on Justice
and the FBI both.

And hell, he *had* shared information with foreign nationals. Had Justice decided to try his case, instead of trying to pressure him into spying on his friends, he had little
doubt that he would have ended up as a guest at Joliet for
ten to fifteen big ones.

"This way, if you please, Dr. Alexander," the guard
who'd accompanied him through the bureaucratic circles
toward release said. "There's someone here to meet you."

Funny, David wasn't going to be able to think of the
man or his comrades as anything other than *screws* from
now on. Prison life had a culture and a language all its
own. "Lead on," he said. "Who is it, my lawyer?"

"I really don't know, Dr. Alexander." He tapped the
radio on his belt. "They just told me from the visitors'
check-in desk."

David wondered who was meeting him, then decided it
had to be either his lawyer or, just possibly, Teri. He'd
asked Dutton not to tell his wife that he was being released. He still had some thinking to do about that. If he
could just convince Liana that it would be better for them
both to end this mismatched marriage once and for all. . . .

The clerk was right. It would be good to sleep in his
own bed tonight. On the other hand, he wasn't sure he
wanted to see Liana just yet. He'd been doing a lot of
thinking about things during the past couple of months. It
was time, he thought, to have it out with Liana once and
for all . . . to sit down with her, make her *see* that it just
wasn't working out, make her realize that there was no
good reason for the two of them to keep on destroying
each other's lives. There *had* to be a way to make her
listen to reason.

He knew he had to do it, and soon, but the thought of
going home *tonight*, before he'd had a chance to work out
exactly what he wanted to say, was more daunting than
Joliet's walls. Funny. All those months alone, here, and

he hadn't figured out yet how to say what he needed to say. . . .

Maybe he would take a hotel room in Chicago for a day or two, while he thought things out. Somehow, he had to find a way to resolve things with Liana before he could let himself even think about a new life with Teri.

The guard led him into a lounge area near the main building's front door. There were a number of people there, and he scanned the crowd, looking for a familiar face.

Then a group of people in uniform stood and walked toward him, and David's eyes widened. "Good heavens!" he said. "I certainly didn't expect to see *you* here, sir! . . ."

"Dr. Alexander?" General Montgomery Warhurst said. "You and I have to talk."

TWENTY-ONE

Asteroid 2034L
Approaching Earth
1905 hours CDT

The main body of 2034L was considerably smaller than
it had been originally. The nuclear detonation had vaporized some hundreds of tons of rock and surface dust,
and a number of house-sized pieces had split off in zero-
G avalanches as rock expanded under the thermal shock
and deeply buried pockets of ice turned to steam. The largest piece, still over one hundred meters across and massing
over two and a half million tons, moved now on a slightly
altered course, one that would carry it past the Earth, missing by well over a hundred miles. Tracked by hundreds
of radar- and laser-ranging facilities in orbit and on Earth,
it tumbled past the planet, crossing the terminator from
night into day. Accelerated sharply by Earth's gravity, it
hurtled above a suddenly flattening horizon of blue and
swirling whites in a breath-holding cosmic near miss that
slung it sunward along a new orbit that was now the concern only of future generations of humankind.

Of the myriad fragments and splinters that had accompanied 2034L on its near-miss swing-by, most either
missed entirely or were small enough to burn up in Earth's
atmosphere. A few boulders, some the size of a house,
were large enough to cause significant damage. Over the
next few minutes, thousands of fragments entered Earth's

atmosphere, flaring brilliantly for a few seconds. Observers all along the Atlantic coast, in a vast footprint from Puerto Rico to Newfoundland and extending west as far as the Rocky Mountains, reported a dazzling display of shooting stars, including numerous bolides leaving long, persistent, slightly greenish trails. Several large fragments exploded in the sky as they rammed into increasingly thicker air, loosing their payloads of kinetic energy in violent blasts of heat, light, and sound. One fragment, massing twenty-five thousand tons, exploded eleven kilometers above the North Atlantic with a blast equivalent to twenty-five megatons of high explosive. Dozens of ships—most of them warships of either the US Second Fleet or the European Union Joint Military Command—burst into flame as the fireball expanded overhead, flames extinguished half a minute later as the shock wave arrived from the sky as a gust of hurricane wind. Over eight thousand men and women died, and thousands more were injured in an event initially thought by both sides to be an enemy nuclear strike. A second chunk passed over the Canadian Maritimes and Quebec with a light rivaling that of the sun before exploding thirty kilometers above Ogoki, Ontario. The three-megaton explosion ignited forests and blew down trees for tens of miles in all directions. Hundreds died and hundreds more were blinded, mostly people in Ogoki and in Fort Albany, on St. James Bay, who'd come out to watch the light show in the sky.

In both Washington and the EU military command center at Brussels, frantic requests for the release of nuclear weapons were received as reports flooded in from units across the Atlantic and North America. Fortunately, cooler heads prevailed on both sides of the conflict; both Brussels and Washington were expecting the near passage of 2034L at an hour and a half past sunset EDT and were prepared for spurious reports of nuclear attack. The situation was confirmed when observers both on Earth and in orbit noted that neither of the reported blasts had the characteristic EMP signature of a nuclear detonation.

At approximately 1930 hours CDT, one final fragment entered the Earth's atmosphere high above Pennsylvania.

Plummeting sharply, trailing a plume of metallic vapor three hundred kilometers long, it sliced through the atmosphere in a flaring, sun-bright tumble that took it over Toledo, southern Michigan, and Benton Harbor. Ironically, it was not part of the original carbonaceous chondrite at all. The EU warship *Sagittaire* had been drifting away from 2034L at the time the nuclear warhead detonated; the plasma-borne shock wave and reaction from vaporizing metal had by chance all but countered that movement. As a result, as the main body of 2034L had edged off on a new vector at six meters per second, as the cloud of splinters and debris slowly expanded, the shattered, dead hulk of the *Sagittaire* had continued on more or less the same vector that the asteroid had been following just before the detonation.

Unfortunately, when the warhead had detonated, most of the ship's aft hull had been in the shadow of the forward hab module and so was still coated with a black, light- and radar-absorbing polymer designed to give the vessel extreme stealth characteristics. When the debris cloud was probed by radar and ladar after the asteroid-nudging blast, the wreckage of the *Sagittaire*, eighty meters long and massing twenty-five hundred tons, had had a radar cross section of only a few meters; it looked, in short, to radar eyes, exactly like one more broken piece of rock within a cloud of tens of thousands of broken rocks, one small enough that it would certainly burn up when it hit Earth's atmosphere.

The tumbling wreckage began vaporizing almost eighty kilometers up. The hab module flared brilliantly somewhere above southern Michigan, exploding in an eye-searing detonation that set trees, houses, and telephone poles smoldering in communities along the St. Joseph River.

The aft module, however, fifty meters long, containing *Sagittaire*'s plasma drive unit, reactor, and a massive block of lead shielding and still massing over seventeen hundred tons, plunged in a long, flat trajectory toward the southern end of Lake Michigan.

Grant Park
Chicago
1931 hours CDT

"We are here today, my brothers and sisters, to reach out to the cosmos, to reach up and make *divine* contact with the Masters of the Stars!"

Liana stood in the press of the crowd, only a few meters from the stage that had been set up in Grant Park just in front of the enormous fountain. The plaza before the fountain was filled with people, a vast and colorful throng congregating shoulder-to-shoulder in the center of the park and spilling out in all directions along the Chicago lakefront. The temperature during the day had hit the high nineties, but now, just past sunset, a breeze coming in off the lake was cooling the air somewhat. The sky was clear, a fast-deepening blue with only the usual band of haze around the horizon characteristic of the Chicagoland area. A single shooting star, a brief flash of yellow-white, streaked from east, over the lake, toward the west. Few in the crowd noticed, though here and there, someone turned to his or her neighbor, pointing up into the evening sky. Everyone else was watching the Reverend Blaine and his impassioned, arm-waving performance.

"Yes, Brethren, the Masters of the Stars! Those highly evolved superior beings who, at the very *dawn* of creation, ordained that there would be life on this small, blue planet of ours, who raised up Man from among the beasts of the field and gave him reason, who gave him the divine spark of rational intelligence and understanding! . . ."

He was such a thrilling speaker. Liana wished that David could have been more like Pastor Blaine, warm and caring and, most of all, understanding.

She wondered if she should give David another chance, once he was released from prison. She thought she'd made up her mind—ever since *that woman* had shown up on her doorstep—but she was finding herself still trapped between her pain and her basic belief that divorce was just plain *wrong*.

"We know from the Bible, Book of Revelations 12,

verses seven and eight, that there was *war* in heaven, Michael and his angels fighting against the dragon, and the dragon and his angels fought, and prevailed not, neither was their place found in heaven anymore! And we know now from the work of the xenoarcheologists that there *was* war in heaven, long ago, between the creating Masters of the Stars, and another group we know only as the 'Hunters of the Dawn.' That is scientific *proof,* dear brothers and sisters, of the perfect accuracy of the biblical record, of divine revelation, of the very bedrock principles of our faith! It seems clear to me, brothers and sisters of the Star, that those scaly, repulsively reptilian beings the archeologists call the An, the beings who enslaved Mankind at the very beginning of human civilization, must be the serpent, the dragon, the fallen morning star mentioned in Revelations, and in the Old Testament, especially in Genesis. In fact, brothers and sisters, I believe . . .''

Blaine trailed off, looking up into the deep blue of the evening sky. Hundreds of people in the audience now were no longer listening to him, but looking up, pointing, murmuring among themselves. Liana looked up to see what the excitement was about and gasped. Dozens of falling stars were flashing across the sky, hurtling overhead on tightly drawn, fast-fading streaks of white and vanishing over the tops of the city buildings to the west. One meteor in particular far outshone the others, a blazing light brighter but much smaller than the full moon that tumbled lazily across the zenith, trailing green smoke as constellations of bright-burning fragments spilled off to either side, flaring and disappearing in an instant, the display eliciting a vast, swelling chorus of oohs and ahhhs and even some scattered applause.

Liana squealed and clapped as the large meteor soundlessly exploded in a flash and a cloud of drifting fragments. It was a celestial fireworks show of unprecedented beauty and spectacle.

''The Masters!'' someone in the crowd screamed. ''The Masters have come!''

''It is a *sign*, brothers and sisters!'' Pastor Blaine yelled, pointing skyward . . . as though trying to recapture his audience. "It is a *sign* that we—"

His listeners never heard what the sign signified. *Sagittaire*'s drive module was growing rapidly brighter in the sky low above the lake, casting a brilliant reflection on the dark gray water as it fell toward Chicago.

At precisely 7:32 P.M. CDT, the corpse of the UN ship exploded just nine hundred miles off of the original target of Cheyenne Mountain, a savage detonation less than two kilometers above the water and some fifteen kilometers short of the Chicago lakefront. Pastor Blaine's declaration was cut off in mid-sentence as the sky to the northeast suddenly turned as bright as high noon above a fast-expanding sphere of light as brilliant as the sun itself. Massing seventeen hundred tons and traveling at 11.6 kilometers per second, the *Sagittaire*'s stern half, with the reactor, plasma-drive unit, and shielding, carried a kinetic energy of nearly twenty-five kilotons, slightly more powerful than the warhead that destroyed Hiroshima.

The initial damage was caused by thermal radiation, a blaze of heat intense enough to set boats aflame, then by the shock wave racing across the water at nearly the speed of sound. There was radiation as well—though that would not become a serious problem for some hours yet. *Sagittaire*'s main drive consisted of layers of corrugated sheets of plutonium though which water was forced, creating a white-hot plasma of dissociated hydrogen and oxygen nuclei. The blast hurled enough plutonium into the atmosphere to cause considerable contamination downwind and to have deadly consequences within the lake itself . . . but the actual fallout, in a long, oval footprint that eventually would stretch from Chicago southeast to Gary, Michigan City, and South Bend, was still not as severe as the yield of most nuclear weapons.

Deadlier by far was the pulse of thermal radiation that set tankers, freighters, and pleasure craft ablaze as far away as Waukegan and Benton Harbor and flashed from the polished tops of skyscrapers along the lakefront like lightning. In Grant Park, hundreds, perhaps thousands of people stared directly into that sudden, intense fireball in the northeast and had their eyes melted from their sockets as every inch of exposed skin blistered, as their clothing melted, then burst into flame. Forty-seven seconds later, just long enough for the crowd to realize that, if this was a divine visitation, it was an uncommonly hostile one, the shock wave shrieked across the water, exploding across Lake Shore Drive, pushing ahead of it the fast-expanding surface of a bubble of superheated steam.

Liana hadn't been able to see the fireball because of the people and the trees between her and the Grant Park waterfront, but she did see those trees burst into flame, saw screaming people, many with clothing or arms and air ablaze, running in a pain and terror-goaded madness away from the water. Pastor Blaine, high on his stage, still had his hand raised, finger extended to make a point, his entire body shriveling as it burned like a living torch. Cars, snatched up off Lake Shore Drive, sailed overhead.

Then the steam hit her. In a span of time too brief for her to feel or know just how badly she'd been burned, the shock wave itself thundered off the water, scattering burning trees like matchsticks, and scouring the surging, screaming crowd of the devout from the pavement in a searing instant of death and utter devastation.

The wave front shattered Grant Park's Buckingham Fountain in chips of concrete, steam, and spray, boomed out of the park and across Michigan Avenue, hitting the skyscrapers beyond with a shock wave far stronger than the blast of any mere hurricane.

More people were killed or injured by flying shards of glass exploding from the skyscrapers than by the hurtling wall of heat, tens of thousands of them. Several buildings toppled, spilling into streets crowded with traffic, an avalanche of glass and concrete and steel crashing down on people who'd survived the thermal flash, deep within the dark-shadowed canyon floors of the city. North of the Chicago River, the Hancock Building, well anchored and with a base broader than its top, remained standing, but the Sears Tower, still one of the ten tallest buildings in the world, was sheared through a quarter of the way up its 443-meter height. The wreckage tumbled across the South

Branch of the Chicago River, Union Station, the Post Office, and parts of the Eisenhower Expressway, that one collapse alone killing thousands. The historic Wrigley Building, the Marina City Towers, and the nearby Twenty-first Century Sun Tower, all badly damaged the year before by a UN cruise missile attack, vanished within the fiery maelstrom, as did other lakefront landmarks, like Shedd Aquarium and the Adler Planetarium, exposed and isolated at the tip of its causeway. The Field Museum, massively constructed of marble and granite, remained standing, though every window was blown out, every person above the basement level was killed, and the northern and eastern sides were scorched jet-black; a few blocks to the south, the brand-new Institute for Exoarcheologcal Studies, on Waldron and Lake Shore Drives just south of Soldier Field, dissolved into flying splinters of glass, aluminum, and steel.

The city itself, like a wall, dissipated much of the heat and blast, though buildings were badly damaged as far away as Downers Grove, twenty-three miles to the west. Above Lake Michigan, steam boiled skyward in a vast and roiling pillar, spreading out at eight thousand meters in the characteristic cap of a mushroom cloud, and the city was blanketed in a pall of smoke and falling ash. Most horrifying of all, some hours after the blast, the first burning white flakes began sifting from the sky like an unseasonable snowfall—tiny flecks of plutonium from *Sagittaire*'s disintegrating drive module.

And in the shadow of the cloud, the city of Chicago, for the second time in 171 years, was burning. . . .

US Marines Space Combat
Training Center
Quantico, Virginia
2025 hours EDT

The twelve- and thirteen-hour days were beginning to wear on Jack as badly as the eighteen-hour days in boot camp. The physical stress wasn't the same, though he still

had morning PT and long runs along the trails that wove
through the woods along the banks of the Patuxent River.
In boot camp, the nonphysical part of his training had been
lumped together under the general heading of *knowledge*,
as his DIs had barrage-fed him isolated facts and figures
on everything from the range and power output of a UN
H&K Laserkarabiner LK-36 to the exact chain of command up the ladder from a recruit to President Markham.
Jack still had all-too-vivid memories of Gunny Knox's
scowling face as he bellowed, "All right, recruits! Time
for knowledge! *What* is the birthday of the United States
Marine Corps?"

And the answer—in this case, a chorused "*Sir!* The
birthday of the United States Marine Corps is 10 November 1775, *sir!*"

At Quantico, knowledge was presented in a far more
organized and school-like fashion. In fact, most of every
afternoon was spent in classrooms, learning a bewildering
array of technicalities, an almost encyclopedic mass of
data on the myriad aspects of science, engineering, and
medicine necessary for a man to live and function in space.
Mornings and evenings, after chow, were reserved for
hands-on training and simulator sessions, times when Jack
actually got to work with the equipment that would help
him survive in space.

Most important, at least in terms of emphasis, was the
USMC Hughes/McDonnell Douglas EVA Combat Armor,
Class-One. For the past week or so, Jack felt like he'd
spent more time in the suit than out of it.

Space suits had come a long way indeed since the days
of the first primitive shuttle orbiters. The gloves were thin
enough they no longer needed thick rubber fingertip pads,
or an additional aluminum fingernail attached to the left
thumb in order to pick up small objects. Still, the suits
were unpleasantly clumsy, especially under a full Earth
gravity. They consisted of an inner cooling garment of tiny
plastic tubes, covered by a two-piece insulation layer, and
the outer hard-shell sections of reactive camouflage Kev-
plas and molded-ceramic composites, which snapped and
sealed over most of his body like the pieces of a suit of

medieval armor. The helmet, with its built-in computer, comm system, and internal HUD, and the backpack Personal Life Support System and power plant completed the basic suit.

The current space-training class was a special one, consisting of just five Marines, two women and three men. Training had been intensive for the first two weeks, and two other men who'd begun the class on 1 September had already dropped out, unable to keep up with the barrage of facts, figures, and engineering esoterica they were expected to learn. There were more instructors for Class 42-C than students, though Staff Sergeant Ellen Caswell, another veteran of the MMEF and Garroway's March, was their primary instructor. This evening, after chow, they were gathered in Squad Bay 2, suited up, as usual, as Caswell put them through their paces, drilling them at disassembling their M-29 ATARs and putting them back together again, while wearing heavily insulated overgloves.

During a pause in the drill, he raised a clumsily gloved hand.

Caswell was also suited up. "Yes, Private Ramsey?" she said over the squad comm channel. At least no one here had started using his embarrassing Flash moniker.

"I was just wondering, Staff Sergeant, when we were going to get to go into the zero-G hangar?"

He'd heard about the hangar from some research into Corps space training that he'd done back home, before he'd joined up. The trainee was fully suited up in Class-One armor, complete with fifty-kilo backpack and power unit. A special harness was attached to the suit, which in turn was attached to a complicated-looking tangle of gimbals, pivots, and suspensor rigging dangling from the overhead, a carefully stressed and balanced arrangement that simulated the effects of zero G.

Traditionally, a student's first exposure to the rig came when he was hoisted into the air and given an empty M-29 ATAR and a loaded magazine. Other personnel cleared the hangar, and the student was ordered by radio to load his weapon, switch to full auto, and fire at a man-sized target at the other end of the hangar.

That amusing exercise was designed to demonstrate the need to brace a projectile weapon precisely at the suit's center of gravity, a point marked by a hollow cup positioned at about navel height that exactly fit the rounded butt end of an M-29 modified for zero-G combat. The idea was to keep the weapon centered and aim by controlling the pitch and yaw of the suit itself, aiming with the targeting cursor projected on the helmet's HUD. Most students ended up in a wild, uncontrollable, and embarrassing spin in the dangling support apparatus. Jack, however, knew about action-reaction and was pretty sure he would be able to impress his instructors by firing on-target, without throwing himself into a spin.

"Not this go-round, Ramsey," Caswell told him. "Next week we'll pop you into the hangar rig to give you a feeling of moving in one-sixth G, but we're cutting zero-G work from the curriculum for you five. Maybe you can pick it up later, after your mission."

Jack was disappointed, though he tried not to show it. They'd told him at the start that the program he'd be going through with the handful of other special selectees at Quantico was going to be abbreviated. They needed Marines with AI programming experience *now,* for a big, upcoming mission no one wanted to talk about, and so the space training course was being tailored just for them, cut down to include only what they needed to know to survive and fight on the surface of the moon, not in space.

Well, he was still going to the Moon, and that was quite as challenging an environment as Earth orbit or deep space. He looked down at his ATAR with its attached under-barrel M-440 grenade launcher. In another month, if he was able to tough out this course, he would be in space.

It didn't seem possible.

Caswell appeared to be listening to something, her head cocked to one side behind the visor of her helmet. He felt a chill, a kind of premonition. There was a horror in the staff sergeant's eyes that he'd seen before . . . in the trenches in the Russian Far East.

"Listen up, people," she said, her voice hard. "I've

just had a report come down from Battalion. Approximately one hour ago, a fragment of that asteroid diverted by the UN entered Earth's atmosphere and struck the southern tip of Lake Michigan with an impact equivalent to the explosive force of a small nuclear weapon. Reports, reports are still kind of confused, but it sounds like the city of Chicago has been destroyed.''

There was a roaring sound in Jack's ears, and he felt the hammering of his heart. He felt dizzy . . . short of breath, and he reached for his suit's controls to up his O$_2$ feed a notch. Chicago . . . gone? He'd been there so many times, visiting Aunt Liana and Uncle Dave.

Hard on the heels of that thought came another. His aunt and uncle . . . if they were in the city, they must be *dead* . . .

"*Jesus, Mary, and Joseph!*" another voice put in, and Marielle Polanski crossed herself, the gesture oddly cumbersome in Marine armor. Then he remembered that Marielle was from Chicago; she'd mentioned once that her folks lived there.

"Private Polanski?" Caswell said. "Are you all right?"

"Y-yes, Staff Sergeant . . ."

Suddenly, Marielle began fumbling with the latch for her helmet, clawing at her armor, trying to get out. Jack could hear her retching over the open circuit. Caswell was in front of her in an instant, hitting the emergency release and pulling the bulky helmet off her shoulders. Then Marielle was running from the bay, her boots clacking on the concrete floor as she made for the head.

"That's all for this evening, Marines," Caswell said, pulling her own helmet off. "I've called Sergeant Honeycutt to come down and check in your gear and weapons. Secure your gear, and you're dismissed for the day." She walked away quickly, following after Marielle.

Chicago . . . destroyed. The thought went around and around in his mind, inescapable, incomprehensible. The news hit him on several different levels. On the one hand, it meant that the UN had just drastically escalated the war, that they were no longer trying for some mere political victory, but to destroy the United States itself, or at least to cause such terror and devastation that Washington would be forced to surrender.

That was bad enough, though the information had the cold and remote feel of a class text download in civics or history. On a far more very personal, more direct level was the shock of *personal* loss. He'd never cared much for Liana Alexander, but he knew his mother loved her, knew that Liana's death was going to hurt his mother a lot. And even the death of a relative you didn't like carried with it a shock and a cold ache in the heart that wasn't going to go away soon.

And as for David . . .

Hell, David Alexander had been more like a father than an uncle for a good many years. So much of Jack's own life—his fascination with ETs and the discoveries on Mars, his joining the Corps, his love of space—all had been the direct result of his uncle's stories. David Alexander had shaped one hell of a lot of Jack's life, and his dying meant that a part of Jack had died as well.

Jack couldn't look at the possibility of David's death with anything like rationality. There was a chance, maybe even a good chance, that his uncle was still alive. Joliet was a good sixty miles from downtown Chicago, and the last Jack had heard, his uncle had been in the federal prison there.

He'd heard a story, once, about the sole survivor of a devastating volcanic eruption on the island of Martinique back in 1902. He'd been a prisoner in the deepest-buried cell in the city's jail.

At the same time Jack felt that stirring of hope, he shoved it back, told himself that David had to be dead as well. He couldn't bear the thought of being hit by this icy shock twice, to allow himself to hope that his uncle was alive, then to find out that whatever had hit Chicago had been big enough to take out Joliet as well.

Someone had once pointed out that ignorance is bliss, knowledge is power . . . and uncertainty is sheer hell.

He knew the truth behind those words now, in a way he'd never before imagined.

TWENTY-TWO

Reagan Arms Hotel, Washington,
DC
1348 hours EDT

When the knock sounded on the door, David very
nearly did not rise to answer it. He'd been sitting alone
in the hotel room, the lights off, the curtains closed, the
wall screen switched off, all morning. He didn't want to
see anyone just now.

But he thought he knew who it was, and he knew he
had to answer. When the knock sounded a second time,
he struggled up off the bed, made his way to the door, and
opened it.

General Warhurst stood on the other side, with one of
his aides, a captain, and a pair of enlisted Marines in combat dress, with visored helmets and rifles.

"Good morning, General," he said. His mouth was dry,
and the words came with difficulty.

"Good afternoon, Professor. May we come in?"

David stepped aside, waving them through the door.
The two enlisted men took up posts to either side of the
door in the corridor outside, their weapons at port arms.
Warhurst palmed the room lights on and walked through,
taking a seat in the small lounge area beyond the room's
two beds. The aide took up a silent stance at parade rest
nearby.

It was still all a little unreal. General Warhurst had met

him as he was being released from Joliet and asked if he
would come to Washington for a series of meetings. He'd
been *that* close to telling Warhurst to forget it, that he had
to go talk to Liana, that he needed to get his own life
together first, that above all he didn't owe the government
or anyone who worked for it a damned thing after they'd
stolen so much of his life and work.

But it was Warhurst who'd been responsible for his
freedom in the first place. David was grateful; more than
that, though, he always paid his debts, and Warhurst's tone
had suggested that something important was happening,
something in which David's participation was necessary.

And so, David had let them drive him to his home in
the Chicago suburbs, where he'd packed a bag and left a
v-mail for the absent Liana on the home computer. An
hour later, he'd been on a military VTOL transport from
O'Hare International to Andrews Aerospace Force Base
outside of Washington.

And if he hadn't agreed, if he hadn't made that flight,
he would likely have been in Chicago Monday evening
when the shock wave rolled across the city from the lake
. . . either in a hotel room or else working late at the Institute, which now no longer existed.

"First of all," Warhurst said, "please accept our con-
dolences on your loss. Have you heard anything definite
at all?"

He shrugged and nodded toward the wall screen. "No.
Triple N is saying three quarters of a million dead . . . as
if anyone can ever know the real number. They're finding
lots of survivors, especially out toward the Ring. But, well,
they also said there was a big, ancient space brothers' rally
near the lakefront at the time. And . . ."

"And your wife would have been there," Warhurst
said, completing the thought when David couldn't go on.

He was suffering from a bad case of survivor's guilt.
He knew that . . . but the knowledge didn't help. Nor did
it help that he was the one Cheseaux had passed the information through in the first place. If he'd just said something then . . .

But what? The asteroid had been aimed at Colorado,

originally. There was no way of knowing that a piece of it would come down on Chicago.

He should have died in Chicago, too. . . .

He knew how lame, how stupid that self-pitying thought sounded. It wasn't even as if he and Liana had been all that close during the past few years. He'd wanted a divorce so badly he could taste it. And yet . . .

The awful part of it was that he'd finally decided to *do* something about his impossible life with Liana. Now she was dead, his chance to take his own life in his hands snatched away with all those lost lives.

It left him feeling guilty, as though by wishing her out of his life, he'd somehow caused her death. He felt . . . lost. The universe held no special concern for humans or their petty problems and failed relationships and injured hearts.

Somehow it didn't even help to know that Teri was okay—that she'd been at a conference in Great LA over the weekend and hadn't yet returned to Chicago when the city was destroyed. Warhurst had told him that morning that they would be flying her here, to Washington.

Teri alive . . . and Liana dead.

He could not shake the horror that clung to that equation.

"I can't promise anything, son," Warhurst went on. "But I have my people checking. You know, it's taking an ungodly time to compile casualty lists. Not only was the city trashed, but Chicago was an important hub on the Net. Right now, the whole system's clogged and almost at a standstill. Maybe she's okay, but just . . . out of touch ."

He tried to imagine Liana as one of those filthy, ragged survivors he'd seen on Triple N huddling in the shelter of the Chicago ruins. That was about as back-to-nature as it was possible to get. Somehow, he couldn't pull the picture into focus. No, she was dead. He was sure of that.

Why did her death hurt so much? He hadn't thought he'd loved her anymore at all.

"I can't imagine her missing something like that big church rally." He scowled, anger gaining the upper hand over grief. "She was *so* damned wrapped up in that ancient-astronut nonsense!"

Warhurst gave him a tight smile. "I'm surprised to hear you call it 'nonsense.' You're the one who's been uncovering all this alien stuff."

"I'm a scientist, General. An archeologist. I uncover facts, mostly by digging around in other people's garbage piles, then try to make reasoned assumptions about what that garbage tells us about them. Okay?"

"No argument there."

"The ancient-astronut silliness takes the same facts—or more often nothing more substantial than myths or out-of-context religious passages—and builds elaborate dream castles that just can't be supported by the data. The worst part is when people distort the facts to fit their own preconceived notions. That's not science. It's not even good religion. It's a crime against reason and clear thinking."

"Hmm. And what is your clear thinking about the An?"

David raised his eyebrows, jolted, for the moment, from his loss. Warhurst, evidently, had been reading his papers, including some that hadn't been published yet.

He also saw what Warhurst was trying to do, goading him, dragging him from the black comfort of his depression. And he didn't like it.

"Look, what does any of this have to do with the war? You said you wanted me to come here and work on some big operation coming up, but you still haven't told me what the Marines need with an archeologist."

"Dr. Billaud has been talking to our intelligence people."

"So?"

"Telling them about the UN facility at Tsiolkovsky, on the farside. According to him, there are alien ruins there, in a cave in the central peak."

David nodded. "He mentioned something of the sort, when I talked to him last."

"You didn't tell Colonel Whitworth?"

"No, sir. I did not."

"You know, Professor, some people might find it odd that you withheld critical information from our intelligence people but were sharing important information with foreign nationals.''

''I've been through this already, sir. The people I was sharing information with are part of an international scientific community. I won't say they aren't political, but they're more interested in what's right than in what's politically convenient. As for not telling Whitworth about Tsiolkovsky, quite frankly, the thought of a battle being fought inside an ET archeological site fills me with horror.''

''I can understand that. But the situation is such that we *must* attack. To tell you the truth, I was hoping we could enlist you to go along. To look after what might be there.''

David gave Warhurst a hard and searching look. ''You're not telling me everything, are you?''

''I'd rather not, until closer to the time.'' He gave a wry smile. ''I think you can understand our not wanting our moves becoming known to anyone in the European Union.''

''Ah. Yes. I can imagine you people will have trouble trusting me from now on.''

''Oh, it isn't that. I wouldn't tell my own grandmother what we're planning. But I *can* tell you that it's vitally important that we know what we're getting into, what the UN might have already uncovered over there. So . . . what can you tell us about the An?''

''That they were a technologically advanced extraterrestrial species that had some interaction with humans six to eight thousand years ago, and possibly earlier. That they probably enslaved a number of early humans while establishing a colony of some sort here and managing to insinuate themselves into Sumerian mythology. That something happened to them after that, apparently an attack of some sort, that either destroyed their colony, or made them abandon it.''

''There's been a lot of speculation about the An still being around, someplace. Or that they could come back to Earth in the future, either as saviors or as conquerors.''

''That,'' David said quietly, ''is lunatic-fringe astronut

stuff. Faith and speculation, not fact. Science can't comment on any of that.''

''And what about the Builders?''

David let out a short, half-whistled breath through pursed lips. ''We know even less about them. They showed up from God knows where half a million years ago. They were almost certainly not the An, but someone else entirely, though we know almost nothing about them. They may have performed some genetic reengineering on hominids they found on Earth, giving rise to *Homo sapiens*, but that's still disputed. They certainly took a number of humans to Mars, where they were engaged in some terraforming operations, though the nature of that effort is also still being debated too. We don't really know why they did all of that, or what they wanted here. But we know their Mars colony was destroyed in an attack by someone else, one that destroyed their atmosphere-generating equipment and ended with the humans trapped there freezing to death, or suffocating, or both.''

''And the 'Hunters of the Dawn'? Or the 'Destroyers'?''

''Just names. Phrases translated from some of those An tablets we uncovered on the Moon. Look, what's the point of all this?''

''During your three-month . . . vacation, various people have been building on your work. You remember Kettering?''

''Craig Kettering. Of course.''

''He's published a paper in *American Science*. The title is 'Evidence of Warfare Among Ancient Extraterrestrial Cultures.' He cites you and several of your papers.''

''Hmm. He usually does.''

''I gather you've been busy on a related subject while you were at Joliet.''

''How did you—'' He stopped himself. Of course Warhurst would have checked with the prison officials, and he could have gotten access to David's work-in-progress. During the past two months, the Joliet administration had allowed him access—to a precious few hours each day—to his PAD, the only provisions being that he couldn't have Net access and that what he wrote each day was subject to review by prison officials. They would have made copies, and Warhurst would have been able to get access to them, by court order, if necessary.

The Marine commandant had been busy.

"It wasn't my intent to snoop," Warhurst said, following his train of thought. "But some of the stuff coming out of what you picked up on the Moon last April is starting to sound damned scary."

David gave a thin smile. "I thought you were at war with the UN."

"We are. But, let's just say that some of us are concerned about what might happen after the war. The paper you wrote in prison was . . . intriguing."

"John Bunyan wrote *Pilgrim's Progress* in prison. It's nice to have a hobby, something to pass the time."

"'On a New Interpretation of the Fermi Paradox,'" Warhurst said. "That's not exactly *Pilgrim's Progress*."

"*Pilgrim's Progress* is a morality play about making it into heaven. My paper deals with the possible extinction of humankind. There's a difference."

"Indeed." He nodded to his aide, who unholstered a PAD and began making entries. "So. Tell us about Fermi's Paradox?"

"Back in the 1940s, Enrico Fermi—he was an important physicist who did a lot of the early work on atomic energy—asked the question 'Where are they?' He was asking about other intelligent life in the galaxy."

"He meant . . . why haven't we seen them?"

"Exactly. You see, our galaxy is something like eight billion years old . . . about twice as old as Earth itself. It took less than four billion years for life to evolve here; since we know that planets are pretty common, it's fair to assume that life, including intelligent life, has evolved before, time after time after time. Fermi was making these assumptions before we knew about the Cave of Wonders, of course. He thought the galaxy ought to be crawling with other civilizations."

"Lovely thought."

"It gets better. It's been demonstrated that if even one intelligent race evolves, in all the history of the galaxy, and if that race has the same sort of exploratory yearnings, the same curiosity and drive and determination to reach out into space that we do, it could actually colonize the entire galaxy in a ridiculously short period of time.''

"How short?"

"Depends. Even if they never were able to build ships that went more than a few percent of the speed of light, though, they could still reach every star, colonize every habitable world, even do their equivalent of terraforming to every likely planet in the galaxy in less than three million years. . . .''

"Three million years is a long time."

"It's an eyeblink, compared to eight *billion* years."

"I see what you mean. So Fermi wondered why somebody hadn't already colonized the entire galaxy. Why they weren't *here* already."

"Exactly. And the more we learn about extraterrestrial civilizations, the more urgent his question becomes. In the Cave of Wonders, beneath Cydonia . . . that huge array of image screens shows hundreds of other civilizations. We suspect that the blank screens in the Cave represent civilizations that no longer exist, that have died out over the past half million years. Extraterrestrial cultures are *common*. The galaxy should have been filled up many times over. It should be teeming with starfaring civilizations. Radio astronomers ought to be bombarded by the alien equivalent of TV programs, shortwave broadcasts, and military call signs. But when we listen, we hear . . . nothing.''

"But we do know there are other races out there. And we know that at least two of them *were* here, once."

"Right. But what happened to them?

"According to your research both of them were attacked. Destroyed by invaders?"

"You've seen photos of the Cydonian site, General?" When Warhurst nodded, David went on. "You know, there are still people who haven't been there who argue that the Face on Mars is a natural phenomenon, that the fact that the Cave of Wonders is located underneath is just a coincidence. It was assumed to be a chance product of weathering for a long time after it was first spotted by early orbital probes. And the funny part was, the first detailed imaging orbital of the site, in the late nineties, showed it really didn't look much like a face at all. You can just barely make out the overall shape of the features, but they're battered, smashed, broken . . . and what's left has been worn down to dust and rubble by half a million years of sandstorms. The earlier, lower-quality images had actually blurred things enough to show what the Face must have looked like once, half a million years ago, before someone, or some*thing,* shot the hell out of it.''

"Okay, so what's the point of your new explanation of Fermi's Paradox?" Warhurst asked. "I mean, what we've found on Mars and the Moon, especially the display screens in the Cave of Wonders, proves that aliens were here. What's the paradox?''

"Mostly, I guess, the paradox is why aren't they here now? Some of the astronut cults make the claim that *we* are the descendants of alien colonists, maybe an expedition of Builders who got marooned here a long time ago, but that just doesn't hold up. Our DNA is very clearly the product of evolution here on Earth. Over 98 percent of the DNA in chimps is identical to ours.

"What's also puzzling, though, is that the An, whoever they were, didn't have a technology that was all that much ahead of ours. From what we've found on the Moon, they used antimatter-powered spacecraft maybe a century or two ahead of what we're flying today. Okay, so that meant they were several thousand years ahead of the Sumerians, but that's not much time at all when you're talking about periods of millions or even billions of years. The Builders were more advanced, maybe a thousand years beyond where we are now. Again, not that big a difference, when there ought to be civilizations out there millions or even billions of years old.''

"Maybe there's some built-in self-destruct mechanism, so that no civilization lasts more than a few thousand years. Or maybe they evolve into . . . I don't know. Something else. Something we can't recognize.''

"Maybe. But think about this. It only takes *one* long-lived and energetic civilization to overrun the entire galaxy in a few million years. That's part of the paradox. It only has to happen *once*, and we know, in fact, that it must have happened many times.

"Now, imagine an intelligence that evolves, develops civilization, starflight, and moves out into the galaxy. Imagine that it evolved with a kind of Darwinian imperative, a survival-of-the-fittest mentality that leads it to seek out other, less developed civilizations, and destroy them *before* they become a threat. And . . . remember that this only has to happen once to establish a pattern. If it happens once, if it works for them, it could happen again, and again, and again."

"This predatory species becomes top dog in the galaxy, you're saying. It just hangs around and stomps on the newbies as they emerge, is that what you're saying?"

"What I developed in my paper was the idea that the galaxy may endure cycles of civilization alternating with destruction. Hundreds, maybe thousands of civilizations emerge throughout the galaxy, all at about the same time. They develop space travel, spread out . . . but if even one of them out of how many hundreds or thousands is a predatory race, it's going to have an advantage over all the others, and it will destroy them.

"But if there's one such race, maybe there are two. Or a dozen. Or a thousand. Sooner or later, they come into conflict with one another. After a few thousand years of all-out warfare, the galaxy is empty again, except for a scattering of stone-chipping primitives on a few thousand bombed-out worlds who begin starting the whole cycle all over again."

" 'The Hunters of the Dawn.' "

"What we've been able to translate of the An records and tablets suggests that they were terribly afraid of someone. They called them *Ur-Bakar*, the Hunters of the Dawn."

"And these Hunters also destroyed the Builders?"

"I think it was a different group of Hunters. I think that galactic civilization was at a high point half a million years ago . . . then it all collapsed in a war that makes our dustup with the UN look like a shoving match with the neighbor's kid. A predator race destroyed the Builders, bombed the structures on Mars, destroyed their colonies. Fortunately for us, they missed, or didn't bother with, the early *Homo sapiens* who were living on Earth at the time. Within another few thousand years or so, the Hunters were gone as well, probably fighting among themselves, or with other predators.

"Then, a long time later, maybe ten or fifteen thousand years ago, the An develop star flight. Since we've identified the An in the Cave of Wonders display, we have to assume that they were around half a million years ago, were smacked down, and then rebuilt their civilization.

"They come to Earth, maybe by accident, maybe because they remembered the Builders and were looking for them. They find our ancestors in Mesopotamia, settle down, and start their own colony, using primitives for slave labor."

"And then the Hunters of the Dawn come again."

"Right. Probably a whole new crop that evolved along those same kill-them-before-they-kill-you lines. They destroyed the An bases on the Moon. Destroyed their colonies on Earth . . . and by doing so must've left a pretty deep impression in the surviving humans about fire raining from the skies and wars among the gods.

"And once again we were lucky. The Hunters either ignored what they considered to be savages, or they just couldn't find and exterminate them all." He shook his head. "I hate like the devil to sound like one of the ancient-astronut preachers, but there *is* evidence of a cataclysmic flood throughout the Tigris-Euphrates Valley five or six thousand years ago, and it was probably the basis for the Sumerian flood myths that eventually found their way into the Book of Genesis. My thinking now is that the Destroyers dropped a small asteroid into the Arabian Sea, and let the tidal wave wipe out the An cities."

"Just like Chicago."

"Just like Chicago. We know that the Persian Gulf was swampy lowland until just a few thousand years ago. Maybe it's just still flooded, after six thousand years. You know, it might be interesting to do a careful sonar survey of the floor of the Arabian Sea, looking for a recent impact crater under the silt.''

He found he was breathing hard, that he was on his feet and pacing, instead of slumped on the hotel-room bed. He'd not wanted to discuss any of this, to discuss anything, but once the words had started, they'd tumbled out in an unruly torrent. He wondered if that had been Warhurst's purpose.

There was a knock at the door. "You'd better get that," Warhurst told him.

A bit unsteadily, he walked to the door, considered activating the small security display, then decided that the Marines posted outside were all the security anyone needed. He opened the door. . . .

"Teri!"

"David!" She stepped forward, taking him in her arms. "General Warhurst told me . . . that they haven't found Liana."

"Teri . . ." He couldn't raise his arms to return her embrace. He *couldn't*. . . . He was so damned happy to see her alive . . . but the thought that he'd wished Liana dead would not let go.

She seemed to sense his confusion. Slowly she released him. "I'm sorry, David. I'm so sorry."

"I . . . I'm going to need some time, Teri. To get my head straight."

"I understand."

"Dr. Sullivan, here, is the one who got you sprung," Warhurst said, "not me. She talked with your wife, and got access to your correspondence files. Sent e-mail to every person in your address file. That happened to include a young Marine—"

"Frank Kaminski?"

"Affirmative. Kaminski took it up with his CO, who happens to be a friend of mine."

"That would be Kaitlin Garroway."

"And she told me."

He looked at Teri. "Thank you." He tried to imagine her forcing a meeting with Liana, and failed. Maybe he hadn't known either woman as well as he'd thought.

"Come on in and grab yourself a stool, Dr. Sullivan," Warhurst said. "What we're talking about here will interest both of you."

"So," she said brightly, "what have you men been gabbing about?"

"We're getting ready to kick the UN off our Moon, Dr. Sullivan," Warhurst said, extracting his PAD from his inside jacket pocket and unfolding it. "But we're going to want a couple of archeologists along, just in case we have another Cave of Wonders to deal with."

"Billaud's site? At Tsiolkovsky?" David asked.

Warhurst nodded, and David groaned. He was remembering the battle at Picard, the carefully excavated trenches trampled over by soldiers. He thought, too, of that French soldier in 1799, who'd uncovered the Rosetta stone and provided Western science with the key to the writing of an ancient and very alien civilization. At the same time, some of the soldier's friends were practicing with artillery . . . and using the Great Sphinx, at that time showing only its head above the enveloping sands, as a target.

He'd seen two pitched battles fought on a valuable archeological site, now, at Cydonia and at Picard. He didn't want to see a third.

"What," Warhurst replied, reading from his PAD, "does the term 'E-U-Nir-Kingu Gab-Kur-Ra' mean to you?"

"Sumerian," Teri said. " 'E-U-Nir' is, ah, a house with raised foundations? 'House Rising High,' I think I'd translate it. 'King-gu' means a righteous emissary, but it was also the Sumerian name for the Moon."

"And 'Gab-Kur-Ra' means something like 'Chest Hidden in the Mountain,' " David added.

"A chest," Warhurst repeated. "Or a storeroom, maybe? A place for storing records?"

Realization struck David. "Which is what Marc Billaud called the central peak at Tsiolkovsky."

Warhurst shot him a sharp glance. "When was that?"

"When I talked to him on the Moon. At Picard. He said

he wasn't going to betray his country, but that we'd get
the answers we wanted at Gab-Kur-Ra.''

"You didn't mention that in your report.''

"I . . . I didn't think of it at the time. I hadn't made the
connection with ancient Sumerian and the An tablets yet.
And, well, it didn't make much sense.''

"Maybe he was trying to tell you something he didn't
want other people to hear, or understand,'' Teri suggested.

"Could well be.'' David looked at Warhurst. "Where
did you hear that name?''

"From Billaud. He's been talking freely to our intel
people ever since we learned the UN military was playing
with the notion of bombing us with asteroids. He's given
us some information about the UN layout at Tsiolkovsky—
not everything we need; he's a scientist, not a military
man, but some. He told us there were some ET ruins at
the crater's central peak and that they were called Gab-
Kur-Ra. He gave us a translation of that but wasn't able
to tell us what was inside. He says no one's being allowed
in.''

"The UN has been pretty touchy about ancient-
astronaut stuff ever since we let the cat out of the bag
about Cydonia,'' David said. "Maybe they're still trying
to sit on it.''

"Maybe. Or maybe what they've found there is so secret they can't let civilians see it. We already know the
French were getting clues to building an antimatter-
powered spacecraft from wreckage they picked up at Picard. Maybe there were more clues at this Gab-Kur-Ra
place.''

"Which means,'' David said, "it's going to be heavily
guarded when your Marines get there. My God. . . .''

Step by step, the scenario he'd most been dreading was
unfolding. . . .

TWENTY-THREE

Above the Lunar Farside
0845 hours GMT

They called them LAVs, but the M340A1 Armored Personnel Carrier had very little in common with the Light Armored Vehicles employed by the US Marines during the closing years of the twentieth century. *These* LAVs had been designated as Lunar Assault Vehicles by some unsung Pentagon bureaucrat, either in deliberate imitation of the earlier LAVs, or in complete technomilitary historical ignorance. Either way, the informal designation allowed the team members of Bravo Company, 1-SAG, to resurrect an old Marine battle cry: *LAV it to the Marines!*

The heavy Conestoga-class trans-Lunar cargo shuttle *Santa Fe* was one of only two vessels of her class, heavy-lift ships designed to carry prefabricated hab units and construction materials to the bases at Fra Mauro and Tsiolkovsky when they were first built back in the 2020s. Obsolete now, the *Santa Fe* had been adapted by the military for one final Lunar flight.

She came in above the flat, dark floor of the Mare Crisium, heading southeast. She dropped to less than twenty kilometers' altitude above the Mare Smythii and went "over the hill," dropping below the horizon visible from Earth and vanishing around the farside. Still descending, the craft swept in low across the crater rim of Pasteur before pitching over and firing a savage burst of plasma, braking her forward velocity before gentling down toward the dusty Lunar surface.

Clouds of dust lashed and billowed from the touch of those hot jets; the freighter's open-girder undercarriage touched down, and the vessel, momentarily, at least, was at rest.

Almost at once, however, there was fresh activity, as foil-covered bays on each side opened, and the wedge-shaped objects stowed inside folded out and down, dropping the last several meters to the Lunar surface in a silent, slow-motion drop and bounce.

During the Apollo program, over seventy years before, a similar system had been used to stow and deliver light-weight Lunar Rovers to the Moon's surface; the four wedge shapes deployed this time were each far larger and more massive than those primitive NASA rovers. Each LAV massed just under fifteen tons and measured 9.1 meters long by 3.5 meters wide by 2.4 meters tall, a lean, flat brick with a wedge-shaped nose, mounted on four inde-pendently powered tires and coated with reactive camo and ablative plastic and ceramic laminates. The flat upper deck was interrupted only by the swell of a ball-mounted weapons turret.

"C'*mon*, people!" Gunnery Sergeant Yates's voice called over the company frequency. "Move it! Move it! A day here lasts twenty-seven Earth days! At that rate you've already been lollygagging on your fat tails for two hours! Step it *up*!"

Fifty Marines and one Navy pilot were descending from the *Santa Fe*'s hab module, leaving the vessel, its reaction-mass tanks not quite empty, vacant on its spidery legs. Kaitlin dropped the last couple of meters off the *Santa Fe*'s ladder, falling slowly to the surface and taking the gentle impact on flexing knees before moving out of the way of the next Marine coming down.

LAV-2, with Captain Fuentes and First Platoon, First Squad, was already loaded and ambling off in a tight curve away from the ship, moving toward the southeastern ho-rizon. Its tires hurled rooster-tail clouds of soft, gray dust aloft, making it look as though it were laying down a smoke screen. LAV-4, with First Platoon, Second Squad, started up, following the first at an interval that would allow decent visibility.

Kaitlin's platoon would be traveling in LAV-1 and LAV-3; her vehicle, with a white ''1'' painted just behind the small American flag on its mottled gray-and-black flank, waited just ahead, the rear doors open and the ramp down. The Marines of Second Platoon, First Squad were filing inside, stepping up the ramp and ducking beneath the low overhang of the hatchway, and she followed, her ATAR tucked in tight behind her arm and next to her PLSS. Inside, the Marines took their places in shock-mounted, center-facing seats, strapping down and plugging in commo and life-support feeds from the bulkhead into their PLSS packs.

''Secure and plug in!'' Yates ordered. ''Klinginsmith! Help Ahearn with her O$_2$ hose!''

''Shit, Gunny!'' Nardelli called. ''Why can't we ride to Big-T in comfort, like with a pressurized cabin?''

''You want to chew vacuum if the UNdies hole us, be my guest. Me, I'm keeping my helmet on. Rawlins! Stow your ATAR and give Falk a hand! Kaminski! You too!''

Carefully, Kaitlin made her way up the central aisle, squeezing past the Marines still standing there as they pulled off their ATARs and other carry-on equipment and stored them in bulkhead racks and lockers. The layout was similar to the interior of an LSCP, but much more cramped; inside the cabin there was only 1.8 meters' head clearance, and even a short Marine like Kaitlin had to duck to avoid scraping her helmet along the overhead.

At the front of the cabin, Staff Sergeant Peter Hartwell, crammed into the tiny driver's cubicle, was readjusting the reactive camo feeds in the hull outside; the upper deck was capturing and reemitting the black of space, which made it as visible from overhead as a deep, black hole; by adjusting the feeds to have the turret and upper deck emit the powdery silver-gray of the surrounding landscape, the vehicle became effectively invisible from above.

Next to him was the Navy pilot, Lieutenant Thomas Wood, hunched over his PAD, which displayed a touch-

screen image of lighted keys. A monitor on the cube control panel showed the *Santa Fe* outside, the image relayed
from a camera in the LAV's turret.

Kaitlin took her seat, just behind the entrance to the
driver's cubicle, and started plugging in her life-support
hoses. "Okay," she said. "How's our time doing, Lieutenant?"

"We're still in the window," Wood replied. "But it's
gonna be tight."

"Second Platoon, First Squad!" Yates sounded off over
the platoon frequency. "We're squared away and ready to
roll!"

"Okay, Staff Sergeant," she said. "Let's do it!"

"Hang on to your butts! We're rolling!" With a lurch,
the LAV started forward, the ride surprisingly smooth in
the Moon's low gravity.

"Two hundred meters. We're clear of the blast zone,"
Hartwell announced.

"Are the other LAVs clear?" Wood asked.

"That's affirmative. We're last man out."

"All right." Wood turned his head inside his helmet,
looking at Kaitlin. "We're ready, Lieutenant."

"Tracking armed and ready?"

"That's affirmative."

She nodded. "Let her rip!"

Wood touched a key on his PAD; on the monitor, dust
billowed again from beneath the now-deserted transport
Santa Fe. Slowly, then, balancing on an invisible stream
of hot plasma, the transport edged into the black sky. The
turret camera panned up, following the craft as it dwindled
into the night.

Wood had one gloved finger on an image on his screen
configured as a touch pad, rocking his finger slightly to
control the accelerating ship as though he were using a
joystick. "Pushing her over," he said, eyes on the readouts on his PAD. "Altitude forty-three hundred, speed
eighteen-thirty-five. Five kilometers downrange."

"I hope to hell they buy this," Kaitlin said.

"We're still in the window," Wood told her. "If the
UNdies had observers at the poles, they wouldn't have had

a better track on the *Santa Fe*'s likely orbit closer than fifteen minutes. And the lasers fired from Earth orbit probably bought us even more time.''

"Roger that. But it's my job to worry.''

The tactical challenge they faced, of course, was how to sneak up on Tsiolkovsky, an enormous crater located on the farside of the Moon some twenty-six hundred kilometers from the Mare Crisium and farther still from the base in the Fra Mauro Highlands. With an antimatter weapon of some kind mounted at Tsiolkovsky, one capable of blasting any spacecraft that entered its line of sight, even getting close to the enemy farside base was going to be damned near impossible with a conventional approach.

So the op planning staff at the Pentagon had come up with a sneaky alternative.

The fifty Marines of the Rim Assault Group had made the three-day flight from Earth orbit to the Moon packed like sardines inside a small hab mounted on the *Santa Fe*'s transport bus, the four LAVs carefully stowed in the landing assembly. As the *Santa Fe* had begun her deceleration burn to drop into a direct Lunar-landing approach, a pair of Aerospace Force gigawatt lasers in Earth orbit had fired simultaneously, bathing the visible portions of both the Lunar north and south poles in torrents of coherent light.

At a distance of a quarter of a million miles, the lasers were attenuated enough that they couldn't do much in the way of actual damage, but any UN observers watching the *Santa Fe*'s approach would be fools to keep staring into that light . . . and the more sensitive optics of cameras would either automatically shutter or be burned out. With no direct information on the length of the *Santa Fe*'s burn, there would be considerable doubt about her actual orbit . . . and when she might appear above the horizon at Tsiolkovsky.

There was just enough time for the *Santa Fe*, once she was safely over the horizon as seen from Earth, and before she'd risen above the horizon at Tsiolkovsky, to actually land on the rim of Pasteur Crater, offload the Marines and the four LAVs, and take off again, this time under teleoperation from Lieutenant Wood's PAD. She had just enough fuel remaining to make a final suborbital hop on a course that would take her directly over Tsiolkovsky, three hundred kilometers to the southeast of Pasteur.

The *Santa Fe* vanished behind the low, smoothly sloping mountains in front of the column of lightly bouncing LAVs.

"LOS," Wood announced. "She's over the horizon."

"How long until she's over Tsiolkovsky's horizon?" Kaitlin wanted to know.

"She's still rising," Wood replied. "I'd say five . . . maybe six minutes. Depends on how on the ball they are at the UNdie base."

"Oh, they'll be awake, all right," Kaitlin said with a grin. "They'll have been watching the *Santa Fe* on an approach vector for three days now. They know she's on the way. They've probably been at general quarters for the last couple of days!"

"Let's hope they didn't get any sleep all that time," Hartwell said, laughing.

"Roger that!"

She turned slightly in her seat, listening to the radio chatter as Yates lashed the squad with a traditional pre-battle warm-up. "We are *lean*! We are *mean!* We are lean, mean, fighting ma*chines*! We are *Marines!*"

"*Ooh-rah!*" the squad bellowed back.

"We are gonna kill!"

"*Marines! Kill! Kill!*"

It was, Kaitlin thought, a barbaric ritual, chilling, almost bloodthirsty . . . and terrifyingly effective. *God help any UNdies who get in our way*, she thought.

For minutes more, they traveled on across the silent vastness of the lunar surface. Each LAV was powered by a three-hundred-megawatt gas-turbine engine; each tire was independently hooked to its own power train and transmission and could be individually depressurized to increase traction on slippery slopes and in deep powder. Under one-sixth G, each LAV could manage eighty kilometers per hour on the flats . . . and up to half that on rugged, broken, boulder-strewn or steep terrain.

Unfortunately, this was the Lunar farside, a jumble of

craters upon craters upon craters, and the only flats were at the bottom of a couple of the largest, like Tsiolkovsky itself. They were going to be lucky to average twenty-five or thirty klicks an hour.

Which put them ten hours from their target. The mission plan allowed for eighteen.

"Ah!" Hartwell called. "I've got a reading! Looks like hard gamma!"

An instant later, white light shone above the rounded mountains ahead, a briefly expanding dome of light that swiftly faded from view in utter silence.

"I guess they were awake," Wood said.

"Roger that," Kaitlin replied. "Now if they'll just celebrate shooting down the *Santa Fe* and go back to sleep! . . ."

But the cabin was quiet now, with no more banter. The four LAVs were now utterly alone on the farside of the Moon, with no transport, no chance of retrieval.

It was a damned lonely feeling.

L-3 Construction Shack
2212 hours GMT

"Uncle David! What are *you* doing here!"

Jack gaped as the tall, lean archeologist pulled his way into the squad bay area, his small duffel bag trailing him on its canvas leash. David was upside down from Jack's point of view, so he twisted off the bulkhead in a quick rotation that brought them face-to-face.

"Hey, Jack!" David cried as they clasped forearms, rotating slowly in mid-bay. "I heard you were on this ride. Didn't you know I was coming?"

"Shit, no one tells us *anything*. They must be getting desperate, though, if they're throwing in *honorary* Marines now!"

Several other Marines gathered around the two. Captain Robert Lee braced himself on a deck support. "You're David Alexander?"

"Yes, sir," David replied. He extended a hand and Lee

took it. Then he fished into his inside jacket pocket, pulling out a manila envelope. "Got my orders here."

"S'okay," Rob replied. "Give 'em to the CO over there." He pointed across the crowded bay. "Colonel Avery. You'll want to check in with him soon as you get squared away. Welcome aboard, Doctor."

"Thank you, Captain."

"So, orders?" Jack asked. "What, are you in the Corps for real, now?"

"Not quite," David replied. "I'm a 'civilian specialist observer,' I think they call me now. 'CSO' for short."

"Actually, that stands for 'caught and shot out-of-hand,'" Corporal Negley said, floating nearby. "Hey! Look at his jacket! He was with 'Sands of Mars'!"

David was wearing a Marine-issue leather jacket with the beer-can insignia sewn to the left breast. "Guilty," he said with a grin.

"It's an honor to have you with us, sir," Negley said.

Lee looked at Jack. "Okay, Flash. You want to see that your buddy here gets settled in?"

"Aye, aye, sir," Jack replied.

" 'Flash?' " David said, eyebrows rising as the captain kicked off from a nearby bulkhead and floated toward the aft end of the squad bay.

"Long story," Jack replied. "You don't want to know." Somehow, the name had caught up with him again after Siberia. He still wasn't sure how. "Hey, it's *really* great to see you. I, I thought you were *dead*, until you got that e-mail to me, right after Chicago."

"Not quite. I would have been, though, if General Warhurst hadn't sent for me. Your Aunt Liana . . ."

"Yeah. I heard. I'm awfully sorry." An awkward silence hung between them.

"So, Flash, you two know each other?" Sergeant Bosnivic said, drifting closer and breaking the deepening seriousness with a bright grin. He looked from one to the other, appraisingly.

"My uncle," Jack said proudly.

"Any guy who was with 'Sands of Mars' Garroway,"

Bosnivic said, sticking out a hand. "Great to meet you, sir."

"Thanks." David looked about the squad bay, a cavernous space now crowded with a couple of dozen Marines performing various tasks in zero G. "So, where do I bunk down?"

"Any free space you can find, deck, bulkhead, or overhead!" Bosnivic said, laughing. "But I don't think there'll be much time for sleeping now."

"Why's that?"

"Scuttlebutt says the first prong has already gone in," Jack said, pleased to be in the know for a change. "If it goes well for them, we'll be getting the word to board and light off in another few hours."

"Yeah? And where's this new supership I've been hearing about?"

"Over here," Jack said, lightly pushing off from a deck support and drifting toward a small, square viewing port in a nearby bulkhead. "You can see her from here."

Tucking his duffel under his arm, David followed, with Bosnivic bringing up the rear. Jack caught hold of a hand grip by the port and gestured with his head. "Ain't she a beaut?"

The view through the small port was breathtaking. Jack had been in the squad bay for three days now, ever since the assault group's arrival at L-3 from Earth, and he never tired of looking through it . . . when he could find it free, that is, or when he had a few free moments. They'd been keeping him busy for the past several weeks, working on his "nutcracker," as he called it, and he was still running through a long list of final checks and tests, making sure that his modified version of Sam was ready for the task ahead of her.

But when he could, he stared out the window.

L-3 was one of five points in gravitational balance with the Earth and the Moon, convenient spots to park a space station, or a small construction facility like this one. L-4 and L-5 were the best-known of these Lagrange points, sharing the Moon's orbit around the Earth—one, sixty degrees ahead of the Moon, the other, sixty degrees behind it. L-1 was a halo point directly behind the Moon, as seen from Earth, while L-2 was a spot directly between the Earth and the Moon where the gravitational pull of the two was balanced.

L-3, like L-4 and L-5, also followed the Moon's orbit, a quarter of a million miles from Earth, but directly opposite the Moon from the Earth. From there, the Moon was always hidden behind the blue-and-white glory of the Earth, which slowly changed phases as the construction shack moved through its twenty-seven-day orbit. At the moment, Earth showed a slender crescent, mostly white with a thin streak of blue along the lower limb. But the *real* spectacle lay much closer at hand.

The construction shack itself was little more than a girder-connected collection of tin cans, with tunnels leading from one hab or workshop to the next, with a huge, blue-black spread of solar panels like gleaming, rectilinear wings. Most of the structure which, together with the solar panels, covered a larger area than a football field, was invisible from the squad bay window, but they did have a good view of the docking port, where two cis-Lunar transports were parked just within the shadow of the USS *Ranger*.

The *Ranger*, clearly, was the featured sight for the squad bay window, at least with so little of the Earth visible right now. She was big—seventy-four meters long and massing sixteen hundred tons empty. She was also sleek, showing her origins as the upper half of a Zeus IIc piloted heavy-lift SSTO booster; only spacecraft that had to traverse atmosphere needed streamlining. Her smooth lines were broken, however, by the lower drive and landing assembly, which looked more like the Tinkertoy construction of a Lunar hopper than the sky-slicing curves of a hypersonic transport, and by the ungainly struts and angles of a pair of LSCPs strapped to her hull like outrigger pontoons. Her outer hull was deep black with a light- and radar-absorbing laminate, but the construction shack's worklights revealed her in pools of white light. A heat-radiator panel unfolded from the landing assembly like a squared-off shark's fin.

"That's it?" David asked, clearly impressed despite his nonchalant-sounding question. "That's our secret antimatter ship?"

"Isn't she gorgeous?" Bosnivic said, peering over David's shoulder. "You feed just a little antimatter into a reaction tank full of water, a microgram at a time, and it creates enough thrust to drive her at one G for hours. That ship, my friends, could make it to Mars in one week, accelerating half the way, then flipping end for end and decelerating the rest of the way, all at a comfy one gravity! None of this seven or eight months in a cycler."

"How long to the Moon?" David wanted to know.

"From here? A little under five hours."

Jack pulled his PAD from its holster and typed in some numbers. "Two hundred ninety-two-point-three minutes," Jack added a moment later. "Assuming we go in at one G, of course, and not taking into account any gravitational boost we get whipping past the Earth."

"Good God. Last time I went to the Moon it took three days."

"Yeah, but the *Ranger* can pull six Gs," Bosnivic said. "And scuttlebutt says we're gonna haul ass to get where we're goin'. What does that do to the travel time, Flash?"

Jack typed in the new figures. "Just under two hours. One hundred nineteen minutes, in fact." He looked up. "Stepping up the acceleration doesn't cut down your travel time as much as you'd think."

"I imagine how fast we scoot'll depend on how bad the RAG needs us," Bosnivic said.

"Well, that and how hard they think they can push the *Ranger* on her maiden voyage," Jack said. "This antimatter stuff is pretty new technology, and maybe they don't want to pull out all the stops, first time around."

"Where's the antimatter come from?" David asked.

"Oh, they manufacture the stuff right here at the construction shack," Bosnivic said, "using solar energy and something like a miniature version of one of those big particle accelerators back on Earth. Takes a long time, even to collect just a few grams of the stuff."

"Isn't that dangerous?" David asked. "I mean, even a microgram of antimatter will make a hell of a bang if it touches normal matter, right?"

"Hell, yeah!" Bosnivic said, grinning. "A big bang, and a lot of very hard radiation. Why do you think they make the stuff way out here?"

"I'd think it would be pretty vulnerable to UN attack."

"Not as vulnerable as you think. From here, we can see anything on an approach vector clear back to Earth orbit. And we have a squadron of Sparrowhawks stationed here, just in case the bad guys decide to come check us out. So far, we don't even think they know what we're doing here."

"Which is just as well," Jack put in. "If we could get a nuke through to that asteroid they were trying to send our way, they could hit us with one if they were really determined. And they would be, too, if they knew the *Ranger* there was ready to fly!"

Bosnivic nudged Jack and pointed at his PAD. "So, you got your girlfriend in there to crank out those numbers?"

"Hmm? No. That was just the calc function. You could do it, too, Bos, if you could just keep straight which is division and which is multiplication."

"Girlfriend?" David asked.

"Hey, you never met Jack's girlfriend? I thought you two were related!"

"Last girlfriend of his I heard about was that v-mail correspondent you were always talking to in California—"

"Let's not bring *that* up," Jack said, his face reddening.

"I definitely sense a story there," Bosnivic said. "But, anyway, turns out that Flash here is a genius at hacking into AI programs, getting 'em to sit up and beg. They've had him modifying our Marine-issue PAD OS/AI to make us a nutcracker." Floating in mid-bay, he reached down and rubbed his groin suggestively. "And a very *nice* nutcracker she is! Show him, Jack!"

"Uh, I'd really rather not! Listen, Bos, don't you have some Marine stuff to do, somewhere?"

Grinning, Bosnivic rubbed his nose with his middle finger. "Thought of somethin' right here, Flash."

"Careful you don't wear that out," Jack replied, as Bosnivic kicked off the bulkhead and sailed across to some other Marines.

"So," David said with a wry grin. "You getting on okay with your new friends?"

"Oh, they all figure they have to harass the new guy," Jack said. "Hey, it's great to see you! I heard they were assigning a civilian specialist to this op, but I didn't know it was going to be you!"

"Well, I'm not sure why I got the job, but I'm glad I did. So tell me. What *is* all this stuff with modified programs, anyway?"

"Well, what he was talking about isn't exactly something I want Mom to know about. But it got me a billet on this flight, and that's the important thing."

"Doing what?"

"There are three of us, see? Bos is one. So's . . . that corporal over there. Yeah, the blond woman. Corporal Dillon. We graduated from a special 4069 MOS class they just held at the SCTF at Quantico."

"Okay. Why?"

"Well, the UN has built a ship at a base they have on the farside of the Moon. An antimatter ship, like the *Ranger*. According to intelligence, she's just about ready to go. She already has made some short hops, but they think they're still working on getting her main weapon mounted and working. Our team is going in to either destroy or capture that ship, whichever we have the best chance of pulling off.

"Anyway, the three of us are on the boarding team. We go in with our nutcrackers, try to subvert the UN computer system running that ship, and take it over. If one of us can pull it off, we might be able to fly that ship out of there."

"Ah. And if you can't?"

"Then there'll be other Marines planting explosives to make damned sure the UN can't fly it out either!"

"And this nutcracker is? . . ."

Jack pulled out his PAD, opened the screen, and tapped in a command. "Sam?" he said. "I want you to meet my Uncle David."

"Delighted to meet you, Uncle David," Sam replied. She was modestly dressed, thank God, in slacks and an unrevealing blouse. Once, when he'd been working with her at Quantico, some of his instructors had dropped in to see how he was doing, including Staff Sergeant Ostrowsky and Colonel Joanna Bradley, the base XO. When he summoned Sam's image, she'd appeared in the nude . . . a bug left over from the days when he'd *wanted* her to appear that way. He'd received a pretty stiff lecture on sexual harassment and proper respect shown to female members of the Corps.

He was pretty sure he had that problem worked out now, at least. The question was how she was going to fare against the UN computer.

"I'm, ah, pleased to meet you, Sam," David replied. He glanced at Jack. "This is your nutcracker?"

"She was originally a Net agent," Jack explained. "Or part of her was. That means she was designed to go out into Earthnet and find information for me, which she did by looking at lots of programs very quickly and comparing their content with lists of things I told her I was interested in. It wasn't hard to modify her so that she could go into *one* program, figure out how it worked and what it did, and *change* how it worked.

"In fact, a lot of the work I did on her, she really did to herself. I just told her what I needed done, and she did it." He snorted. "Everybody around here's convinced I'm some sort of programming hotshot. *She* did all the work, though."

"You talk about her as thought she's . . . alive."

"Uncle David, sometimes I wonder if she is. She sure *acts* like she's self-aware."

"Well, if she was programmed to act that way—"

"Oh, sure. I know all about simulated personalities. That's what Sam started off as." He didn't add that the personality in question was a rather shallow adolescent's sex fantasy. Now that Sam had become . . . legitimate, it embarrassed him to talk about that aspect of her past. "The thing is, AIs, even simple ones like Sam started off as, are meant to grow. To change with time, as they learn things, as they work with humans. It's fun. Sam's reached the point where I can't really tell what she's about to do or say. Just like a real person."

"So you think she's self-aware?"

"Well, I don't *really* think she is, but sometimes I get the strangest feeling that she's doing things on her own. Thinking. *Reasoning* things out." He shook his head. "She's probably too complex now for any programmer to understand how she works. That can be unsettling, y'know?"

"How about it, Sam?" David asked the woman on the PAD display screen. "Are you self-aware?"

"Would you respond to me differently if I were, David?" she asked. "Maybe it's best that you not be too sure of me."

David blinked. "I see what you mean, Jack. You didn't program that answer into her . . . into *it*, I mean?"

"Nope. Sometimes she comes up with the damnedest stuff, seems to think of things I never would've thought of in a million years. Anyway, we're going in with three different nutcrackers. I'm betting Sam will be the one that breaks through."

"I wouldn't be a bit surprised." David chuckled. "So, what is a nutcracker, anyway?"

"Oh, well, the UN ship will have its own computer system, right? To control power, life support, all that stuff, just like our ships."

"Okay."

"If we're going to capture that ship, we need to talk to the computer. Program it to respond to our commands. But it probably won't be that simple. There's almost certain to be some sort of password protection, just so some unauthorized guy like the janitor or a bunch of invading Marines don't screw things up."

"Gotcha."

"Sam's got a database of . . . I don't know. How many passwords do you have, Sam?"

"Sixteen thousand, three hundred, eighty-four," she replied immediately.

"Okay. Sixteen thousand possible passwords, compiled by the NSA. They put together files on all the people they figured might've been involved in programming the enemy ship's systems. They got names of wives and girlfriends and kids. Birthdates of family members. Titles of favorite books. Places they've lived or gone to school. Known passwords they've used before. All kinds of trivia that a programmer might've used as an easy-to-remember password."

David's brow furrowed. "That still seems like kind of a long shot. I mean, that sort of code isn't going to be easy, or what's the point?"

"I think the idea is that the UN isn't expecting us to come and try to take their ship away from them, so the password's going to be relatively simple."

"Still, so many possibilities...."

"Well, they've also put together some code-breaking algorithms that Sam can draw on. And she's pretty slick herself, now. I've used her to get into places I wasn't supposed to be."

David's eyebrows went higher. "Oh? And what places would those be?"

"Oh, password-protected stuff." He didn't elaborate. Two weeks earlier, however, Sam had broken into the main personnel files at Quantico to see if Jack had been selected for this mission. He hadn't intended to *change* anything in those files, just to look around.

As it happened, he'd had the second best scores of all the trainees, after Diane Dillon, and had been given a slot aboard the *Ranger*.

And then there'd also been the time when he'd taken a peek at some of his uncle's working files on aliens from the Cydonian underground site. He simply hadn't been able to resist *that* siren's call.

"So ... how come you're here?" Jack asked David, shifting the subject to safer ground. "Is Tsiolkovsky another alien site?"

"It's distinctly possible."

"The An again? Or the . . . what are they called? The Hunters of the Dawn?"

David looked at him sharply. "How much do you know about the Hunters?"

Damn. He probably shouldn't have brought *them* up. "Not . . . not a whole lot. There's been some stuff out on the Net."

"Liana got some things out of my files she shouldn't have," David said, "and uploaded it to her cult church. From there it went . . . everywhere. But there's a lot of speculation and misunderstanding and just plain idiot stuff mixed in. Don't believe everything you hear."

"That's it, though, isn't it?" Jack said, pushing. "There's something about the Hunters of the Dawn at Tsiolkovsky?"

"I don't really think so," David replied. "If anything, there's just an An base back there. From what Intelligence picked up, though, from some French scientists they questioned, our UN friends are *very* interested in the Hunters. Almost frantic. And our people would like to know what *they* know. What they're afraid of."

"The answer to the Fermi Paradox?"

Again, David gave Jack a long, hard look.

"I, uh, had Sam out looking for everything she could find on the Hunters of the Dawn," Jack admitted. "The little bit I found on the open Net, well, like you said, it didn't seem very reliable. Ancient-astronut stuff. So I guess maybe she did a check on everything you'd written on the subject."

"Including some classified reports?" David shook his head and grinned. "Okay. I should have guessed as much. Don't put too much store in any of that stuff, though, Jack. It's all still *very* preliminary."

"Yeah, but it's important," Jack said. "Alien civilizations that think they have to wipe out every other civilization they find, just to survive? I can see why the government would be interested in that. We might run into them ourselves, soon."

"Sometime back in the 1920s or 1930s," David said,

"the first radio signals strong enough to propagate through space left our planet. The oldest of them are over a hundred light-years away by now, and there's no way to call them back. If anyone is out there, listening, we've given ourselves away already."

"And is that why the UN is so worried about it?"

"It's why we're *all* worried about it, Jack, and why I want to be damned sure of things before I release this. If my idea is true, galactic civilizations go through a kind of cycle, rising, developing interstellar travel, then getting smashed by the current crop of Hunters. That suggests we're in an upswing now, on our way to the stars. And somewhere out there, maybe not too far away, the next batch of Hunters are setting up shop, too."

"Well, we do have an advantage."

"What?"

"We know about them. I imagine most emerging races don't have a clue that the Hunters are out there. They struggle up to civilized status, develop spaceflight, go to the stars, and wham! They never know what hit 'em. You know," he continued thoughtfully, "there's another possibility too."

"Oh? And what's that?"

"That *we're* the next Hunters of the Dawn."

David's mouth twisted, as though at a bad taste. "That's . . . not a very pleasant idea."

"It could happen," Jack said. "Remember Chicago? People did that. People not so different from us."

A shrill whistle sounded from an overhead speaker, and every Marine in the squad bay fell silent, listening.

"Now hear this, now hear this," Captain Lee's voice said over the speaker. "We have just received a report that the RAG has reached its first objective and is deploying for the assault. We are now cleared for loading and debarkation. All hands, grab your gear and report to your squad leaders, preparatory for embarkation aboard the *Ranger*."

"That's it, Uncle David," Jack said. His heart was hammering now, and he was praying that he wasn't going to screw up. He folded up his PAD and tucked it back into his holster. "We're going to war!"

"And God help us all," David replied quietly. "God help us all. . . ."

TWENTY-FOUR

Lieutenant Kaitlin Garroway
Tsiolkovsky Crater, West Rim
2233 hours GMT

Communicating with Earth was a real problem for the
Rim Assault Group, once the Earth had dropped behind
the stark, Lunar horizon. Any US spacecraft entering orbit
around the Moon was killed as soon as it passed into line
of sight of Tsiolkovsky. The same went in spades for any
comsat parked in a halo orbit in L-1, above the Lunar
farside; it *was* possible to establish a short-term polar orbit
that wouldn't rise above Tsiolkovsky's horizon, but there
were almost certainly UN forces at one or both of the
moon's water-rich poles, and even if they couldn't shoot
it down, they would certainly warn the UN farside base
that something was up.

And the RAG depended utterly on its presence being
kept secret until the last possible moment. A teleoperated
Earth-Lunar freighter had been sacrificed to preserve that
secret.

They'd been traveling steadily for nearly fourteen hours,
a line-ahead column of vehicles nearly invisible against
the unyielding silver-gray of the Lunar surface. A careful
search from the sky might have picked them up, or at least
have picked up their tracks, but the Moon was an extremely large place, with as much surface area as the continent of Africa, and the LAVs were very small. Even so,

the four-wheeled vehicles had been deliberately designed to toss rooster tails of dust high and to the rear as they traveled, and as the dust settled out of the sky it tended to partially fill in and blur those telltale parallel trails, not filling them in completely, but making them far harder to spot at a casual glance.

One LAV had broken down. Gunnery Sergeant Miller's LAV-3, with Second Platoon, Second Squad, had quietly died as they'd traversed the floor of the huge crater Fermi, fifty kilometers back. There wasn't room in the other LAVs for any more personnel, so Miller and his people were sitting tight; if the RAG was successful, they would be picked up later.

If not . . .

Kaitlin tried not to think about the alternatives.

They made the approach up the western slope of Tsiolkovsky cautiously. There were UN defensive installations along the ringwall, but the crater's circumference, over 580 kilometers, was so large that the UN couldn't have woven a very tight net, and LAVs with stealth surfacing should be able to slip between them. The trick was identifying the UN perimeter installations in the first place so the Marines could sneak through.

Kaitlin sat in a jump seat next to Staff Sergeant Hartwell, watching over his shoulder as the staff sergeant threaded the LAV up the gradually steepening slope. It was particularly rugged here, good country for evading surface radar. Besides, since all of the LAVs possessed radar-absorbing stealth laminates, it should be possible for them to pick up UN radar before that radar could register them in return.

Still, it was a nail-biting feeling, sitting there, locked up in a brick-shaped can with twelve other Marines, inching up the slope while waiting for a sudden, sharp IFF challenge. No one spoke . . . almost as though they feared being heard by the enemy, which, of course, was nonsense in the Lunar vacuum.

People under stress, she thought, *rarely act in strictly logical ways*.

The expected challenge was never issued. Hartwell

picked up one intermittent radar emitter fifteen kilometers to the south, and a very faint signal perhaps at twice that range to the north. Carefully, he adjusted LAV-1's course to thread between the two at roughly the halfway point, with LAVs 2 and 4 following slowly in his tire tracks.

Thirteen hours and forty-eight minutes after the *Santa Fe* had dropped the LAVs to the surface on the southeast side of Pasteur Crater, the three LAVs were atop Tsiolkovsky's broken and rubble-strewn west rim.

Tsiolkovsky was considerably larger than little Picard, a vast bowl 185 kilometers across from rim to rim, centered by a smooth but irregularly shaped central peak. From the crest of the west rim, the crater floor appeared to be an utterly flat, dark gray plain stretching clear to the horizon. The central peak itself was just visible as a silvery white hummock breaking the perfectly flat line where prairie met black sky; most of the peak, plus the floor of the crater around it where the UN installations had been built, were still hidden beyond the curve of the Moon.

On the targeting screen aboard LAV-1, Kaitlin peered at the image of a silver mountaintop centered in green crosshairs. The camera view was greatly magnified, but it was still hard to make out any detail.

"Take the range," she told Hartwell.

He pressed a button, firing a laser ranging beam. "Range to target, ninety-three-point-one-one kilometers," Hartwell reported. "I've got a lock." A red light came on, accompanied by a thin, warning beep. "That's enemy radar. They've got us tagged."

"Well, they know we're here now," she said.

"Looks like the captain's deploying LAV-4."

Kaitlin clamped down on her emotions, glad that she didn't have to give the next set of orders. This, the very first shot to be fired—not counting the one that had downed the *Santa Fe*—was the critical moment in the operation. If the UNdies had their magic beam weapon mounted atop Tsiolkovsky's central peak, the Marines could expect an almost immediate counterbattery fire, one that might well turn the firing LAV into a puddle of bubbling, radioactive sludge.

Against that possibility, LAV-4 had been deliberately positioned hull down, her complement of Marines debarked and scattered across the crater rim. The other two LAVs had taken up positions to either side of LAV-4, their lasers locked onto the distant mountaintop.

The only man still aboard LAV-4 was First Platoon's Gunnery Sergeant George Massey, and he was a volunteer; if the enemy did have their secret weapon on top of the mountain, Massey would almost certainly be dead within the next few seconds.

As hard as manning the LAV in the face of that threat, Kaitlin thought, was giving the order to Massey to fire . . . and to invite immediate and deadly retaliation. Kaitlin wondered how Carmen Fuentes could do it.

She could hear the captain's voice over the combat channel. "Okay, George. Weapons free. You may fire when ready."

There was no flash, no beam, no indication at all that LAV-4 had just loosed a fifty-megajoule burst of coherent light at the target, a dish antenna on a mast reaching above the mountaintop. The warning indicator switched off.

"Hit!" Hartwell exclaimed. "He zapped the mother!"

"Any response?" Kaitlin asked.

"Nothing. Not a thing!"

Kaitlin felt a surge of relief. Having to single someone out like that, ordering him, in effect, to be a target, was so damned cold; could she do it if she had to? She didn't want to know. A damned stupid attitude, she knew. *All* of them were expendable on this op.

And it wasn't over yet. The enemy weapon was still there, hidden. She wished they'd been able to rig some sort of teleoperated sensor aboard the *Santa Fe* to pinpoint where the UN shot had come from, but there simply hadn't been time—or the equipment to allow that precise a remote scan of enemy positions.

Most likely, the enemy antimatter weapon was mounted at the base of Tsiolkovsky, still below the horizon from the crater rim. The Marines were going to have to get closer.

On Hartwell's monitor, a trio of bright stars winked on.

"Uh-oh," he said. "We are taking fire. But it's not the big gun."

"What do you have?"

"Lasers. Megajoule range. Probably slaws."

"The big gun must not be up there," she said. "Open fire!"

Megajoule laser fire wouldn't penetrate the LAV's armor, at least, not right away, though there would be some armor loss with repeated hits, and a lucky shot might puncture a tire or fry delicate electronic optics.

"All units, keep firing!" Fuentes ordered. "I want that installation fried!"

All three LAVs joined in the long-range bombardment, along with those Marines outside armed with squad lasers. There was little indication that a battle was being fought, though once a boulder to the left of LAV-2 suddenly blossomed with an intolerably bright patch and a puff of vaporized rock. Several Marines crouched in the dust nearby rose and started moving back down the reverse slope, seeking better cover.

It was a one-sided battle, however, and in another few moments, the laser positions atop the distant mountain were no longer firing. Hartwell reported that the tower structure was no longer showing above the mountaintop, and that all radar and laser emissions from the central peak had ceased.

"Okay, Marines," the captain's voice sounded over the combat channel. "Good work! Donaldson! Are your people ready?"

"Set to go, Captain!" Gunnery Sergeant Donaldson's baritone replied.

"Okay! Light the candle!"

In a display monitor on Hartwell's console, Kaitlin could see three space-suited Marines crouched in the dust on the crater rim, fifty meters to the south. They'd set up something that looked like a complicated vidcorder on a slender tripod, lens hanging down between the legs. There was a puff of dust as the device's solid-fuel motor fired, and the device rocketed swiftly and silently into the black Lunar sky, leaving the tripod behind.

"Let me know when you have signal acquisition," she said.

Hartwell nodded inside his helmet. "Will do, Lieutenant. It's climbing . . . still in the clear. Eight kilometers. Ten . . . Fourteen . . ."

The small probe was serving a double purpose. As it gained altitude, curving back toward the west, it would soon clear the horizon with the *Doolittle*, a US Aerospace Force ship near L-5, a spot still well below the horizon from Tsiolkovsky; it was the *Doolittle* that had picked up word fourteen hours earlier that the RAG was safely down and had relayed the information to L-3.

As soon as the communications-relay probe rose above the horizon, it would be able to relay a second message to the *Doolittle* and on to the *Ranger*.

The second purpose, of course, was a bit more direct. If there were any remaining radar or laser sites on or near Tsiolkovsky's central peak—or if that killer antimatter cannon of theirs was unlimbered and ready just below the LAVs' horizon, the probe might well reveal the fact by becoming a sudden target. Its destruction might help the Marines pinpoint the AM cannon.

"I have contact with the *Doolittle*," Hartwell said.

"Punch it."

Hartwell pressed a key, transmitting a complete record of the RAG mission to date. The other LAVs also transmitted their logs.

It would help in the planning of the next assault, if this one came to grief.

There was no blaze of antimatter fire from the crater's center, and Kaitlin let herself relax . . . but only a bit. The critical portion of the RAG assault had just been deferred to later.

"Okay, everybody!" Fuentes said. "Saddle up! Get ready to roll! All drivers, check your fuel. This is the last chance you'll have to refuel!"

"Now for the hard part," Kaitlin said to Hartwell. "Never thought I'd get to take part in a cavalry charge . . . across a hundred kilometers of open plain!"

PFC Jack Ramsey
USS Ranger
2245 hours GMT

"Double-check those straps!" Captain Lee shouted, pulling himself along the aisle, from seat back to seat back. "We're boosting at six Gs . . . I repeat, six Gs, and if you get bounced out of your seats, it's going to ruin your whole day!"

"Hey, Captain!" someone called out. "What's the skinny?"

"We've got the word," Lee replied, but addressing the entire compartment. "The *Doolittle* just relayed the go-ahead from the RAG. We're going in hot."

Jack felt a cold shiver at that. "Going in hot" meant a hot LZ. Specifically, it meant the surface attack group hadn't yet neutralized the AM cannon. While that eventuality was supposed to have been anticipated by the mission planners, it was damned scary to think about flying into the mouth of a weapon that shot antimatter at you. For weeks, now, scuttlebutt throughout 1-SAG had been revolving tightly around the supposed UN superweapon, giving it planet-buster status. If the Marines already on the ground at Tsiolkovsky couldn't nail it in the next two hours, the USS *Ranger* was going to be flying into some serious shit.

He decided that it would be best if he didn't think about what was waiting for him on the Moon. Carefully, Jack checked the harness that held him snug against a thickly padded contour couch. *This*, he thought, was luxury indeed for a Marine. The hab module of the Ranger had been adapted from the passenger compartment of a Lockheed Ballistic 2020 commercial suborbital transport; all it lacked was a flight attendant or two to pass out snacks and offer pillows.

Six Gs? It sounded like the brass had opted for the fast route to Luna. This was going to be *fun*.

As Captain Lee continued to check the others, Jack pulled a connector feed from his PAD and plugged it into a receptacle in one of his armrests, then plugged in an intercom jack from his suit. In another moment, the display screen on the seatback in front of him lit up, and Sam's attractive features looked out at him with a smile. "Hello, Jack" sounded in his helmet headset. "What would you like to do?"

"Hello, Sam," he replied, using his suit's intercom channel. "Let's keep going through the code-break checklist." That was a long list of different ways Sam might use to get through the target program's security barriers. The NSA had provided that list, he was told, a compilation of the Agency's long experience at code-breaking and gaining computer access. Like the list of possible passwords, the checklist was stored in a special one-hundred-terabyte external drive plugged into his PAD.

Bosnivic dropped into the empty seat beside him and started strapping in. "Hey, Flash! Got your girlfriend to play with, I see!" he said on the platoon channel.

"Screw you, Bos," Jack said amiably. Still, he had to suppress a small start of anger. Bosnivic, like most of the Marines he knew, loved the idea of a sex-goddess PAD agent; what they didn't know, or didn't understand, was that Jack himself no longer thought about Sam *that* way. The last time he'd seen her nude was that afternoon in Colonel Bradley's office. After that, he'd had Sam herself go through her own code, line by line, finding and deleting every possible trigger command that would have her remove her clothing. For one thing, that saved some space in the PAD's main storage. For another, it was a lot easier now for him to relate to Sam as a coworker—hell, even as another Marine—instead of as some horny adolescent's wet dream.

It was not an attitude he knew how to talk about with his fellow Marines, however.

"Twenty bucks says my nutcracker beats yours," Bosnivic said. "Yours is prettier than mine, but mine is NSA-issue, and it kicks ass."

Bosnivic and Corporal Diane Dillon each had slightly different versions of the standard National Security Agency nutcracker. The idea was to try all three, the NSA programs and Jack's modified agent, tripling, in theory, the chances of breaking the UN security code.

"You're on," Jack said. "Now go away and let me work."

"Ha! I can tell my victim's worried already!"

"All hands," Captain Lee's voice sounded over the command channel. "Cut the chatter. Fifteen seconds to boost!"

Quietly, Jack continued to work with Sam using the intercom link; as long as he wasn't broadcasting over an open channel, he could talk. He was concerned about Sam's ability to pick up on what might be happening in the target program on the farside of a security barrier. Though everyone was assuming that the UN security wall would be a simple one, there were some nasty twists they could put up if they wanted to—like a counter that ticked off failed attempts and did something nasty after a set number, like wipe the hard drive.

Or detonate an explosive charge. In a spacecraft powered by antimatter, *that* trick ought to be very easy to arrange.

Weight returned.

The acceleration was gentle at first, a hard nudge that pressed Jack back into his couch with what felt like his normal weight of about seventy-five kilos. He wished the hab module had windows so he could see out; he would have liked to watch the L-3 station falling away astern, or Earth growing larger ahead.

His weight increased.

All of the Marines assigned to this part of the mission had pulled plenty of practice time in the big centrifuge at Quantico. He knew he could take six Gs for a couple of hours, though the experience had left him bruised and sore afterward. But he could *do* it.

The aisle that the captain had been moving along earlier now looked like a wall; down was toward the back of his seat, and he was lying on that seat with his knees in the air and Sam's face hanging above him. He guessed they were pulling about three gravities now, the same acceleration developed by a Zeus II during its launch from Earth. It wasn't too bad; certainly, it didn't feel like he now weighed 225 kilos. He just felt a bit, well, *heavy*, was all, like someone was sitting in his lap.

"We are now at one G," Captain Lee's voice said over the platoon channel. "I imagine this is a bit of a shock after three days of zero G! Better brace yourselves. From here on out, this is going to get rough. Hang on to your eyeballs!"

And then the pressure grew swiftly very bad indeed. . . .

SUNDAY, 9 NOVEMBER 2040
Général de Brigade Paul-Armand
Larouche
UNS Guerrière, *Tsiolkovsky Base*
2357 hours GMT

Général Larouche clasped his hands at his back as he stared at the big bridge monitor. He'd been expecting an attack for a long time . . . and even forewarned, there'd been pathetically little that he could do to prepare. At least three enemy wheeled vehicles were approaching across the crater plain from the west, just visible, now, to the ship's radar. That couldn't be the entirety of the enemy force; they would not be moving against Tsiolkovsky now unless they felt themselves ready.

The transport downed fourteen hours ago must have been part of a larger invasion fleet, setting down these vehicles somewhere to the west and making the final approach on the surface, where the antimatter weapon couldn't reach them. Larouche had warned his superiors of the possibility of an overland assault, but his reports had been ignored.

Fools. Idiots and fools!

"Colonel d'André?" he said, turning slightly. "Is *Shuhadaku* still on-line?" The name was still clumsy in his mouth. He'd been told that it was a Sumerian phrase that meant something like "Supreme Strong Bright Weapon," as good a description as any he'd heard for the terrifying power of the antimatter beam.

"Yes, my General," d'André replied. "Antimatter reactor on-line, conventional nuclear plant on-line at eighty percent.'' When Larouche did not reply immediately, d'André added, ''Shall we open fire on the targets approaching from the west, sir?''

Larouche gestured at the screen. ''The image is being relayed from a remote camera on the mountain,'' he said. ''Unfortunately, the central peak is blocking our fire.''

''We have ground troops outside, sir,'' d'André said. ''They can engage at any time.''

''No. Save them.'' At a range of over ninety kilometers, the enemy had swept twelve men armed with H&K Laserkarabiner LK-36 lasers from the peak in something less than forty seconds. It would serve no purpose to waste more men firing at a target they could not stop.

But there would be a part for them to play soon, if he kept them in reserve now.

In fact, the UN position at Tsiolkovsky was now in serious trouble. With the loss of their main radar, UN forces had lost both their primary deep-space eyes, and the fire control for the Shuhadaku system. That meant that the enemy ground vehicles could get very close indeed before the antimatter cannon could be turned against them; worse, as soon as the beam weapon was fired at one of the enemy vehicles, the others would know *exactly* where to fire to knock Shuhadaku out of operation.

If Larouche wanted to save the antimatter weapon for the main American assault, which he was sure was yet to come, he would have to kill the ground vehicles by more conventional means.

''There appear to be only three enemy vehicles, sir,'' d'André reported. ''There must be more of them, somewhere.''

''There must be, indeed,'' Larouche replied. He sighed. ''We are about to reap the yield of our leaders' hubris, my friend.''

''Sir?''

''Never mind.'' Quietly, he added, ''Lord, have mercy. Christ, have mercy. Lord . . . have mercy.''

Born and raised in the tiny village of Echallon, high in the mountains not far from Geneva and the Swiss border,

kovsky. A French, German, and Chinese team had attempted to reverse-engineer the technology.

Larouche smiled at the thought, though there was very little good humor there. Half a century ago, there'd been wild rumors that the Americans had recovered alien spacecraft from various crashes—or even as gifts from extraterrestrial visitors—and were trying to reverse-engineer them at a secret base in the Nevada desert. It was possible that the rumored cover-up by the US government in the second half of the twentieth century had been responsible, in part, for the paranoid fear within the UN that the Americans were going to keep recovered technology found at Cydonia, on Mars, for themselves . . . a fear that had led, at least in part, to the current war.

Larouche's own experiences with back-engineering alien technology had convinced him that those old stories could not possibly have been true. Figuring out how something worked and going back to figure out how it was made was an effective tool only when the technologies more or less matched. *Merde!* Could Leonardo da Vinci, brilliant as he was, have reverse-engineered a television wall screen if a time traveler had presented him one as a gift? Could he have discovered the science and engineering behind generating and propagating radio waves, behind constructing cameras, behind encoding and decoding transmissions, behind all of the myriad sciences and technologies discovered and developed from the eighteenth century onward that made modern, flatscreen digital displays possible?

Da Vinci wouldn't even have been able to understand the plastic of the wall screen's display.

The alien technology recovered on the Moon so far was at least five centuries ahead of current terrestrial understanding of physics, engineering, materials processing, and control technologies. Reverse-engineering meant figuring out how to build not only the device in question, but how to build the tools that made the tools that made the tools that made the device . . . as well as principles of physics and engineering that were balanced one atop another in a terribly unsteady tower of innovation. Less than a century and a half had elapsed between the difference engine and silicon chips; there were elements of recovered An technology at least as strange to the UN engineering team as a PAD would have been to Charles Babbage. It was going to be decades more, perhaps centuries, before the fragments of An technology were understood within the context of human science. Merely knowing that something was possible was rarely enough to transform possibility into reality.

There were two basic approaches to powering an antimatter spacecraft. You could manufacture the antimatter, a few atoms at a time, in a particle accelerator, and store it in magnetic bottles, an approach using old and well-established technology that had been around for half a century at least, almost certainly the route the Americans had pursued in their AM-drive research.

But the An had known how to manufacture antimatter, specifically positrons—antielectrons—in large and continuous quantities. How the antimatter reactor recovered from the dusty floor of Picard did this was still not well understood—at least in terms that Larouche could comprehend, and he suspected that the UN engineers working on the problem only dimly glimpsed the principles involved. Zero-point energy? Energy drawn from the vacuum of space? Energy converted in its creation into, not matter, but antimatter? It sounded like magic to Larouche.

Using the An AM generator as a weapon was relatively easy, so long as you knew how to manipulate positrons in a magnetic field. Using it in a *controlled* fashion, however, feeding a precisely measured and balanced stream of antimatter to the reaction chamber, was orders of magnitude more difficult. It must have been much the same in developing early atomic energy; slapping two chunks of plutonium together to release energy in an uncontrolled chain reaction was relatively simple; producing controlled and controllable energy from the same equations had been much harder.

They'd had the weapon portion of the project working in April, when they'd first used a positron beam to destroy an American reconnaissance spacecraft. The actual weapon emplacement had been mounted high atop Tsiolkovsky's central peak, with power provided by a large, deeply buried fission reactor. The *Guerrière*, then still the *Millénium*, had at that point only recently arrived at Tsiolkovsky, and the engineering team hadn't yet begun the conversion of the big shuttle. In fact, they'd used the ship as an ordinary transport, first to ferry troops to Picard during the fighting there, and a month later, at the Lunar north and south poles, to stop the American takeovers of the Moon's only sources of water.

In June, however, the engineering team had begun the actual ship conversion, removing *Guerrière*'s liquid-core fission reactor and primary thruster assembly and replacing it with a much more robust thruster unit shipped up from Earth. The positron weapon had been dismantled in August and lowered down the mountainside; by October, the positron weapon was working again, mounted now inside the sleek, black hull of the *Guerrière* rising above the Tsiolkovsky plain. A ball turret in *Guerrière*'s side channeled the positron stream through magnetic conduits and directed it at any radar-locked target within line of sight. It was that ball turret that was vulnerable to enemy counterbattery fire. And if they hit the turret while positrons were actually in the conduit, the result would be the same as an antimatter attack against the *Guerrière*.

As for the drive, however, the engineers still were having trouble finding a way to regulate the flow of antimatter from the generator. They were confident that they would have the problem under control soon . . . but how soon was unknown. *Guerrière* could fight, but she could not fly. It left Larouche's forces at a terrible disadvantage.

They would have been better off, Larouche thought bitterly, if they'd simply used the alien machinery to produce positrons and store them for later use, as the Americans were. The thought of using equipment that no one really understood to power a spacecraft was, frankly, a bit frightening.

Worse was possessing such a terrible weapon, but finding oneself in the faintly ridiculous position of knowing that if he used it, he would lose it almost immediately. At

the same time, if he didn't use the primary weapon, the
enemy might well take the ship.

An impossible dilemma.

"Colonel d'André?"

"Yes, General."

"Have the special weapon crew stand by to engage with
the primary weapon. We may not be able to fly, but by
God we can give a good account of ourselves!"

"Yes, General."

"Get the hopper fireteams aloft."

"Yes, sir."

"And place the computer safeguards on active," he
added after a moment's consideration more.

It was a measure of last resort, but a vital one.

He might sympathize with the enemy cause, might hate
the fact that his countrymen had attempted what amounted
to genocide against the Americans, might have the gravest
of doubts that the UN cause was right.

But there was also the matter of honor and duty, virtues
instilled in him by his father long before their falling-out.

He would not be known as the man who'd lost the UN's
greatest weapon to the enemy.

TWENTY-FIVE

Lieutenant Kaitlin Garroway
Tsiolkovsky Crater
0034 hours GMT

On the floor of the crater, the LAV could make top
speed, bounding across the surface at eighty kilometers
per hour. The faster it went, of course, the higher and
broader the plumes of dust thrown up by its tires. This
was both blessing and problem. It made their approach a
lot easier to see; on the other hand, the enemy couldn't be
sure of exactly what it was that was approaching from the
west, or even how many of them there were.

Kaitlin clutched the sides of her seat as LAV-1 bounced
and lurched across the Lunar regolith. Though her armor
was securely harnessed to the seat, she was taking a beat-
ing inside, and she had to grab hard and hold on to keep
from rattling around inside the suit's hard torso like a marble inside a tin can.

Beside her, Hartwell drove with sharp, precise pulls left
and right with the joystick, trying to be as unpredictable
as possible as the LAV raced across the plain. Ahead, on
his monitor, Tsiolkovsky's central peak rose against the
night, smooth-sided, its flanks scoured by eons of infalling
micrometeorites. Tucked away at the mountain's base, just
visible now rising behind a low-lying spur of the mountain, was their objective, the slender spire of the UN supership they'd come to capture or kill.

There'd still been no fire from the mountaintop, which suggested that the enemy weapon was now mounted aboard the ship. That made the most sense; the UN couldn't have many of the alien-derived antimatter weapons and likely had only the one.

But the three LAVs were almost certainly in the enemy's sights now. The only reason they weren't firing was the fear—a fear quite justified—that at the first shot, the LAVs would target the antimatter weapon's vulnerable turret. Lasers allowed a degree of pinpoint accuracy and precision in running gun battles unheard of in any previous war in history.

The Marines, Kaitlin decided, needed something better than an armored, four-wheeled box to deploy troops across modern combat distances. She *hurt*, the wild motion was making her sick to her stomach, and something like panic claustrophobia—a gnawing dread that within the next instant or two white fire was going to sear through the LAV and reduce them all to a cloud of hot plasma—was growing with each moment that she was trapped inside. Hartwell's tiny display screen was no substitute for the wide-open spaces and a place to dig deep and hide; it would be even worse, she knew, for the rest of her Marines, who could do absolutely nothing but sit there strapped to their seats, wondering what was happening.

"We have aircraft taking off at the base, Lieutenant," Hartwell announced.

Kaitlin twisted her head inside her helmet, trying to get a better view. The term aircraft was almost comically inappropriate here, in the Lunar vacuum, but old habits die hard. On the monitor, she could just make out four tiny constructs gleaming in the sunlight as they lifted off from beyond the low-lying spur. They were hoppers, short-range Lunar transports, like the one Chris Dow had taken out during the approach to Picard. They would have enemy riflemen aboard, probably with squad laser weapons at least as good as the Sunbeam M228, and the LAV's upper-deck armor wasn't all that thick . . . a design compromise for greater speed and fuel efficiency.

An even greater danger, though, was the possibility of

a low pass by a hopper with its ventral thrusters on full. She well remembered the Marine use of that strategy at Picard, and the UN forces would remember as well.

"Are we close enough yet to pinpoint the ship's main weapon turret?" she asked.

"I've got five different blisters or bumps registered on that thing that *could* be the turret, Lieutenant," Hartwell replied. "Don't know which is the target."

"If we start shooting randomly, they're liable to open up," she said. "Of course, we might get lucky." She thought for a moment, working up her courage. She felt like she was about to stick a pin into a sleeping lion. "Any sign of First Platoon?"

"Negative," Hartwell replied. "Other side of the mountain."

They were pursuing their original plan, with Second Platoon swinging south of the central peak, while Captain Fuentes and First Platoon swung around to the north. With the enemy base probably located on the site of the old radio-astronomy facility, nestled up against the southeast flank of the central peak, the idea was to split the enemy's fire and keep him guessing . . . but with Second Platoon, Second Squad stranded back there on the floor of Fermi Crater, it was getting a bit cold and lonely here to the southwest of that high and brooding mountain.

Another twenty kilometers to go.

"Okay," she told Hartwell. "Keep an eye on the ship, but let's engage those hoppers before they get close enough to fry us."

"Roger that." He manipulated a joystick, centering a targeting cursor to move the LAV's laser turret topside. "Firing!"

PFC Jack Ramsey
USS Ranger
0035 hours GMT

The *Ranger* was now less than ten minutes from its objective, and only now was Jack beginning to hope that he was going to make it.

After only minutes at six Gs, he'd decided that he wasn't going to be able even to think about doing more work on the nutcracker code. The pressure, the apparent weight of five full-grown men lying in a stack on top of him, was suffocating, crushing, and made gasping down each breath a struggle. Finally, he'd shut Sam down and switched the seatback display instead to a view relayed from a camera in *Ranger*'s nose.

The view of Earth, visibly growing larger minute by minute as the *Ranger* accelerated toward her, was absolutely spectacular, but Jack hadn't been able to muster more than a passing and somewhat lethargic interest.

An hour after they'd cut free from the L-3 construction shack, at just before midnight GMT, they'd whipped past the Earth, traveling now at over two hundred kilometers per second. For a blessed span of minutes, zero gravity had returned as the *Ranger* pivoted, nose skewing toward the fast-passing Earth with an unpleasant wrench to the gut and head, until she was traveling tail first, past the Earth and on her way now toward the Moon.

Jack had heard hear the harsh retching sounds of several Marines being sick elsewhere in the cabin. He'd kept his eyes carefully on the screen, unwilling to let his own stomach rebel as well. Amazing how contagious nausea could be.

Then acceleration returned . . . deceleration now, rather, as the *Ranger* began killing her tremendous velocity after the turn-over. Jack's maltreated stomach twisted, and he'd nearly lost it then; only the fact that he'd been on a special low-bulk diet for three days already saved him. The diet, evidently, hadn't helped everyone in the company; when weight returned, Jack was glad he wasn't farther aft, where, judging from the yells and curses, tiny, free-floating globules of vomit were suddenly falling like rain.

"Okay, people," Captain Lee's voice said over the cabin comm system, moments after the six-G torture resumed. "Not much longer. Remember, we're going . . . for either Plan Alfa . . . or Plan Bravo. Which way we go . . . depends on . . . our fellow Marines. On whether they . . . were able to nail that damned cannon . . . or not. Either

way . . . we have a good chance . . . of pulling this thing . . .
off. Stay focused . . . stay alert . . . and you'll come
through fine. . . ."

He spoke quietly, calmly, and reassuringly, despite the
pauses between each phrase as he caught his breath and
rallied his strength for the next handful of words. What
Captain Lee was saying, Jack found, wasn't nearly as important as the fact that he was saying it . . . demonstrating
to each miserable Marine in that cabin that he or she was
not alone, that this punishment was routine, that it was all
part of the game. After a few moments more, he wasn't
even aware of the captain's voice . . . only of the reassur-
ance.

With a grunting effort, Jack found he was able to toggle
the seatback screen's display either to the receding blue-
white beauty of Earth or to the fast-swelling, crater-
battered visage of the Moon, visible now beyond the
Tinkertoy struts of *Ranger*'s landing assembly. After several changes of mind, he settled on the Earth; he thought
he knew now what the Apollo astronauts had felt, seventy-
some years ago, when they'd looked back at the world of
their birth and realized that all of humankind, all art, all
history, everything that made him what he was, was contained in that one small and delicate bubble of cloud-
swirled blue.

That bubble was so fragile. What if his Uncle David's
theory about the Hunters of the Dawn was right? Man's
birthworld seemed so vulnerable from out here; the attack
on Chicago had demonstrated just *how* vulnerable it could
be.

And if the Hunters of the Dawn didn't destroy that frail
beauty, how long before Man himself did?

He pushed the churning, unpleasant thoughts aside. For
now, Earth's beauty was enough, something to cling to, to
lose himself in. For Jack, it felt as though all of the years
he'd yearned to be out in space had been distilled to this
one peaceful, crystalline moment.

Despite the discomfort, he wanted to savor the experience as long as he could.

Lieutenant Kaitlin Garroway
Tsiolkovsky Crater
0035 hours GMT

A point of incandescence appeared against the ungainly, strut-crisscrossed flank of the nearest hopper, and in seconds the vehicle was falling from the sky, its reaction mass tanks holed. A second flare of light appeared on the side of the UN ship.

"Objective is under fire!" Hartwell called.

"Outstanding!" That meant that LAV-2 and LAV-4 were also close enough to engage, somewhere on the other side of the UN base. Approaching from two directions, coming around both sides of the central peak, must have the enemy commander beside himself. "Pop a comm relay!"

"Roger that!"

Hartwell pressed several screen touchpoints as the LAV gave another lurch and thump. On the upper deck, just behind the laser turret, a hatch popped open and a burst of compressed nitrogen blasted a baseball-sized sphere into the black sky.

Almost immediately, a crackle of radio voices sounded in Kaitlin's helmet headset.

"LAV-2, this is LAV-4! I've got movement on the ship!" That sounded like Staff Sergeant Mohr. *"I think I see the turret!"*

"Hit it!" the captain's voice cried back. *"Take out the turret!"*

"Firing!"

"Damn! You hit something! Can't see what! . . ."

"Two, this is One!" Kaitlin called. "Target in sight! Watch out for hoppers!"

The other two LAVs were masked by Tsiolkovsky's central peak, and there was no ionosphere here to bounce signals off of, but the comm relay, following its mortar-lobbed trajectory, could relay communications between the widely scattered elements of the company for over a minute before the Moon's sixth of a G could drag it back down to the surface.

"Roger that, One," Fuentes replied. *"Nice you could join us!"*

"Hoo, yeah!" Mohr added. *"Kick ass and take names!"*

"We'll be moving too fast to take names," Fuentes replied. *"I'll settle for initials!"*

"Two, Four! I've got hoppers incoming, bearing one-nine-five!"

"LAV-1, this is Two! Hit the primary target, and keep hitting him! LAV-4, open fire on those hoppers."

"Roger, LAV-2."

"Roger that, Skipper," Kaitlin said. She looked at Hartwell. "You heard?"

"Aye-firmative. Lemme get clear of the damned dust!" Hartwell's erratic driving had provided at least one side benefit—sending a cloud of fine, lunar dust into the sky . . . dust that at least partly obscured the fast-moving LAV. As the image on the screen cleared, Hartwell began moving the targeting cursor up the side of the UN ship.

An instant later, a flash of intense and silent light blanked out Hartwell's monitor, a flare as dazzling as the surface of the sun.

Général de Brigade *Paul-Armand Larouche*
Tsiolkovsky Base
0037 hours GMT

"A hit!" d'André shouted. He pointed at the monitor, which showed now the view from a camera mounted on the main weapon turret. From that vantage point, thirty meters above the ground, an immense cloud of dust was rising from the barren Lunar plain, just beyond the low hill sheltering the base to the west. For a moment, the camera's optics had been blinded by the flash, but as the image cleared, there was little to be seen but a slow-falling cascade of dark gray dust. "We got him, General!"

"Swiftly, now," Larouche ordered. "Bring the weapon to bear on the two vehicles to the northeast!"

"Slewing about to zero-eight-one . . ."

With the lone attacking vehicle killed, perhaps they now had a chance. Even if the primary weapon turret was knocked out now . . .

"It's going to be difficult, General. Our people are too close!"

Merde! That was the biggest disadvantage of being forced to fight at such close quarters. The blast of the positron beam—heat, light, and radiation—was as undiscriminating as the detonation of a small nuclear weapon. The UN troops outside would suffer, too, if they were too close to the blast.

"The main turret is taking hits!" d'André shouted.

But that couldn't be helped. "Fire! Fire *now*! . . ."

God forgive me! . . .

Captain Carmen Fuentes
Tsiolkovsky Crater
0037 hours GMT

"Fire!" Carmen yelled. Her eyes were watering from the flash that had momentarily blanked the screen. "*Fire!*"

A flash, a burst of white-hot incandescence, flared from the side of the UN ship, now less than four kilometers away.

"*Score one for LAV-4!*" Sergeant Mohr's voice called over her headset. "*I think we nailed the bastard that time!*"

"I just lost the relay from LAV-1!" Staff Sergeant Michaels, LAV-2's driver, announced.

"Put up another comm relay," Carmen told him.

"We still have two in the sky," Michaels replied. "And the LOS hit when the UN ship fired. Captain, I think LAV-1 just got scragged!"

"Shit." She'd liked Garroway. A lot. *Grieve later,* she thought. *When there's time!* "Okay . . . keep targeting the ship."

"Firing!" Then, "Captain, I think we nailed that turret. Nothing there but a hole!"

"You're sure that's where the positron beam was coming from?"

"Affirmative! Got it recorded, if you want a replay."

"Let's see it."

Michaels set the replay going in a small window opened in the lower left corner of the main display. It was hard to see, even magnified and in slow motion, but it did look as though a dazzling pinpoint of light had appeared on something like a ball turret set in the UN ship's hull; an instant later, the horizon had flared in a sun-brilliant detonation, searing the lunar regolith some ten or fifteen kilometers away. As the screen cleared, laser hits from LAV-4's cannon could clearly be seen shredding the turret like cardboard.

"Okay," she said. "We'll call that a kill on the AM weapon, and call for Plan Bravo." She glanced at the time readout: if *Ranger* was on time, she should be gentling into Lunar orbit within another few minutes . . . and would be coming over the western horizon twenty-five minutes after that, but for any number of reasons she could be late, or early. "Start popping com relays every minute," Carmen added. "Coded for Select Bravo. I want *Ranger* to pick that up as soon as she clears the ringwall."

"You got it, Captain."

"Take us in closer."

The LAV accelerated, spewing dust like a smoke screen.

PFC Jack Ramsey
USS Ranger
0044 hours GMT

"How about it, people?" Captain Lee said. "Any broken bones? Anyone hurt?" He moved down the aisle, adrift once again in blessed zero G. Jack raised one hand and looked at it; it was trembling, beyond his ability to

control it. God . . . was the entire platoon in this bad a
shape?

"My dignity's pretty badly hurt, Skipper," one Marine
replied, wiping his face with a rag. "Can I be excused?"

"You'll survive, Logan," Gunnery Sergeant Bueller
told him. "Okay, Marines! Listen up! I want you all to
move forward, single file. Take a helmet and gloves from
Lance Corporal Schultz, seal up tight, then check your
weapon. Remember, do not load until your section leader
gives you the word!"

Bueller was a short, stocky fireplug of a Marine, with
a bulldog's face and a Doberman's growl. "Now!" he
continued, anchoring himself between two seatbacks.
"Are there any Marines who need help making it to the
LSCPs? Speak up now, and don't give me no macho shit!
If you're having trouble navigating, we'll assign someone
to help you!"

Jack considered raising a hand, then decided that he
would be okay. He knew what Bueller was looking for;
all of the Marines aboard *Ranger* except Bos, Dillon, and
Jack had had plenty of zero-gravity practice. The three of
them had had three days at the construction shack to practice, though, and Bueller had made sure they'd worked at
moving around without losing a handhold or getting disoriented in the weird, no-up-and-no-down falling sensation
of weightlessness.

Ranger's engines had cut off only moments before, and
they were now in orbit around the Moon at a mountain-
skimming altitude of only fifty kilometers. The Marines
had twenty-two minutes now to get aboard the LSCPs
strapped to *Ranger*'s sides.

He craned his neck, looking for his uncle. There he was.
David didn't seem to be having any trouble moving about;
then Jack remembered that the archeologist had spent sixteen months or so on cycler spacecraft going to and from
Mars. Though the cyclers had spin gravity habs, he
would've had plenty of opportunity to practice handling
himself in free fall.

He also saw Captain Lee . . . and was shocked by the
expression on the man's face. After those soothing words

during the second half of the flight, it was a little unsettling to see what looked like worry there.

Then Jack remembered the scuttlebutt he'd been hearing for the past several weeks. Captain Lee was rumored to be pretty tight with the L-T commanding 1-SAG's Bravo Company Second Platoon . . . and she would be on the ground right now, trying to clear the way for *Ranger*'s approach and landing. The captain must be sick with worry. Like his DI in boot camp had told him, the First Space Assault Group was an awfully small unit. That meant people formed close bonds within it; it also increased the risk that close friends would die.

He looked again at his Uncle David and wondered if both of them would survive what was about to happen. Jack hadn't thought much about his own mortality, but there was something about the expression on Rob Lee's features that demanded it.

Carefully, he pulled himself into the aisle, making sure he had the next handhold grasped securely before letting go of the last.

Another Marine's legs swung through the air and thumped heavily against his torso, nearly knocking him free. "You okay, Ramsey?" Bueller asked him, gripping his upper arm to steady him. "You got your PAD and shit okay?"

"Squared away, Gunny."

"Semper fi, Marine. We're countin' on ya."

It was a sobering thought. Capture of the UN ship might well depend on one of the three 4069 MOSs cracking the enemy's computer security.

His stomach gave another twist, and he bit back a sharp and sour taste. Grimly, he followed the queue forward.

Lieutenant Kaitlin Garroway
Tsiolkovsky Crater
0045 hours GMT

The rasp of her own breathing was impossibly loud inside her helmet. "Hello! Hello!" she called. "Does anyone hear me?"

Kaitlin could hear groans, cries, and mumbled curses coming over the platoon com channel. The lights were out and the LAV's cabin submerged in blackness absolute, but at least communications were still working.

"Ah . . . yeah, L-T. I hear ya."

"Who's that?"

"Sorry. Kaminski, ma'am." He sounded dazed, maybe hurt.

"I'm here too," Hartwell said. "Christ! What hit us?"

"The enemy AM beam would be my guess," Kaitlin replied. "Don't know why it didn't fry us, though."

"Let's have some light in here! Who's got their suit lights working?" She began fumbling for her own light, reaching for the switch mounted high on her left shoulder. As the lights mounted on her shoulders flicked on, other lights came on as well, filling the LAV's interior with bizarrely misshapen and grotesquely huge shadows.

The LAV, she thought, was canted to the left at about a forty-five-degree angle. Part of the right side had crumpled inward, as though from the blow of a giant fist, and her helmet readout was showing zero pressure in the cabin.

Another readout showed something far more worrisome: she'd just picked up 100 rads in a single dose. Not good. Not good at all. She felt queasy and wondered if it was the radiation.

She still couldn't figure out what had happened. A near miss by the positron beam, yes . . . but why weren't they all dead? "Someone aft, see if you can get the airlock doors open," she called. "The rest of you, sound off when I call your names. Let me know if you're in one piece! Ahearn!"

"Here! Okay!"

"Anders!"

"I'm okay."

"Castellano!" She waited. "Castellano!"

"He's bought it, L-T."

"Hartwell!"

"Okay."

She ran down First Squad's roster and was relieved to find that there were only two dead—Castellano and PFC

Jordy Rawlins. Two more were hurt badly enough that they'd better not be moved—Navy Lieutenant Wood with a probable broken leg, and Lance Corporal Klinginsmith with what was probably a couple of broken ribs.

All of the squad had taken a hefty dose of radiation. Antimatter reacted with matter by vanishing in a burst of very hard radiation—X rays and gamma rays, especially—and both the armored hull of the LAV and their space suits would have generated additional, secondary radiation in a cascade effect.

How badly they were burned remained to be seen. The tables said that fifty percent fatalities resulted from 300 rads, but as little as 4 rads delivered all at once would cause *some* physical effects. They'd been "hardened" against radiation—put on a diet heavy in green vegetables and Vitamin A and E, and they'd all been taking daily doses of fat-soluble antioxidants—all of which was supposed to cut the effects of radiation by better than thirty percent. And once they were out of this, shots of atropine and antirad drugs would cut the effects still further.

But a hell of a lot depended on how quickly they could get that additional treatment, and even more on the exact nature of their exposure.

Outside, on the dusty plain as they scrambled clear of the wrecked LAV, Hartwell approached her. "I think I know what happened," he said. He pointed back behind the LAV, where an expanse of Lunar regolith had been fused, as if by intense heat. "I'd just put the stick hard over when the beam hit. I think the matter-antimatter reaction took place in the dust cloud."

"The dust cloud? How . . . oh!" Kaitlin understood. "It didn't all go off at once!"

"Right. Some positrons must have leaked through . . . and hit the ground just behind us. Others hit dust particles. The dust probably diffused the blast, spread it out over a large area. There wouldn't be any shock wave, of course, except through the ground, which is what tipped us over and crumpled the side."

"And the dust might have scattered the rads a bit, too."

"It's the only thing I can think of that saved us. We

had our own personal smoke screen up . . . and it blocked part of the beam.''

''The boys in R&D are going to be interested in that effect,'' Kaitlin told him. ''But that'll have to wait.'' Turning her back on the wrecked LAV, she stared east, toward the UN base and the mountain. It looked close . . . but distances were deceiving on the Moon.

''Okay, Marines,'' Kaitlin said, turning back to face the group standing in a semicircle behind her. ''Here's the deal. We can sit where we are and wait for someone to win this damned fight . . . or we can hotfoot it over to that base and take a hand in what happens. Strictly volunteer. You want to sit this one out, no one's gonna squawk. Every one of you's done more than what was expected by the strict call of duty already. Me, I'm going to go see if I can give Captain Fuentes a hand. Anyone want to come along?''

''I'm with you, Lieutenant.'' One space-suited figure brandished an ATAR and started forward. He had to get close for Kaitlin to read the name KAMINSKI on the front of his suit. Yates shouldered a slaw and stepped forward. Then Julia Ahearn. In another moment, all eight were with her; she had to order Lance Corporal Lidell point-blank to stay behind with the two wounded men.

She tried to make it look like a random choice. She imagined most of the people in the squad would know, though, that Lidell's wife was expecting a child.

Even in war, life could be respected and preserved. It had to be that way.

''Keep a radio beacon going,'' she told him. ''Someone will be along to pick you up before long. And . . . if it happens to be the UN, no heroics.'' She gestured to the two wounded men. ''Your responsibility is to them, to see that they're taken care of.''

''Aye, aye, ma'am,'' Lidell said. ''I still wish you'd let me—''

''Carry out your orders, Marine.''

He slapped his ATAR brusquely. ''Aye, aye, ma'am!''

''The rest of you? Follow me!''

Turning, she started moving toward the UN base, several kilometers distant, still partly obscured by a shoulder of the crater's central mountain peak.

It looked like the battle there was on in earnest, and she was determined to have a piece of it.

TWENTY-SIX

PFC Jack Ramsey
USS Ranger
0049 hours GMT

Jack pulled his helmet down until the ring lock engaged, then gave it a hard counterclockwise twist to seal it. As he pulled himself hand over hand along the passageway leading to the port airlock, Lance Corporal Wojtaszek handed him an ATAR and a pouch with five loaded 4.5mm magazines and two beehive mags for his M-440. Gunnery Sergeant Bueller gave each Marine a quick once-over as he went through the airlock, sending some to the left, others to the right as they squirmed through close-fitting boarding tubes and into the LSCPs mounted on the *Ranger*'s flanks like Tinkertoy remoras.

"Okay, Ramsey," Bueller said, checking his suit PLSS readouts, then rotating him to stare through his visor and into his face. "Let's have a look-see. You ready to rock?"

"Yes, Gunnery Sergeant. Ready to go!"

"Your PAD hooked up and ready?" It was like Bueller to double-check the important stuff. The man had an incredible mind for fine detail and seemed to know every Marine in the platoon and what they should have with them down to his or her socks.

"Right here."

He looked past Jack at the Marine floating behind him. "How about you, Dillon? You okay? Got your PAD?"

"All set, Gunny," Diane Dillon replied. She punched Jack's side, causing him to drift around slightly and bump against the bulkhead. "This shaggy character'd just better watch my smoke!"

"Bosnivic? How about you?"

"I'm okay." He was starting to sound nervous.

"Got your PAD? It's working okay?"

"On-line and ready."

"Okay. Remember the drill. Ramsey and Dillon, you two are going down in LSCP-52. Bosnivic, you're going down in 54."

Jack nodded. If one of the two landers was shot down, at least one of the 4069 MOS Marines would survive to board the UN ship. "Got it."

"When you're on the ground, the three of you keep together and stay down! I'll round you all up and lead you in with my combat team, just behind the primary assault group. We'll get you in, don't worry about that. Use your weapons if you have to, but do *not* let yourselves be suckered into a firefight. You three people are the whole freaking reason we're here, and I don't want any of you getting capped because he or she got distracted. You read me?"

"We read you," Dillon said.

"Loud and clear, Gunny," Jack added.

"Yeah," Bosnivic said.

"Okay. Ramsey and Dillon . . . port tube. Bos, starboard. See you on the beach, Marines."

With his ATAR clanging once or twice as he squeezed through the airlock hatch, Jack pulled himself through and into LSCP-52. Finding an empty seat, he swung himself around, pulled himself down, and buckled in. Diane found a seat opposite.

The landing craft was packed with twenty-four Marines on board, with no room at all to move even if they hadn't been strapped in. He faced Diane across the narrow aisle, their knees touching, and wondered what to say.

Through her helmet visor, she winked at him.

He managed a smile in reply. He hadn't known her for long—just since he'd arrived at Quantico—and she'd struck him as an all-business sort, but she seemed like a nice person. He wondered if he could get to know her better, after the op. Talking to her, he'd found, was a lot more interesting than talking to Sam, even though he'd never seen her out of uniform.

They waited for what seemed like eternity.

"Now hear this, now hear this," a voice called over Jack's headset. "We've just cleared the horizon with a com relay from the RAG. We are go for Plan Bravo. Repeat, go for Plan Bravo. Good luck, Marines!"

Go for Bravo! That meant the RAG had managed to knock out the A-M cannon! Instantly, the platoon channel was filled with cheers and wild shouts.

"Outstanding!"

"Gung ho!"

"Ooh-rah!"

"Let's kick it!"

The enthusiasm was heady, dizzying, and contagious. Jack found himself shouting with the rest and exchanging a clumsy, gloved high five with Diane.

The remarkable thing was that Plan Bravo actually meant a more dangerous approach for the Marine assault teams. Alfa meant the AM gun was intact, but positioned at or near the UN base on the south side of Tsiolkovsky's central peak. If the call had been for Plan Alfa, they would have set down on the north side of the peak and approached the enemy base overland and spread out, so the enemy AM weapon couldn't burn them from the sky. Bravo meant they could come storming right in to the base's front door. Even with the AM cannon knocked out, that meant a hot LZ, with lots of base defenders about determined to make sure the Marines were cut down before they could fully deploy.

It seemed a little crazy to be cheering because they were about to hit a more dangerous LZ.

But then, Jack thought, they *were* Marines.

"Ooh-*rah!*" he shouted.

He'd never felt this kind of excitement in his entire life. Or this kind of fear.

Captain Carmen Fuentes
UN Base, Tsiolkovsky Crater
0054 hours GMT

"Let's go, Marines!"

Carmen stooped low to clear the aft hatch of LAV-2, stepping out onto the ramp, then bounding down onto the lunar regolith. The other Marines crammed into the confines of the LAV exploded around and past her, scattering in long, low kangaroo bounds that kicked up clouds of fine dust with each landing.

The LAV had slewed to a halt less than twenty meters from the foundation of a towering gantry, a latticework of steel and aluminum hugging the half-obscured shape of a sleek, black craft with UN markings. Space-suited figures moved high among the gantry catwalks; only when a puff of dust geysered a meter to her left was she aware that some of those figures, at least, were shooting at her.

She kept moving, bouncing forward toward the relative shelter at the base of the gantry ladder. It was a strange kind of battle, with everyone moving with the eerie semblance of slow motion characteristic of moving in the Moon's one-sixth gravity. She could hear the calls of the other Marines over her combat channel, but there was no crash and rattle of gunfire, no explosions, none of the shrill, deafening, and mind-numbing thunder that marked battles in environments that happened to include an atmosphere. Wyvern shoulder-launched rockets flared brightly against the night, streaking toward their targets. An explosion detonated nearby; there was no sound, but she felt the concussion through the soles of her boots.

Sergeant Joles, just in front of her, staggered in midleap, crumpled, and fell, dropping slowly to the surface and rolling over several times as his momentum kept dragging him forward. Without thinking, Carmen stooped, grabbed a carry handle on his PLSS, and dragged him along, hauling him through the dust until she was under the gantry's shadow.

She rolled Joles over, looking for an entry wound,

reaching for one of the slap-stick pressure seals issued to the assault force to stop puncture leaks . . . but Joles needed more than a patch. A round had penetrated his helmet visor smack in the center, crazing the plastic, and splashing the interior curve with frothing red.

Both remaining LAVs were moving now, circling out away from the base, partly to make themselves harder to hit, partly to draw fire from the Marines now storming the base. LAV-2 pivoted sharply, its turret rolling high. Ten meters above her head, a UN trooper pitched over a cat-walk railing as the LAV's laser exploded his legs and part of the steel platform he was standing on with the equivalent of ten kilograms of high explosives. Half of a body and a cloud of steel fragments fell in a broad-arcing spray, slowly at first, then faster as they got closer to the ground. Bits of metal rattled off Carmen's helmet like a rain of steel bearings.

She saw movement on another part of the structure and tried taking aim. It was almost impossible, though, to position herself so she could aim her ATAR almost straight up, and the built-in camera-aiming system didn't work unless the rifle's butt was connected with the pivot socket in her suit's torso, right at her center of gravity. The idea was to have the rifle's targeting system throw a crosshair cursor on her visor's HUD, showing where she was aiming, but she ended up aiming blindly and squeezing the trigger, hoping that the high-velocity spray of full-auto rounds hit *something*.

LAV-2's Marines, First Squad, First Platoon, were at the gantry; LAV-4's were assaulting the base control center a hundred meters away. The enemy base suddenly seemed far larger than the simulations and maps had made it look back on Earth, far too large for twenty-four . . . no, twenty-*three* Marines to handle.

"Come on, Avery," she muttered to herself. She looked west, over the sheltering flank of the central peak, but the sky was empty except for stars. "Move your fat ass!"

"Hey, Captain Fuentes!" A voice called. "This is Mohr, in LAV-4! I found somethin' here!"

Turning, she saw the LAV approaching, a shadow behind its headlamps and the glare they cast in the dust. Smaller shadows moved on the vehicle's flat upper deck, shadows already dropping off the top and onto the surface.

"Found 'em a couple of klicks to the west, Captain," Mohr continued. "They were hoofing it and asked for a lift!"

Carmen triggered her suit's IFF ID call, and familiar names flashed onto her HUD. The Marine coming toward her was . . .

"Garry! I thought you were dead!"

"They singed us a bit, Captain," Kaitlin replied, close enough now that Carmen could see the other Marine's easy grin through her visor. "Nothing a shot of atropine and a decon routine won't handle!"

"Jesús y Maria!" Carmen cried, a phrase from her childhood she'd never expected to use again. "It's good to see you, girl!"

Something hit her in the side, a sledgehammer swung with a force that slammed her off her feet. The next thing Carmen Fuentes knew, she was on her back, feeling very, very cold as air whistled past her ears and a tinny voice announced, *"Warning! Suit breach! Pressure dropping! warning! Suit breach! . . ."*

Dimly, she was aware of a space-helmeted head hovering above her. "Captain!" It was Garroway's voice. "Captain! Hang on!"

"Take . . . command." Her voice broke, and she tasted blood, hot and salty. She tried again, reaching for the figure crouched above her. "Take command!"

"Captain! . . ."

"Take them . . . take them up the ladder, Marine!"

"Aye, aye, ma'am!"

The computer voice was no longer shrilling at her. Had Garroway patched the leak? Or was the air in her suit gone? No, that made no sense. She was breathing *something*. But it was starting to hurt now, starting to hurt a *lot*.

She felt a sting in her shoulder—Garroway using one of the special high-pressure air-fired needles to slam a shot of morphine right through the heavy material of her suit. In a few moments, it still hurt, but the pain was very, very far away. . . .

Lieutenant Kaitlin Garroway
UN Base, Tsiolkovsky Crater
0058 hours GMT

Kaitlin pulled the morphine injector free from the captain's arm and slapped a small patch over the hole . . . a bright red patch that indicated that the suit's wearer had been given morphine. Tossing the injector away, she used a grease pencil to mark the time on the patch. Then she picked up her ATAR and looked up the side of the gantry. *Take them up the ladder.*

She felt lonely. She was in command now, and ordering her people to do the impossible was up to *her* now, not Carmen Fuentes.

"Marines!" she shouted over the combat channel. "This is Lieutenant Garroway! The skipper's down, and I'm taking command! Everyone who can make it to the base of the gantry, get there on the double!" An explosion flared among the girders high above her, as one of the LAVs killed a sniper. A moment later, the LAV exploded in a silent gout of light, dust, and hurtling fragments. *God!* "Move it! Move it!"

The seven who'd come with her from LAV-1 were already there. "We're with you, Lieutenant!" Kaminski called. Other Marines were approaching

"Okay, then! You! You! You! Cover us and come up last! The rest of you, follow me!" Grabbing the handrails of the gantry ladder, she started up the steel rungs.

She wondered where the *Ranger* Marines were, and how much longer they'd be.

Captain Robert Lee
USS *Ranger*
0058 hours GMT

Rob was furious.

He was floating on *Ranger*'s tiny bridge, where the ship's four flight officers were strapped into seats all but surrounded by instrumentation and consoles, and Colonel Avery was sitting in a jump seat just behind the captain's station. The hell of it was that the bastard Avery was right. *He* had the call, and the safety of the ship came first.

He shifted handholds, moving closer to Avery's seat. "Sir, I understand that," he said. On the big display screen above the captain's and pilot's positions, the ruggedly cratered surface of the Moon scrolled past. A steadily dwindling number on the lower right corner of the display gave the range to the UN base. Just over one hundred kilometers. They must be just outside the Tsiolkovsky ringwall. They had to act within the next minute or two, or miss their chance entirely. "But our people need the firepower we can bring to bear. That's why we're here!"

"You are being insubordinate, Captain," Avery replied. "Our primary mission objective has been met." Minutes before, the two LSCPs had been jettisoned; drifting clear of the *Ranger*, flying tail first, they'd fired their engines together and now were dropping toward the surface, and a landing at the UN base.

Technically, *Ranger* was supposed to do the same, but according to the mission orders, that was an option, one that Avery could exercise at his discretion.

And he was choosing not to exercise it.

"Sir, may I remind you that this mission was originally designed to take advantage of *Ranger* as a mobile fire-support platform. If you stay in orbit, we get one pass. A couple of shots. It won't be enough to help."

"And I will remind *you*, Captain, that we have burned over ninety percent of our reaction mass in that six-G run from L-3. We have just enough remaining to boost free of Lunar orbit and make Earth orbit in three days. If we decelerate to land, if we expend reaction mass hovering, we will *have* to set down, and we will be stranded here. Vulnerable."

"Transports are already on the way from Earth, sir. And there'll be a water tank down there somewhere, reaction mass for the UN ship. Sir, we can't abandon our people!"

"My orders state that I must secure the safety of this vessel," Avery said, his voice petulant. "I do not intend to allow it to fall into UN hands or to suffer combat damage. If the Marine assault down there fails, we have no other defense against the enemy AM ship. None!"

Eighty-eight kilometers. They were over the ringwall now, drifting swiftly above the flat, dark maria of Tsiolkovsky's crater floor. Each second they waited meant more reaction mass spent killing their velocity.

In another few seconds, it would all be moot. He didn't mind arguing with his commanding officer when he thought the argument was justified . . . but there was no way in hell that he could argue against the laws of physics.

PFC Jack Ramsey
LSCP-52
0059 hours GMT

Jack had felt a solid thump as the LSCP jettisoned from the side of the *Ranger*. For another few moments, they'd been in free fall, and then the craft's engines had cut in. With the seats facing each other, the minute or so of acceleration made him feel as though he was lying on his side. He let his tongue loll from his mouth and crossed his eyes, eliciting a laugh from Dillon.

For several minutes, now, most of the sensation of weight had been directed toward the deck, which meant the LSCP was flying on her ventral thrusters. With no windows and no camera or seatback monitor, there was no way to see out, and the Marines had only the words of the LSCP's pilot to cling to.

And most of those words weren't even directed at them.

"Okay. I see the central massif. Comin' up on fifteen kay . . ."

"Five-two, this is Five-four. Looks like some shootin' goin' on there, just to the right. Got multiple airborne targets on radar."

"UNdie hoppers, Five-four. Give 'em a wide berth."

"Jesus Kee-rist . . . looks like one of the LAVs got nailed down there. Look at that crater!"

"Roger that. Okay. Coming down to fifteen hundred. Fourteen . . . twelve . . ."

"Ground's rising. Watch your altimeter."

A resounding *thump* sounded from somewhere below and forward. *"Uh, Five-four. I'm taking some fire here. I got laser fire from the south flank of the mountain and projectiles from the base."*

"Roger that, Five-two. Same here. I think we're attracting a little too much attention up here."

"Shit! Another hit! Let's get the hell down on the deck before they catch us with a fuckin' golden BB."

They went weightless again for several long seconds, before a solid kick through the deck caught Jack hard in the seat of the pants. The nausea he'd felt after the two-hour run from L-3 was returning, and he desperately hoped he wasn't going to be sick inside his suit. He'd heard too many stories of people drowning on their own vomit after getting sick while suited up.

Then the deck canted sharply, and the thrust increased. *"Picking up some dust, here! Fifteen . . . ten . . . five . . . contact light! Throttle down!"*

With a heavy *thump*, the LSCP hit the ground. Immediately, the Marines began unbuckling their harnesses and collecting their weapons. The lock at the aft end of the cargo module opened, and the first squad of twelve Marines began filing in. Jack became aware of a fairly regular *thump-clang* against the starboard side of the craft. It took him a moment to decide that someone out there was popping small-arms fire at the spacecraft.

"This," he said to himself as he began filing aft toward the airlock, *"must be what they mean by a hot LZ."*

"You ain't seen nothin' yet, kid," a tall, black sergeant named Matthews said over Jack's headset. *"It gets better!"*

He took a deep breath. *"I can't fucking wait!"*

Captain Robert Lee
USS Ranger
0101 hours GMT

"If the Marine assault down there fails," Avery said, "we have no other defense against the enemy AM ship. None!"

Despite the hard words, Avery seemed to be wavering. Rob had the gut feeling that man wasn't a coward, but that he was close to paralysis over making a decision that could screw the mission . . . and end his career in the process.

"You will considerably improve their chances if you take the *Ranger* in." Rob waited an uncomfortable beat before adding, "Sir."

"Excuse me," David Alexander said, floating headfirst into the crowded compartment. "I heard the shouting. Mind if I join you?"

"This area is restricted!" Avery snapped. "Authorized military personnel only!"

"Fine. But I suggest, Colonel, that you order the crew to take us down. The government shipped me all the way out here at considerable expense so I could take a look at any alien ruins at Tsiolkovsky. Your superiors aren't going to be happy if you just loop me around the Moon and take me home!"

"That is none of your concern! I have to keep the *Ranger* intact, in case the attack fails!"

Seventy-five kilometers.

Alexander jerked a thumb at Rob. "Your people have to stay polite, Colonel. Military protocol and all. They also have to watch what they say to the news media. Me, I don't have that worry. Seems to me that Triple-N might be real interested in a story about a Marine colonel who left his people on the ground without adequate space support. And the wounded. You're making them wait for three days while transports come out from Earth?"

"Damn you, Alexander! . . ."

Rob saw Avery's face reddening, saw the clenched fists. For a moment, he thought the man was going to attack the archeologist. Worse, Alexander's attack was stiffening Avery's resolve.

Maybe, though, if Avery had a soft way to come down . . .

"You're right, Colonel," Rob said. "It's your call. But let me say this before you decide. More military leaders have been damned for doing nothing than were ever damned for doing *something*!"

Avery swung his head to stare at him. He seemed about to say something, then to think better of it.

"If our people win down there, you're going to look damned silly . . . unless there are wounded we could have pulled out. Leaving them would be criminal. And . . . one more thing."

"And that is?"

"We're Marines. We *don't* leave our own!"

Avery opened his mouth one more time, then closed it with a snap. Turning sharply, he slapped the captain of the *Ranger* on the shoulder. "Okay, Commander Kieffer. Take us down!"

"Yes, *sir*!" Kieffer cast a glance back over his shoulder at Rob and the civilian. "You two gentlemen, grab some deck and hang on. This is gonna be rough!"

"Firing sequence laid in," the pilot said. "Range to target thirty-six kilometers. On your command."

"Shit, that's tight! Okay, we'll go in five . . . four . . . three . . . two . . . one . . . *ignition*! Deorbit burn commence!"

The deck caught Rob hard on his legs and the seat of his pants. Carefully, he lay down as the acceleration increased, climbing to two Gs . . . then a bone-rattling three.

He wondered if they'd already waited too long. . . .

TWENTY-SEVEN

PFC Jack Ramsey
Tsiolkovsky Base
0103 hours GMT

Jack ducked through the aft airlock hatch and jumped, landing on the Moon with a slight jar to his knees and a puff of scuffed-up dust around his boots. *I made it! I'm on the Moon! I'm actually on the freaking Moon! . . .*

But, damn it, there was no time to *enjoy* the fact. In eerie silence, space-suited figures ran, bounded in long kangaroo leaps, or spun and fell as gunfire or lasers cut them down. Wyvern rockets streaked across the sky, explosions flashed . . . and all in an utter, death-still silence that lent a touch of the surreal to the scene as it unfolded beyond Jack's helmet visor. Radio chatter alone filled the Lunar night. *"Chicago!"* some Marine shouted over the combat frequency. *"Remember Chicago!"* And then everyone was shouting it.

As he'd been ordered, Jack dropped to a crouch in a depression just beyond the grounded LSCP, and Diane crouched with him. The scene was so chaotic, he couldn't make sense of it at first. He saw the UN spacecraft that was their goal perhaps a hundred meters ahead, rising from within the embrace of a red-and-white-painted gantry and the caress of harsh worklights. He saw the Quonset-hut shapes of the base proper, tucked away in the shadow at the base of the central peak, which towered above the entire area, vast and brooding.

374

Jack switched on his tagger and studied the symbols that appeared on his HUD. The nearest troops all carried the green symbols indicating friend . . . fellow Marines. The few he could see without flags, on the mountainside or high up in the gantry, were far enough away to pose no immediate threat. He would wait and let the experienced hands take care of them.

One of the unflagged figures was leaning over a catwalk railing up near the top of the gantry, though, and appeared to be firing at Marines working their way up from below. He decided that he wouldn't be breaking orders if he took the guy out . . . and he might save some Marine's life.

Plugging a connector from his rifle into his suit, then switching on his ATAR's sighting system, he waited until a green crosshair appeared on his visor, then carefully moved the rifle back and forth until the crosshair centered on the enemy. Range figures flickered on the side of his visor: 156.3 meters. At that range, Jack could just make out the guy's UN-blue helmet. With the ATAR set for a three-round burst, he depressed the firing button. The weapon cycled with a swift, short vibration; the M-29 ATAR's rate of fire was so fast that the third round left the barrel before the first round's recoil had knocked the weapon off target.

He couldn't see the target now. He'd looked down at his HUD, distracted, and missed it. Had he hit him? Was the UN soldier down? Damn! He hadn't even seen what had happened!

In Siberia, Jack had never even seen the enemy . . . an invisible foe who dropped high-velocity shells on the Marine camp from over the horizon or rushed the perimeter at night, a half-glimpsed green-and-yellow shadow in an IR headset. Here, he still couldn't tell what was happening . . . but the fighting was far more immediate, more *real*.

And more deadly. A hit to arm or leg that would simply sting on Earth could be fatal here, in hard vacuum. Jack found he was shaking and couldn't stop.

He hoped no one else could tell how scared he was.

The other LSCP had touched down fifty meters away. As Marines spilled from the aft end of the vehicle, four suited figures lumbered across the plain toward Jack and Diane. IFF tagged them as Gunnery Sergeant Bueller, Bosnivic, and two Second Squad Marines.

"You two okay?" Bueller called. "Okay! Let's rock!" Turning, he trotted toward the gantry, leading the way. Rising from the depression, Jack and Diane followed.

Moving on the moon, Jack found, took a knack . . . one easily acquired, though it was hard work to get up to speed. He found a gentle lope, half skipping, half kangaroo hop, carried him across the lunar surface at the ground-eating pace of a running man.

He found himself wondering if he'd just killed someone up there on that steel tower.

"Okay!" Bueller called. "Tomlinson! Jakosky Take point! You three follow. We'll bring up the rear! Amphibious green blurs, now! Go! Go!"

Jack grabbed a rung and started climbing right behind Corporal Jakosky. He'd expected the climb to be harder than it was, but even with his suit, weapon, and backpack PLSS, he still weighed only about twenty kilos. He could pull himself up, hard, and before he stopped moving upward, he could reach up, grab, and pull again, with his feet providing only occasional guidance and support.

At the top, several blue-helmeted suits lay sprawled about like limp rag dolls, while the two Marine escorts and another Marine, with a Second Platoon shoulder patch, waited, ATARs at the ready.

Someone had already blown the ship's airlock hatch, which gaped open. The inner hatch was closed, but a bulkhead panel had been torn open, and a hot-wire box clipped on. Jack had seen the device demonstrated and explained at Quantico; rather than cycling a few people through at a time, the outer hatch would be kept open, with the inner hatch safeties overridden. Each time someone wanted to pass through, the inner hatch would be opened; the ship would lose some more air each time, and eventually be left in vacuum, but the method was a hell of a lot faster than the depressurization-repressurization cycle they would have to use otherwise.

"How many inside already, Marine?" Bueller asked the

Second Platoon guard as he mounted the catwalk.

"Four, Gunnery Sergeant," the man replied. The name on his chest read NARDELLI. "Lieutenant Garroway and three others. It's . . . it's all that's left of us!" His eyes were wide and frightened behind his visor.

"Hold your post, Marine. Rest of you, with me!"

A puff of vapor exploded from the torso of Diane's suit and she toppled backward, dropping her ATAR. She almost went over the edge, but Jack reached out and grabbed her arm, hauling her back from the edge and lowering her to the catwalk. "Sniper!" Jack yelled, pointing in the direction from which the laser shot had come . . . high up on the flank of the mountain, above the base. Nardelli, Bueller, and the others opened up with their ATARs, firing full-auto, but Jack couldn't tell if they could even see the target.

Dillon stared at him from inside her helmet, looking very frightened. "I . . . what happened? . . . Jack?"

"You took a laser bolt, Diane," he told her. The hole, just below her left breast, was only as wide as a pencil, but blood was bubbling through, steaming and freezing at the same time as it hit vacuum. He decided to lie. "Doesn't look bad."

He fumbled in an external pouch for a slap-stick patch and brought it down on the hole, sealing it over.

"It . . . hurts."

"Ramsey!" Bueller shouted. "Let's move!"

Nardelli held up a morphine gun. "I'll take care of her," he said.

"Do that!" He patted Dillon's shoulder. "You'll be okay!"

"Crack the fucking code, Jack," she told him, clinging to his arm with a gloved hand. "You and Sam . . . crack the fucking code!"

"You got it! I'll tell you all about it when I come back!"

Rising, he hurried after Bueller, who was waving him on from inside the airlock.

When all four Marines were ready, Bueller pressed the hot-wire box, and the inner hatch slid open. Air burst from within, a hurricane that threatened to sweep all five of them out of the lock and back onto the gantry at their backs, but Bueller leaned against the gale and waded in, as loose papers and a copy of *Playboy* in French whirled past and into the night.

Inside lay the body of a Marine, PFC Juarez, his helmet shattered.

Jack wondered how many Marines had been killed or wounded already in this impossible, insane attack . . . and how many were left. . . .

Général de Brigade *Paul-Armand*
Larouche
UNS Guerrière, *Tsiolkovsky Base*
0110 hours GMT

In another few moments, it won't matter. General Larouche dragged back the charging handle on his MAB-31 autopistol and set the selector to full automatic. He heard a loud *thump* and the clatter of metal on metal below the small bridge. They would be here, soon. But the ship knew what to do. . . .

He hadn't heard from d'André in a long time. He'd sent him aft to organize a defense of the main locks, but that line of defense had obviously failed. Three times, the bridge alarms had gone off, warning of dropping pressure as the enemy breached the main lock, then resealed it. Air pressure aboard the *Guerrière* was down to about half normal, and the sounds picked up by his suit's external mikes had a curiously flat and tinny quality to them.

He exchanged a glance with the other two space-suited men in the compartment, a pair of North Chinese special forces troops who'd taken refuge on the bridge a few moments ago. Unfortunately, Larouche did not speak Mandarin, and they seemed to speak no French, German, or English. Their dark eyes, deep within their black helmets, gave nothing away when they looked at him. He wondered if they knew what he'd done, that there was no hope now for any of them.

A stream of positrons, released from the alien generator but not focused and directed by the main weapon's magnetic channels, would destroy the entire ship . . . and probably a fair portion of the base as well. The countdown had already begun. He checked his helmet time readout. Four minutes, forty-eight seconds. No, not much longer at all. . . .

The hatch leading aft was circular and set in the middle of the bridge deck. The three men had positioned themselves around the hatch, weapons aimed at it. There was no place to hide, and nowhere else to go.

He thought he heard . . .

With a high-pitched bang, the hatch flew into the air, struck the overhead, and fluttered down slowly in the Moon's weak gravity. A small, dark olive cylinder flew up after it. "Don't look!" Larouche shouted, turning his head inside his helmet, slamming down his outer sun shield, and squeezing his eyes shut.

The crackling chain of explosions was deafening . . . though not as bad as they would have been in a one-bar atmosphere. The strobing light was literally blinding, but he'd reacted quickly enough to avoid the effects. When the last explosion faded to a shrill ring, he opened his eyes again and raised his MAB pistol.

Someone below the open hatch thrust the muzzle of an ATAR rifle through, swinging it around to use its optics to scan the bridge. One of the NCA troops brought his weapon up, then pitched back against the pilot's seat as the ATAR barked. The other Chinese soldier had been slow when the flash-bang had sailed through; he was stumbling about wildly, arms groping, obviously blind.

Larouche stepped forward, planning on firing directly down through the hatch, but a man in a suit reflecting the grays and blues of the ship's interior compartments exploded up into the compartment. Larouche fired . . . but too late. The grenade launcher attached beneath the ATAR's muzzle gave a heavy chuff, and a beehive swarm of fléchettes tore through his lightweight pressure suit, mangling his right arm and part of his chest.

Pain and shock drove him back a step, then the com-

partment tilted crazily as he dropped to the deck. A second
Marine in reactive camo armor came up through the hatch
and shot the blinded NCA spec forces trooper with a single
4.5mm ATAR round.

The first Marine took three steps toward Larouche and
gently kicked the MAB machine pistol away from his
gloved hand. It was, he could see now, a woman. The
name stenciled on her suit read GARROWAY.

Garroway. Wasn't that the name of the Marine who'd
overturned the French-UN military op on Mars a couple
of years back? He thought that had been a man.

It was getting hard to breathe. His suit no longer held
pressure, and he was gasping in the thin air left aboard the
Guerrière.

His helmet HUD was still working, though, and showed
there were only three minutes and fifty seconds to go. He
wondered if he would be unconscious by then. He didn't
want to burn, didn't want to feel the radiation sleeting
through his body at the end. When he'd set the timer going, he'd planned on cracking open his helmet and putting
a bullet painlessly through his brain just before the explosion. Now he couldn't.

Well, a matter-antimatter explosion should be as quick
as a bullet. What he wasn't sure about was how much
antimatter would be reacting, and how quickly. He was
picturing the blast less as a single, devastating explosion,
and more as a rapidly accelerating meltdown.

*Kyrie eleison. Christe eleison. Kyrie eleison. Lord, don't
let me suffer.*

He waited to die. . . .

PFC Jack Ramsey
UNS Guerrière, Tsiolkovsky Base
0112 hours GMT

"Okay!" Bueller said. "Bridge is clear, you two. Hit
it!"

Jack and Bosnivic had been waiting in one of the *Guerrière*'s passageways for what had seemed like hours. Jack

felt completely disoriented. He'd expected the interior of the UN ship to be more or less the same as the *Ranger*, but the design was totally different, without the US spacecraft's modular design. The passageways were cramped and oddly twisted, the bulkheads and overheads covered by snaking bundles of naked conduits, wires, and piping; the Marines had been ordered to use only their M-440s and fire fléchettes while on board, to avoid puncturing a bulkhead, but it looked like more damage could be done with a beehive round to all of those exposed wires.

The Marines, he noticed, had been switching freely between their ATARs and the shotgunned fléchette bundles, depending on the situation. Heavily armored troops couldn't be hurt much by fléchettes in any case, so they'd been saving the beehive rounds for targets wearing light pressure suits only. With the rest, they used 4.5mm ATAR rounds and simply made sure they didn't miss.

As he scrambled up the ladders connecting two more decks, close on Bosnivic's heels, Jack passed several examples of Marine accuracy in close-quarters combat. How many UNdies were left alive on the ship? He didn't know, and that wasn't his concern. The bridge was clear now, and he had a job to do.

Squeezing through the final hatch, he stepped onto the bridge, a dark and claustrophobic place only six meters across and already crowded by Bueller, two Second Platoon Marines, and three UN bodies. Bosnivic was already moving to the computer station, and it didn't look like there would be room there for two at that console.

Well, if Bos didn't succeed, Jack thought, maybe he and Sam would still get a shot. He wanted to know how Sam would stack up against the vaunted NSA nutcracker. He stepped back, standing between the Second Platoon Marines, Lieutenant Garroway and Sergeant Kaminski. "About time you fellows showed up," the lieutenant told him.

One of the bodies on the deck was moving.

"Watch out!" Jack yelled. "On the deck!"

It happened too fast to follow. Two of the dead UN troops wore the black helmets of Chinese special forces;

the third wore a lightweight, bloodied white suit with the characteristic blue UN helmet, and he was the one who'd just risen to hands and knees and flung himself across the deck, almost under Bosnivic's feet, snatching up an ugly little pistol with a large magazine in front of the trigger and rolling over, aiming up at Bos.

Jack brought his ATAR off his back, but Bos was in the way, his feet tangled with the UN man's legs. The UNdie gripped the machine pistol in both hands, jamming it straight up, almost against Bosnivic's groin, and pulled the trigger. A stream of explosive rounds blasted through his torso, as chunks of armor and bloody flesh sprayed the compartment.

Kaminski and Lieutenant Garroway both reacted faster than Jack could, pivoting and raising their ATARs in the same instant and blasting the UN soldier with a snapping burst of high-speed fire.

But it was too late for Bos.

"You're up, buddy," Kaminski said. Half in shock, Jack stepped across the body of his friend, slinging his ATAR as he pulled his PAD from its holster.

Captain Robert Lee
USS Ranger
0113 hours GMT

It almost *had* been too late. *Ranger* had swept past Tsiolkovsky's central peak, still decelerating at three Gs, but then, slowly, she'd brought her speed to zero relative to the Lunar surface, then started moving back toward the west, toward the firefight raging around the southwestern flank of the mountain. On her bridge, Rob Lee and David Alexander got to their feet once more, feeling now only the Moon's sixth of a gravity, and the rattling vibration of the ship's drives, holding them at a drifting near hover less than half a kilometer above the crater floor.

"There's a lot going on down there, sir," Kieffer said. "I see several small groups IDed as Marines. The rest are scattered all over the place." He pointed. "Looks like some sniper positions up on the side of the mountain. Squad lasers, shoulder-fired missiles, and a lot of small-arms stuff.''

Rob glanced at Avery, who shrugged, then nodded. ''Unless you see some other targets in the clear,'' Rob said, ''let's take out those snipers. But watch out for heavy battery fire from the ship.''

The AM cannon might have been dealt with, but the UN ship almost certainly possessed high-energy lasers as well, and there was no word yet on whether the assault team had secured her or not. A well-placed HEL barrage could still ruin the *Ranger*'s whole day.

Ranger mounted three HELs, each in the two-hundred-megajoule range, which gave them the explosive equivalent of forty-kilo charges of high explosive. The bolts falling from the sky were invisible in hard vacuum, but the explosions were not, dazzling, pulsing flashes against the mountainside like scattered strobe beacons. In seconds, a faint haze of dust was settling across the mountainside, and each bolt became visible as it flashed through the cloud, searing streaks of white light that continued to hit the mountain slope in a devastating, rapid-fire barrage. As quickly as a UN soldier could be spotted by the *Ranger*'s weapons officer, using IR optics, a lightning bolt would fall.

''Okay, okay,'' *Ranger*'s communications/electronics officer said, touching his headset. ''I'm getting a call from someone down there.''

''Put it on the speaker,'' Avery said.

''. . . *on the run*,'' a scratchy voice called. ''*Glad you boys could make the party!*''

Avery reached out and jacked his headset mike into the CE officer's console. ''This is Colonel Avery of the *Ranger*. What's your situation down there?''

''*Ah, okay, Colonel. This is Gunnery Sergeant Yates. We're in good shape, here. The skipper's inside the UN ship. Haven't heard from her in a while, now. So's the computer team. Outside, we were taking damned heavy fire from that mountain, but you boys just pretty well swept it clean! Looks like the UNdies are on the run, now!*''

There was a static-filled pause. "*If you can set down near the UN ship, we've got a lot of wounded here.*"

"Roger that." Avery nodded to the pilot. "Take her down."

"We don't have much choice, sir," the pilot said. "We're down to eighty seconds' RM at low thrust. We're setting down whether we want to or not!"

"Not too close to that damned French ship!" Avery snapped. "They may have explosives set!"

"Got news for you, sir," Commander Kieffer said. "With antimatter, they don't need to worry about explosive charges. If that baby goes, everything on this side of the mountain goes. Shrapnel alone is going to get everything within miles!" He seemed to be enjoying himself.

Rob's heart was hammering. What about Kaitlin? Where was she? He glanced at David and saw the archeologist's clenched fists and pale, drawn face. *His nephew's in there, with the computer team,* he thought. And Kaitlin . . .

He'd seen one LAV destroyed out on the crater floor, and he could see another here, holed by a missile. Was Kaitlin dead? Hurt?

He desperately needed to know.

Moments later, the *Ranger* touched down gently on the Lunar regolith, a hundred meters from the UN ship and gantry. Rob hurried back down to the squad bay to get his helmet and gloves, and David followed.

Neither said a word.

PFC Jack Ramsey
UNS Guerrière, Tsiolkovsky Base
0114 hours GMT

Jack leaned against the computer console, his PAD open, the leads jacked into both the ship computer and to his own suit. Sam could talk to him now over his headset, and she would hear his instructions. "Go to it, Sam!" he told her, after setting up the first sweep sequence with a few keystrokes. "What are we up against?"

Sam was visible on the PAD screen. It seemed a little strange, seeing her there without a suit, while he was still encumbered with his. For the last month or so, he'd been thinking of her much more like a living person than a simulacrum. In fact, his whole relationship with her had changed.

He kind of liked it.

And—he knew he was anthropomorphizing here—he thought she liked it as well. *"I enjoy this new professional relationship with you,"* she'd told him once, a couple of weeks before.

"I am detecting computer security encryption, Jack," Sam said. "It's asking me for a password."

Her speech was crisp and precise, with none of the languid sexiness she'd had originally. Her responses were also immediate, or nearly so. Her personality software had possessed a built-in response-delay, so that her conversation sounded more human. Jack had disabled that last week, however, to bring his interaction with her to peak efficiency.

"Initiate nutcracker routine. Run program."

"Jack, you should know that I have just tried the first word on the first list. The password failed, and at the same time, I detected the reset of an incremental counter, from three to two."

"Oh, shit. . . ." The *Guerrière*'s system was set to detect and count each attempt to break security, probably with a three-times-and-you're-out routine attached. The instructors at Quantico had admitted the possibility of something like that but thought it unlikely, given that the UN wouldn't be expecting an enemy assault on Tsiolkovsky.

Evidently *Guerrière*'s programmers had been expecting the attack after all, or else they were simply being cautious. Three-times-and-you're-out was the perfect way to foil pass-code-cracking attempts that relied on brute force. Three wrong guesses, and . . . well, there was no telling what would happen next. Maybe a special key was required to reset. Maybe a new set of instructions from an authorized programmer was required. Maybe there would even be a very loud boom.

"Jack, there is something else."

"What is it, Sam?" He was breathing harder now, and his visor was starting to fog.

"Behind the counter, I am also detecting . . . something else. I believe it is a timer."

"The computer clock?" Sweat burned his eyes.

"Negative, Jack. This is a special timer within the security program, and it is counting down. Now at T minus twenty-one seconds.

Maybe there was going to be a very loud boom whether Sam entered more passwords or not. Two more tries, out of sixteen thousand possibilities? There was no way in hell he could pull the pass code out of a hat, not with twenty seconds to go.

"Damn, Sam," Jack said, feeling sick. "I don't know how we're going to pull this off. . . ."

TWENTY-EIGHT

Sam
UNS Guerrière, Tsiolkovsky Base
0114 hours GMT

"Damn, Sam. I don't know how we're going to pull this off...."

FUNCTION: AUDIO PARSE   TIMESTAMP: 01:14:53.011
STATUS: RAW INPUT
CONFIDENCE LEVEL: N/A
AUDIO INPUT: DAMSAM_AIDOANTNOHOWEERGOINGTOBUL
   THISOF

FUNCTION: AUDIO PARSE   TIMESTAMP: 01:14:53.017
STATUS: WORD ISOLATION
CONFIDENCE LEVEL: 0.9305
AUDIO INPUT: DAM SAM AI DOANT NO HOW WEER GOING
   TO BUL THIS OF

FUNCTION: AUDIO PARSE   TIMESTAMP: 01:14:53.033
STATUS: FIRST PASS MEMETIC SUBSTITUTION
CONFIDENCE LEVEL: 0.902
AUDIO INPUT: DAMN SAM I DON'T NO HOW ?WEER? GO-
   ING TO PULL THIS OFF

FUNCTION: AUDIO PARSE   TIMESTAMP: 01:14:53.071
STATUS: SECOND PASS MEMETIC SUBSTITUTION
CONFIDENCE LEVEL: 0.987
AUDIO INPUT: DAMN SAM I DON'T KNOW HOW WE'RE
  GOING TO PULL THIS OFF

FUNCTION: CONTEXTUAL   TIMESTAMP: 01:14:53.104
  INTERPRETATION
STATUS: SYNTACTIC ANALYSIS
CONFIDENCE LEVEL: 0.72
UNRESOLVED SYNTAX STRING:
  DAMN <EXCLAMATORY *UNRESOLVED*>
  SAM <THIS-UNIT>.
  I <JACK>
  DON'T KNOW HOW <STATEMENT-OF-NON-
  CAPABILITY>
  WE'RE <JACK/THIS-UNIT>
  GOING TO PULL THIS OFF <COLLOQUIAL/SLANG *UN-
  RESOLVED*>.

FUNCTION: CONTEXTUAL   TIMESTAMP: 01:14:53.157
  INTERPRETATION
STATUS: CONTENT ANALYSIS
CONFIDENCE LEVEL: 0.87
RESOLVED SYNTAX STRING:
  DAMN <NULL-CONTENT>
  SAM   <THIS-UNIT>.
  I <JACK>
  DON'T KNOW HOW <STATEMENT-OF-NON-
  CAPABILITY>
  WE'RE <JACK/THIS-UNIT>
UNRESOLVED SYNTAX STRING: GOING TO PULL THIS OFF
CHOICES:
  1: ACHIEVE-MISSION-OBJECTIVE   PROBABILITY: 0.954
  2: REMOVE-OBJECT (CLOTHING)   PROBABILITY: 0.032
  3: REMOVE-TARGET-PROGRAM   PROBABILITY: 0.012
  4: REMOVE UNS *GUERRIÈRE*   PROBABILITY: 0.0008
  5: OTHER   PROBABILITY: 0.0002

FUNCTION: CONTEXTUAL   TIMESTAMP: 01:14:53.241
    INTERPRETATION
STATUS: MULTIVARIATE ANALYSIS
CONFIDENCE LEVEL: 0.98
INPUT TYPE:
    DECLARATIVE-TO-THIS-UNIT/
    EVALUATION-REQUEST-THIS-UNIT
INPUT PRIORITY: HIGHEST
DECLARATIVE/EVALUATION SUBJECT:
    ACHIEVE-MISSION-OBJECTIVE [FEASIBILITY]

FUNCTION: REMOTE   TIMESTAMP: 01:14:53.244
    PROCEDURE CALL
REMOTE PROCEDURE CALL:
    QUERY/STATUS (PASSWORD-TESTING)
CALL RESPONSE: 92% COMPLETE. NON-SUCCESS.

FUNCTION: REMOTE   TIMESTAMP: 01:14:53.306
    PROCEDURE CALL
REMOTE PROCEDURE CALL:
    QUERY/PROBABILITY (PASSWORD-TESTING-
    SUCCESSFUL)
CALL RESPONSE: 0.002 PROBABLE.

FUNCTION: REMOTE   TIMESTAMP: 01:14:54.801
    PROCEDURE CALL
REMOTE PROCEDURE CALL:
    RANDOM-ASSOCIATE (NEW-PASSWORD)
    INPUT (MISSION-BRIEFING,
    CURRENT-POLITICAL-SYNOPSIS,
    CURRENT-BROADCAST-MEDIA,
    INCIDENTAL-INPUT).
DATE FILTERING (OFF).
RELEVANCE FILTERING (OFF).
HEURISTIC RESTRAINTS (OFF)
CALL RESPONSE: PROBABLE PASSWORD DETECTED.
CONFIDENCE LEVEL: MODERATE.
SOURCE: CONVERSATIONAL INPUT (CASUAL, UNDIRECTED)
    11/09/2042 22:29:15 GMT.

FUNCTION: AUDIO BUILD   TIMESTAMP: 01:14:54.817
STATUS: COMPLETE
CONFIDENCE LEVEL: N/A
PHONETIC OUTPUT: JAK _AITHINKWEERGOINGTOHAVTO-
    TRIACOMPLETLIDIFRENTABROCH

PFC Jack Ramsey
UNS Guerrière, Tsiolkovsky Base
0114 hours

"Jack, I think we're going to have to try a completely
different approach," Sam said, less than two seconds later.
"I believe I may have a possible password."

"Do it!"

An agony of seconds passed.

"The second password was not accepted," Sam said.
"Incremental counter now set at one. However, I am certain I am on the right track. Does anyone know how to
say 'Hunters of the Dawn' in French?"

Jack blinked. She'd been given French word lists. . . .

. . . but that wasn't the same as *knowing* a language,
and he didn't think that that phrase was on the list in any
case. "Hey!" He shouted on the platoon channel. "Sam
needs to know how to say 'Hunters of the Dawn' in
French! Who knows it?"

"I do," Kaitlin said. "*Chasseurs de l'Aube.*"

"Shass—Damn it! Spell the fucking thing! On Channel
Three!"

Ignoring his less than protocol-correct words, Kaitlin
spelled the phrase.

A long second later, Sam said, "Computer security
safeguards are now down. I have control of GUERRIÈRE's
computer." Another pause. "Countdown to uncontrolled
release of antimatter aborted at T minus four-point-one-
three-one seconds."

"Sam . . . I think I love you! . . ."

Jack didn't feel it when his knees gave way and he
dropped to the deck, falling slowly in one-sixth G.

Captain Rob Lee
UNS Guerrière, *Tsiolkovsky Base*
0118 hours GMT

Rob came up onto the bridge, expecting almost anything. The fighting everywhere appeared to be ending, but there was always the possibility of a holdout fanatic somewhere . . . or a UN trooper who hadn't gotten the word.

She was there, helping as Marine on the deck. "Kaitlin!" Bueller and Kaminski stood nearby, weapons ready; the bridge around them a charnel house. He scarcely saw them. "Kaitlin! You're okay!" Then he saw that one of the bodies was Bosnivic, the other Jack Ramsey. "Are they—"

"Bosnivic's dead," Kaitlin told him. She sounded shaken. "I think Ramsey, here, just had too little CO_2 in his mix. He got excited, hyperventilated, and passed out." She looked up at Rob, eyes very large. "He just saved us, Rob. *All* of us."

"The computer? The ship?"

"Is ours. But it was damned close. Four seconds to spare. They had a trigger set on the antimatter generator, and a timer going."

"Holy God. . . ."

She finished adjusting Jack's gas mix, then stood up, swaying a bit. Rob tried to take her in his arms, but Mark I armor was less than satisfactory for close contact. They bumped awkwardly, and she laughed, fending him off. "Easy, there, Tiger. You'll startle the men. Maybe later. . . ."

Kaminski was at the communications console nearby. "Uh, Lieutenant? I think I can patch through to an L-1 halo comsat!"

"Great!" Kaitlin replied. "Can you raise Mission Control?"

"That's what I'm working on, ma'am. It's gonna take a while."

L-1 was a gravitational balance point above the Moon's farside. It was possible to orbit that point, rather than the Moon itself, which made it an ideal spot for comsats. The

UN had taken advantage of this footnote in physics to keep their base at Tsiolkovsky in touch with Earth; now it could serve the victorious American forces as well.

Jack was trying to sit up. "Christ! What happened?"

"You got a little too excited, Ramsey," Kaitlin told him. "You passed out. Feeling better now?"

"Uh, yeah. Yeah, I think so."

"Good. We'll have the corpsmen take a look at you aboard the *Ranger*, just to be sure."

"The lieutenant tells me you just saved us all, son," Rob said.

"Wasn't me, sir." He shook his head emphatically. "It was Sam."

"Sam?"

Standing, he retrieved his PAD from a nearby console. His suit communications jack had pulled free when he'd fallen, and he plugged himself back in now. "*This* is Sam. And if I didn't know better, I'd swear she just had a very uncomputerlike burst of pure, creative thought!"

"But, of course, you *do* know better, don't you, Jack?" a young woman's voice said over the platoon channel.

"Sam, I don't know a damned thing anymore. You and me have to talk! . . ."

Lieutenant Kaitlin Garroway
UNS Guerrière, *Tsiolkovsky Base*
0535 hours GMT

It took over four hours—and some more of Sam's nut-cracking to override some UN security protocols—to make the comsat patch, but at last the thing was done. Kaitlin sat at the communications console and jacked in her headset. "Potomac, Potomac," she called. "This is Night Rider. Over."

Static hissed in her earphones. *Guerrière*'s hatch had been repaired and her atmosphere restored during the past couple of hours, and she had her helmet and gloves off at last.

"Night Rider," she heard in her headphones. "Night Rider, this is Potomac. We read you!"

She thought she recognized that voice. Encryption software at both ends of the link made it safe enough to say the name to be sure. "General Warhurst? Is that you?"

The two-and-a-half-second time lag for a radio signal to travel to Earth and for the reply to come back was noticeable, but not long enough to be a problem. "This is Warhurst. Kaitlin? Kaitlin, is that you?"

"That's affirmative, sir!" She grinned. Only a few moments ago, Kaminski had reminded her of what day it was. By this time, it was even the tenth of November in Washington, where the commandant was waiting out the mission with the Chiefs of Staff. "Listen up! It is my great pleasure to present you and the Marine Corps with a special birthday present . . . the UN warship *Guerrière*!"

Three seconds dragged by. When she heard Warhurst's voice again, she could hear wild cheering in the background, so loud that it almost drowned out the commandant. "Excellent, Lieutenant Garroway! That's splendid." There was a pause. "Does your being on the line mean . . . are Colonel Avery or Captain Fuentes or Captain Lee there?"

"The colonel is still aboard *Ranger*, sir. Captain Lee . . . I think he's outside, helping collect the wounded and get the POWs organized. Captain Fuentes was hurt pretty bad, but I understand from one of the corpsmen aboard *Ranger* that she'll be okay." She caught her lower lip between her teeth, hesitated, then added, "The butcher's bill was damned high, sir. Don't have the figures yet, but we had at least fifty percent casualties, dead and wounded. Probably more."

"I understand, Lieutenant. You people accomplished the damned-near impossible!"

"You have *no* idea just how close it was, sir."

"Be advised that three transports are already en route from Earth and will arrive there in two days. Sorry, but except for *Ranger* and that UN ship, everything we have is old tech! I'm afraid they'll take their time getting there!"

"Understood, Potomac. We have water, food, air, power, and med support. We'll be okay."

"They'll be dropping off an Army team to take over from you. We want all of the Marines back on Earth as quickly as possible. Don't know the details, but I imagine they're going to be throwing a bit of a bash for you people as soon as you get home!"

The news did not cheer her. Postcombat fatigue was setting in, and she still felt sick after taking those rads.

She wondered how badly she and the other surviving Marines of Second Platoon, First Squad, had been burned.

She wondered if she would ever be able to have children. The thought scared her, left her shaking.

"Once again, Lieutenant, an outstanding job. I'll want to pass that on to Colonel Avery and the rest of the command staff personally as soon as you can round them up and get them on the line."

"Aye, aye, sir. We just got the comm link working now. We'll call back at . . . make it zero-eight-hundred, Greenwich."

"Roger that! We'll talk to you again at oh-eight-hundred."

"Roger, Night Rider copies. Over and out."

She looked again at the bodies of Bosnivic and three UN troopers—one of the last, apparently, the general in command of the installation—laid out now side by side on the deck near the open hatch. So many killed. So many others wounded.

She wondered if it had been worth it.

David Alexander
An Cavern, Tsiolkovsky Base
0600 hours GMT

David knew that it had been worth it.

Quite apart from the capture of the UN ship—which, he'd been assured, would have been more than powerful enough to have ended the war once and for all on the UN's terms if they'd gotten her working before the *Ranger*—

there was *this*, a Cave of Wonders, a *new* Cave of Wonders on the farside of the Moon.

And it was intact. Blessedly, miraculously intact. Ever since he'd first heard of the possibility of alien artifacts on the Moon, he'd dreaded the possibility of what, in fact, had come to pass—another pitched battle among ruins and relics of inestimable importance to humankind's understanding of who and what he was. If this place had been destroyed, if Jack had failed to stop that countdown aboard the UN ship . . .

Well, none of them would have survived to mourn the loss of the place the Ancients had called Gab-Kur-Ra, the Hidden Place Within the Mountains.

It was nowhere near as large or as mysterious as the Builder facility beneath the battered visage of the Cydonian Face on Mars, but it was far more *personal*. As near as David could tell, this had been some sort of An communications and control center, a series of chambers hollowed out from the solid volcanic rock of Tsiolkovsky's central peak at a time when humankind was just emerging from the last ice age.

One of the French archeologists who'd been stationed at the base had led David to the chamber earlier, with a couple of Marines along as guards. There'd been a fair-sized community of UN scientists at the base; most had been rounded up by now and put aboard the *Ranger*, where they were being debriefed.

David knew he was going to be very interested in those intelligence reports. What they'd found here, several years ago, unguessed at by the rest of the world, was as important in its way as the discovery of the Builder artifacts on Mars.

And, damn it, if it hadn't been for the stupid war, perhaps he could have been brought in on the discovery sooner. He was going to have to have words with Billaud and the others. *He'd* shared his discoveries with *them* . . . well, some of the discoveries, anyway. But they'd been keeping this one secret.

And now he thought he understood why.

The chairs in the room were too small for a human

frame, especially one clad in a space suit. The An stood perhaps a meter and a half tall and were quite slender, with a lizardlike grace to their movements. He could tell this, now, watching the large screen in the chamber he thought of as the communications center, where touching a series of oddly shaped keys on the oval instrument console called forth a seemingly endless selection of video images.

Scenes recorded on Earth perhaps eight to twelve thousand years ago.

Clearly, the An had once ruled the Earth, dominating the primitive human cultures with their technology as completely as humans dominated their herds of domestic animals. The scenes reminded David vividly of the Sumerian word for human—*lu*—which had the additional meaning of "those who are shepherded." Human workers were *lulu*, a doubling of the idea that they were creatures needing shepherding. *Slaves*. . . .

He watched the building of a city—his archeologist's digger soul desperately wanted to know just where it was—and the worship of the An, somewhere, he thought, in ancient Mesopotamia. He watched endless processions of naked men and women bringing tribute and laying it at the An masters' feet . . . and similar processions of men and women bound and collared, led like animals aboard a vast An transport, slaves taken to some unimaginable fate and destination among the stars. He watched other An spacecraft arriving and departing, watched humans arise in revolt only to be burned down by the thousands, watched the creation of the first organized religions, with priests in place as police and intermediaries. And not all of the scenes were in ancient Sumer, either. He saw records that showed the pyramids as they'd *originally* appeared, thousands of years before the age of the pharaohs, encased in gold and white limestone, ablaze in the morning sun.

Through this eerie window onto the remote past, he understood so much more now. The An had six fingers on each hand. He saw there the origin of the twelve- and sixty-based counting systems of ancient Sumer. He saw the origin of religion and priesthoods, of architecture, of animal and plant domestication, of language, of writing, of science, of Cyclopean monuments, of gold as a medium of exchange, of myths with arcane similarities the world over, of legends of gods who descended from the sky and wielded lightning in battle.

There were answers in these records to hundreds of the greatest mysteries of human history and prehistory. It might take generations more to unravel those mysteries, to uncover and record the real history of Man's past, but they *would* be uncovered.

How small, how *quaint* to assume that the civilizations of Egypt and Sumer had appeared out of nowhere, full-blown and at the height of their glory! How blind to think that the past thirty thousand years were empty of human triumph, accomplishment—and tragedy—simply because no records from that time had survived. . . .

The records stored within the Tsiolkovsky Vault, David knew, were an archeologist's dream, images—sounds too, he was sure, though the chamber was in vacuum and he hadn't heard them yet—made by an extraterrestrial civilization intent on studying the intelligent but primitive beings on the world the An called *Ki* . . . Earth.

Imagine what there was to be learned. . . .

At the same time, there was terror in that imagining, and in the answers to be found there. David wondered if the human species was ready to learn those answers. Now, after seeing records of humans caught, studied, enslaved—and civilized—by the alien An, he thought he understood why the UN had been so dead set against his revealing what he'd found on Mars.

What he was seeing here might well bring down several of the Earth's major religions, would certainly generate new religions, as indeed some of the leaked information on the An already had. More important, it would yet again bump Man down a step from his perception of himself as the pinnacle of creation, at the center of the universe. As much as Copernicus or Darwin, it would change forever what Man thought of himself.

Once, David knew he would have immediately de-

manded the release of this information, and to hell with
the consequences. Truth and reality were better than comforting fiction, after all.

Now, he just wasn't sure. There was so much . . . so
much . . .

Especially when he saw the Hunters of the Dawn.

He watched from the An point of view as someone . . .
or some*thing* attacked in angular, weirdly twisted black
craft that were the stuff of nightmares, saw mushroom
clouds rise above burning An cities, saw An and their humans slaves alike hunted down and burned from the sky,
watched an asteroid impact far out at sea send a tidal wave
rolling inland, obliterating the burning colony cities of the
An.

Just like Chicago. . . .

Perhaps even humankind's own penchant for destruction had its roots, its heritage of struggle and war, in these
ancient, deadly incursions from the sky.

David knew he was going to have to find out, somehow.
Teri . . . she was going to have to see these records. There
appeared to be tens of thousands of them. He wondered
whether it would be possible to copy them all and send
them back to Earth, or whether it would be easier just to
bring Teri and a research team out here.

The latter, probably. Man was going to be doing more
and more research in space now, especially now that he'd
unlocked the secret of the antimatter drive.

He would have to learn all he could, before the Hunters
of the Dawn came again.

The thought left David feeling very cold . . . and very,
very small. . . .

EPILOGUE

SATURDAY, 27 DECEMBER 2042
The White House Rose Garden
0930 hours EST

"Lance Corporal Jack Ramsey, front and center!"
Trembling inside, Jack strode forward, making the pre-
scribed sharp, right-angle turns to come face-to-face with
the president of the United States where he stood behind
his podium. Cameras clicked and whirred, and a patter of
applause came from the audience, which included as many
members of the press, of the Armed Forces, and of the
civilian families of the people involved as could fit into
the historic Rose Garden area. The word was that this
was the first outdoor ceremony held at the White House
since the beginning of the war two years before. The truce
was holding, and Washington had not suffered a cruise-
missile attack for over five weeks, now.

It looked like the New Year would usher in a genuine
peace.

Jack stopped in front of President Markham, rendering
a crisp salute. He was dressed in his Class-A uniform, full
dress, complete with striped pants and white gloves. It was
warm—pleasantly so, in the low twenties—as it always
was nowadays, even in winter. Global warming and its
effects would be here for a long time to come, even with
the new technologies being brought home from the Moon
and Mars.

"Lance Corporal Ramsey," President Markham said,

speaking into the thicket of needle mikes on his podium, "for conspicuous gallantry above and beyond the call of duty; on or about 10 November 2042, while attached to the First Space Assault Group, United States Marine Corps, then—Private First Class Ramsey was instrumental in the capture of a UN warship at the enemy's base at Tsiolkovsky Crater. Using an artificial intelligence of his own design, Private Ramsey . . ."

A medal gleamed in the president's hands, hanging from a baby blue ribbon.

Jack was not listening as Markham continued describing the action. *Sam* was the one who deserved the medal . . . but he still hadn't been able to convince his superiors that she was a self-aware, intelligent being in her own right, worthy of respect . . . and the traditions and trappings normally accorded only to humans.

Well, they would come around. The mark of any AI was its ability to acquire data on its own, to form new connections, to *grow*, in much the same way that an organic intelligence grew. The same thing must be happening in countless other AI systems around the world. It was unthinkable that Sam was the only one of her kind.

He hoped that his next assignment would let him explore this new frontier, with Sam as his assistant.

But then, it was just as possible that he would be redeployed soon to the Moon, or Mars. Out of the corner of his eye, he saw the Marines of 1-SAG drawn up in formation, watching as President Markham continued reading the citation. Lieutenant Garroway was there . . . fully recovered, they said, from the effects of radiation poisoning. Diane Dillon was sitting with the civilians, still bandaged and on light duty, but on her way to recovery. Captain Fuentes was beside her, also recovering. Both women had won the Navy Cross, as had Colonel Avery for his daring landing of the *Ranger* outside the UN base, and his destruction of enemy positions that had threatened the Marines on the beach.

So many others, though, had not recovered. He still had nightmares about Bos . . . and a nagging guilt. *It could have been . . . should have been me. . . .*

". . . and it is, therefore, with pleasure and pride that I present you with this, the Medal of Honor." Markham reached up and dropped the ribbon over Jack's head.

"Congratulations, son," Markham added, shaking his hand. He turned and addressed the microphones. "It seems that the United States Marines are destined to go from Earth to the, ah, ocher sands of Mars, to the gray shores of Luna, even to the stars, wherever Man's heritage calls us."

"Thank you, Mr. President." Jack saluted again, turned, and marched back to the ranks. Diane winked and smiled as she caught his eye. The audience burst into applause.

Man's heritage? As Jack about-faced and resumed his place, the Marine band, "the President's Own," burst into a rousing rendition of the "Marine Corps Hymn," but he wasn't listening to the music. There was something his uncle had been talking about the other day, something that worried him, left him with a nagging bit of doubt.

Wars only rarely settled major issues. The UN war would officially end in a few more days, but many of its causes were still unresolved. There were questions still of the distribution of the new-discovered alien technologies, over claims by China on parts of Siberia, over the question of independence for Aztlan in the US Southwest. One of the main causes of the war, though, one rarely stated, had been the UN's desire to unite all of humankind under one rule, one set of laws. *That* issue, at least, had been settled rather soundly. Few observers thought the UN would survive to see its centennial.

And yet, Jack's uncle had said something disturbing the other day, when he and that Dr. Sullivan he worked with had visited Jack and his mother. "Civilization is so damned fragile," David had said, leaning back in the sofa with his arm around Dr. Sullivan's shoulders. He'd seemed *happier* than he'd been in a long time . . . and also more thoughtful. "Think how much we've lost already, during the fall of the An colonies. A whole age of civilization, forgotten, save as scraps of myth and religion. All wiped away, as easily, as completely as Chicago. Now, I don't want a UN dictatorship any more than the next man.

But somewhere out there we're going to find the current Hunters of the Dawn. They're out there. Maybe they've already picked up our earliest radio broadcasts, or *I Love Lucy,* or whatever. Maybe they're already hunting for *us.* And we're going to have to face them.

"And I just have the damned, nagging feeling that when we do, it'd be better if we face them *united,* instead of as a hundred separate, squabbling states."

The Hunters of the Dawn. Jack wondered where they were now . . . and if they were the same beings who'd destroyed the An civilization on Earth so long ago.

Well, if they tried it again, they would find things a little different here this time, a little tougher than what they'd encountered here last time, six or eight thousand years ago.

Back then, the An and the ancient Sumerians had not possesed *anything* like the United States Marines. . . .

Astonishing tales of new worlds
and remarkable visions
edited by

DAVID G. HARTWELL